To Forgive, Divine

TO FORGIVE, DIVINE

A Novel

Melissa Lea Leedom

iUniverse, Inc.
New York Lincoln Shanghai

To Forgive, Divine
A Novel

iUniverse, Inc.

For information address:
iUniverse, Inc.
2021 Pine Lake Road, Suite 100
Lincoln, NE 68512
www.iuniverse.com

ISBN: 0-595-29495-2

Printed in the United States of America

This book is dedicated to my mother, who always knew I could do it.

For if you forgive men when they sin against you,
your heavenly Father will also forgive you.
But if you do not forgive men their sins,
your Father will not forgive your sins.

—Matthew 6:14–15

Acknowledgments

The bulk of *To Forgive, Divine* was written as a thesis to fulfill the requirements for a master's degree at Towson University in Maryland. I owe a debt of gratitude to several people who were involved in that project.

Heartfelt thanks go to Helen Jean Burn for her support, encouragement, and affirmation. I thank her for being the first to say "yes" to working with an inspirational novel as a thesis project; she made it all possible. I thank her for her open mind and giving spirit. I thank her also for the "kid gloves" she used to help me make my writing better. Rarely have I been critiqued with such tact.

Thanks also to Drs. Harvey Lillywhite and Dan Jones for agreeing to serve on my thesis committee. Special thanks go to Dr. Lillywhite, not only for what he has done for the Professional Writing Program at Towson and for me as my professor, but for supporting me in my bid for a Graduate Student Association grant. I appreciate his willingness to go the extra mile when the lines of communication at times broke down.

I would also like to express my appreciation to the Towson University English Department: the secretaries for their help in walking my signed proposal to the graduate school, and Ms. Clarinda Harris for "pinch-hitting" when signatures were needed. You all went above and beyond the call of duty on my behalf, and I am grateful. Thanks go also to Hannah Smith of the Towson University Graduate Student Association for working so diligently to see that I received my grant funds.

I would be remiss if I did not also thank two professors at Troy State University at Dothan, Alabama, who influenced me and my writing tremendously: Dr. Carolyn Holdsworth, for planting the idea of going to graduate school in my head when I felt like I was working on my bachelor's degree on the hundred-year plan; Dr. Alan Belsches, for his unfailing encouragement and enthusiasm for my writing.

Words cannot adequately express the gratitude I have for and indebtedness I feel to my husband. Had it not been for his unstinting support and willingness to "hold down the fort" with our two children while I attended class, went to the library, and spent endless hours at my computer, I could never have reached this point. I have been richly blessed, and I thank you, Dennis.

Melissa Lea Leedom

CHAPTER 1

Bonnie Callaway glanced uneasily at the thunderous, dark navy clouds hovering on the horizon of the April evening sky as she entered the Coffee Shoppe. She wondered whether she should go home and just skip her once-a-month dinner with the other members of the Benevolent Board; it looked like a monsoon was brewing. She might miss getting caught in a deluge later, but then she would also miss her chance to have the gang buy her dinner. With one last, uneasy look at the spindly fingers of lightning flittering down to earth in the distance, she let the restaurant door close behind her. As things would turn out, Bonnie would still miss the dinner with her friends that she'd been looking forward to, and she would still get caught in the pouring rain. And she would certainly wish she had gone straight home.

First to join her in the large booth with its round table was Father Norman Blake, rector of St. Alban's Catholic Church. An imposing figure in his mid-fifties, he put one in mind of Orson Welles. Father Blake was also jokingly known as "Doctor Father." In addition to his duties as a parish priest, Father Blake, who held a doctorate in religious studies, also taught courses in world religion and philosophy at Chandler City Community College.

"Wouldn't be surprised if the power goes out," he told Bonnie with a nod toward the window.

"I'm afraid you might be right," Bonnie agreed, following his glance.

Not far behind Doctor Father were John Reeves, the young pastor of Chandler A.M.E., and Carolyn Perkins, an attorney in her mid-thirties who attended Franklin Unitarian. John and Carolyn had parked next to each other and dashed in together. Their clothes were dotted with raindrops.

"It is *not* looking good out there, folks," Carolyn informed them, scrunching her hair to rid it of water.

Last to arrive was Dr. Jeff Wells, a forty-ish widower who pastored Foster Road Baptist Church, where Bonnie Callaway was a member. "Anybody ever hear of an umbrella?" he asked, brandishing his before the group with a smile.

"Just like a Boy Scout," kidded Doctor Father, holding his own aloft. "Always prepared."

As Bonnie watched her fellow members of the Chandler City, Georgia, Benevolent Council laugh and joke with each other, she realized with a twinge of sadness that she was going to miss these people who had become such an important part of her life. It was a tradition of long standing for Council members to have dinner together after their once-a-month meetings, and she was really going to miss those, too. The bill was usually Dutch treat, but remaining Council members always chipped in to buy dinner for those rotating off after their two years of service. On this night, the group was to buy dinner for Bonnie and Jeff.

"Anybody need menus tonight?" asked Della, their favorite waitress, as she distributed a glass of ice water to each member of the party. Della, a pleasantly round redhead in her early fifties, was practically an institution at the Coffee Shoppe. She waited on the Council members every month when they came in and, by now, had a pretty good handle on who would order what. Doctor Father would have a BLT and iced tea, John Reeves and Carolyn Perkins were always good for the Monday night pancake special, Dr. Wells usually ordered the fried seafood platter, and Bonnie would have the spaghetti dinner. Everyone always took menus as if they really needed to see what was there, and everyone usually ordered what they usually ordered.

"Not for me," said Father Blake. "I really only have time for a quick cup of coffee tonight. I've got to teach an eight o'clock class. Spring quarter starts today."

"No menu! And I'll bet Andy's already got your BLT ready in the kitchen," Della teased.

"Why, Della, are we that predictable?" returned Father Blake, flashing her a smile through his salt-and-pepper beard and a wink at the rest of the group.

In reply, Della pointed with her pen at each person at the table, her other hand on her hip, and recited in a deadpan voice, "Pancake special, pancake special, seafood platter, spaghetti dinner, BLT. Coffee, coffee, iced tea, ice water, iced tea." With that, she swaggered triumphantly away to get Doctor Father's coffee.

"Looks like she's got us pegged," said Dr. Wells with a grin. "Oh, and Norman," he continued with a mischievous smile, "if you're going to leave early, don't forget to leave your share of our dinner tab with John and Carolyn."

Bonnie reveled in the relaxed and jovial atmosphere of these post-meeting gatherings The Chandler City Benevolent Council grappled with trying to feed and shelter homeless or indigent families, provide an after-school program for latchkey kids, and place potential students with adult literacy volunteers (and struggled to find the funding with which to do it all). After all that, it was good just to kick back with the group and debate about which were the best desserts at the Coffee Shoppe or laugh about the latest little foible among their various congregations.

Doctor Father usually had more than one hilarious tale to tell about the youngsters who served as acolytes at St. Alban's: they all looked positively cherubic in their white robes, but their exploits were usually anything but angelic. Then there was the story of how the Foster Road Baptist church bus, carrying the Senior Adult Choir home from their last tour, broke down on the outskirts of a small town in front of a pool hall and bar populated by leather-jacketed bikers. That was the subject of conversation for two consecutive after-meeting dinners. Jeff Wells had been driving at the time, and he fully expected the Legend of the Church Bus Snafu to outlive his tenure at Foster Road.

When Della returned, she poured Father Blake's coffee, set the pot aside, and poised herself to take orders. "Okay, everybody ready?"

As if nothing at all had been mentioned about it before, Carolyn Perkins peered at her menu, tucked one side of her neatly trimmed pageboy behind her ear, and said thoughtfully, "Hmm, I just can't decide. I don't know, I guess I'll have the pancake special. That looks good."

When everyone, including Della, burst into laughter, Carolyn looked up from her menu, mystified. "Did I say something funny?"

"Della, we just don't know ourselves how predictable we are, do we?" laughed Father Blake.

"Boggles the mind, don't it?" Della said, shaking her head as she marked down Carolyn's order.

Father Blake gulped down the last of his coffee and said, "I hate to drink and run, folks, but a class full of young minds is waiting to be enlightened."

"Oh, were you planning to bring the Dalai Lama with you?" rejoined Dr. Wells.

"Cute, very cute," called Doctor Father over his shoulder as his large form trundled toward the cash register.

When he had gone, it was Jeff Wells who remarked, "Hey! He forgot to chip in his share for our dinners. I'll have to razz the old dog about it next month."

"You won't be here next month," Bonnie reminded him gently. "The farewell dinner is the whole point of him paying, remember?"

The rest of the group looked with mild surprise at Bonnie, who more often than not silently observed their conversations instead of participating in them. They all assumed she enjoyed these dinners: she kept coming each month. She smiled at everyone's jokes and funny stories; she just never had much to say. Since Bonnie had joined the Council two years ago having been recently widowed, the other members had interpreted her silences as a symptom of her grief. It would be nice to think that perhaps at least part of that grieving process might be coming to an end for her.

Jeff turned to Bonnie, his eyes holding hers for a long moment.

"Gee, I guess you're right," he said, as if it were just now registering with him that he really was rotating off the Board. A thoughtful look crossed his face and he turned to his other table-mates. "You know, I'm really gonna miss this. It's been a real treat getting to know you all and forming such great working relationships."

"Well, don't think you're going into permanent retirement, buddy," said John Reeves. A recent seminary graduate and by far the youngest of the group, John Reeves seemed to look up to Jeff Wells: Dr. Wells was the kind of pastor he hoped to be one day himself. "We'll rotate you right back onto the Council next year if you're still here and put you right back to work."

"Hey, I said I'd miss you, not the work," Jeff laughed.

"'If you're still here'?" echoed Bonnie with a questioning look at Dr. Wells. It had never occurred to her that he might be leaving Chandler City. Her blue eyes registered concerned surprise.

"Oh, I get feelers from pastor selection committees at other churches now and then, but I haven't really had any offers I'm interested in taking. Not yet, anyway. Still, after eight years in one place, maybe it's time to let the church benefit from some new blood. I've really been waiting to let Jeff Junior graduate from high school before I look at anything seriously. It would be cruel to move a kid to a new school for his senior year if you really didn't have to, don't you think?"

Just then, Della came back to the table, a look of concern on her normally playful face, and said to John, "Joanna just called. Says she's gone into labor and she wants you to come home."

John looked slightly panic-stricken. "What? Already? The baby's not due for another three weeks!" Having been through the birth process with his wife twice before didn't seem to lessen its aura of emergency for him any.

"Well, tell that to the baby, darlin'," Della drawled. "He—I mean she—don't know it ain't time yet." Della had made her feelings clear early on that since John and Joanna Reeves already had two boys, it was time for them to have a girl.

"Would you like me to come and stay with the boys?" Carolyn offered. The Reeves boys were three and five. "Joanna's folks haven't come in yet, I'm sure."

"Oh, Carolyn, thank you, that would be great. Della, could you—"

"Cancel those orders. I'm way ahead of you. Go take that wife of yours to the hospital."

"Here, take my umbrella," offered Jeff. "You'll need it more than I will."

John gave Jeff a grateful look and took the umbrella. "Thanks."

A moment or two after they had gone, Jeff Wells turned to Bonnie, his sole remaining table partner. As if self-conscious about being suddenly alone with Dr. Wells, she seemed preoccupied with sliding the paper cover from her straw through her graceful, slender fingers, so he could see only the top of her blonde head. He tried breaking the ice with, "Well, this is going to be some farewell dinner. All the buyers have thought up excuses to get out of paying!"

Bonnie looked up, her eyes revealing shy amusement. If there was one thing she knew Jeff Wells didn't have to worry about, it was money.

"My, my, aren't *we* Mr. Sensitivity? I have a few extra pennies in my purse if you need help paying your tab."

"Well, that's good to know," he said, feigning relief, but also pleasantly surprised at this newly revealed sense of humor in Bonnie. How had he missed noticing those wonderful dimples when she smiled? Maybe it was because she didn't smile enough. He'd just have to do something about that, wouldn't he?

He knew that Bill's sudden death had been a shock from which Bonnie had not yet completely recovered, just as it had been an awesome hurdle for him to confront his wife's death. No one really questioned Bonnie's lack of involvement in the rowdier conversations among the board members; still, it was good to see her smile. As he had remarked to himself more than once recently, a man could get lost in a smile like that. He looked intently into her eyes with a warmth in his own that made Bonnie turn nervously back to her straw cover. A little puzzled by her reaction, Jeff tried gently to draw Bonnie into conversation, remarking that babies seemed to pick the most inconvenient times and the worst weather conditions to make their entrances, speculating about whether the new Reeves baby would be a girl or not, and wondering what John and Joanna would name her if she were.

Gradually, Bonnie began to relax in Jeff Wells's company. It struck her that she couldn't remember how long it had been since she had felt this way—comfortable in a man's company. She thought once again how nice Dr. Wells was and marveled at how he always seemed to be able to put her at ease. These monthly group dinners were picker-uppers for both Bonnie and Jeff. Here, they could relax for a while, even, in Jeff's case, laugh out loud. It was only after Bonnie had playfully reminded him that this would be the last time, at least for a long while, that he would participate in them, that he realized how much he would miss them—and how much he would miss the opportunity of seeing Bonnie Callaway outside of church. Too soon, it seemed to Jeff, Della arrived with their salads.

"Ranch for you and vinaigrette for you," said Della as she presented them their salads with a flourish, with the same knowing tone she had used earlier that reminded them she had not needed to ask them their preferences.

"I'd say she's made her point, wouldn't you?" said Jeff with a wink at Bonnie. Bonnie agreed with a rueful smile.

"Hey, Della, do you have any shaky cheese?" As soon as she had said it, a shadow fell across Bonnie's face.

"Come again?" Della asked with a quizzical look.

Bonnie could feel her face redden. "Um, you know, the grated cheese for my spaghetti," Bonnie explained, trying to hide her embarrassment. When Della left to retrieve the requested item, Bonnie, her eyes riveted to the plate of pasta before her, murmured to Jeff, feeling obligated to explain to somebody, "That…that was a term Bill coined, I guess because he thought the kids wouldn't be able to say parmesan, or maybe because he thought they'd like the sound of 'shaky cheese' better."

At the mention of Bill, Bonnie's late husband, the shadow fell across Jeff's face also. Since Jeff had lost his wife, Terri, later the same year that Bill had died, Bonnie knew that he truly empathized with the pain she was feeling. Still, she felt terrible for dredging up memories, even bittersweet ones, especially when they had just been enjoying themselves so much. Then, in that comforting voice that was so familiar to her, he said softly, "Well, it is kind of logical when you think about it. At our house we still call pancakes 'can-cakes' and hot dogs 'how-dows' because that's how Jeff Junior pronounced them when he was learning to talk. And he's almost seventeen now!"

Leave it to Dr. Wells to know just what to say. Even with all the sadness he had endured in his own life, he showed so much courage. Around Jeff Wells, she could feel that memories didn't always have to be painful. Maybe that's what made him such a good pastor—his ability to put people at ease, to say the right thing. She looked up into his eyes and saw kindness and understanding there.

He smiled gently, and she was reminded again of the laugh lines that framed his gray-green eyes. Since she usually saw him only from a distance as he stood in the pulpit on Sundays, it was almost like seeing him up-close for the first time, each time she did.

No one would ever call Jeff Wells devastatingly handsome, it was true. He wasn't terribly tall, a couple of inches shy of six feet, but he had kept himself in reasonably good shape and didn't really look all of his forty-three years. He still had most of his sandy brown hair; some of it near his temples and sideburns was now sporting a little gray. Rarely seen without a suit and tie, Dr. Wells always looked like the Pastor of Foster Road Baptist Church: distinguished without being stuffy, impressive without being slick or flashy.

Jeff Wells also had a trait few people can resist: that of making the person he was speaking with feel that he or she had Jeff's undivided attention. People were drawn to Jeff by his warmth, his genuine concern for others, and a sense of humor born of a keen intellect. When Bonnie met his gaze just now, though, there seemed to be special meaning to the warmth in his eyes—was she imagining it? She looked away quickly, feeling herself coloring.

Jeff turned to look out the window of the restaurant after a particularly loud clap of thunder. The rain was now coming down in gusty sheets.

"Shall we return thanks?" Jeff reminded her gently.

Without thinking, Bonnie extended her hand to Jeff and he looked at it quizzically. Bonnie looked at her hand; her eyes widened and she jerked it back.

"I'm so sorry," she said, closing her eyes and shaking her head in embarrassment. "Force of habit. We always hold hands when we pray at home."

"Well, I think that's a fine idea," said Jeff, now holding his hand out to Bonnie. She looked at it ruefully, not meeting Jeff's eye, and laid her hand tentatively on his upturned palm. He folded his large, masculine fingers over her small hand, closed his eyes, and began to pray: "Father, we thank You for this food and our time of fellowship together. Be with John and Joanna as they bring a new life into the world. Be with Father Blake that he might bear witness to You even as he teaches. Be with us that we might grow to be more like You each day. Amen." Bonnie tried hard to listen and murmured her own "Amen" when Jeff had finished, but she was keenly aware of the warmth of Jeff's hand enfolding hers.

Just as Bonnie was picking up her fork, Clara Adkinson, accompanied by her friend Mertis Hargrove, stopped next to their table. Both ladies, in their mid-sixties, were members of the Senior Adult class at Foster Road Baptist.

"My, my, my! Look who's out on the town on a Monday night!" Clara's face had probably never been an attractive one; the haughty, mincing look she usually gave people did not help matters. A thin smile stretched across her lips now, but there was a knowing tone in her voice and a steely glittering in her lashless brown eyes that made Bonnie's cheeks begin to burn all over again.

As if Jeff could see the wheels turning in Clara's mind, he took matters in hand.

"Well, good evening, Clara," he said broadly. "How are you, Mertis? Hope you enjoy your dinner, ladies. You ought to try the pancake special. It's delightful and not too rough on the ol' budget."

Clara smiled derisively at Jeff; the very idea of her having to live on a budget was ludicrous. Mertis's kindly face acknowledged her pastor's greeting gratefully. As Della hurried Clara and Mertis off to a table in the back of the restaurant, Clara called back, "I'll be seeing you in the morning about the plans for our banquet, Dr. Wells."

Was it Bonnie's imagination, or was that a look of smug satisfaction in Clara's parting glance at Bonnie? It was as if the red glow of Bonnie's cheeks served somehow to affirm the suspicion implicit in Clara's glance. Della caught Jeff's eye and rolled her own as she led the older ladies away.

"You know, I don't think Clara ever has forgiven me that the church bus broke down in front of that bar, or that we all had to wait inside with a bunch of bikers and other assorted shady-looking characters," Jeff said with a conspiratorial smile. "I think that if it hadn't been so cold that night, she would've stood outside and waited for the bus we had to rent to get home."

"Oh, I'm sure Clara doesn't hold that against you," Bonnie replied. Jeff saw, much to his chagrin, that Bonnie was avoiding meeting his eyes again. What a time to run into Clara! "How could she blame you for something you had no control over? Besides, I think you're just about one of her favorite people, judging by the way she brags on you all the time."

She tried to sound casual, but inwardly she was mortified, her racing thoughts jumbled and confused. It wasn't that she didn't want to be thought of as being on a date with Jeff Wells; it was just that the thought had never crossed her mind! And how would it look for Dr. Wells? Yes, he was single, too, but…It was just that the look in Clara's eyes had made her feel guilty somehow, even though she knew perfectly well she had nothing to feel guilty about!

"Well, it's nice to know *somebody's* saying something nice about me behind my back," Jeff joked, but Bonnie barely heard him. Even though the damage had been done—Clara had seen them together, hadn't she?—she just had to get out of that restaurant and away from sitting alone at a table with Jeff Wells.

Eating as little of her meal as she felt she could without seeming too obvious about leaving the rest, she said, "Well, I guess it's time I got on back to the boys. Amanda Summers is babysitting on a school night, so I shouldn't keep her out too late. We'll see you Sunday."

And, not even giving him a chance to swallow the food in his mouth so he could reply, she took her check to the counter, paid, and dashed out into the pouring rain.

Ben and Josh were pleasantly surprised when their mother arrived home in time to tuck them in, seeming not even to notice her soggy appearance. Amanda Summers, their favorite babysitter and the daughter of Bonnie's best friend, Cheryl, usually had them in bed by the time Bonnie returned from her monthly Benevolent Council meeting and dinner.

"Hey, you're back early!" Ben grinned, his mouth full of toothpaste, as Bonnie arrived at the boys' bathroom. "Now you can read us our story."

"Were you guys good for Miss Amanda?" Bonnie teased, ruffling Josh's newly washed hair. The damp, white-blonde strands stood up in spikes around his head. Both boys had inherited their mother's blonde hair, but, apart from that, each was a miniature of Bill.

"Wow, that looks cool!" Josh said, admiring himself in the mirror and flashing a partially toothless smile at his mother.

"Looks like Joshie's going punk on us," laughed Amanda. "Well, guess my work is done here, huh?" She seemed as surprised as the boys at Bonnie's early arrival, but was tactful enough not to ask questions.

"I left your money on the counter, along with the information for the newsletter I promised your mother," Bonnie told her. Amanda was that most valuable of commodities: the babysitter who can drive herself home. "Thanks again for sitting on a school night."

"For these guys, anytime." Amanda tousled Ben's hair, too. "Now we've got twin punkers!" She laughed and waved goodnight.

When the house was quiet, and Ben and Josh had stopped thinking of "one last things" to stave off the inevitable and reluctantly gone to their beds, Bonnie went to the kitchen to fix herself a cup of herbal tea with which to warm the chill from her bones and relax in the tub.

Not that she felt very relaxed. Bonnie could still see the look in Clara's eye as she had made her innocuous-sounding comment about her and Jeff Wells being "out on the town." What a thing for her to have said! What must have gone through Dr. Wells's mind?

Bonnie set her cup down on the window seat behind the tub and turned the water on. She had, out of conscious choice, not dated anyone in the two and a half years since Bill had died. The only "men" in her life were her nine- and seven-year-old boys.

She stared at her toes, squishing bubbles in and out between them, and breathed out a long sigh. She reflected on the way she had carefully orchestrated her life to keep her contact with men, especially single men, to a minimum. The pain of losing Bill had left no room for new feelings of affection for anyone else. So, even though Tom Givens, Foster Road's Singles Minister, had waited a thoughtful three months after the funeral to invite her to join the Singles' Sunday School class for her age group, she had sequestered herself in a ladies-only class and felt safe there.

Bonnie wrapped herself in a plush terry robe and began to cleanse her face. For perhaps the millionth time, she mentally recited her litany of reasons why her life was just perfect the way it was: Bill had provided well for her and the boys, so she was able to continue building the small word processing and computer services business she had started at home after Josh was born, without really having to worry about making ends meet. Her clients were mostly small business owners with no secretarial help and, not coincidentally, mostly women. She was active in the boys' parent-teacher association, whose meetings were attended mostly by mothers. She and the boys spent their weekends going to movies and for pizza or working on school projects and, of course, going to church. Life was busy and, she had convinced herself, full.

As she pulled up the covers of her mostly empty king-size bed, though, Bonnie admitted to herself that there were times, times like tonight, after Ben and Josh had gone to bed and the house was quiet and she was alone with her thoughts, when she still felt Bill's absence acutely. She missed his companionship, his sense of humor. She missed his arms holding her deep in the night.

She had no desire, though, she had told herself repeatedly, for anyone new in her life. And now here was Clara, acting as if she and Dr. Wells were some kind of item!

As she clicked off the lamp on her nightstand, she wondered: would Clara tell anyone that she had seen Bonnie and Jeff out together? Was there any doubt in her mind that Clara would? After all, seeing the pastor out on what looked like one of his first dates since his wife died was quite a scoop. Gossip didn't get much juicier. Bonnie stared into the dark, envisioning her carefully planned world of detachment crumbling around her, knowing there wasn't a single thing she could do about it.

CHAPTER 2

In the morning, after getting Ben and Josh off for school, Bonnie walked drowsily to the kitchen counter to fix herself a second cup of coffee. She'd had trouble getting to sleep the night before, and her dreams had been filled with disturbing images.

She was sitting next to Jeff Wells in the Coffee Shoppe. He said a blessing while he held her hand, and Bonnie experienced again the warmth she had felt at his touch and the look in his eyes when he had smiled at her the night before. Instead of releasing her hand when he finished his prayer, though, he brought it up slowly to his lips and kissed her palm tenderly. In the dream, Bonnie eyes locked with Jeff's, her heart pounding with the sheer surprise of it all, and he leaned over to kiss her. Just before their lips met, however, Bonnie looked up and saw Clara Adkinson's face, seeing that same look Clara had had in her eyes when she had referred to Bonnie and Dr. Wells as being "out on the town." Bonnie forced herself awake, astounded that she could have such thoughts about Jeff Wells in the first place, only to dream again and again of Clara "catching her in the act" of being with him as she drifted in and out of uneasy sleep.

What had been so wrong about it, anyway, Bonnie thought a little angrily. Weren't she and Dr. Wells both single? She knew that a lot of the older widows at church wouldn't think of seeing another man now that their husbands were gone. They, like Clara, seemed to view those who did with a suspicion born of some sort of distorted sense of moral superiority—as if it were a betrayal of the departed spouse still to need companionship, still to want love. Was that what was going on in Clara's mind?

But Bonnie had always thought it was so sweet when she saw older couples together, holding hands like teenagers: men who had outlived their wives and widows lucky enough to find someone their age with whom they felt compatible.

Clara just needs to mind her own business, Bonnie fumed to herself. Why shouldn't people be allowed to find companionship after they've grieved for a lost spouse?

Not, of course, that *she* was ready to look for such companionship…

The phone rang, jarring Bonnie from the argument she was having in her head. It was Carolyn Perkins.

"Just thought you'd like to know that John and Joanna had a false alarm last night. Turns out the baby wasn't quite ready for a change of scenery."

"Oh, boy, that's frustrating!" Bonnie sympathized. "Those false labor pains aren't very false, I can vouch for that."

"Well, the Reeves crew is pretty pooped after spending most of their evening with Joanna hooked up to a monitor and then getting sent home well after midnight. Anyway, I just thought you'd like to know."

"Oh, yes! Thanks for filling me in, Carolyn."

"Listen, I'll call and let Doctor Father know, but do you think you could pass the word along to Dr. Wells? That'd be one less call I'd have to make, and you'll probably be talking to him at church soon anyway, right?"

Just the mention of his name was enough to send the color rushing to Bonnie's face and her pulse thumping in her throat. "Oh! Well, sure! I…I guess I'll be talking to him Wednesday. Sure, I'll be glad to let him know."

"Great, thanks. Hey, let's do lunch soon, okay?"

Bonnie smiled and shook her head as she hung up, silently chiding herself for being such a goose. Carolyn had probably never given it a second thought that she and Dr. Wells had been left alone together last night. Once again, a ringing phone jarred Bonnie from her reverie.

"Hey, Bon, what's up?" It was Cheryl Summers, Bonnie's best friend.

"Mm, just having a little coffee and trying to wake up," Bonnie replied sleepily.

"Oh, come on. Jeff didn't keep you out that late last night, did he?"

Bonnie was awake instantly. She felt her throat constrict.

"Wha-a-at?" Bonnie croaked.

"No need to hide it from me! I heard you were out with Jeff Wells last night," teased Cheryl, who seemed not at all to doubt what she was saying.

"And, frankly, I'm a little hurt that you didn't even tell me you guys were dating. I'm supposed to be your best friend, aren't I?"

"How in the world…? Who told you…?" Bonnie spluttered.

"Clara Adkinson called early this morning, *supposedly* to give me her input on the Missions part of the Auxiliary newsletter." At the mention of Clara's name, Bonnie closed her eyes and felt herself re-living all her nightmares of the previous restless night. "But *I* think she just couldn't wait to share her juicy morsel of information. She usually waits until I call her." Bonnie could just see the smile on Cheryl's face: mischievous but not malicious. "Or maybe she was trying to see if I had any more information on you guys—Of course, it was all news to me, and I told her so. But I'll bet half of Chandler City knows you two were out together last night," Cheryl kidded her, "and the other half is finding out right now!"

Bonnie knew Cheryl was just playing with her, but inside she was mortified. Cheryl was probably exactly right. How could Clara! The old joke about the fastest means of communication came to mind: telegraph, telephone, and tell Clara.

Then she remembered: Mertis Hargrove had been with Clara. She wondered with a sinking feeling whether Mertis's tongue would be as loose as Clara's apparently was.

"We were *not* out together last night." Bonnie struggled not to put too much vehemence in her voice. "The Benevolent Board members always have dinner together after the monthly meetings, but Dr. Father, John Reeves, and Carolyn Perkins had to leave. Clara just happened to see us there after everyone else had gone. What a conclusion for her to jump to!" Bonnie moaned.

"Hmm. *I* certainly never would've pictured you and Dr. Wells together, it's true," Cheryl mused. "But it's not like it would be the end of the world for you to be out on a date, either! I'd kind of like to see you meet someone nice. I know you still miss Bill, Bonnie, and I know you'll always love him, but…you're just a young woman."

"Thirty-five doesn't *feel* so young sometimes," Bonnie muttered. "Even so, I just hate the idea of anyone gossiping about me. Or Dr. Wells! I mean, you know how people can be. He's such a good pastor. I'd hate for anyone to be saying catty, malicious things about him. For all we know, he may be seeing someone. Wouldn't it be a shame if this gossip got to her?"

"Well, it's been a little over two years since he lost Terri," Cheryl replied. "The man is certainly entitled. Don't you think we would've heard something about it, though, if he were seeing someone?"

"Not necessarily. Dr. Wells impresses me as a man who likes what little privacy his very public life affords him." Then she caught herself. "Listen to us! It's none of our business who or even *if* the pastor is dating. I just know it isn't me!"

"Well, now that I think about it, why *not* you and Jeff Wells? I can't think of a nicer lady than you," Cheryl finished brightly.

"Puh-lease," said Bonnie. "Trust me. The subject has never, ever come up. I don't know if Jeff Wells has dated anyone since Terri died or not, but I do know that he has never asked me out. And last night was no exception!"

"Maybe, maybe not," Cheryl teased. "Clara's a pretty unimpeachable source!" She laughed at her own joke and then said, "Listen, I'll let you go. I just had to call and see if Clara Adkinson was off her rocker or what. I didn't really think you'd start dating again and not tell me first."

"If and when it happens, you'll be the first to know," promised Bonnie, shaking her head with a smile. "Will I see you guys at Fellowship Supper tomorrow night?"

"The Summers gang will be there in force. Amanda and Carrie are getting so excited about the retreat this weekend. They're having some kind of pre-retreat meeting for the counselors. I think we may have a budding romance between Amanda and Jeff Wells, Jr." Cheryl sighed at the thought. "By the way, aren't Ben and Josh going?"

"Yes, my *babies* are going on an overnight retreat!" Bonnie said in mock sorrow. "I can't believe they're already old enough."

"Oh, it happens quickly, I know," Cheryl said with sympathy. "Listen, why don't you come over for dinner with Jack and me Friday after we drop them off at church?"

"Are you sure you guys wouldn't rather spend the time alone?"

"Nah," Cheryl scoffed. "We haven't had you over in ages. Come on. We'll play a hot game of Scrabble over dessert!"

"That'll be great. Want me to bring dessert?"

"You don't have to ask me twice! Make some of that decadent Chocolate Mousse Pie for me you're so good at. Listen, we'll see you guys tomorrow, okay?" As if she couldn't resist a parting shot, she added, "Let me know if you and Dr. Wells have any more dates!"

Bonnie shook her head with a derisive smile. That Cheryl! No sooner had she hung up the phone and turned to retrieve her coffee from the other side of the counter, when the phone rang yet again. *That's going to be one cold cup of coffee*, she thought as she picked up the receiver.

"Hello?" she answered, half expecting it to be a telemarketer. This seemed to be the time of day for it.

"Bonnie, this is Jeff Wells." Her heart gah-lumped in her chest at the sound of his voice. What on earth was wrong with her? All this talk about dating and Jeff Wells had her completely discombobulated.

"Good morning, Dr. Wells." She struggled to sound nonchalant.

"Um, listen," he said, sounding unsure of what to say. This, from Dr. Wells, was highly unusual. "I, uh, I wanted to let you know that the, um, the bank statement for the Benevolent Fund was in this morning's mail."

"Oh, okay," said Bonnie, a little mystified. He usually had Sandra, his secretary, call to let her know things like that. In fact, the one and only time Jeff Wells had personally called her for any reason was to ask her to consider taking on the Council treasurer's job after he had become Benevolent Council president. Now that Carolyn Perkins was going to be taking over the treasurer's job, there was even less reason for him to be calling her about this. "I can pick it up and drop it off at Carolyn's office this morning when I'm downtown if you'd like."

"Man!" He sounded chagrined. "Why do I keep forgetting that we're rolling off the board? Must be a mental block with me! Are you sure? I'll just give Carolyn a call."

"No, no, I don't mind at all," Bonnie assured him. "As I said, I'll be downtown anyway." There was a long, uncomfortable pause, and then Bonnie remembered Carolyn's news. "Oh, by the way, Carolyn Perkins called this morning to tell me that Joanna didn't have the baby last night after all."

"False alarm, eh?" His voice brightened, as if he were glad for a reason to keep the conversation going.

"Happens to the best of us." There was that silence again.

"Well, uh, I'll leave that bank statement with Sandra, and I guess you can pick it up on your way to church tomorrow night, right?"

"Well, as I said," Bonnie reminded him tactfully, utterly amazed that he had forgotten so quickly, "I have to be downtown this morning anyway. I'll pick it up while I'm there and drop it off at Carolyn's law office."

"Gosh, that's right! I…I don't know where my head is this morning!" There was another long pause.

"Well, okay." Was there something else he wanted? It was hard to believe that Dr. Wells had called her just to tell her about the Council bank statement. "Thanks. 'Bye."

"Um…goodbye," he said, and hung up.

Hmm, thought Bonnie. *That was kind of strange*. Again, she started to reach for her coffee cup and, again, the phone rang.

"Hello?"

"It's me again," said Jeff Wells. Bonnie's heart began a new dance in her throat. "I'm sorry, I'm not doing this very well, I know. It's just that…It's been a long time," he stammered. "I was just wondering, um, are Ben and Josh going on the children's retreat this weekend?"

Bonnie again struggled to sound casual. She knew what was coming, but she still couldn't believe it.

"Yes, they'll be going," she answered slowly.

"Yeah, Jeff Junior's going to be a counselor, so he'll be going, too. The fact that Amanda Summers is also going as a counselor probably played a part in this sudden burst of altruism," he said. Again, a pause. "So," he began again after taking a deep breath, trying without success to sound offhand, "I thought that since you and I were both going to be without kids this Friday, maybe we could share some dinner."

Even though she had somehow known that this was the real reason he had called before, Bonnie was still overwhelmed. Dr. Jeff Wells was actually asking her out! The man she had looked up to for almost eight years as her pastor. The man who had visited her in the hospital when she'd had pneumonia. The man who had helped her bury her husband after the car accident two years ago. The man who had looked at her with such kindness and warmth last night. Had there been something else in his look that she simply had not allowed herself to see?

"I…I…" Bonnie stammered.

"I know this is kind of sudden, but I just got to thinking after you left the restaurant last night that we won't be having any more Board meetings together, and I don't want to stop…I mean, I'd like to see you…I mean…"

Bonnie listened again in amazement as he struggled to find the right words—Jeff Wells, who seemed *always* to know the right thing to say. She felt a sudden, overwhelming desire for this conversation to be over. This couldn't be happening. She wasn't ready for this! She just couldn't believe that, after all this time, she was finally being asked for a date. And by Jeff Wells, of all people! Her legs were barely supporting her. She wanted to yell, "No!" hang up the phone, and just collapse where she stood.

"Dinner Friday night would be nice," she heard herself saying softly, incredulous at her own words. What was she doing? Had she lost her mind completely?

After a pause, not quite long enough to be awkward, Jeff sounded like himself again: "Well, good! How shall we work this out?" As if thinking aloud, he said, "The kids meet in the church parking lot at six. Since I'm so close to the church, would you like to swing by when you drop the boys off, and we can leave from my house?"

"Yes, that'll be fine," Bonnie murmured. Now it was her turn to pause awkwardly. "I...I guess I'll see you a little after six on Friday."

"I'm looking forward to it."

When she hung up the phone, Bonnie just stood staring at the receiver in its cradle, listening to her heart thud in her ears. After two years without a man in her life—two years of holding on to the memory of a husband gone forever, two years of deftly changing the conversation whenever she even *thought* a man might be getting ready to ask her out—she was going out on a *date*.

And not just any date, but a date with one of the most visible, prominent men in Chandler City, the pastor of Foster Road Baptist Church, one of the largest in Georgia. What in the world had possessed her to say yes to him?

True, she had always admired him: he preached wonderfully meaningful sermons; he was a joy to watch with the children of the church; he was gentle and personable with the fragile little old ladies who were the mainstays of the congregation. He wasn't above a sweaty game of basketball with the youth nor, Bonnie had heard, playing practical jokes on the Minister of Music or his own secretary. And, just as in the restaurant last night, he seemed always to have just the right words at his disposal. Words of encouragement when projects seemed overwhelming. Words of praise for jobs well done. Words of comfort in times of sorrow.

She remembered, still, the words he had spoken at Bill's funeral, how he had found just the right combination of Scriptures. His words seemed to break through the pain she was feeling to create a glow of hope and reassurance in her heart. She remembered, too, that when Terri, Jeff's wife, had died not six months later after a shockingly brief battle with cancer, she herself could only mutely grasp his hands in hers, look into his eyes through her tears, and hope that he could feel how she shared his sorrow.

Then she smiled as she thought about this wonderfully articulate man struggling to get the words out to ask her to dinner. It was actually kind of cute.

Cute! How long had it been since she had thought of anyone as being cute? And she realized that, yes, Jeff Wells, with his kind, gray-green eyes and his warm, sometimes impishly playful smile, *was* an attractive man. She'd just never stopped to think of him that way before. "This is kind of sudden," Jeff had said. They had only known each other eight years! And yet, this *was* a sudden turn of events!

Then, she had another, sinking, thought. *Oh, no!* Not two minutes before Dr. Wells had called, she had said she would have dinner with Jack and Cheryl. Now what was she going to do? She would have to cancel—with whom? She knew that Cheryl would understand if she told her, but then she'd have to *tell* her! This wasn't something she wanted to advertise all over Chandler City! Not that Cheryl would break a confidence, of course, but it seemed premature to make announcements of *any* sort, even to Cheryl. To have to tell her she had a date with Jeff Wells after she'd just spent all that energy denying any truth to the rumors Clara Adkinson was spreading! No, she was just going to have to call Dr. Wells and cancel. She just had to—didn't she?

She picked up the phone and dialed Cheryl's number.

"Cheryl, it's me."

"What's wrong?" asked Cheryl, alarmed at Bonnie's tone.

"No, no, nothing's wrong, but you're not going to believe this." Bonnie dreaded actually saying the words.

"What? What is it?"

"I...I know what I just got finished telling you, but Dr. Wells just called and..."

"He asked you *out*?" Cheryl shrieked. They were like a couple of high school girls talking about the captain of the football team.

"There's a problem, though," Bonnie told her.

"Don't tell me you said no. Please tell me you didn't say no!"

"That's the problem," Bonnie said with a rueful smile. "I *didn't* say no. I said yes, and he asked me to have dinner with him this Friday. After I already said I'd have dinner with you guys!"

"Oh, Bonnie, give me a break! Do you really think I care? I am so excited for you I could just scream!" Cheryl seemed truly elated for her. Bonnie just wished she could feel the same elation for herself. All she felt was butterflies.

"So you won't mind if I take a rain check?" asked Bonnie, seeking reassurance.

"Go! Go with my profoundest blessings!"

"Since you're so excited, maybe you should go for me." Bonnie smiled dreamily. "I'm not quite sure what I've gotten myself into."

"Hey, this is *Jeff Wells* we're talking about," Cheryl reminded her. "You know what a wonderful man he is. I would've been upset if you *had* said no to him on our account. You can have dinner with an old married couple anytime. It isn't every day Jeff Wells asks you out."

And thank goodness for that, thought Bonnie.

"Well, I'll see you tomorrow night anyway, right?" Bonnie asked.

"You got it."

"And Cheryl," Bonnie began diffidently.

"Yeah?"

"Not that you would, but please don't breathe a word of this to anyone. Please. Not even to Jack, okay?"

"Bonnie, you ought to know me better than that. My lips are sealed—I won't tell a soul. But," she added with devilish delight in her voice, "you still owe me a Chocolate Mousse Pie!"

"A small price to pay for your silence!" Bonnie smiled, actually a little relieved that she *had* told Cheryl. "I'll see you tomorrow night."

With that, Bonnie was left to contemplate a date. *A date with Jeff Wells.*

Jeff Wells looked without seeing the phone, a bemused smile on his face, when he'd ended his conversation with Bonnie.

Yes! he thought, very pleased with the results of his call. Okay, the second call.

He'd been worried that Bonnie's hasty exit from the Coffee Shoppe last night would mean she'd be too upset about Clara Adkinson's "out on the town" remark to accept his dinner invitation. He could see that Bonnie wouldn't want to feel rushed or pressured, feelings he would have to be careful to accommodate. *After all,* he thought, ruefully remembering the times that Terri had chafed at the fishbowl-like existence they often led as a pastor's family, *it's not exactly like I can do anything in this town without everybody and his uncle thinking they have a say in it. Including Clara. Especially Clara! I don't want her making a big deal out of anything before it even gets started! I've got to find a way to mention it to her when she comes by this morning.*

As if reading his thoughts, Clara Adkinson tapped expertly manicured fingernails on Dr. Wells's door and called, "Yoo-hoo! Am I in time for our little meeting?"

Jeff stood and walked around his desk to greet her. "Good morning, Clara. How are you this morning?"

"Oh, about as well as an old lady like me can expect to be, I suppose," Clara answered airily, a knowing smile on her face. There wasn't a thing decrepit about Clara Adkinson.

"I should be in as good shape as you are," Jeff chided her with a return of her knowing look. He put an arm around her shoulder and led her to the sofa near a coffee table at the front of his office. "Can I offer you a cup of coffee?"

"Thank you, I'd love some." As Jeff went to the coffee maker on his credenza, Clara continued, "Oh, and speaking of coffee, it was so nice to see you out with Bonnie Callaway last night. She's a lovely girl." And then, more archly, "I hadn't *realized* that you'd begun dating again."

With his back turned to Clara, Jeff closed his eyes and stifled a frustrated sigh. "Well, strictly speaking, we weren't *out* together, at least not in the way you mean," he tried to put as much meaning as possible in his eyes as he met Clara's when he handed her her coffee.

"Oh, really?"

Jeff noted with derision the pleased look on her face. *Never known for your subtlety, eh, Clara?*

"Well, then, I'd say that's *her* loss," Clara said primly. Then, with a look that dripped concerned sympathy, "Terri left some awfully big shoes to fill, didn't she? The woman lucky enough to snare you will have to be quite a lady indeed, won't she?"

"Clara," Jeff began, making no attempt to hide his discomfort with this discussion, "I'm *not* looking to fill Terri's shoes…"

"No, no, of course you're not, dear," Clara was quick to counter. "Don't let anyone rush you into anything you're not ready for. After all, a man in your position can't be too careful what he does."

You don't know the half of it, Jeff thought. In an attempt to change the subject, he said, "So what do you have lined up for 'Retro Night?'"

"Oh, Dr. Wells, if I do say so myself, I think this is going to be our best Seniors' banquet ever! Things are really falling into place. And, I have a special surprise for everyone," she said with a conspiratorial twinkle in her eye. "I've persuaded Anna Lee to do a medley of Rosemary Clooney's hit songs! She's working on them already."

Speaking of trying to rush people into things they're not ready for!

"That'll be a real treat," Jeff said, a smile painted on his face. "Your daughter has a beautiful voice."

"And, if it's all right with you, I've arranged to have her sit at our table before and after she sings," said Clara, looking into her coffee cup. "After all, she's doing us a favor as it is, socializing with us older folks. Letting her sit with the only young fella in the room is the least I can do for her, don't you think?"

Jeff could just barely hide his amazement at the look of utter innocence in Clara's eyes as she maneuvered once again to have her daughter in his company.

"That'll be fine," Jeff replied, his voice as non-committal as he could make it sound. "So what else do you have planned for the evening?"

As Jeff listened to Clara enthuse on her preparations for the upcoming banquet, part of his mind was occupied with the realization that, much as he was looking forward to seeing Bonnie Callaway, he was going to have to be as discreet as possible. He didn't want any woman he happened to be with at any given time to become an object of scrutiny and speculation. If last night was any indication, Clara had *already* begun to scrutinize Bonnie. *With her living right across the street from me*, Jeff mused, *she's in the best position of anyone in this church to observe my comings and goings. Maybe I should call Bonnie and have her meet me somewhere else. And how would I explain that to her?*

"By the way, Bonnie," he could just imagine himself as saying, "can we meet on the other side of town from my house? We need to avoid seeing Clara when we go out because she might start to gossip about us."

Yeah, right. Great way to start a relationship.

CHAPTER 3

Bonnie drank the last of her tepid coffee and closed her Bible. It never failed to amaze her that God could speak to her in such timely ways. The scripture accompanying her daily devotion message was from II Corinthians 12: "...there was a thorn in my flesh...I asked the Lord three times that it might leave me...And he said to me, 'My grace is sufficient for you, for My power is perfected in weakness'..." Her grief had been like a thorn in her flesh. She could never have Bill back, so the thorn would never really be gone, but God's strength had sustained her. The words of Paul brought her comfort even as she wondered now what the future held, something she rarely did.

For, as a rule, there was little to anticipate in Bonnie's weeks. When Ben and Josh were in school, she spent her time completing various computer-related assignments for her small-but-growing list of clients. In the afternoons, "Mom's taxi" provided transportation to soccer practice and piano and tae kwon do lessons. The boys spent their evenings after supper doing homework or playing endless rounds of games on the family computer that doubled as a video arcade. With the exception of those occasional evenings when she had a PTA meeting or a Benevolent Council meeting to attend (which she wouldn't anymore for a while), the days flowed by in a pleasant but very predictable routine. In the summers, they took long car trips to visit her parents in New Orleans or Bill's parents in Jackson, Mississippi.

But this week! Suddenly, a towering question mark loomed at the end of it! She began looking forward to her dinner on Friday with a growing sense of excitement and anticipation and, well, not a few misgivings. Her life was not exciting, she conceded, but *comfortable* the way it was. Did she really want to risk changing all that by going out with Jeff Wells?

She remembered only too well her single days as a career woman in New Orleans. She had certainly encountered her share of frogs before she had found her Prince. Three years out of college, she had married Bill. The year after that, they had moved to Chandler City when his company had transferred him. Crazy as it might seem, she still felt a sense of loyalty to Bill. Or maybe, she sometimes thought, it was that she felt guilty that Bill had been the one to go out that late Sunday night for an emergency milk-and-bread run—that he was the victim of the drunk driver and she had been safe at home. She also worried, when she thought about it at all, that the boys might doubt the love she'd had for their father if she began to see anyone new. It had been a moot point, anyway—she had never seen or met anyone she felt remotely attracted to or interested in. Until last night. Had she simply been numb all this time? Was she beginning to feel again? What about all those crazy dreams of almost kissing Jeff Wells? Did that mean she *wanted* to kiss him?

It was true that she had always admired Dr. Wells, but Bonnie was suddenly struck by just how little she really knew about Jeff Wells, the man. He seemed to have quite a sense of humor, judging from the stories and jokes he interspersed through his sermons and the banter he carried on at Benevolent Council meetings and dinners. Bonnie remembered how it was Bill's unfailing ability to make her laugh that had first attracted her to him at Singles gatherings at their church in New Orleans.

Dr. Wells was somewhat athletic; he played basketball on the church's men's team, and he was known for a pretty mean game of racquetball. When Bonnie and Bill started dating, he had persuaded her to go with him on his morning runs through Audubon Park. Once she had gotten her wind and her legs in shape, she had become an avid runner. As a result, she'd had little trouble regaining her figure after the births of their two sons. Even now, Bonnie still felt a sense of closeness to Bill when she ran on "their" old route here in Chandler City.

Bonnie went into her office and turned on her computer. And then it hit her. She was comparing Jeff Wells to Bill! How unfair! No one could replace Bill, and she doubted that Dr. Wells would even want to try. How would she like it if Dr. Wells compared her to Terri? How would *she* measure up?

Again, from the admittedly little Bonnie knew about her, Terri Wells had seemed the perfect minister's wife. She was an attractive yet modest woman who gave of herself unselfishly to various projects and causes in the church. Yet she never gave the impression that she was doing things just because she was The Minister's Wife. She'd had her own ministry.

Bonnie put the diskette for her latest project in the drive and reminded herself that Terri had also been a career woman. She had earned a master's degree and had run a successful freelance art business while raising their two children. When the youngest, Jeff Junior, entered high school, she took an adjunct faculty position teaching art at Chandler City Community College. It was there that Terri had gotten to know "Doctor Father" Blake, who had recommended her for a position on the Benevolent Council. Bonnie knew that, a couple of months after Bill died, Terri had been trying to help her get back into life by nominating her for a seat on the Council, but still she had almost turned Terri down. She hadn't thought she would have the spiritual or emotional energy to do justice to the job.

Looking back on it, Bonnie realized that it was that very participation that had helped her look up out of the darkness of her mourning and into the light of the living. After Terri's death, Dr. Wells had agreed to fulfill the rest of his wife's Council term. It was his participation in the Council that had, for better or worse, put him and Bonnie together at a restaurant table last night and seemed to have been the catalyst for his asking her out to dinner. Bonnie would like to have thanked Terri for bringing something into her life that, in retrospect, had been a source of healing. But how would Terri feel about the fact that the Council seemed to have brought her and Jeff together?

As the computer booted up, Bonnie studied the picture of their family that Bill had digitally scanned and loaded as a wallpaper on the computer screen. She looked at Bill with Josh, still a baby at the time the picture was taken, in his lap. She thought again that, no, it wasn't fair to compare Dr. Wells to Bill, and she didn't want to be compared to Terri. She doubted seriously whether she could measure up. She secretly wondered how long it would take Jeff to figure out that she was not the woman Terri had been. This whole thing was probably just a waste of time. Maybe it would be better if she just saved them both the time and trouble of finding out that she wasn't a suitable partner for Jeff.

Partner! *Get a grip on yourself, girl!* Bonnie thought. All of this projecting into the future, when they had not even spent their first evening together! (If you didn't count last night.) She would call him and cancel. Yes, that's what she should do.

And tell him what? "I'm sorry, Dr. Wells. I just don't think we're suited to each another." She could hear his counterargument: How could she possibly know that? They had to give themselves a chance to find out, didn't they? Jeff would be right, of course. So it looked like she was stuck: now that she had agreed to it, she was just going to have to have dinner with Jeff Wells. It wasn't like he had asked her to *marry* him, after all. It was just dinner. *Just dinner*, she repeated to herself.

Bonnie called up her first document and forced herself to concentrate on her work.

One of the nice things about working for clients who were almost all female, Bonnie thought as she headed downtown later that morning, was that she didn't have to contend with being propositioned for dates by unwelcome suitors. Bonnie remembered only too well her office working days—how the various equipment and supply salesmen she'd had to deal with as an office manager seemed to think it perfectly natural, because she was single, to ask her to lunch or dinner. As if she would be inclined to begin a dating relationship with someone she barely knew from sales visits; as if their business relationship were completely irrelevant; as if the cordial smile she afforded anyone and everyone she had to deal with on her firm's behalf were meant solely for them.

She had always hated it when someone did ask her out because, when she turned him down, as she invariably did, he would be offended, sometimes even asking *why*, for goodness' sake. Thus, the working relationship was forever tainted, the rejected party always assuming a somewhat miffed posture when he had to come in again for periodic sales calls. It was maddening. Hadn't these guys even *considered* that she might turn them down? Hadn't they stopped to think that it would make future sales calls awkward and difficult? Obviously not.

Such concerns were essentially over now. Bonnie had practically handpicked her clients. There were Claire Smith and Betty Anderson, the owners of a breakfast-and-lunch-only shop and catering service. She prepared their menus and fliers and maintained a database of customers for their monthly mailings. There was Margie Bryant, a real estate agent who sometimes needed secretarial work done. She even typed up an occasional will or contract for Carolyn Perkins when the attorney did work for clients privately, or other legal documents for those who came to the Benevolent Council for help. Bonnie had also gotten occasional work when John Reeves or Norman Blake referred people from their churches to her. Even those she considered carefully, though. It was nice to be able to pick and choose her clients, nice not to be desperate for work.

When she had work to deliver to them, as she did today, Bonnie always visited Claire and Betty at Grabbabite at around ten in the morning, after the breakfast business and well before the lunch rush. On this particular morning, parking had been practically nonexistent; she had lugged a big box of fliers advertising Grabbabite's specials for next week a block and a half. When she got to the plate glass door, which pulled out, she leaned against it and looked in. From across the counter and through the rectangular glass window of the kitchen door, she could see Claire and Betty talking to each other. Just as she was about to put the box down to open the door, a cloud of cigarette smoke enveloped her head and a booming male voice behind her said, "Here, baby, let me get that for you."

She turned to see who her overly familiar rescuer was and found his face and his cigarette uncomfortably close to her own as he reached around her, practically engulfing her in his arms, to open the door. She turned quickly away, puzzling to herself that she thought she recognized the man somehow. He was tall—very tall, perhaps six foot three or more—and had dark, curly hair. He wasn't especially good-looking, but was impressive in the way that most well-groomed men in well-tailored business suits are. Where had she seen this man before?

"Well, Bonnie Martin! I thought that was you!" this strange-but-familiar man announced embarrassingly loudly, using her maiden name. "I ain't seen you in a 'coon's age, girl! And I guess you probably don't go by Martin no more since ya went off and got married on me!"

As Bonnie lunged forward to deposit her box on the counter, she looked at him again, certain that this man's voice had probably been heard several blocks away. "It's Callaway now," she said cautiously, still struggling to put a name to the face.

"And I'll bet you don't even remember your old boyfriend, Preston Hardy, do ya, baby?" Why did this man feel compelled to speak as though over a public address system? At the sound of his voice, Claire and Betty turned to look and then started out of the kitchen toward them.

"Hey, mornin', ladies! I'll have my usual," said the stranger, using that everybody-knows-me tone again. Claire turned to pour him a cup of coffee and place a bear claw on a plate. "I guess y'all must know my old girlfriend, Bonnie Martin—I mean Callaway." Bonnie felt herself coloring at the word *girlfriend*. "And ya know what? I don't even think she remembers me!"

You've got that right, mister, Bonnie thought, fervently wishing he would lower his voice.

"Well," he demurred, "I gotta be honest and admit that ol' Bonnie here never really let me get my foot in the door, but it wasn't for my lack of trying! She was on my coffee sales route when I was workin' outta New Orleans. That is, till she up and got married on me and moved off to...well, I guess *this* is where ya moved off to, huh?"

So *that's* who he was! "Preston?" she asked tentatively, "Preston Hardy?"

"Well, there's hope fer you yet, girl!" he mumbled through a big bite of the bear claw.

"Gosh, that was over ten years ago! I'm surprised you remember *my* name. What...what are you doing in Chandler City?" Bonnie asked, reluctant actually to encourage conversation with this man who, she was now beginning to recall more clearly, had always been this obnoxious.

"Oh, I never ferget a name or a face, baby. That's the lifeblood of a salesman," he said, his mouth still full, little clumps of sugar glaze clinging to the corners of his mouth. "I got out of the coffee business, though—not a lotta room fer growth there, ya know? I'm repping for an insurance company out of Atlanta now. I been coming to Chandler City here once or twice a week for the past six months or so. First time I run into *you*, though! Ain't this somethin'! So how's that ol' husband of yours treatin' my ol' girlfriend, anyhoo? And by the way," he added with a mischievous leer, "y'all need any insurance?"

Bonnie wished he would *stop* calling her his old girlfriend, but this man obviously had no concept of his own offensiveness. "He's..." Bonnie struggled to say the word. "I'm a widow now."

"Aw, hey, I'm real sorry to hear that, darlin'." Preston's face was momentarily solemn, but sugar glaze still clung to his chin. "Me, I'm just goin' through a divorce myself. Maybe you and me can get together some night and cry in our beer together." He cracked a big grin at his own tasteless joke.

"Are these the special fliers for next week?" interrupted Betty, coming to Bonnie's rescue. "They look great, as usual. How much do we owe you?"

Relieved at the distraction, Bonnie turned to her customers. "The invoice is on top there."

"Would you care for a cup of coffee?" Claire asked as Betty went to the office area in the kitchen to write a check for Bonnie.

"Oh, no thanks," said Bonnie wistfully. "I have a few more stops to make this morning." Normally, she would have lingered a while, chatting over coffee and a bran muffin. The wonderful smells emanating from Betty and Claire's kitchen—of quiches crowded with savory onions and chickens roasting with rosemary—were practically edible themselves. But she really didn't want to stay as long as Preston Hardy was there.

"Say, what've you got there?" asked Preston, picking up one of the fliers to examine it. "You run a copy shop or somethin'?"

"I have a word processing business. I typeset these using my desktop publishing software," Bonnie answered, not looking directly at him. Preston took no notice. He brushed flakes of glaze from his suit as his cheek bulged with the last half of the bear claw.

"You do any secretarial-type work?" came the muffled question.

"Well, yes, but I—"

"Well, maybe I can throw a little business your way," he said, reaching into his breast pocket for a business card to hand to her. "My company don't provide secretarial service to us reps—we're on our own there. I guess you can imagine that my typin' ain't the best in the world. How'd ya like to do some mass mailin's for me? I'd provide you with a list of potential customers, say five or six hundred names, and you'd type up a 'personalized' letter for each of them. You could do my follow-up thank you letters for the sales I make, too. Sure would be a big help to me!"

Bonnie did a quick mental calculation of the fee that such a project would bring. It was tempting, but to have to work with Preston Hardy…

"I…I really have about all the work I can handle right now," Bonnie lied.

"Here you go," said Claire, coming out of the kitchen again and handing her a check. "And here's the list for next time. By the way, we're going to be going up on some of our prices and adding a few items to the lunch menu. We'd like to have you typeset it for us this time. Can you take a copy of the old one and make us some samples to look at? Use that creative mind of yours—you always make things look so pretty and eye-catching!"

Great, thought Bonnie. *I've just turned Preston down and now two of my best customers are asking me to take on more work.* "Sure, I'll be glad to," said Bonnie weakly, avoiding Preston's eye.

"Well, there, that's what I thought!" boomed Preston. "A good businessman's always lookin' to expand his work base, huh? Or are you one of them wimmin's libbers that makes ya say 'business*person*'? Hey! Why don't we talk about it over dinner tonight? You got any plans for dinner? Maybe now I can finally have dinner with my old girlfriend after all this time!"

Good grief, thought Bonnie. *This man is too much!*

"I really—Some other time, perhaps," murmured Bonnie. "Claire, I'll get back to you about those menus as soon as I can. Have a great day!" Without bothering to say goodbye to Preston, Bonnie rushed out the door.

Even after it closed, she could hear Preston booming, "That girl always was a slippery one!"

Bonnie's next stop was the church office to pick up the bank statement Dr. Wells had called her about. His car was in the parking lot and, her heart pounding, she found herself half hoping, half dreading that she would see him when she went in. But, as he always had in the past, Dr. Wells had left the statement with Sandra, the church receptionist and pastor's secretary. Bonnie made idle chit-chat with Sandra, glancing periodically at the closed door of the pastor's office, hoping he might have reason to come out while she was standing there, until the phone rang.

"Can you hang on a second?" asked Sandra, reaching for the flashing button.

"Oh, that's okay, I'll just run on," Bonnie answered, feeling a little sheepish. Glancing at her watch as she opened her purse for her keys, she saw that it was just about lunch time. She decided to head over to the Coffee Shoppe before going home. Grabbabite would have been closer, but she didn't want to take even the slightest chance that Preston Hardy might decide to go there for lunch, too.

The waiting area of the restaurant was crowded with business people on their lunch hours. She was scanning the faces to see if she might recognize anyone, when a now-familiar voice boomed behind her, "Well, looka there! It's my old girlfriend again! We gotta stop meetin' like this, darlin'!" Preston Hardy swooped one of his long arms around her shoulders and scrunched her in for a huge bear hug. People around them looked on curiously and edged out of the way of Preston's flying arms. To disentangle herself from this decidedly unwelcome embrace, Bonnie bent her knees. She tried to back out from under his arm, but only succeeded in mussing the top of her hair as Preston moved right around with her. As their awkward pivot continued, she suddenly came face-to-face once again with Clara Adkinson.

Clara's eyes flew open with shock and surprise. Then her look changed to one of smug triumph, just like the one she had given Bonnie the night before when Bonnie had blushed at being seen alone with Jeff Wells. "Well," Clara said primly, a glint in her eye, "The Coffee Shoppe must be your favorite place to bring a date these days, eh, Bonnie?"

Eager to make the acquaintance of anyone that Bonnie knew, Preston swung his arm forward to shake hands with Clara. That part of Bonnie's hair that wasn't standing on end now completely covered her face. She could feel herself reddening, as much from Clara's insinuations as from her dishevelment. She heard Preston introducing himself as she tried to restore order to her hair. Clara took Preston's proffered hand, but never took her eyes off of Bonnie.

"Bonnie! Bonnie!" Carolyn Perkins had miraculously appeared from among the crowd, and Bonnie couldn't remember when she'd ever been so glad to see anyone. "Come join me for lunch!"

When Bonnie sat down in a booth across from Carolyn, she glanced back at Preston, who was still trying to listen politely to whatever Clara Adkinson was saying, while searching the restaurant for her.

"What on earth was that all about?" asked Carolyn, unable to contain a smile.

"I think I wish I'd stayed in bed this morning." Bonnie smiled ruefully. "I mean, in two years, I've hardly even spoken with a man, and today I've been asked out twice!"

"This," said Carolyn with a skeptical glance back at Preston, "sounds like a story I want to hear!"

CHAPTER 4

During the next few days, Bonnie would at times find herself preoccupied with thoughts of her upcoming dinner with Jeff Wells. Where would they go? What would they talk about? Would she know how to act, or would that panicky feeling she'd had Monday night after Clara Adkinson's appearance return to haunt her? During her morning prayers, normally a time of focus and purpose, she would find herself praying earnestly for—she couldn't exactly say what for. God's will, to be sure, and wisdom and guidance. But there were unspoken things in her heart that she knew only God could understand and translate into the proper prayer. Her preoccupation even crept into her work. She sometimes found herself staring at her computer screen, seeing not the words and figures on it, but an imaginary table in a restaurant where she and Dr. Wells were seated together. She found it difficult to imagine their conversation, but she saw vividly his smiling, gray-green eyes.

At Fellowship Supper on Wednesday night, Dr. Wells had come to the table where she and the boys sat with Cheryl, Jack, and their girls, but it was only to say his customary, "How's everyone here tonight?" In fact, he'd stood behind her chair, a friendly hand on her shoulder, so they hadn't even made eye contact. Just the same, she had felt herself coloring at his nearness and was keenly aware of the warmth of his hand. When he had gone on to greet those at another table, Bonnie glanced at Cheryl, who wiggled her eyebrows mischievously.

When Jeff finally sat down to eat his own dinner, Bonnie was intrigued to see Clara Adkinson make a beeline for his table, her daughter Anna Lee trailing dutifully behind her. Clara seemed to make a big show of greeting the pastor, her smile unnaturally large, telling Jeff something that made him turn to smile and make a remark to Anna Lee. Anna Lee smiled shyly and Bonnie could see her blush from across the room.

Bonnie sometimes felt sorry for Anna Lee; having Clara Adkinson for a mother couldn't be easy. She sometimes wondered why Anna Lee, a high school teacher whom she reckoned was about her own age, had never married. Although she was somewhat on the plain side (some might even call her dowdy), she had a nice figure and seemed intelligent enough. She appeared to be very shy, though.

Funny how a single phone call could change things. Any other Wednesday night, Bonnie would have been as nonchalantly pleased to greet the pastor in this casual way as anyone else in the congregation. But tonight, knowing that a new dimension had been added to her relationship with Jeff Wells (however untried it actually was), Bonnie caught herself feeling slighted somehow that Jeff's greeting or his acknowledgment of her hadn't been more substantial. Even though she should have known better, she had still been disappointed yesterday when he had left the Council bank statement with Sandra instead of using it as an excuse for her to come into his office to see him.

Get over yourself, she thought. After all, he was a busy man, and his office was hardly the place he would choose to have a really personal conversation with her. But tonight, when he saw her, couldn't he have…

What did you expect him to do? she chided herself. Make a declaration to the whole room that now there's a little more than meets the eye to our pastor-member relationship? Tell everyone that we have a date for Friday night?

As far as the rest of the world was concerned, Bonnie Callaway was just another member of Foster Road Baptist Church, with no particular significance for Jeff Wells. And, with the exception of their phone conversations yesterday morning, that was still largely true. On top of that, she had been mortified when she had learned that Clara Adkinson was spreading rumors about them. She wondered with inward dread just how many people might be buzzing about them all over Chandler City. She had sworn her best friend to secrecy about their date. Why should she be annoyed or hurt by Jeff's apparent desire for discretion?

It was so strange. Until two days ago, except for her memories of Bill, which she considered perfectly natural, she had hardly thought of a man in over two years. Now, after one phone call (okay, two) from Jeff Wells, she seemed constantly preoccupied with thoughts of him. What had she gotten herself into?

When Friday finally arrived, Bonnie conducted her usual morning routine: she got the boys off to school, had her quiet time of Bible study and prayer, did her morning run, then showered and dressed. As she looked in her closet, it occurred to her that she didn't know where they were going to eat that night. She wasn't sure what to wear. With a great deal of reluctance, she realized she was going to have to call Dr. Wells to see whether a dress or jeans were in order. She dialed the number for the church office.

"Foster Road Baptist Church." Instead of Sandra's cheery voice that usually answered at that number, it was that of Dr. Wells himself greeting her over the phone.

"Oh, good morning, Dr. Wells! I wasn't expecting you to answer!" she blurted, a little flustered at hearing his voice so suddenly.

"Well, sorry to disappoint you," he teased. "Sandra's coming in late this morning. Who would you like to speak with?"

"Well, actually, I was calling for you."

"In that case, I can help you." She could just see the smile in his eyes.

"Um, well, when we spoke the other day, we didn't talk about where we were going for dinner. I wasn't sure what to wear."

"Ah, no, I guess we didn't. Well, I thought that, since you won't have a baby sitter to relieve tonight, it wouldn't matter if you got home a little late. I thought we'd take a drive down to Mexico Beach and have some seafood at Captain John's. In fact, since Jeff Junior's not going to be using it, I thought we could borrow his old Mustang convertible and drive with the top down. Enjoy some of this spring air. Maybe even bring it home with an empty gas tank, like he used to do for me! How does that sound to you?"

Bonnie giggled—he could be such a hoot. "That sounds great! We haven't been to the beach yet this year," she said. Then, not really knowing what else to say, she added, "Well, I guess I'll see you this evening."

"I'm looking forward to it," he said warmly, as he had on Tuesday. And she realized that she, too, was really looking forward to their dinner now. She was still nervous about it, yes, but a drive to the beach! That would really be fun.

Bonnie suddenly had the urge to get a new outfit for the occasion. In a way, this dinner with Dr. Wells was a new beginning for her. Something new to wear seemed only appropriate.

She headed for the mall.

That evening, Bonnie made sure that Ben and Josh were properly packed for their overnight trip: missing toothbrushes were packed and superfluous plastic army men were set aside for their return. Wearing a bathrobe over her slip, she served them their favorite impromptu dinner of bagel pizzas, then went off to put the final touches on her make-up and finish dressing. As she looked at herself in the mirror, Bonnie was struck with idea of trying to imagine what Jeff Wells saw when he looked at her. Not bad for thirty-five, if she did say so herself. A natural blonde, there were times when she despaired over the utter lack of curl in her hair. It was silky and shiny, though, which counted for a lot. Tonight, she twisted its just-below-shoulder length into an upsweep from which wispy, feminine tendrils fell to grace her cheeks and the nape of her neck.

With a touch of mascara to her long but nearly invisible eyelashes and a hint of blush on her cheeks, the look was complete. She spotted her favorite perfume out of the corner of her eye and hesitated. When Bill had been alive, she had worn it only when she knew they wouldn't be together; he'd been allergic to perfume. Even now, she seldom wore it except for church occasionally. She reached for the atomizer and, making a sudden decision, spritzed her neck and wrists lightly.

She thought once again what a great choice the sundress had been for tonight. It was one of those flower prints that were in style right now and had a halter top. She was always a little tanned from her running, so the style was a perfect showcase for the flawless skin on her shoulders and back.

When she came out to get the boys to the car, Ben said, "Whoa, Mom! You look cool! And, boy, do you smell good!"

"Yeah," Josh chimed in. "You smell like Sunday!"

"Why're you so dressed up, Mom?"

Bonnie flushed a little. She hadn't told them about her dinner date with Dr. Wells—hadn't told anyone but Cheryl (not even Carolyn Perkins, who had tried to pry it out of her at lunch the other day)—but she hadn't anticipated *this* reaction either.

"Oh, well," she said, trying to downplay the matter, "I'm just going to dinner with some friends from church," she said, only half-truthfully.

With his most devilish grin, Josh said, "Must be a *boy*friend!"

"No way, dork-face," Ben corrected his little brother. "You know Mom doesn't have any boyfriends."

Even though this was technically true, Bonnie felt a little guilty because the situation appeared to be changing. She just couldn't bring herself to tell them anything yet.

"Don't call your brother a dork, Ben," she murmured absentmindedly.

After seeing the boys off to their first overnight trip away from home without her, Bonnie drove the short distance from the church to Jeff Wells's house. She remembered with a smile, as she drove, how her sons had given her reluctant goodbye hugs and kisses, surreptitiously glancing around to see if their friends had noticed. Boys! She also noted that Jeff had managed to see his own son off without making eye contact with her at all. Once again, she found herself fighting off a feeling of disappointment.

You're going to spend the whole evening with him, she reminded herself sternly.

Bonnie pulled into the drive beside Jeff's forest green SUV. She had wanted to be sure he got there first, so she'd spent a few minutes lingering in conversation with Cheryl and Jack. Jack apparently hadn't even been told that she was originally supposed to have dinner with them; Cheryl announced nonchalantly that Jack was taking her to dinner on "parents' night out."

"Speaking of dinner," Jack had said, smiling mischievously at Bonnie, "you look good enough to eat!"

"Down, boy!" Cheryl had smacked him playfully on the shoulder and dragged him away with a roll of her eyes and a wave to Bonnie. With a smile and a shake of her head, Bonnie hoped inwardly that Jeff would like the way she looked as well.

Seeing Bonnie approaching, Jeff opened his front door before she could ring the bell.

"Hi, there. Come on in," he said with a wave of his hand. "You look so nice." She could see genuine admiration in his eyes. In his navy polo shirt and khaki pants, he was rather easy on the eyes, himself. "And you smell wonderful!"

Bonnie felt herself blushing and hoped desperately that she hadn't worn too much perfume. She wished, too, that her stomach would stop jumping into her throat. She was a big fan of seafood, especially the kind you could get at Captain John's, but she wondered if she would be able to eat at all that night.

"I'll just be a second while I set the alarm, and we'll be off."

Bonnie sat tentatively on the edge of the sofa in the comfortably decorated living room. She noted that little had changed since she'd been here for a ladies' tea over four years ago. The backs of the chairs were still adorned with doilies Terri Wells had crocheted herself; the piano had an open hymnal resting on the sheet music shelf (but with their daughter, Becky, away at college, Bonnie suspected no one ever played anymore). The only change that Bonnie could see was that Terri's riotously blooming African violets, which had once graced the seat of the bay window facing the street, were long since gone; plastic ivy now added the only green to the room.

And there on the end table, a few feet to her right, was the family portrait: four smiling Wellses in much happier times—Jeff and Terri standing behind their two almost-grown children, his arm around Terri's waist, his right hand on Becky's shoulder, Terri's hand resting on Jeff Junior's shoulder. The sight of Terri's image, however much she told herself that she could have expected to see it, was almost more than Bonnie could bear.

It was only natural that Jeff should have this picture on display, she reminded herself. Bonnie hadn't put away any of the Callaway family pictures when Bill had died. Yet she knew that, even as she picked up the frames each time she dusted, she never really saw Bill's face. It was just easier not to look. She wondered if Jeff felt the same—whether he intentionally looked without seeing. Since he'd hired a housekeeper after Terri died, maybe he never came into this room at all.

As he entered the kitchen on his way to the alarm system control panel, the phone rang and Jeff picked up the receiver. Bonnie looked across the room and saw him standing facing away from her.

"Oh, I'm so sorry, Ruth," she heard him say. "I know we were expecting it, but it just doesn't seem possible that he's really gone." He paused. "Yes, certainly." Another pause. "Of course. I'll be over shortly."

What? He'd be over *where* shortly?

She stood up and looked at him anxiously as he walked toward her. In his eyes were sadness and profound disappointment.

He took both of her hands in his and a momentary thrill went through her at his touch. "That was Ruth Newton. Art just passed away. I'm terribly, terribly sorry to have to do this, but I've really got to go to be with the family."

Selfishly, Bonnie thought in anguish, *Why, oh, why now? Why tonight?*

Arthur Newton, Chairman Emeritus of the Deacons at Foster Road, longtime member and pillar of the church and community, had been declining with Alzheimer's disease for nearly three years. For the last eight months or so, Art had clung tenuously to life, long after he had ceased to recognize or even acknowledge anyone around him. Lately, his condition had been more a source of suffering for his friends and family than for Art himself.

And now, of all times, he had died, and there were arrangements to be made and family to be comforted. Bonnie knew that Dr. Wells had to go, but railed inwardly at the incongruous timing of events. She berated herself for chatting so long with Jack and Cheryl; perhaps if she'd gotten here sooner, Dr. Wells would have missed this call. Then she immediately felt guilty at having such selfish thoughts. Bonnie looked up into his face with a disappointed smile.

"Rain check?" she asked softly, wanting to look down and see that, yes, her hands were being held by Jeff Wells, but not letting herself.

"At the very first opportunity," he said gently, giving her hands a squeeze. He returned to the kitchen, set the alarm, and walked out onto the porch with Bonnie. His hand rested lightly on her back as he led her through the door before him. She felt a tremor at the touch of his hand on her skin.

"Goodnight, Dr. Wells," she said, making a production of searching her purse for her keys.

On a sudden impulse, he stopped her with his right hand on her waist and looked down at her earnestly.

"I…I know this probably isn't proper since we haven't even really had our first official date, but there's something I've been wanting to do for quite some time now."

Then he leaned over and kissed her. As his arms found their way around her waist, his warm mouth rested gently on hers, her lips parted slightly in surprise. His lips lingered for a long, wonderful moment. When the kiss ended, Bonnie opened her eyes and looked up into the beautiful gray-green of his.

His mouth still very close to hers, he murmured, "You know, you really ought to call me Jeff." He ran his forefinger softly across her cheek. "I'll talk to you soon."

Without a backward glance or a wave goodbye, he was in the car and out of the drive.

In no particular hurry, Bonnie slowly descended the three steps to the sidewalk leading to the driveway, still feeling the warmth of Jeff's kiss and his breath as he'd spoken rather huskily to her, still reeling a little inside from the sheer surprise of it all. How had she gone over two years without being kissed liked that?

As she lifted her head, her glance drifted idly to the house across the street. Suddenly, jarringly, as if being awakened rudely from a wonderful dream, Bonnie realized she was looking straight into the hard, piercing glare of Clara Adkinson! How long had Clara been watching from that window? As soon as their eyes locked, Clara closed the curtain she'd been holding open and moved away from the window.

CHAPTER 5

Bonnie thought she would take advantage of the unusual quiet and solitude that Saturday morning to indulge in her "beauty routine." Once a week or so, she treated her hair and skin, which both tended to be on the dry side, to some intensive care. She prepared a homemade regimen: a slightly warmed mixture of olive oil and egg yolk combed through her hair and wrapped in a plastic cap. She then applied mashed avocados as a moisturizing masque for her face. Ben and Josh had dubbed it "Mom's monster time" and would tease her by screaming and running in mock fright when they saw her. For once, she wouldn't have to contend with their little-boy shenanigans.

After an early-morning run, she administered her treatments, intending to wear them for an hour or so and then shower and dress for Art Newton's wake. The obituary and funeral arrangements had already been published in this morning's paper. After leaving Jeff's the previous evening, she had stopped at the grocery to pick up the ingredients for two Chocolate Mousse Pies: the one she owed Cheryl and one to bring to Ruth Newton.

At the thought of Cheryl, Bonnie decided to call and let her and Jack know about Art Newton's passing if they didn't already. It was Jack who answered the phone.

"Well, good morning," he said, his voice unusually cheerful. Then, in a conspiratorial whisper, he asked, "So…how'd it go last night with Jeff?"

Once again, she reeled inside at how *everyone* seemed to know what she'd prefer *no one* know.

"Excuse me?" was all she could manage to say. Had Cheryl broken her vow of silence?

"Jeff and I played racquetball Wednesday morning. He told me he'd asked you out to dinner. But don't worry," he reassured her, "I haven't said anything to Cheryl. I know you'll want to be the first to tell her—that is, if you haven't already…"

Bonnie closed her eyes, smiling ruefully and sighing. It seemed as if the whole world knew about something that hadn't actually taken place yet.

"Yes, Jack, Cheryl knows."

"Well? So, how'd it go, already? You guys an item, or what?" Jack seemed as excited about the prospect of her seeing Jeff Wells as Cheryl had been.

"To tell you the truth, Jack, it *didn't* go." Bonnie explained about the call from Ruth Newton.

"Gee, poor old Art is finally out of his misery," mused Jack. "How is Ruth taking it?"

"I haven't spoken with her yet. I planned to talk to her at the viewing this afternoon. The family is receiving visitors beginning at one today. Byrd Funeral Home. The actual funeral is on Monday."

"So. You and Jeff didn't get to go out after all. That's a shame," Jack mused. "Have you rescheduled yet?"

"Jack! I think Dr. Wells—Jeff—had a few other things on his mind last night," she chided. "Besides, I'm not entirely sure I really want to. Maybe it was a good thing we didn't get to go out last night. I'm not sure I'm ready to begin…dating." *Kissing Jeff Wells, though, might be another matter entirely,* she thought a little guiltily. She obviously had been ready for *that.*

"Well, I'm certainly not going to tell you how to live your life, but I *can* tell you that I think Bill would've wanted…" He didn't finish his sentence.

"Wanted what?" Bonnie asked, a defensive note in her voice. Even though Bill and Jack had been close friends, she felt a strange flash of anger that Jack would presume to tell her something about Bill. "For me to find someone else when he died? I can't imagine that he ever thought about it."

Jack sighed. "No, I guess most thirty-four-year-old guys don't think a lot about what their widows will do because they figure they'll be around for a while. But Bill was a guy who jumped in with both feet. Life, for him, was complete because of you and the kids. If it'd been *you* who died—I think in time he would've begun seeing people again, and I think he would've wanted the same for you."

Bonnie fought the tears that suddenly welled up in her eyes. Sometimes the pain still seemed so fresh. She knew in her heart, though, that Jack was probably right.

"So how come you never said anything before?" Bonnie managed to ask.

Jack's tone turned gentle when he heard the choke in Bonnie's voice. "Well, partly because I figured it wasn't really any of my business," he began. And then, more playfully, he added, "And partly because you and Cheryl never let me get a word in edgewise when we get together—"

"Oh, Jack, that's not true!" Bonnie laughed through her tears.

"And partly," he said finally, "because I didn't know that two of my favorite people might have a chance at getting together. I just happen to think you and Jeff would make a great couple."

Apparently, Cheryl had come into the room, for he spoke away from the mouthpiece of the phone:

"Yes, it's Bonnie. Is it against the law for *me* to talk to Bonnie once in a while? Thank you very much!"

"You may be right," Bonnie sighed again. "I just don't know if I have the energy."

"Well, take a lot of naps if you need to," Jack teased, "but schedule another date with that boy pronto!"

"Oh, you! Tell Cheryl that I'll see you guys at the funeral home. And tell her I have a surprise for her that involves chocolate."

Jeff finished knotting his tie and sighed. It seemed to him sometimes that he wore a suit and tie every day of his life. He remembered with an inward smile Art Newton in his better days, razzing him about having to wear a suit all the time while he, a self-made millionaire, could dress any old way he pleased. Any old way he pleased was usually a pair of work jeans and a matching denim jacket (except when Ruth made *him* wear a suit to church on Sunday) with the most disreputable pair of cowboy boots he could find on one of his business trips to Houston. Every now and then, after particularly heated discussions at deacons' meetings over which Art had presided, Art would call a beleaguered pastor Jeff Wells aside, put a fatherly arm around his shoulder, and say, "Come to work for me, boy. You'll never have to suffer through another one of these things."

"And what will you do with me when I show up for work tomorrow?" Jeff would answer, grateful for the comic relief.

"Well, you can wash windows, can't you?" Art would say with a grin and a slap on Jeff's back.

Jeff couldn't help but think that Art would have thought it quite a joke, him waiting until a Friday evening to die so Jeff would have to wear a tie on a Saturday. Jeff smiled at himself in the mirror and thought, *Messed up my date with Bonnie, too, didn't you, Art?*

He thought again about Bonnie: how she had looked last night, her hair all soft and wispy around her face, smelling like—man, he had to find out what she wore and make sure she had a steady supply of it!

Remembering how shaken Bonnie had been the other night at the Coffee Shoppe when Clara Adkinson had seen them together and made such a big deal over it, he worried a little that he might have scared her off, kissing her like that. She hadn't *seemed* to mind, he thought with an inward smile. But Bonnie was special. He wanted to do this right. Shrugging his suit jacket on and adjusting the lapels and collar, he reached for his keys and wallet. Then he heard the doorbell ring downstairs.

Wondering who might be calling this early on a Saturday morning, Jeff headed down and saw the shadowed outline of a feminine figure through the smoky, beveled glass windows flanking the front door. He opened it to see his across-the-street neighbor, Clara Adkinson. The look on her face was pensive, as if she were troubled about something.

"Hi there, Clara. What brings you over this morning?"

He was surprised to see Clara gave him a look that seemed filled with sympathy. "If you have a free moment, I'd like to have a word or two with you."

"Why, certainly," he said. "Come on in. I'd offer you some coffee, but I usually only have instant when it's just me here at the house."

"No, no, I'm fine." Clara walked ahead of Jeff and sat down on the living room sofa. She looked around her a bit and sighed. "This room still looks like Terri could just walk right in, doesn't it?"

Jeff made no reply. He had been a minister for over twenty years, but he could still be amazed at the thoughtless things people could say. What was Clara getting at, making such an obvious remark? To Jeff, every stick of furniture, every picture, every knickknack in the room cried out Terri's presence. *What is your point?* he thought, not a little angrily.

Clara waited, that odd, sympathetic look on her face, as if she expected him to agree with her. After a moment, when he said nothing, she gave a small shrug and began again.

"I'm not sure why you'd feel the need to lie to me, Dr. Wells. I thought that you and I have been good friends ever since you and your family moved in across the street from me." The sympathetic look had turned to an injured one.

"Lie to you? What on earth would I lie to you about?" Jeff was alarmed; Clara had been a little nosy and a lot pushy at times, but he had always written that off as just being her way. Now, though, he wondered what he could have said that she had construed as an untruth. She seemed genuinely hurt.

"I can understand that a man in your position wants to maintain his privacy," she began again in that prim little tone that was beginning to grate on his nerves. "I just wouldn't have thought you'd feel the need to lie to *me* about your relationship with Bonnie Callaway." There was accusation and recrimination in her voice.

Jeff thought back. Clara had mentioned seeing him and Bonnie together last Monday night when she'd come to his office for their planning meeting Tuesday morning. As he recalled, he'd said something to the effect that he and Bonnie hadn't been out on a date together, which had been true.

"My relationship? I'd hardly call—"

"Dr. Wells, there's no need to hide from me what I already know. Being, as I am, across the street from you, I am often in a position to see you leave from and arrive at your house."

I'll just bet you are.

"I know you were with her last Monday evening, and I saw that you were with her again last night." She paused, waiting for Jeff to react. Though he watched Clara intently, he said nothing. "I can understand why you might want to see a woman like Bonnie Callaway, of course. She *is* quite attractive, I suppose. But as a friend and a member of your congregation, I feel I must tell you that it's almost certainly *not* in your best interest."

Jeff's eyebrows met in a frown. "I don't follow."

"Well, of course," there was that hurt look again, "I know that in *this* day and age, most folks don't bat an eye if a woman goes out with several different men at once, but I think *you* deserve better. And I don't think it would do much for your reputation as a pastor if people knew that one day Bonnie is in the arms of one man and the next day in yours."

Jeff's heart began to pound. Could he have misjudged Bonnie that badly? He'd been sure that Bonnie Callaway hadn't been seeing anyone until he asked her out. There *had* to be some misunderstanding.

"I know this must come as something of a blow to you, dear," she said, reaching over and patting the back of his hand lightly. Jeff fought the impulse to move his hand away. "But I really felt you had to know. I saw Bonnie Callaway out with another man just this week."

"Perhaps you were mistaken," Jeff said, remembering the conclusion she had jumped to last Monday about the two of them. "Maybe it wasn't what it—"

"Mistaken? About what?" She laughed derisively. "Do you think that just because I'm an old lady, I don't know what I see when I see it? No, dear, it was *quite* unmistakable. The fellow—Preston I believe he said his name was—very openly spoke of Bonnie as being his girlfriend. Had his arm around her and everything, right in front of a crowd of people at the Coffee Shoppe. Mertis was with me. She was as shocked as I was at the brazenness of it all. After all, we'd seen you two together there just the night before!"

This was too much. There *had* to be some mistake. But why would Clara make up a story like this? Was it really possible?

"His arm around her?" he repeated weakly.

"In plain view of everyone," she confirmed. "And...from the looks of her hair that day...I'd say there had probably been more than an arm around her waist before they came into the restaurant. She was quite a sight to behold!"

Clara watched Jeff's face carefully, gauging his reaction. She noted his shocked expression, barely concealing his rising anger, with grim satisfaction.

"I'm sorry to be the bearer of such bad tidings, but really, dear, don't you think it's better that you found out from a *friend* before things went any further between you two? I'd hate to see *your* reputation tarnished by association."

"Mertis saw them, too?" Jeff was fishing desperately for confirmation that this could really be true.

"And any number of people standing in the lobby waiting for a table." The sympathetic look was back. After a moment's hesitation, Clara began again. "Which brings me to a little bit more delicate matter."

Now what?

"Bonnie Callaway holds some rather prominent positions of leadership, both in our church and in the community. I think this is rather unseemly behavior to be tolerated in the Chair of the Women's Missions Auxiliary and a member of the Chandler City Benevolent Council. Her actions this week have certainly put her in a bad light. I feel strongly that she should be asked to step down, especially from her position on the Women's Auxiliary. She obviously has other priorities right now."

Jeff was still trying to take it all in. He just looked at Clara, trying to focus on what she was saying, but having difficulty seeing anything but the misty way she had looked at him last night when he'd kissed her. How could he have been so wrong?

"Really," Clara continued, her eyes not meeting Jeff's, "as pastor of the church and chair of the Benevolent Council, I think it would certainly be your place to speak to her about stepping down before she is publicly embarrassed. Word about this kind of thing travels very fast, let me tell you."

You'd know all about that, wouldn't you? Jeff fumed inwardly.

"Clara, people can't be asked to resign from positions of service because of who they're dating."

"Are you saying that you don't think this kind of behavior is inappropriate? I can't *believe* you'd condone it!"

"I...I think we need to hear Bonnie's side of things, don't you?"

"Well, surely you don't think I'd make such a story up!" Clara wore her best shocked expression.

"No, of course not, but—"

"Because, let me tell you," she interrupted, "until the other day, I had nothing but the highest regard for Bonnie Callaway. No one could've been more shocked to see her acting that way in public. But then, when I saw her kissing *you*, right out in front of your house for anyone to see, well, I knew I had to say something!"

Jeff rubbed his eyes and pinched his nose with his thumb and forefinger. Why couldn't he have had the impulse to kiss her while they were still standing in his living room?

"Are you saying you're not going to ask Bonnie to step down from the Auxiliary?"

Jeff sighed, weariness descending on him. "I'll speak to her, Clara. I'll speak to her about it."

Clara looked at Jeff sadly again, as though she had the utmost sympathy for the awkwardness of his position. After a moment, she patted his hand again and said, "Well, dear, I can see by the way you're dressed that you're probably on your way over to the funeral home to be with Ruth. I won't delay you any longer."

Jeff walked her to the front door, his mind still reeling.

"Perhaps I'll see you later, then," she said.

He looked at her intently, not knowing what to say. "Thanks for stopping by" certainly wasn't it. An absentminded "Yes" was all he could manage.

Clara walked down the steps, turning to look once again at Jeff, her eyes exuding sympathy, and then turned and completed her journey back across the street.

In a shocked daze, Jeff went back into the house, set the alarm, and walked out again. As he turned his key in the lock, his throat beginning to constrict with anger, he chided himself for so naively taking Bonnie's demure demeanor at face value. Did she value his reputation as a pastor so little that she hadn't even *considered* what her actions might mean for him? And if she was already seeing someone, he asked himself in frustration, why on earth had she agreed to go out with *him*? He certainly would have understood if she had told him someone had beaten him to the punch.

However disappointed he might be, Clara was right about one thing: this wasn't something he wanted to be associated with in any way. If word about this got around, Bonnie would be *persona non grata* at church and, most likely, even around town. Chandler City, like most Southern towns, could be highly judgmental about things like this, especially if Bonnie was being as open about it as Clara had described.

He just hoped that Clara, if she was as concerned about his welfare as she claimed to be, would be discreet about having seen him with Bonnie last night. The only other person he had told about his intention to see Bonnie was Jack Summers, and Jack was no gossip. Perhaps this business could be contained. The only thing left to do was to let Bonnie know that, since there was already someone else, he was removing himself from the picture. Immediately.

As Bonnie began assembling the ingredients for her pies, she had much to think about. To her great dismay, Jeff's kiss was still on her lips, and it didn't take too much imagination to conjure up the warmth of his nearness. In her dreams last night, the kiss had gone on and on, and she had wrapped her arms around Jeff's neck. She relived again and again the closeness of his mouth as he had said, "Call me Jeff." Had she been missing this all along and just not been able to admit it?

But another inescapable, recurring image was that of Clara Adkinson's scowling face. She had been watching them through the curtains, for goodness' sake! How could she be so nosy? If Clara had been gossiping about just seeing them in a restaurant together, what wouldn't she do about seeing them kiss? Bonnie closed her eyes and sighed deeply.

Placing two graham cracker crumb crusts in the refrigerator, Bonnie had just gotten the double boiler going to melt the chocolate when the doorbell rang. She glanced at the clock. Ten-thirty. Had Ben and Josh neglected to tell their neighborhood buddies that they would be away for the day? She hated the thought of going to the door looking the way she did. Little boys could be so silly. And she still hadn't showered after her run this morning; she had probably smelled better in her life. She toyed with the idea of not answering the door at all.

Wiping her hands on a dish towel, Bonnie peeked through the drapes of the front window. The plastic cap on her head crackled as it brushed against the material. She was surprised to see an Overnite Express truck parked in front of her house.

Now, who would have sent her an express package? Bonnie thought hard. She had no out-of-town clients, and she hadn't ordered anything from a catalog in a while. Could it be something from her parents or from Bill's family? No one had a birthday coming up. Still, if it had been sent Overnite Express, it must be important. No matter what she looked like, she really ought to accept the package.

Dreading the look on the delivery person's face, she unlocked the door and opened it to see Jeff Wells standing there! He was dressed in his best Sunday suit and looked as attractive as she had ever seen him look. She gasped, frozen to the spot. Jeff's eyes widened. When he pursed his lips, Bonnie could tell he was trying not to laugh. Over Jeff's shoulder, Bonnie could see the man from Overnite Express standing on George Owens's porch across the street, holding a package while George signed for it. She felt herself blushing through the mashed avocado on her face.

"Oh, dear, Bonnie," said Jeff, mirth in his voice. "I should've called first. I am so sorry! I was just on my way to the funeral home, and I thought I'd stop by to talk with you, but really, it can wait."

Bonnie had shrunk back behind the door and was barely peeking around it now. "It's okay to come in," she lied, then quickly added, "although I'm kind of right in the middle of cooking something."

And whatever it is, Jeff thought, *it's just about the most heavenly chocolate scent I've ever smelled.*

"Oh, no," Jeff said kindly. "You're clearly not ready to receive visitors." Then his face turned serious. "But we do need to talk. Can you meet me in my office tomorrow afternoon, say around four?"

"Your office at church?" Bonnie was puzzled. What did he need to discuss that required an office visit? Why couldn't they talk over, say, dinner?

Jeff sighed. "Yes," he said, looking as though he would like to say more but thought better of it. "Listen, I'll see you tomorrow, then. And, really, I apologize for coming by unannounced this way. I…I should've called."

"'Bye," Bonnie murmured, closing the door. She smiled. *No impromptu kisses today, eh, Jeff Wells?*

Jeff had said, "See you tomorrow," but in fact, Bonnie saw him twice more that day. Much to her disappointment, though, on neither occasion did she have the opportunity to speak with him. Indeed, if Bonnie hadn't known better, she would have thought that Jeff Wells was actually *avoiding* her. True, there had been a crowd of people at the funeral home, so it seemed natural enough that Jeff had his hands full helping Ruth Newton greet them all. Still, it seemed that he could have at least managed to make his way over to say hello. She wanted to try somehow to erase from his memory the sight of herself with a green face and a plastic bag on her head.

Among those in the crowd at the wake were Father Norman Blake and John Reeves. The Chandler City Benevolent Council had been the brainchild of Art Newton over twenty-five years ago. It had been his idea to form a group that was non-denominational, one oblivious to racial and social boundaries, to foster a spirit of cooperation among Chandler City Christians. He had formed an organization that helped people put their faith into action or, as Art himself had put it, "Put legs on their Christianity!" He had given generously to the Council through the years, both monetarily and by providing materials from his various businesses, and land and office space for Council operations from his own real estate holdings. Word of what the Council had been able to do, not just for people in Chandler City, but for those in the entire tri-state area, had spread, so that even those from organizations and churches not specifically Christian, like Carolyn Perkins from the Unitarian church, were moved to get involved. Caring about easing the sufferings of one's fellow human beings was the sole criterion for Council participation.

Doctor Father had been there with Art at the Council's small beginnings, using his own connections with his church and at the Community College to garner support and participation. He had rotated on and off the Council Board of Directors over the years, but had never ceased to work with Art to oversee its operations nor to be an active participant in what the Council tried to accomplish. When Art fell ill several years ago, Father Blake took it upon himself to see that Art's vision was carried on. Today, he was saying goodbye to an old friend and ally, his "partner in do-gooder crime," as Art had once put it. John Reeves, a relative newcomer to the Council, had not known Art before his illness, but knew of his legacy. He had come with Doctor Father to pay his respects to a man who had been the silent partner in bettering the lives of hundreds, if not thousands, of people.

Cheryl found Bonnie at the back of the funeral home chapel and stood beside her. Leaning toward Bonnie's ear, Cheryl whispered, "Heard about last night. Bummer."

Bonnie smiled wanly at Cheryl, glad for her friend's closeness, but said nothing. Jeff was at the front of the room reading the Twenty-Third Psalm. As he looked up from his reading, it seemed that his gaze went directly toward her. For an instant, their eyes locked. Jeff seemed to be searching her face, but for what, Bonnie couldn't say. Then the moment was gone. Jeff was busy being Dr. Wells right now. Bonnie saw, and started inwardly at the sight, that Clara Adkinson was sitting on the front row, not five feet from Jeff. On her right sat Anna Lee.

Bonnie saw Jeff again from a distance in the church parking lot later that afternoon as the children disembarked from the bus after their overnight retreat. She was surprised at how her heart gave a little jump when she saw him, as if she were a high school girl catching sight of some cute boy. Was one kiss melting away two years of numbed feelings?

Ben and Josh ran to her excitedly, waving the t-shirts they had painted and decorated in the arts and crafts sessions of the retreat.

"Hey, Mom!" called Ben. "Look at the cool designs they showed us how to make!"

"Look, Mom!" cried Josh. "They let us put our hands in the paint to make handprints and everything!" Bonnie crouched down to inspect the shirts more closely and complimented each on his artistry. Then, before they could protest, she wrapped a boy in each arm and hugged them tightly.

"Oh, I missed you guys! That house is too quiet with both of you gone!" Bonnie told them.

"Aw, Mom," said Ben. "We were only gone one day!"

"Well, I'm still glad you're back," she said as she led them to the car.

Josh noticed that she was quite dressed up. Bonnie hadn't gone home to change, but had gone straight to church from the funeral home.

"Hey, Mom, you're all dressed up again," Josh remarked. "Are you going out to dinner again tonight?"

Bonnie smiled. There was nothing wrong with this little guy's memory.

"No, sweetie," she answered softly. She told him about Art Newton.

"I remember Mrs. Newton from when we went Christmas caroling at the nursing home," said Ben. "She was visiting Mr. Newton, but I don't think he even knew we were there. He was just kind of lying there with his eyes open. It was…scary."

"Yes," said Bonnie. "Think how hard it must've been for Mrs. Newton to see him that way." She gave Ben's arm a little squeeze, then closed his door.

As she walked around the car to get in herself, she glanced over to where she had seen Jeff standing before, waiting for his own son, but he was no longer there. She scanned the parking lot quickly, but saw no sign of his green SUV. She sighed, a little disappointed at again not having had the chance to talk to him, and annoyed with herself for feeling that way.

With another rueful glance at Jeff's empty parking space, Bonnie got in the car and drove home with Ben and Josh.

CHAPTER 6

❀

As Bonnie had feared, Clara Adkinson had done an amazingly thorough job of spreading whatever it was she was telling people about Bonnie and Jeff. Almost as soon as she walked through the doors at Foster Road Baptist the next morning, one person after another greeted her in one of two ways: some would either wink at her knowingly and greet her with an apparent mixture of surprise and merriment: "Well, helloooo there, Bonnie!" Others would come up to her and whisper conspiratorially, "What's this I hear about you and Jeff Wells?" Stunned at every inquiry, Bonnie could only look at her questioners with shocked surprise. Some would respond to her silent stare with, "Oh, you don't have to look so surprised! Everybody knows you and Jeff Wells are going together now! I think it's just great!" By the time she arrived at her Sunday School class, Bonnie was walking in a sort of stupor of embarrassment and panic.

Even Nancy McLin, her Sunday School teacher, couldn't seem to help leaning over to her ear and asking, as they stood in the church parlor for the departmental opening assembly, "Can it possibly be true?"

With an urgency in her eyes that seemed to beg for mercy, Bonnie whispered back, "I don't know what you've heard, but I *really* don't want to talk about it."

Nancy seemed to understand, and no more was said, but Bonnie could feel and occasionally *see* the surreptitious glances of her fellow class members. By the time Sunday School was over, she felt a headache coming on.

As Bonnie sat next to her children in their usual seats in the balcony of the sanctuary for the morning service, her surroundings took on a kind of surreal look and feel. She had been a member of this church for eight years and had attended—how many?—hundreds of services. Yet today, she looked down at Jeff Wells standing in his pulpit and saw a different man—a man who had expressed an interest in dating her. *A man who had kissed her.* A man who everyone in Chandler City—or at least everyone at church—seemed to *know* had kissed her!

She realized that it would be difficult, at best, for Jeff to make eye contact with her from this distance, but still, Bonnie found herself looking intently at his eyes, as if she could will them to meet hers. It didn't happen.

When the service was over, Bonnie could have answered correctly, had she been asked, that the sermon topic was forgiveness, but could not have discussed the points Jeff had made in any detail, so preoccupied had she been with Jeff himself. Something about the Prodigal Son, something about a judge and a debtor, something about lost sheep. As she leaned over to pick up her purse and her Bible (she had even neglected to look up the scripture passages from which the sermon had been taken), Bonnie saw that Clara Adkinson was first in line to shake the pastor's hand when the service was over. Anna Lee, as usual, stood shyly by.

Just as Bonnie was going to lead Ben and Josh toward the aisle, she saw another figure approach Jeff Wells. This lady, one Bonnie had never seen before, was impeccably dressed in a red suit that was tasteful and yet very feminine and attractive. She was tall, almost as tall as Jeff, and carried her height gracefully; she could have been a model. Gold jewelry, not gaudy but expensive-looking nevertheless, glinted from her throat, wrists, and ears. Even from this distance, Bonnie could see how expertly manicured was the hand this perfectly coifed female extended for Jeff to shake, and how warmly she smiled at him.

"Are ya gonna go or not, Mom?" asked Josh, giving her a little nudge.

"Hmmm? Oh, yes, sorry, sweetie," Bonnie answered. "Let's go."

Just then, Cheryl walked up. She was blotting under her eyes with a tissue. "Oh, Bonnie, that sermon was so wonderful! I've got to tell Dr. Wells how much it meant to me."

Bonnie felt a little embarrassed and even more ashamed. In her preoccupation with her new relationship with Jeff, she had probably missed something *she* needed to hear herself.

"Yeah," she fibbed. "It was really great." She made a mental note to call Jeff's secretary, Sandra, to order a cassette recording of today's service so she could hear what she had missed. She really *had* to get a grip on herself.

"Looks like I'd better get in line if *I* want to tell him anything," said Cheryl.

Bonnie followed Cheryl's gaze to the line of people waiting to speak with Jeff Wells. The beautiful brunette, Bonnie saw with some alarm, was still talking to Jeff; she still held his hand in a handshake and, in fact, her left hand rested atop their clasped hands. Jeff was nodding his head affirmatively about something she was saying. At last, their handshake broke, this new person walked lithely away, and Jeff turned to grasp the hand of the next person in line.

"Hmmm," observed Cheryl. "Who's that?"

"I couldn't say," Bonnie said, more dryly than she would like to have sounded.

"That's Sherry Niles," Jack informed them brightly. "She's a new client representative for Chandler City Bank." Bonnie and Cheryl stared at him in amazement, Cheryl not a little accusingly.

"What?" he asked, mischief in his eyes as he feigned surprise at their response to his knowledge of this attractive newcomer. "I was on duty at the greeter's desk when she came in, so sue me," he grinned. "I had the distinct pleasure of escorting Ms. Niles to the Single Adult Sunday School Department. It was probably the highlight of my entire life!"

"Oh, you!" said Cheryl with an exasperated but good-natured grin. "Do you see what I have to live with here?"

Single, thought Bonnie. *Why am I not surprised?*

"Mo-om, c'mon!" nagged Josh. "You're holding up traffic!"

"Okay, okay," she said, following Jack and Cheryl to the stairwell that led to the lower level of the sanctuary. Maybe they could all have lunch together.

Jack and Cheryl begged off her invitation to join them for lunch, claiming to have a refrigerator full of leftovers. "Besides," Cheryl had added with a wicked little smile at Bonnie, "we have this *wonderful* dessert waiting for us!"

In the car, as they were driving out of the church parking lot, Ben asked if they could have lunch at Golden China House, a local restaurant featuring an all-you-can eat buffet on Sundays. Bonnie often took the boys out for dinner on Friday nights, but they had missed this past Friday because of the children's retreat. And *she* certainly hadn't gotten to eat out, as things had developed. "Sure," she agreed, smiling at Ben. "Good idea."

There was a knot of after-church diners crowded into the tiny entry area of the restaurant. Covenant Methodist let out at 11:30, Foster Road Baptist's service ended at noon, and the late Mass at St. Alban's was over at 12:30. From the time it opened for lunch at 11:00 on Sunday until about 1:30, a steady stream of customers poured into Golden China House. It wasn't unusual to have to wait for a table; depending on the size of the crowd, the wait could be considerable. But the tantalizing aromas of garlic and ginger floating on the air kept people coming and enjoying their wait.

Not wanting to waste her afternoon waiting for a table in a restaurant, though, Bonnie was just about to ask the boys if they could take a rain check on Chinese food when she heard a voice calling from across the dining room:

"Hey, Bonnie! Over here! Come join us!" Bonnie looked in the direction of the voice and saw Tom Givens, the Singles Minister from Foster Road. Three long tables had been pushed together; seated at them were a number of people she recognized from the Singles Department at church. Tom, a tall, pleasant-looking man in his late twenties, had respected Bonnie's preference for staying in a ladies' Sunday School class rather than joining a co-ed Singles class, but he had still put her name on the Singles mailing list. Now she got their monthly newsletter and notice of all of their upcoming activities. Often, when he saw Bonnie in the halls at church, Tom would find a way to mention some singles event that had either recently taken place and was just *tons* of fun, or one coming up at which they would love to see her. She knew Tom was just doing his job since she was, after all, single, and she admired his persistence. But sometimes she *did* wish that he would give it up.

Bonnie thought wryly that if they accepted his invitation to eat at the Singles' table, Tom would almost certainly think he had finally made headway in getting her to participate in Singles activities. But a table *was* a table: she wouldn't have to disappoint the boys, and she wouldn't have to go home and put lunch together—the afternoon wasn't getting any younger.

"Hey, guys, there're some folks from our church," Bonnie told Ben and Josh. "Why don't we go sit with them so we won't have to wait so long?"

"Glad you could join us!" Tom said, pulling out a chair for Bonnie at his table.

If he had heard the gossip circulating about her and Jeff, he didn't let on. Much to Bonnie's relief, the other singles at the table also seemed unaware of the local buzz. Anna Lee Adkinson, in what must surely be a rare public outing without her mother, sat several places away and across from Bonnie; Bonnie had no doubt that Clara had filled her daughter in on what she had seen Friday night.

After they had seated themselves and placed their drink orders with the waiter, Bonnie corralled the boys over to the buffet line. She filled her plate and helped Josh, who couldn't quite reach across the steam table, fill his. As they headed back, they arrived just in time for Bonnie to see Jeff Wells walking toward one of the tables with Sherry Niles. Heads turned as she passed gracefully through the restaurant. Sherry Niles, Bonnie could now see at close range, was a strikingly beautiful woman about her own age, or perhaps just a bit younger. Sherry, herself, seemed coolly oblivious to the minor sensation her presence caused. Bonnie's heart gave an excited leap when she saw Jeff. But then came the same twinge of disappointment she had felt last Wednesday night as Jeff waved a friendly but general hello to everyone in the Singles group and went to sit with Sherry at the other end of her table.

Bonnie's seat was on the opposite side from where Jeff sat down; Sherry sat across from him. Although she had a clear view of Jeff's face from where she sat (as Bonnie was sure he had of hers from his seat), not once did she see him look her way during the meal. Between their trips to the buffet line, Sherry seemed to dominate conversation with Jeff. As the meal progressed, Bonnie felt her cheeks flushing at the realization that, for some inexplicable reason, Jeff was avoiding speaking to or even making eye contact with her. It wasn't her imagination: on his way back to his seat after going for refills, Bonnie noted, he made a point of greeting the other singles and their children who had joined the group for lunch, but never ventured near Bonnie and her boys. Ben and Josh, of course, took no notice of the slight whatsoever, but they did see that their mother wasn't eating very much.

"What's the matter, Mom?" asked Ben. "I thought Chinese was your favorite."

"Guess I need to have a smaller breakfast if we're gonna eat out for lunch," she said with a weak smile. She had been hungry enough when they had first come in. "I'm ready to go whenever you guys are finished."

On the drive home, Bonnie remembered abruptly that Jeff had asked her to meet with him in his office that afternoon. She wondered if his sudden avoidance of her had anything to do with what he wanted to talk to her about.

At a large church like Foster Road Baptist, it was rare to find fewer than twenty cars in the parking lot at any given time of the day or evening, seven days a week. Jeff Wells had made it clear from the start of his pastorate that he didn't want to be the head of a "Sunday-only" church. Sunday School rooms served as daycare and preschool classrooms from Monday to Friday. Various groups held non-denominational Bible study classes on set days of the month. Many of Foster Road's Senior Adults volunteered as literacy instructors or taught English as a Second Language for the Benevolent Council using other empty Sunday School rooms. On weekdays, Friday nights, and all day on Saturdays, the church gym was host to individual walkers and weight trainers, aerobic exercise groups, and team sports from basketball to volleyball, with participants aged six to seventy. On Sunday afternoons, any number of committees met between services: the Deacons, the Nominating Committee, and the Women's Missions Auxiliary, of which Bonnie was Chair.

And so it was that when Bonnie turned her car into the church parking lot later that day, she saw the usual array of cars belonging to meeting-goers and afternoon exercisers. It was no surprise to see them, of course, but she had imagined that meeting Jeff in his office at four o'clock on Sunday afternoon would be a little more private somehow. The more she had thought about Jeff's behavior at lunch, the more misgivings she had about what it might be that Jeff wanted to discuss. She had been willing to write off not being able to speak with him yesterday, either at the funeral home or when they picked up the kids after the retreat, as the result of his simply being too busy with the matters at hand to have a real conversation with her. She hoped that was what Jeff wanted: to wait until he could speak with her alone, so that they could begin really getting to know each other. They couldn't do that with crowds of people around.

But today, at lunch, it seemed to her that he could have at *least* sat down with her for a minute or two to say hello. Since he had made a point of speaking with nearly every other Single there, it was almost conspicuous to her that he *hadn't*. She tried, mostly successfully, to rid her mind of thoughts tinged with jealousy at the way Sherry Niles had dominated nearly all of his time at the restaurant. More often than not, Sherry had leaned conspiratorially across the table when she spoke to him, holding her head far too close to Jeff's for Bonnie's comfort, as if what she had to say was extremely confidential. What could she have been talking to him about so intently? It seemed to Bonnie that Sherry was working awfully fast to—

Bonnie shook her head to erase the thought from her mind. Whatever it was they had been discussing, it was none of her business. After all, Bonnie reminded herself, Jeff had asked Bonnie out to dinner on Friday; that had to count for *something*. Then the doubting thought would come again: *Maybe that was before he met Sherry.*

As Bonnie approached the church office, she was surprised to see Sandra, Jeff's secretary, at her desk.

"Working on a Sunday, San?" Bonnie asked with a smile.

Sandra looked momentarily uncomfortable. "Oh! Well, Dr. Wells asked me to come in because he, um, had some appointments this afternoon. I…I had work to catch up on anyway."

A little puzzled at Sandra's discomfort, Bonnie said, "Yes, well, I guess I'm one of those appointments!" She sounded a little too perky, even to herself. She wondered, if Jeff did indeed have other appointments this afternoon, with whom they might be.

"Oh, yes, Dr. Wells is expecting you. He should be with you in just a few minutes."

"Hey, listen, while I'm here," said Bonnie, suddenly remembering her lapse of attention to the sermon that Cheryl seemed to have enjoyed so much that morning, "I'd like to order a tape of this morning's service."

"Consider it ordered," Sandra said, jotting a note to herself on her desk calendar. "It should be ready for you to pick up Wednesday night before supper."

Just then, Jeff opened his office door. He greeted Bonnie, his right hand outstretched. Bonnie looked at it, mystified, until she realized that he meant to shake hers. She grasped his hand hesitantly and searched his eyes for any sign that he might be aware of the fact that the two of them were currently the objects of local gossip, but could see none. That he wanted to shake her hand, though, struck her as extremely odd, especially in light of the tender way he had kissed her as they'd parted on Friday night. Bonnie still trembled a little inside each time she thought of it. She found herself hoping wistfully, knowing that it probably wasn't possible in his office, that their meeting today would end in another kiss. As they walked in and sat in the chairs around the coffee table across from Jeff's large desk, Bonnie told herself to snap out of it; Jeff obviously had something he wanted to discuss with her.

The heady scent of Bonnie's perfume drifted toward Jeff as she passed him, and he faltered momentarily as a small voice inside him asked if he really *had* to do what he was about to do. Then he steeled himself with the thought that had dogged him since yesterday morning: the mental image of Bonnie in some other man's arms just days before she was to go out with him for the first time.

"Thanks for taking the time to meet with me this afternoon, Bonnie," Jeff began. His tone seemed awfully formal to her. "As I mentioned to you yesterday," his eyes seemed filled with mirth for a moment, and Bonnie knew he was remembering the sight that had greeted him as she'd answered the door, "there's a bit of a problem."

"Oh! What kind of problem?" To Jeff's amazement, her expression reflected genuine puzzlement. Did she really have no idea that he would object to there being someone else?

For a moment, Jeff looked very uncomfortable. He seemed to be searching her face again, as he had done yesterday, almost as if he expected *her* to speak first. He seemed at a loss as to how to begin.

Bonnie viewed his discomfort with some alarm. "What...?" she started to ask.

"Of course, you know Clara Adkinson," Jeff finally began.

At the mention of Clara's name, Bonnie felt her throat go dry, and she guessed that the gossip had, indeed, already gotten back to Jeff. But the truth was much worse.

"Bright and early yesterday morning," he began again with a sigh, "as I was preparing to go to Art Newton's wake, I had a visit from Clara."

Bonnie looked intently at Jeff, bracing herself for what must be coming next, but said nothing.

"I guess you know, um, that Clara lives right across the street from me, don't you?"

Bonnie nodded her head slowly, watching Jeff's face.

"Well," Jeff cleared his throat, "she said that Friday night, she, um, happened to have seen us, uh, *together.*" Jeff was clearly embarrassed.

"'*Happened* to have seen us?'" Bonnie echoed, not a little angry at how innocently Clara had characterized what amounted to out-and-out spying. "Do you realize she was practically peering out of her front window at us?"

"Oh, you saw her?" Incredibly, Jeff seemed relieved somehow that Bonnie had seen Clara. "I...I must've been so intent on getting to the funeral home that I didn't see her, myself."

Still, she waited. Jeff's apparent lack of concern that Clara seemed to have positioned herself to "catch them in the act" put Bonnie on her guard.

Then Jeff appeared to take another tack: "I'm sure you must realize that, if you'd told me you were already seeing someone, I would certainly have understood if you had declined my dinner invitation."

Now Bonnie was stumped. "'Seeing someone,'" she echoed in a hollow voice, completely mystified.

"Clara also mentioned seeing you and your, uh, *friend* at lunch the other day. At the Coffee Shoppe. Said you seemed to be quite an, uh, *affectionate* couple." He looked pained at the word and avoided meeting Bonnie's gaze.

Bonnie closed her eyes and shook her head. This was too much to be believed. That ridiculous encounter at the Coffee Shoppe, when she had been trying vainly to extricate herself from Preston's arms, was actually coming back to haunt her. At least, Clara was trying to *make* it haunt her. It took little imagination to guess how Clara had taken the truthful details of what had happened and twisted them into a story that Jeff quite plainly believed.

Jeff saw the look of chagrin on Bonnie's face and took it as confirmation that what Clara had told him was true.

"The point is," he said, hating the discomfort he knew he was causing Bonnie, "she'd actually come over to say that I should ask you to step down as an officer of the Women's Missions Auxiliary and as a member of the Benevolent Council for what she called 'unseemly behavior.'"

Bonnie stared at Jeff, dumbfounded. She suddenly understood more fully the knowing look she had seen in everyone's eyes this morning: Clara had been insinuating, apparently to anyone who would listen, that she was some kind of loose woman!

"Naturally," Jeff continued quickly, "I told Clara I thought she was being a little precipitous. It's certainly no *crime* for a single woman to date more than one man if she so chooses."

Bonnie had little time to begin feeling any relief, though, for Jeff's next words were, "However, in view of the fact that Clara seems determined to cause some little stir over this, I think it only prudent that I defer to your previous relationship and allow you to continue seeing him without complicating matters with my attentions. I'm sure you'll agree that that's the wisest course."

CHAPTER 7

Bonnie opened her mouth to speak, her eyes searching Jeff's for some sign that this wasn't as final as he was making it sound. She could think of no adequate response. Her mind was a sea of anger and hurt and disappointment.

"A little precipitous," he had said. *A little precipitous!*

She averted her eyes; she couldn't bear to look at him anymore. How could this be happening? Had she *asked* for any of this? Had she asked to have a man invite her to dinner? Had she asked to be kissed? To have the desire to have a man in her life rekindled? *No!* was the frustrated cry in her own mind. So why, now that she had finally opened her heart to the possibility, now that she had opened her heart to Jeff, *why* was everything being yanked out from under her?

And the insinuations Clara was making! How could she? How dare she! And how could Jeff possibly take them seriously? How could he give any credence at all to such ridiculous accusations?

She thought of several sarcastic things to say: *Does Clara want me to wear a scarlet A as well?* But she said nothing.

Jeff's began again, as if only to break the terrible, uncomfortable silence in the room: "I…I know right now you must think this isn't really necessary, that I should just ignore Clara."

Bonnie looked up. Tears had welled in her eyes, but she didn't care. She felt it only right that Jeff have some idea of how much this was hurting her. Jeff cast down his eyes down when he saw them.

"But as a pastor," he continued, his voice softer now as he examined one of his fingernails, "everything I do, everything I say, even every friendship I have…*everything* is subject to the scrutiny of the people in my congregation, sometimes even in the whole town. It was the one thing that Terri struggled with most as a pastor's wife. I think all pastor's wives do. And, of course, as we are seeing with Clara, some folks scrutinize a little more closely than others. As a pastor, though, I have a responsibility to my church and to other pastors who face the same scrutiny, to avoid even the *appearance* of impropriety."

Still, Bonnie said nothing. Here he sat, talking about pastors' *wives*, for goodness' sake, when they hadn't even had a real date! What good would it do to try to explain about the buffoonery of Preston Hardy when Jeff was so concerned about his public image? And really, what would be the point anyway? Did she really want to fight for a relationship that had never actually gotten started, when Jeff seemed only too willing to break it off? She had even told Jack Summers that she didn't think she was ready to begin dating. Maybe this was God's way of telling her that she was right; she wasn't ready. *This*, however, was anything but an easy out.

But, oh, she was so disappointed! The thought of never having that dinner with Jeff, of never taking that long, leisurely drive down to the Gulf Coast with him, of never having him kiss her tenderly again—it hurt so much!

Bonnie felt a sudden urgency to be out of Jeff's office, to be *away* from him. She stood up quickly. Looking intently in her purse for her car keys, Bonnie made a point of addressing him formally: "I understand your position perfectly, Dr. Wells." Her voice choked with tears. "I won't take up any more of your time. I can assure you, I wouldn't *think* of tarnishing your—"

She couldn't finish her sentence; she was sorry she had started it.

Without another word, Bonnie turned and rushed through his office door. Behind her, she could hear Jeff say, "Bonnie, I hope—" but she didn't acknowledge him. Jeff watched Bonnie leave his office and felt a piece of his heart tear away from him.

Bonnie cast a furtive glance at Sandra. The sympathetic look in her eyes told Bonnie that Jeff's secretary knew everything. Was there *anyone* in Chandler City who didn't know about her and Jeff? How long would it take, she wondered, for word to get around that the whole thing was off?

Bonnie couldn't remember having experienced this much turmoil in her whole life. Her quiet, peaceful, slightly boring existence had been turned inside out, and she knew somehow that nothing in her life would ever be quite the same again. This church, that she and Bill had attended ever since they had moved to Chandler City, that had embraced her so warmly and comfortingly when he died—she felt like she wanted to run out of its doors and never come back! The stares and knowing smiles of her fellow church members were bad enough, but how could she come Sunday after Sunday now and look at Jeff, even from afar? How could she listen to him preach, feeling so much anger toward him, knowing his attitude about "keeping up appearances?" Yet even as he had lost a great deal of credibility with her, she was consumed with disappointment that things had turned out this way. Their brief time together Friday night had seemed to hold such promise.

And how could she *not* come back? She and her family had been involved in so many areas of church activity from the start. Her boys were forming friendships that would outlast any they made in school. Indeed, almost all of her own friendships had been made through this church. How could she ever explain an abrupt switch to Ben and Josh, when they knew nothing of her relationship with "Pastor Jeff," as they called him, to begin with? She dreaded staying; she couldn't bear the thought of leaving.

Clenching her keys in her hand, Bonnie realized with a start that, much as she would love to get in her car and drive straight home, she wasn't going anywhere. The boys would be going into their evening children's program soon, and she knew she could offer no reasonable explanation to them for wanting to go home before activities actually started. Lifting the outside flap of her purse and dropping the keys back in with a sigh of resignation, she made her way to the church staff break room, where a pot of coffee or the makings for instant could usually be found. Rather than attend her own Sunday evening Bible study session, she felt that she needed some time alone to think, to pray. Having opted for hot tea, she was dunking her teabag absentmindedly up and down, the homey scent of chamomile mildly comforting to her, when Tom Givens stopped in the doorway as he was passing down the hall.

"Well, hey, there, lady!" he said with pleased surprise. "Didn't expect to see *you* in here during Bible Study," he said, a smile of pleasure on his face. "By the way, we sure were glad you and the boys could join us for lunch today. I knew if I worked hard enough, I could get you to—"

He stopped short when she looked up. Bonnie's was one of those faces that show the after-effects of crying far too long after the fact; there was no point in pretending she hadn't been upset.

"Hey, what's wrong? Are you okay? Has something happened?"

Bonnie smiled a rueful little smile. "Oh, I'll be fine," she said with a trembling voice. "This thing with Jeff has gotten a little out of hand. I just needed a few minutes to myself before I go back out among everybody."

"Jeff? You mean Dr. Wells?" Tom seemed genuinely not to know anything, not to have heard the gossip. She smiled inwardly at the irony of having been the one to spill the beans to the one person who *didn't* know what she would give anything to have been kept secret.

"You must be the only person in town, or at least in church, who doesn't know that Dr. Wells and I were going to go out to dinner together on Friday night." She managed a weak bravado.

"Well, you've gotta remember," Tom answered softly, "that the Singles are sometimes pretty detached from the rest of the church. For better or worse, they tend to keep to themselves, so usually the only gossip they hear is about other Singles. You said, 'Going to go out.' What happened?"

Bonnie took a deep breath and sighed.

"I can't *begin* to imagine why, but Clara Adkinson seems to have a problem with the idea of Jeff having a relationship with me. She's convinced him that somehow I'll do damage to his reputation."

It was bad enough that she had to explain this much; Bonnie refused to go into any of the sordid details.

"*You?*" Tom shook his head incredulously. "Man! I knew she was a determined woman, but I never thought she'd stoop this low."

"Determined? Determined to do what?"

Again Tom shook his head. He hesitated a moment, then said, "No, I've probably said too much already. I will say this, though: I wouldn't take it personally if I were you. Clara would have a problem with *anybody* Dr. Wells wanted to date if it wasn't…" He stopped himself again. "Look, just try not to take this too personally."

Bonnie gave Tom a wan smile.

"If you knew the things Clara's saying about me, you'd see why I have trouble taking this any way *but* personally."

"But surely Dr. Wells isn't going to let something *Clara Adkinson* said stand in the way of seeing you, is he?" He said her name as if Clara were somehow inherently untrustworthy.

"It would appear so, Tom," she murmured. "I think they've been pretty close since Terri died. She seems to have become a sort of mother figure to him. I guess that's probably at least partly because she lives so close." She tried not to make this last statement with too much derision—she couldn't shake the mental image of Clara peering through the window at them from across the street. A smile struggled to break through the sadness in her eyes.

"But, you know, it's really okay. Maybe Clara did me a favor. I wasn't seeing anyone before Jeff called me, and so now things can just go back to the way they were."

What a lie, she thought.

"But Bonnie, it doesn't have to be that way," Tom said, a note of urgency in his voice. "Let me tell you, there are any number of guys in the Singles Department who'd *love* the chance to go out with you."

Bonnie's eyes snapped up to Tom's.

"Excuse me?" was all she could manage to say.

With the exception of sitting at the table with them at lunch today, she had never done the first thing to get to know any of the Singles group at Foster Road Baptist Church. How could any of them know *her*?

Tom gave her a gentle smile. "Don't act so surprised, lady. In case you hadn't heard, it can be pretty lonely out there for singles who only want to date other Christians. You may not know who *they* are, but there are a number of fellas in this church who definitely know who *you* are."

Bonnie couldn't help laughing a shy, girlishly embarrassed laugh. She felt herself blushing. Searching Tom's eyes, she saw that he was quite serious.

"In fact," Tom continued in a confidential tone, "I've had more than one guy ask me what I thought about them asking you out. I've always told them I thought they'd be wasting their time. Interesting that *Jeff* never asked me my opinion, but then, him being my boss and all, I guess he wouldn't."

Shaking her head in wonder, Bonnie said, "All this time I thought you were trying to rope me into the Singles Group, and here you were actually protecting me from it!"

Tom came and sat down across from her and put his hand over hers. "Bonnie, you know I'd love nothing better than to see you get involved with the Singles, if only because I think you have so much to offer. You'd be a wonderful example for some of our other single parents who really struggle. But I know you have to be ready. I try to be encouraging without being pushy."

"Well, you aren't always completely successful on *that* score," she teased him, "but I do appreciate your patience with me. Maybe it's time I did think about getting involved in the Singles Department."

"Well, hot dog!" said Tom, genuinely elated. "You can start tonight! We're having a get-together at Jenny Pierce's house after the evening service. Kids are welcome, 'cause so many of the singles have children."

"Whoa! Whoa!" laughed Bonnie, "I said I'd *think* about it. Don't sign me up *too* fast!"

"Rats," he said, snapping his fingers. Then, something else seemed to occur to him. "Well, here's something to *really* think about. We're going to be having our annual Singles Celebration Conference over Memorial Day weekend. Would you consider being one of our session leaders?"

"Me? What would I lead a session on?"

"Why, the trials and joys of single parenting, of course!" Tom said it as if he'd never considered anyone else for the session.

"Gosh, I don't know," Bonnie said. She tapped the side of her cup in thought.

She didn't want to turn him down too quickly. She still had reservations about jumping full-tilt into the Singles group, certainly, but she wanted always to be open to opportunities to serve God. Perhaps this was something God did want her to do. Perhaps God was going to take this debacle with Jeff and turn it into something useful and good after all. But Memorial Day was coming up awfully fast!

"How do you think the Singles would feel about having a newcomer start out by being a group *leader*?"

"Knowing all of the other areas you've served in at this church, I think they'd feel just fine about having you lead a session. To be honest," he said with a rueful grin, "most folks are glad for *anyone* to lead a group as long as they don't have to do it themselves."

The irony of Tom's request didn't escape Bonnie: Clara Adkinson was doing her best to see that she *lost* her places of service in church, and Tom Givens was doing his utmost to get her to take on *more*.

Bonnie looked at Tom and smiled. "You're a determined man," she said. "Let me pray about this and give it some thought. How soon do you need to know?"

"As soon as you can tell me. We're going to be getting publicity fliers out to Singles groups at other churches in the tri-state area. Our big draw is that we'll be featuring a special mystery guest. I'd like to know if we can put you down as one of our session leaders before the flier gets printed up."

"Okay, I'll try to let you know by Wednesday."

"Good deal," he said, preparing to leave.

"Well, hey, don't keep me in suspense—Who's this big mystery guest?"

"Oh, no you don't!" He grinned. "You wanna know, you gotta come to the conference!" Abruptly, Tom changed the subject. "Hey, you sure I can't talk you into Jenny's get-together tonight?"

"Tom…" she said in a mock-menacing voice.

"Okay, okay, I'll quit while I'm ahead."

With that, he left her to finish her tea in solitude.

For the second time that day, Bonnie sat through a worship service with anything but a worshipful attitude. Dr. Wells appeared a little more subdued than usual, but otherwise no worse for wear; he continued his weekly Bible book study on the chapter they had left unfinished the previous Sunday night. Bonnie, however, would leave the sanctuary no more knowledgeable about the book of Ephesians than she had been when the service began. She'd sat down in a pew as close to the back of the sanctuary as she could get and hoped that Cheryl wouldn't be too curious about why.

But Josh wanted to know: "Why are we sittin' way back here, Mom? I can hardly see what's goin' on!"

"Well, honey, I'm just not feeling very well tonight. I thought we'd sit back here in case I need to slip out during the service." This was not entirely untrue.

While the rest of the congregation had pored over their Bibles, following Jeff Wells verse by verse, Bonnie had stared at the pages before her without seeing any of the words. She was still mentally wrestling with how she would cope with coming to church Sunday after Sunday, listening to Jeff preach (she *would* start listening again, she told herself) and facing the wondering looks she knew she would encounter when news finally got around that she and the pastor were, after all, *not* an item. She remembered the inquiring looks on the faces of the other women in her Sunday School class that morning and seriously considered joining a Singles class, if only until this whole thing blew over. It *had* to blow over some time.

Ben nudged her. "Mom, it's time to turn the page," he whispered, giving her a questioning look.

She glanced at him, feeling her face color. "Oh," she whispered back. "Sorry."

She even thought there might be a way to avoid going to some of the church services: she could volunteer to work in the church nursery. If she could persuade Jack and Cheryl Summers to let the boys sit with them…

Bonnie's eyes filled with tears. She couldn't *believe* she was sitting there trying to think of ways to avoid going to church! How could things have gotten so mixed up so quickly? Bonnie handed her Bible to Ben so that he could continue following along, then slipped out of the pew and out the back door. She made her way to the ladies' room tucked away in the narthex.

What was wrong with her? How could she have lost control of things so completely? She realized she had relinquished control the second she had said "Yes" to dinner with Jeff Wells.

And why on earth did Clara Adkinson seem so intent on humiliating her? Bonnie had never done anything remotely unkind to Clara. They knew each other distantly from having served together on the Women's Missions Auxiliary, but they were neither close nor unfriendly. They'd had, until this recent turn of events, little more than a nodding acquaintance. Tom Givens had told her not to take Clara's malicious actions personally, that Clara would have a problem with *anyone* Jeff dated. Why should Clara care if Jeff was dating anyone?

By the time Bonnie had pulled herself together and felt she'd gotten her nose to the point where it didn't glow too redly, the congregation was singing the closing hymn. She slipped in beside Ben and mouthed the words, not daring to try to make song come from her constricted throat. Ben looked up at her with concern. When the song was over, he returned the hymnal to its holder, then grasped Bonnie's hand in his. Bonnie looked down lovingly at him. What a sweetheart he was.

When the benediction was spoken, Ben turned to her and asked, "Are you okay, Mom?"

"Yes, sweetie," she said, apology in her voice, thinking how unfair it was to confuse him with feelings about a situation he knew nothing of. "I'll be fine."

"Hey, Ben, didja ask Mom about going to Jason's house?" Josh asked his brother.

"No, I didn't get a chance yet." Then, turning to Bonnie, he said, "Hey, Mom, they're having kind of an after-retreat fellowship at Jason Pierce's house tonight. Everybody that went on the retreat is invited. Can we go?"

Bonnie looked at her watch reflexively, although she knew it was seven o'clock because the service had just ended. "Well, guys, it *is* a school night, you know."

"Aw, Mom, it won't last too long!" Josh wheedled. "Mr. Wilkins said we'd be finished by eight or eight-fifteen."

"Yeah, Mom," intoned Ben. "We really wanna go, okay?"

"Sure," she relented.

She, herself, would like nothing more than to go right home, have a quick sandwich, put the guys to bed, and soak in a hot tub. But why should Ben and Josh miss out on being with their friends just because *she* was miserable? Anyway, if they did leave right at eight, the boys would still be in bed on time.

"Let me get the directions to Jason's house."

CHAPTER 8

Bonnie hadn't put the two names together, but Jason Pierce's mother was Jenny Pierce, the hostess of the Singles get-together to which Tom Givens had invited her that afternoon. Since Jenny was going to be entertaining anyway by having the children's group over, and since a number of the parents of the children who had gone on the retreat were part of the Singles group, she thought she'd kill two birds with one stone and just have everyone over at once. The Singles could entertain each other while the kids had their meeting.

"Hi, there, I'm Jenny Pierce." When Bonnie saw the warmth in Jenny's smile, she wondered fleetingly what she had been so afraid of in avoiding the Singles group all this time. "The post-retreat meeting is just getting started. I'll take the boys to the den for you."

Bonnie watched Jenny walk down the hall with Ben and Josh, then turned with a quiet sigh to the dining room table, where an array of snack foods presented itself. Choosing a celery stick and idly biting off a piece, she glanced around at her fellow singles—and realized she knew no one. *Well*, she thought, *this is going to be a lot of fun.*

Then the kitchen door opened and Tom Givens and his wife, Lisa, walked in. Tom's face lit up.

"Bonnie!" The surprise in his voice was unmistakable. "I thought you said you didn't want to come tonight." Lisa watched this exchange, her curiosity piqued.

Bonnie gave a rueful smile. "Children's retreat meeting. Circumstances seem to conspire against me everywhere I go."

"Well, hey," he shot back, "we like you, too."

Lisa walked up and crooked her arm in Bonnie's.

"Well, I, for one, am glad she's here. It's about time Bonnie joined us at one of these little parties."

A little embarrassed, Bonnie murmured, "I guess I still have a hard time thinking of myself as single, exactly."

A look came across Lisa's face, as if she were just remembering something.

"From what *I* hear, you're about the *only* one who doesn't think of you that way!"

Bonnie's eyes flew open and her mouth parted in surprise. Tom took matters in hand:

"Hey, Lisa, why don't you see if Janet needs any help in the kitchen while I try to meet the newcomers."

Bonnie didn't try to detain her. Although she'd been glad to see a familiar face at first, she definitely didn't like the turn the conversation had taken.

Bonnie glanced around again. Tom Givens was now talking and laughing with a small group of men and women in the living room. She felt a little guilty about not joining them and introducing herself, but something held her back. She wasn't really here as an "official" single person, anyway, she rationalized. If it hadn't been for the after-retreat meeting that Ben and Josh wanted to attend, she wouldn't even be here.

Then, the front door opened and Anna Lee Adkinson walked in, a group of six or seven men and women coming in behind her. Bonnie quickly turned back to the buffet table before Anna Lee could see her, hoping she wouldn't be recognized from behind.

She knew in her heart that Anna Lee almost certainly hadn't had anything to do with her mother's actions this past week, but Bonnie still felt unequal to making small talk with her, of pretending that she hadn't been deeply hurt by the turn of events Anna Lee's mother had orchestrated. As she looked down at the table, pretending to study the crackers and Melba toast, she watched through her hair as Anna Lee passed through the kitchen door, apparently unaware of Bonnie's presence. She was just about to sigh with relief when that voice, that booming voice that now filled her with dread whenever she heard it, announced to the crowd:

"Well, lookee here, y'all! I'm runnin' into my old girlfriend *again*! You gotta quit follerin' me around like this, gal, or folks're gonna start ta *talk*!"

Preston Hardy engulfed her once again in one of his fearsome, hair-mussing hugs. Bonnie knew from experience now that resistance was useless, so she waited until Preston's arm relaxed around her and then stepped aside to look up at him. *How* she wanted to tell him to please, please stop calling her his girlfriend! Did he think he was being funny, or did he somehow delude himself that if he persisted, she might relent and decide to give credence to the name? But they were surrounded now by other Singles suddenly discovering the food. Regardless of how vocal he was about it, to Bonnie it was a private matter; there was no way she would try to broach the subject in this crowd.

"So, what brings *you* here tonight?" Preston boomed. "Ain't never seen you at one of these wing-dings before."

Bonnie looked up at him with surprise.

"Have you been part of the Singles group long? I didn't even know you attended Foster Road."

Preston leaned over confidentially and said to Bonnie's ear in the closest he could come to a whisper, "Well, to tell you the God's-honest truth, babe, I ain't all that interested in that church stuff, know what I mean? Place'd prob'ly fall in on my head if *I* ever walked through the door. But these Singles parties are a great place to meet nice-lookin' women. Like *you*, fer instance!"

He jabbed her playfully in the side with his elbow, underestimating his strength as usual. Bonnie stumbled and winced a little. When she had regained her balance, she couldn't help but ask, "Well, if you don't attend Foster Road, how did you find out about the Singles group?"

"Well, ya know, that's kind of a funny story. I met your pastor in a real interesting way." Seeing the intrigue on Bonnie's face, he continued, "One Sunday night, right before Christmas last year, I was on a two-week canvassing trip up in Westdale. I was havin' a couple of brewskis and checkin' out the local pool tables at a place called Duck Inn.

"It's a real cold night, right? So the door opens, and in walks what looks like the local chapter of the AARP. Buncha old ladies and a coupla old guys comin' in ta get outta the cold 'cause their *church bus* broke down. Hoo-whee! Can you imagine it?"

Bonnie's eyes flew open. She knew instantly that Preston was talking about the bus from Foster Road Baptist; she had heard the story over Benevolent Council dinners enough. She saw the others around the table glance curiously at Preston. He was *so* loud!

"Well, Duck Inn is kinda out in the middle a' nowhere, so it was prob'ly the only place they could find to stop. You shoulda seen the looks on some of their faces when they walked into that pool bar, though. You'da thought they was walkin' through a cesspool!" Preston laughed at his own obnoxious remark.

"Well, anyways," he continued, "I gotta hand it to that pastor of yours. That boy's on the job twenty-four-seven. He buys everybody a Coke and then starts chattin' it up with all these dudes and biker chicks all around the room, like they was members of his congregation or somethin'! Came up to the table where I was playin' pool an' struck up a conversation with me. 'Course, me, I'm on the job all the time, too, 'cause *everybody's* a sales prospect, right? So I gave him my card an' asked him if he needed any insurance. Said he was pretty well taken care of in *that* department, but he gave me his card right back."

Preston reached into his back pocket, pulled out his wallet, and thumbed through it until he found a dog-eared, white business card. He handed it to Bonnie, and she read:

Jeffery D. Wells, Th.D.
Pastor, Foster Road Baptist Church
"Caring and Sharing in Jesus' Name"

Somehow, just seeing his name in print brought a fresh surge of disappointment at how abruptly things had ended this afternoon.

"Dr. Wells is a dedicated man, all right," she murmured, more to herself than to him, as she handed back the card.

"Yeah! Didn't look like it fazed him one bit to be in that bar. Some of the old ladies in the group sure looked pretty steamed about it, though." Preston tucked his wallet back into his pocket. "Well, anyways, like I said, I owe him one for steerin' me in *this* direction 'cause the pickins are mighty fine in this group. Food ain't bad, either," he said through the chips and dip he'd just stuffed into his mouth. "Hey, listen, I need to run outside and have a smoke. Wanna come with me?"

"Thanks, but my kids are in the den having a little meeting. I need to stick around in case they get out," she fibbed. They had just gone in; she knew it would be a while yet before they finished.

"Suit yourself, sweetheart. Be back in a few."

Bonnie could see people sneaking surreptitious glances at her, as if to see whether she were really with that loud guy. She picked up another celery stick and tried not to notice. Then she heard Tom Givens above the rest of the conversation in the room:

"Hey, there, Dr. J! Looks like we're having all kinds of newcomers here tonight!"

"Down, boy! Down!" Jeff Wells said with a grin as he came through the kitchen door. Following close behind him was Sherry Niles. "You've always been after me to come to one of these things, so here I finally am!"

And then, turning to Sherry, he re-introduced her to Tom. Bonnie overhead Tom say something about having met her that morning in Sunday School and having seen her at the Chinese restaurant that afternoon.

Bonnie's heart was pounding. What would she say when Jeff saw her? Would he say anything to her? Would he have the nerve?

"Actually, Tom, I'm here on business," Jeff said. "Dave Wilkins asked me to come by and talk with the kids about some of the things that went on at the retreat."

"Aw, rats," replied Tom. "Thought we'd finally converted you."

Tom might have been disappointed, but Bonnie was tremendously relieved. If Jeff wasn't going to mingle, then maybe she wouldn't have to worry about how to act in front of him. Out of the corner of her eye, she saw Jeff walk past the table on his way toward the den. For the briefest instant, their eyes met. Bonnie saw Jeff start with surprise, but he never broke stride. Then Tom Givens was at her side.

"Bonnie, have you met Sherry Niles yet? She's the newest addition to our group."

Wondering why Tom was making a point of introducing her to Sherry Niles given their conversation that afternoon, but willing herself to smile and be friendly nevertheless, Bonnie turned to Sherry and extended her hand in greeting. She had to look up to see Sherry's face; Sherry was quite a tall woman.

Up close, Bonnie was a little startled at the make-up Sherry wore. From a distance, Sherry was incredibly attractive, and she was still beautiful up close, but in a painted-on kind of way. Sherry wore the full gamut: lipstick, foundation, blusher, shadow and eyeliner, and a good layer of powder covering it all. They looked as though they had been professionally applied, but with a rather heavy hand.

"I'm kind of a newcomer myself," Bonnie said.

"Well, I ain't joined yet or nothin' like that," Sherry drawled.

She had one of the twangiest Southern accents Bonnie had ever heard; when she thought about it, it was very much like the one Preston Hardy spoke with. Bonnie saw Tom, behind Sherry, give a little wave and go off to chat with another group in the room.

Thanks a lot, Tom, she thought ruefully.

Hiding her surprise at how much differently Sherry sounded than she looked, Bonnie asked, "Are you new to Chandler City?"

"Oh, yeah. I'm originally from New Roads. That's a little town not too far from Baton Rouge. That's in Louisiana," she informed Bonnie helpfully.

"Oh, yes, I know!" Bonnie replied, hiding a smile. "I'm from New Orleans originally."

"You don't mean it! Ain't it a small world!"

"Yes," Bonnie agreed. "How about that? As a matter a fact, I graduated from LSU. That's in Baton Rouge." Bonnie regretted that last remark. She didn't mean to be mocking. If Sherry caught it, though, she didn't let on.

"Oh, I know! I went there for two years myself! One of these days, I'd like to go back and finish, but I don't know…Some of them classes was pretty hard."

Bonnie wasn't quite sure what to say to this, so she tried changing the subject.

"Have you found a job here yet?"

This was a bit of a fib on her part; she remembered quite well Jack Summers informing her and Cheryl that Sherry was working at a local bank. Sherry reached into her purse, pulled out a business card, and handed it to Bonnie.

"Oh, yeah! My daddy runs a fishin' camp in New Roads, and he got to be good friends with one of the men who goes there a lot on fishin' and huntin' trips. Turns out, he's the president of Chandler City Bank."

Bonnie frowned a little, trying to follow the story.

"Well, I was livin' in Atlanta and…" Sherry hesitated, as if uncertain of how much detail to reveal. "…and I was gettin' ready to move back to New Roads. But my daddy called up Mr. Blankenship and asked him if he knew where I might could find some work. Mr. Blankenship just happened to have a openin' for an Account Representative."

Sherry pointed to the words "Account Representative" on the card Bonnie held as she carefully pronounced the title.

"I see," Bonnie said with a smile.

Though she had been prepared not to like Sherry, there was a sweetness about Sherry's naïveté that Bonnie found endearing.

"I only been there two weeks so far," continued Sherry, her face clouding a little with doubt. "I…I know I got to be trained an' all, but so far I ain't done much but answer the phone some and make copies on the copyin' machine."

Once again, Bonnie was at a bit of a loss as to how to continue the conversation. She picked up a paper plate and extended it to Sherry.

"Why don't you help yourself to some snacks?"

"Oh, thanks! I ain't had nothin' to eat since lunch."

Bonnie remembered quite well what Sherry had had for lunch. If Sherry recalled having seen Bonnie at Golden China House, though, she didn't let on. As they made their way around the table, Bonnie's glance went momentarily to the kitchen. She saw Anna Lee Adkinson standing by the sink; she seemed to have been rather frankly watching Bonnie and Sherry as they had been talking. Bonnie gave Anna Lee a quizzical look and Anna Lee smiled back weakly. Remembering again the sight of Anna Lee's mother as she'd been looking at her the other night, Bonnie couldn't return Anna Lee's smile. She turned away.

"Excuse me," Bonnie said to Sherry. "I need to go check on my kids."

"Oh!" Sherry sounded disappointed. "Well, it was real nice meetin' you. Maybe you and me could have lunch one day."

Bonnie thought of Jeff and how he'd apparently had eyes for no one except Sherry that afternoon, and, sweet as Sherry seemed to be, she doubted seriously that she could be friends with someone she knew was seeing Jeff.

"Yes, maybe so," she murmured. Avoiding meeting Sherry's eyes, she slipped away to make her way towards the hall. Just as she was about to pass the front door, Preston opened it and walked in again. The acrid smell of cigarette smoke emanated from him.

"Hey, girl! Did ya miss me?" He chucked her, none-too-gently, on the shoulder. "I'm ready for some more eats. In fact, I was thinkin' about—"

Bonnie looked up at Preston to see why he had stopped mid-sentence. She followed his gaze and saw that he was looking in the direction of the buffet table. Who was it that had caught his attention? Was it Sherry Niles?

"Well, lookee what the cat drug in," he finally managed to mutter, his smile gone. Turning back to Bonnie with a grimace, he continued, "Like I was gettin' ready to say, I ain't gonna make a meal outta no finger food. I'm gonna go find a restaurant and get some real food. I'd invite you to come with me, but I know you got your kids with you."

And before Bonnie could even agree with him, he had gone right back out the door. Everyone turned to look when they heard the door slam. Sherry was standing stock-still, looking as if she were about to cry. Impulsively, she set her paper plate on the table, left the serving line, and headed into the bathroom just off the kitchen. Apparently, Sherry Niles and Preston Hardy had met.

Just then, a parade of boys and girls came streaming down the hall from the den. Bonnie picked Ben and Josh out of the group and smiled.

"Hey guys, why don't you go fix yourselves a plate of food and eat. We need to get going."

"Okay, Mom," they said, barely missing a beat as the crowd of children converged on the dining room table. Bonnie could see Jeff Wells coming down the hall. She turned towards the table, but not quickly enough. As Jeff passed by, he hesitated a moment.

"Good evening, Bonnie," he said softly.

"Dr. Wells," she said, allowing her eyes to meet his as briefly as possible.

Even though he had never called her anything else, it suddenly bothered her that he should call her "Bonnie." It was a small thing, she knew, and he called everybody in their congregation by his or her first name. It just seemed so inappropriately intimate now. For her part, she was determined to keep their relationship strictly formal; she would always call him "Dr. Wells."

Why is he even speaking to me? she fumed to herself. *He gave me my walking papers, didn't he?*

Having escaped the onslaught of children, Sherry Niles walked up. She seemed to have recovered from whatever had upset her a few moments before.

"Oh, Jeff, I guess you probably know, uh, *Bonnie*, was it?" she looked at Bonnie apologetically.

"Oh, yes." Bonnie smiled enigmatically now at Jeff. So, he was on a first-name basis with Sherry, too, was he? "Dr. Wells and I go back a ways."

"Well, I sure do appreciate the way he's made me feel so welcome," Sherry enthused, unaware of the looks Bonnie and Jeff were exchanging. "It ain't easy bein' new in town."

Jeff Wells looked decidedly uncomfortable. He thought he could decipher the look on Bonnie's face exactly. But why should it bother her if she thought he was with Sherry, he asked himself defensively. Wasn't she involved with someone else herself?

Still, as if to disabuse Bonnie of the notion that he was actually *with* Sherry, Jeff looked at his watch and said, "Well, ladies, the night's not getting any younger. I think I'll call it a day. Can you find your way home from here okay, Sherry?"

"Oh, yeah, I think so," Sherry said, again sounding a little abandoned. "But ain't—aren't you gonna have anything to eat?"

Bonnie couldn't help but notice that Sherry made an effort to correct her grammar for Dr. Wells.

"Thanks, but I'll just fix myself a sandwich at home. Good night, ladies."

With an enigmatic parting glance at Bonnie, he walked out the front door.

CHAPTER 9

As if the day's events hadn't given Bonnie enough to think about, Ben haltingly announced to his mother on the drive home from Jenny Pierce's that he thought he was ready to make his profession of faith.

"I've been thinkin' about it a lot, Mom," he told her, as if he felt the need to justify himself.

"Oh, honey, I think it's wonderful," she reassured him. "Did you make your decision on the retreat?"

"Well, kind of, but I've been thinkin' about it for a while. Seems like it kind of hit me this past Christmas, when Pastor Jeff talked about what it really means to celebrate the birth of Jesus, and how He left us in charge of fulfilling His mission after He went back to heaven." Ben was staring at his hands folded on his lap. "But tonight, Pastor Jeff said some things at the meeting that made me know I'm making the right decision. I mean, I don't know if I'll ever be as good a preacher as Pastor Jeff, but I think that's what I want to do. I want to spend the rest of my life tellin' people about Jesus and how he came to save us all, and how he came to show us how to live together in the world."

Bonnie's heart swelled with love for this sweet little boy, speaking now with insight that seemed beyond his years. Her eyes misted when the thought occurred to her that Bill should have been hearing this conversation. Bill would have been so proud to see his firstborn make his profession of faith.

"I think that's just wonderful," Bonnie said again through her tears.

"Hey, Mom, are you okay? Seems like you been kinda upset all day. Weren't you cryin' in church tonight?"

Ben was so observant, so aware of his mother and her feelings. How could he be just nine years old?

"No, sweetie, I'm fine." She smiled sadly. "I was just thinking how proud your dad would've been."

Ben said nothing, but continued to stare at his hands.

Hoping she hadn't marred the moment by bringing up his father, Bonnie hastened to add, "Will you go forward next Sunday?"

"I'd like to, if you think it's okay."

Although Josh was still a little too young to grasp the full import of his brother's decision, he had obviously been listening to the conversation in the car. That night, as the three Callaways held hands to say their evening prayers, Josh closed his eyes and intoned softly, "And God, please tell our Daddy about Ben giving his heart to Jesus. He would've wanted to know." Ben smiled indulgently at his mother and Bonnie winked at him in reply.

After tucking her boys in, Bonnie headed toward the kitchen to make herself a cup of tea to sip in the tub. As she turned to the pantry, she heard a soft tapping at the kitchen door and froze.

Bonnie turned toward the door slowly, half dreading what she might see, yet hoping against hope that somehow Jeff might have reconsidered his decision and come to see her again. Nothing could have prepared her, however, for seeing Anna Lee Adkinson looking at her through her kitchen door window. After a moment's hesitation, Bonnie walked over and unlocked the door.

"Guess I'm probably about the last person *you* ever expected to see at your door," Anna Lee said with an ironic smile.

Bonnie ignored the comment, but remarked to herself that perhaps Anna Lee was not so shy after all.

"Please, come in. I'm just about to have some tea. Would you care for some?"

"Sure, that sounds great."

Anna Lee sat down at the kitchen table and waited for Bonnie to finish preparing their tea. Dress for church on Sunday evenings was always casual, but the sweatshirt Anna Lee wore over her jeans did little for her figure. Bonnie recognized her running shoes as one of the more expensive brands, but they weren't very new or clean. Anna Lee just didn't seem to care much about her appearance. Her glossy auburn hair, which was beautiful despite its relatively neglected state, hung to just below her waist; she alternately wrapped and unwrapped a long strand around her forefinger as she slouched in her chair. Bonnie set two steaming mugs of tea on the table, sat opposite Anna Lee, and waited to find out what had brought Clara's daughter to see her.

Holding her mug with both hands, breathing in the fragrant aroma of chamomile, Anna Lee looked thoughtful for a moment and then began:

"I didn't get a chance to talk to you at Jenny's tonight, but I did want to talk to you. Guess you're wondering why."

Bonnie acknowledged this truth with a nod.

"I know you realize that I have no control over what my mother does."

Bonnie sighed and looked into her teacup.

"I just wanted you to know how very sorry I am that you had to get caught in the middle of all of this."

Bonnie looked up, her eyes searching Anna Lee's face.

"All of what? What's going on?" Maybe now Bonnie would find out what was behind Clara's interference in Jeff Wells's affairs.

"I can't tell you how embarrassing it is to have my mother so brazenly trying to get the pastor interested in marrying me. It's like she has no shame whatsoever." It was Anna Lee's turn to look down into her own cup.

"*Marrying* you?" Bonnie was incredulous.

"Too much, huh?" Anna Lee shook her head in disgust. "Ever since Terri died—Well, I guess Mom did have the decency to wait about two months. But ever since then, she has been almost constantly asking Dr. Wells over to dinner or bringing him cookies or cakes or casseroles. And she *lies* and tells him that *I* made them!"

"You're not serious!"

Bonnie laughed and shook her head in amazement. This must have been what Tom Givens had been referring to earlier that afternoon. She had no trouble at all picturing Clara standing at Jeff's door with her daintily covered casserole dishes, bragging on her daughter's wonderful homemaking skills. How obvious could you get!

"Oh, yes, I'm quite serious," confirmed Anna Lee. "She's even arranged it so that he's going to be my 'date,' as she calls it, for the annual Seniors Banquet! I don't know how she pulled that one off, but I'm sure that poor Dr. Wells had no say in the matter." She paused a moment, then looked at Bonnie as if seeking some sort of affirmation, then said, "When Terri died and left Dr. Wells all that money, my mother was determined to have a crack at it. As I say, it's really been embarrassing."

"Ah, so it isn't just Dr. Wells's pretty face, eh?" Bonnie smiled mischievously.

Anna Lee smiled back. This Bonnie Callaway, she was all right.

"Oh, I guess he's an okay-looking guy, but I mean, he's like forty-one or forty-two. I'm only twenty-seven! He's a little old for me, don't you think?"

Bonnie started inwardly, but said nothing. She had not realized that Anna Lee was quite as young as that. She had thought they were much closer together in age. Perhaps it was the clothes Anna Lee wore, always so plain and unflattering. Or perhaps she had just reasoned that Anna Lee had to be older because her mother was in her early sixties. Clara apparently hadn't started her family young.

"I figured that, eventually, Mom would see that Dr. Wells has no interest in me and give up. I mean, it's only been two years!" She sipped her tea. "Up till now, though, Dr. Wells hasn't been dating anybody, so I guess she thought there was still a chance. I just don't know why she thought that Dr. Wells and *you* were dating."

Bonnie's eyes were riveted to Anna Lee, and she wondered how Clara could be so sure about who Jeff did or didn't date, but she revealed nothing of Friday night's events.

"I mean, she told me about seeing you guys at the Coffee Shoppe last Monday night, but I think it's a bit of a leap for her to say that you guys were out on a date."

Bonnie certainly agreed with that.

"Everybody knows that the Benevolent Council eats there after their monthly meetings. Where *was* everybody else?"

Bonnie explained about Doctor Father's new class and Joanna Reeves's false labor.

"I think she was making a big deal out of nothing just because she's *so* worried that Dr. Wells and his precious money are going to slip through her fingers."

So, apparently, Clara hadn't said anything to Anna Lee about seeing them together Friday night. Bonnie wondered why.

"It should be pretty obvious after today, though, that Dr. Wells has a thing for that new woman, Sherry Niles. I mean, he was with her at lunch, and then they were together again tonight at Jenny Pierce's. And I've never even *seen* Dr. Wells at a Singles function before."

Bonnie didn't mention to Anna Lee that they had come in separate cars or that Jeff had left the gathering long before Sherry had. She didn't want even to *appear* to be interested in whom, or even *whether*, Jeff Wells was dating.

"Isn't she one of the most disgustingly beautiful women you've ever seen?"

Bonnie smiled in spite of herself. This conversation was certainly showing her a side of Anna Lee she hadn't known existed—she had *never* seen her this animated around her mother.

"Ya gotta give her credit—she works fast," Anna Lee continued. "I'm pretty sure Dr. Wells hasn't dated anyone else since Terri died. Wait till Mom hears about Sherry Niles. Now she's really got something to worry about!"

Once again, Bonnie refrained from making any comment, but couldn't help noting that Anna Lee hadn't avoided her mother's penchant for drawing hasty conclusions. At least, in this case, she hoped they were hasty. Bonnie debated with herself about whether she should tell Anna Lee about Jeff asking her out to dinner last week. She would feel less than honest if she let Anna Lee continue to think that there had been no basis at all for her mother's suspicions, but she knew that nothing would really change things between her and Jeff. Why tell her about something that had turned out to be a non-event? Truth be told, she just didn't think she had the energy to tell Anna Lee the story anyway. Let sleeping dogs lie.

Anna Lee was thoughtful another moment. "But, hey, this is good news for you! This gets you off the hook with my mother! Now, she'll have to find something else to gossip about. It wasn't anything personal against you, you know? She just wants you to keep your paws off of Dr. Wells!" She laughed at her own joke.

Bonnie smiled and shook her head. Tom Givens had told her essentially the same thing.

"I can't say that it won't be a relief not to feel like Hester Prynne around church anymore. But isn't there anything you can say to her that would convince her to give up her crusade to marry you off to Dr. Wells? Have you tried telling her that you're not interested in *him*?"

At this, Anna Lee's face clouded. She said nothing at first, but just looked intently into her mug. She took another sip of tea, as if buying herself time.

Then, almost in a whisper, she said, "I almost got married once. A long time ago. Someone I met in college."

Bonnie watched Anna Lee, fascinated.

"I brought him home to meet Mom over spring break in our senior year. He was going to enter the seminary in the fall. He wanted to be a minister of music."

Anna Lee set her mug on the table and looked at Bonnie, fire in her eyes.

"Well, Mom had a fit. She said there was no way she was going to let her daughter throw herself away on some preacher so she could be poor as a church mouse. No pun intended, I'm sure." She smiled a sardonic little smile.

"Your mom's kind of fixated on money, huh? Did your dad not leave you guys much when he died?"

Bonnie really didn't think this could be the case, given the model of car Clara drove and the size of the house they lived in across the street from Jeff Wells.

"Died?" Anna Lee looked at Bonnie incredulously. "My dad isn't dead! He lives in Jacksonville, Florida. Where'd you get the idea that he was dead?"

"I...I don't know," Bonnie stammered. "I guess I...I just *assumed* that your mother was a widow. Like her friend, Mertis."

It struck Bonnie that she, too, had been guilty of drawing hasty conclusions. Now that she thought about it, she realized that she couldn't recall ever speaking with anyone on the subject. She had simply assumed Clara was a widow because most of the women in the Senior Adult group *were* widows.

"Oh, no, Mom and Dad have been divorced since I was about nine or ten. He was a sales rep for a textbook publisher before he retired. One Monday morning he left to visit campuses in northern Florida. He called to check in every night that week, just as he always had, and then on Friday evening, he called to say that he wasn't coming back. Mom was furious, of course, but I have to say, it was hard to blame him. Even as young as I was, I could see she led him a dog's life. He married a woman he met in Jacksonville about two years after the divorce was final. Her name is Shirley—she was one of the math professors he sold textbooks to. They've been happily married going on fourteen years. I don't get to see him as much as I'd like to, but I'm happy for him."

Anna Lee drank the last of her tea and set her empty cup on the table.

"The problem was, Mom was the one who had money. I don't know all of the details, of course, but she apparently had to settle quite a large sum on him when they split up. She's very bitter and doesn't believe that he ever loved her. She thinks he was always after her money, which is kind of irrational—they were married over twenty years. They were married twelve years before she finally had me."

Then, after a thoughtful pause, she continued, "Still, if people thought she was a widow, I can see where she wouldn't go out of her way to set them straight. She's never forgiven Dad for making her a divorcee.

"Well, anyway, as soon as I was old enough to date, she tried to instill in me the importance of finding a man whose family had money so he wouldn't be after mine." Anna Lee rolled her eyes at the memory. "It was such a relief to go away to college and not have to have her pass judgment on every guy who asked me out. Because, believe me, there weren't that many to begin with."

She paused and bit her lip pensively, then continued softly: "Then, I met this guy, and we fell in love. It wasn't love at first sight or anything like that. We were good friends at first. For a couple of years, actually. We met at the Baptist Student Union on campus. We both played guitar and sang, although he was *much* better than I was. We began to sing duets together at BSU events and local churches and for weddings. We just got along great—and we were really in demand. We were pulling in some pretty good money for a couple of college students. Then, one night..."

Anna Lee's face was transformed. She was in a place and time long left behind, but obviously not forgotten.

"One Friday night, he'd driven me back to my dorm after we'd sung together at a wedding. I turned to say goodnight, as usual, and it was like BOOM! We looked at each other like it was the first time we'd ever seen each other. He kissed me, and we both wondered how we'd missed each other before."

There was amazement in her eyes at her memory of the moment.

"Oh, Bonnie, if you could've known him. He was so wonderful. Such a strong Christian. And he was *gorgeous*. All the girls in the BSU were half crazy over him. Why he liked someone like *me*, I'll never know. But after that kiss, there was some serious chemistry between us!" Her eyes were far away, remembering.

"Don't sell yourself short," Bonnie murmured.

"Well, looks didn't cut any mustard with my mother. Nor did the fact that he was a sweet, wonderful, Christian man. *Her* daughter wasn't going to marry a poor seminary student wanting to be a poor preacher, and that was that."

"Kind of ironic that now she's moving heaven and earth to get you *to* marry a preacher, isn't it?"

Anna Lee laughed derisively. "Yeah, only this preacher's got bucks." She paused, playing with a strand of her long, auburn hair. "And I guess—Oh, I don't know! My mother has always been so intimidating!"

Bonnie could vouch for that.

"She had me doubting my own judgment. She said that college romances wouldn't last because we lived in a make-believe world, that I wouldn't know what real love was until I'd lived in the real world, whatever *that* means."

Tears streamed down Anna Lee's cheeks now. The words tumbled out of her, as if she had wanted to tell this story to someone for a long time.

"She asked me how I could be so sure about being in love when I'd never dated anyone else seriously before. She kept reminding me about my dad leaving her and getting all that money from her. I mean, Mark didn't even *know* our family has money. I knew he liked me just for *me*, but somehow, I let her talk me into breaking off our engagement, anyway."

Bonnie was stricken for the young Miss Adkinson, defenseless against her mother's intimidation tactics.

"Mark was his name?"

"Yeah," she whispered. She looked at Bonnie, gratitude in her eyes, as if it meant a lot to her that Bonnie understood her side of the story. "So, if you ask me why I haven't told my mother that I'm not interested in Jeff Wells, I guess I'd have to say, experience has taught me she hasn't always been too concerned about what *my* preferences were."

"Oh, Anna Lee!"

"Those last two months of school were awful. I'm lucky I graduated. I was so depressed, I could hardly study anymore. I had to quit going to the BSU so I wouldn't see him. People couldn't understand why we weren't available to sing together anymore, but no one really knew that we'd been seeing each other, you know, dating each other."

She plucked a paper napkin from the holder in the center of the table and wiped her eyes and blew her nose. She began again with a sigh: "After we graduated, he went home to Nashville and I came home to be a teacher." Through her tears, she smiled enigmatically. "I guess in a lot ways, I've never really gotten over him. I've never felt even remotely the same about anyone since Mark."

"Did you ever hear from him again over the years?"

"Not *from* him," she answered slowly. "I don't think he ever was able to forgive me for breaking up with him. Can't say that I blame him. But I've certainly heard *of* him. Instead of going into church work, he got involved in a Christian singing group that became very popular, and then he went out on his own. Joke's on my mom, I guess, 'cause now he's pulling down some seriously big money. He's probably worth several million by now." She paused and looked at Bonnie. "Maybe you've heard of him. His name is Mark Miller."

Bonnie was thunderstruck.

"You were engaged to *Mark Miller*?"

He was only one of the most popular contemporary Christian singers in the country. In fact, he had a crossover hit, a re-make of the seventies rock anthem, "Spirit in the Sky," on the Top 40, Country, and Christian radio stations right now. Bonnie knew that he even had a couple of Grammy awards to his credit.

"Believe it or not," she answered, resignation in her voice. "Not that anyone knows about it but Mark, my mother, and me. I doubt seriously that he told anyone that a mousy little girl like *me* turned him down."

It pained Bonnie to hear Anna Lee talk that way about herself. Anna Lee looked at Bonnie through tear-swollen eyes.

"Even though your husband died," Anna Lee began again slowly, "you were lucky to have married the man you loved and known happiness with him. I hope you never have to go through falling in love with someone you'll never be together with. I hope you never have the pain of feeling there's someone you'll never be over."

As Bonnie thought once again about the kiss she and Jeff had shared Friday night and felt again the sinking sensation in her stomach she'd had when Jeff had told her he didn't want to see her anymore, she fervently hoped so, too.

CHAPTER 10

If Bonnie had thought that avoiding Jeff Wells was going to be easy, she was in for no little surprise in the days and weeks that followed their meeting in his office that Sunday afternoon. Was she imagining things, or was she really running into Jeff much more frequently now that seeing him had become so uncomfortable? The irony of it was that, before the day Jeff had called to ask her to dinner, Bonnie rarely saw him outside of church. Now it seemed she saw him everywhere she went!

First, of course, had been the Singles get-together at Jenny Pierce's house. It would be difficult to say who had been more surprised to see the other, Jeff or Bonnie. Anna Lee Adkinson had said that that was the first time she had ever known Jeff Wells to attend a Singles function. What a way to kick off her *own* participation in the group!

Then there was Art Newton's funeral the following day. It was no surprise for them to see each other there, of course, but it was painfully awkward nevertheless. She'd had every intention of sitting in the back of the church, as she had done in the previous evening's service. And she would have had no trouble doing so: the sanctuary was filled to capacity with those who had come to say goodbye to Art. On her way in, though, she ran into Cheryl in the ladies' room.

"Hi!" Cheryl said, genuinely glad to see her friend. "Please come sit with us. Jack's already gone in to find a place."

And what a place he had found: two rows from the front, right smack in the middle. Had she been trying, she couldn't have picked a better place to be directly in Jeff's line of vision. There was no way to avoid making *some* eye contact with him, but he was definitely looking directly at her far more than the law of averages would have allowed.

At the cemetery, there was a much smaller group. Jack and Cheryl had decided not to be there for the interment, and she didn't see Doctor Father or John Reeves either, so Bonnie found herself on her own. She approached Ruth Newton to condole with her once more as they all waited for Dr. Wells to arrive.

"Ruth, please let me know if there's anything I can do," said Bonnie. "Why don't we have lunch together soon?"

"I'd like that very much."

Ruth's eyes were dry, but the sadness was there. This was the end of a long, difficult journey for Ruth. At that moment, Jeff Wells walked up.

"I'm ready to begin whenever you are," he told Ruth gently.

Nodding her assent, Ruth turned to walk toward the grave site. Jeff hesitated a moment, then murmured, "Good morning, Bonnie."

Bonnie looked at him, surprised and confused that he had even spoken to her. Did he expect her to behave as if nothing had happened between them?

"Dr. Wells," was her wooden reply.

She walked over to stand where she felt she would be least likely to be in Jeff's line of sight. The momentary meeting of their eyes, however, had been full of meaning; there was resignation and a touch of sadness in his, reproach in hers.

After the funeral, Bonnie put off going home right away. For the first time in a long time since Bill's death, she found herself hating the idea of going home to any empty house. She had plenty of work to do, that was for sure. Her thoughts had been so filled with anticipation last week—anticipation of what she had thought would be a nice evening in the company of a man she had been looking forward to getting to know better. As a result, she had been much less productive than usual.

Now, quite frankly, she just didn't want to be alone with her thoughts. She didn't want to think about Jeff, and she *certainly* didn't want to think about Jeff with Sherry Niles. She didn't want to think about Clara Adkinson and the things she had Jeff and everyone else in church believing about her. Either set of thoughts made her alternately depressed and angry. What was even worse was that she felt utterly helpless to do anything about them. Putting off the inevitable, she decided to treat herself to some lunch at the Coffee Shoppe.

It was just after eleven thirty, and the lunch crowd was beginning to gather. Looking anxiously at how many people appeared to be waiting for a table, she was just about to re-think her decision to have lunch out, when the unmistakable voice of Preston Hardy thundered over everyone's head:

"Hey, Bonnie! Bonnie Martin! I mean, Callaway! Come on over here. My table's almost ready. Sit with me, and you won't have to wait for a table!"

Heads turned to look in the direction from which Preston was shouting, and Bonnie felt herself cringing inside. The best way, perhaps the *only* way, to quell this noisy summons, she thought, was simply to answer it. She made her way through the crowd toward Preston, trying not to meet the curious looks of those she passed, and he swooped his arm around her as soon as she drew near.

"We gotta quit meetin' like this!"

That must be the only joke he knows, Bonnie thought with an inward groan.

Eyeing Bonnie in the black dress she had worn for Art's funeral, Preston told her with his usual lack of discretion, "Hoo-whee, girl! You're a sight for sore eyes today!"

Bonnie ignored his comment as the hostess led them to a table in the row of booths closest to the reception area and handed them menus.

"Now, maybe we can have that little talk about you doin' some work for me!"

Bonnie's expression was one of surprise mixed with insuppressible pleasure; she had been worried that Preston would somehow construe her acquiescence at having lunch with him as a sign that she wanted to see him socially. It was a relief to hear him mention work.

"I gotta tell you, though," he said, gravity in his voice, "it's gonna have to be strictly business with us."

"Oh?" Another surprise. Bonnie tactfully refrained from informing him that there had never been any other possibility.

"Yeah, I know I just invited you out to dinner last week and all, but well…last night kinda changed things."

"Last night?"

Bonnie thought back on the previous evening and tried to imagine what Preston might be referring to. She'd spoken with Preston briefly before he had gone out for a cigarette, and when he came back in, he'd left in something of a huff, apparently the result of seeing Sherry Niles.

"Yeah, well, I guess you probably remember me tellin' you last week that I was goin' through a divorce."

"Yes, I remember."

"Well, after seein' Sherry last night, well…I guess you could say we're thinkin' about givin' it another shot."

"Sherry? Sherry Niles is your *wife*?" There was no mistaking the shock in Bonnie's voice.

"Well, she didn't always go by the name of Niles. She started using her *maiden* name again when we got separated." He sounded extremely resentful of the fact.

"Yes, I guess that's fairly common." Bonnie tried to sound sympathetic, but it was Sherry who had her real sympathy if she was married to Preston Hardy. "If you don't mind me asking, how did you and Sherry both come to be in Chandler City?"

"Oh, it ain't as big a coincidence as it might seem. We lived in Atlanta for two years after I transferred from New Orleans. Then, about six weeks ago, she decided she'd had enough and left. I thought she was gonna go back home to live with her folks."

"In New Roads?"

"Well, yeah! How'd you know she was from New Roads?"

"Tom Givens introduced us last night, and it came up in conversation." Bonnie recalled now, though, that Sherry's being married had *not*. Suddenly, it occurred to her to wonder if Jeff Wells knew that Sherry was married. Was Jeff unknowingly going out with a married woman? "Sherry told me that a friend of her father's had gotten her a job at Chandler City Bank."

Preston snorted with derision. "Yeah, ol' Jesse Niles, he's always Johnny-on-the-Spot when it comes to Sherry."

Bonnie didn't know what Preston was implying by that remark, so she said nothing.

"Sherry's a sweet girl, and she's pretty dang good-lookin', too, but she ain't the brightest bulb in the box, if you know what I mean," Preston began again.

Bonnie looked down, amazed at Preston's offhand manner of insulting his wife.

"It's okay," he assured Bonnie. "I think she knows herself she ain't no rocket scientist. But she sure knows how to wrap her daddy 'round her little finger."

The waitress came just then to take their orders.

"Just a chef's salad and some iced tea for me," said Bonnie, handing her unopened menu back to the waitress.

"Let me have a steak sandwich, some French fries, and a chocolate milk-shake."

Whew! Bonnie thought. *Counting fat grams must not be one of* his *worries.*

"But you say now that you're thinking about reconciling?" Bonnie continued when the waitress had gone. "I think that's great. I really hope you can work things out." In spite of her own aversion to Preston, she meant it. "How did the two of you meet?"

"Oh, me and Sherry met when I was quarterbackin' for LSU and she was homecomin' queen on the Tri-Delta ticket. She was a sophomore and I was a senior."

"Yes," Bonnie said, "Sherry mentioned that she'd attended LSU. That's where I went to school, too."

"Are you kiddin'? Well, ain't that somethin'!" Then, he was struck by a sudden thought. "Listen! Wait *right* here. I got somethin' I want to show you!"

With that, he was out of the booth and striding towards the entrance of the restaurant. Bonnie looked after him in puzzlement as he jostled his way through the crowd waiting to be seated. She'd rather hoped that her remark about being a fellow LSU grad might have prompted Preston to tell her why Sherry hadn't finished school as well, but he didn't seem to have caught the hint.

With amazing speed, Preston was back at their table, carrying a large, purple-bound book under his arm. He held it out for her inspection and set it down in front of her, heedless of the rings of water from their glasses on the table.

"An LSU yearbook!" she exclaimed. Then she looked at the date. "Is this the year you graduated?"

"Sure is!"

"I can't believe it! We graduated the same year. What was your major?"

Preston looked a little sheepish.

"Well, to tell ya the truth, doll, I was pretty busy with football most of the time, so it was kind of hard concentratin' on much else. Got a degree in General Studies. Guess you could say I'm a Jack of all trades!"

Bonnie nodded a silent confirmation. Then it struck her how strange it was that he should have, of all things, his college yearbook with him.

"Preston," she began slowly, "Do you always carry your yearbook around with you?"

"Oh, yeah, babe," he confirmed, as if the question, and not the practice itself, were surprising. "Georgia, Alabama, Florida, and Louisiana are college football country! If I can work it in that I quarterbacked for LSU during a sales call, you can't believe how many doors that opens! With guys, anyways," he added a little more quietly. "Many's the times I whip out the ol' yearbook and take 'em on a little stroll down memory lane."

"Ah," said Bonnie, not sure how else to respond. *Theirs or yours?* was Bonnie's unspoken question.

Then she began to peruse the thick, glossy pages of the heavy book. She had one of these herself, packed away in a box at home somewhere. Unlike Preston, however, she hadn't looked at hers in years. Why was he so focused on things that had happened almost fifteen years ago?

She came to the section on the homecoming court for that year. A full page was devoted to a formal portrait of Sherry as the queen. She was beautiful, absolutely radiant. Then, there was a smaller shot of Sherry being escorted to midfield at the homecoming game. Preston Hardy, wearing his football uniform with the number Eight, stood next to her. Sherry had one arm crooked into Preston's; the other held a fabulous bouquet of flowers. They both smiled widely.

"So this is how you met, eh?"

"Yep. We started goin' out when we met for the homecoming court, but it's kinda hard to keep a romance goin' when you're playin' football all the time. Things really heated up between us when football season was over, though."

Bonnie could imagine the homecoming queen and the campus big-man becoming a couple.

"That was the year the Tigers played Penn State in the Sugar Bowl, so I was gettin' a lot of good press. I was bein' courted by a couple'a pro teams for the fall draft, and Sherry had won the Miss Louisiana pageant earlier that year. She was headed for Miss America in Atlantic City that September. She was hopin' for a modeling contract out of it or somethin'."

"Wow," murmured Bonnie.

"Yeah, that was the year we had the world by the tail."

Bonnie wondered at his sardonic tone. Preston peeled the paper cover from his straw and pushed it deep into the milkshake the waitress had just placed in front of him.

"And then we got stupid."

Bonnie frowned, confused. "Stupid?"

Preston leaned back against the booth and slid his long, lanky body into a slump under the table. "Yeah, by the time graduation rolled around in May, Sherry was about three months pregnant."

Bonnie's eyes widened. Was this why Sherry hadn't finished her degree?

"And, of course, being a good Catholic girl and all, there was no way she'd even *talk* about an abortion."

Bonnie squelched her inward disgust that it had seemed a viable option to Preston.

"Her daddy was some hot when he found out, boy."

"Yeah, I guess so." Bonnie hardly knew what to say.

"Well, that was the end of Miss America, I guess you can imagine. We got married a week after I graduated."

"You never mentioned that you had children," Bonnie commented softly.

"I don't." Preston bounced his straw up and down slowly in the thick liquid in his glass. "Turned out to be one of them tube pregnancies. Had to have surgery to remove it. The doctor said her chances of getting' pregnant again are pretty slim." He shrugged. "Been married almost fifteen years, and it ain't happened yet."

"Oh, I'm so sorry." And this time, she truly was. She thought of Ben and Josh and breathed a silent prayer of thanks for her blessings.

"Yeah, well, Sherry and her folks was pretty broke up about it, too." He gave a snort of derision. "They was mad 'cause she *got* pregnant, then sad when she *wasn't*. Go figure."

If he couldn't figure it out on his own, Bonnie was not about to try explaining to him how potential grandparents might feel, regardless of the circumstances, if their child were to lose a baby.

"Well, how about you? How did you feel?"

Preston said nothing for a moment. He was staring into the swirling pattern he was making with the straw in his milkshake.

"Hard to say," he shrugged. "I mean, I can't say that I didn't ever want to be a daddy, but right at that particular moment, I wasn't too thrilled at the prospect. 'Course, I couldn't tell that to Sherry."

I should think not, Bonnie thought, not a little angrily. He actually seemed relieved that Sherry had lost the baby!

"Well, anyways, we was already married, ya know?"

Bonnie didn't want to think about what that statement implied.

"And, I figured it couldn't hurt, bein' married to Miss Louisiana, and all. I was offered contracts from Tampa Bay and the Saints in the draft that fall. I took the job with the Saints since New Orleans is closer to where our families are. Maybe you heard of me while you was there." There was a hopeful look in his eyes.

"Oh! Well…I'm not much of a sports fan," Bonnie admitted. "Sorry."

Preston shrugged, not hiding his annoyance well.

"No big deal. I was only on the roster for two seasons. About the middle of my second year, in a game against the Buccaneers, interestingly enough, I dislocated my shoulder. Put me out for the rest of the season."

"Oh, dear! That must've hurt!"

"No, what *really* hurt was that when my two-year contract was up, the Saints didn't renew me. So that was the end of my illustrious football career." He stared with disgust into his milkshake, dunking his straw up and down even more vigorously now.

Again, Bonnie was at a loss.

"Well, of course, Jesse Niles, being the owner of one of the state's most popular fishin' and campin' sites, he's got connections all over. He got me on as a coffee sales rep for Downtown Coffee Services, there in New Orleans. Great ending, huh? From quarterbacking to pushing cream and sugar on offices to boost my commissions." His laugh was again filled with derision.

Then, a thought, a shocking thought, hit Bonnie.

"Wait a minute. Do you mean that you were *married* when you were working for DCS? When *I* knew you back then? When you asked me *out*?"

Preston gave Bonnie a sheepish little smirk. "Oops!"

"Oops? Is that all you can say? *Oops*? Is *that* why you never wore your wedding ring, so you could see other women?"

"Never had a wedding ring," he answered defensively. "Had to borrow money from my old man to buy Sherry's wedding band, as it was. 'Course, I bought her a big ol' hairy diamond when I signed on with the Saints. I don't suppose she was wearing it last night, huh?"

"You didn't answer my question," Bonnie said coldly.

"Aw, now, don't go gettin' all judgmental on me," he said, annoyance in his voice. "Sherry knew she wasn't my first when we was datin'. I hope she didn't think she'd be my last! Even *she* ain't that dumb."

"What, you mean, just because you got married?" Bonnie said it with as much sarcasm as she could muster.

Preston looked coolly unconcerned.

"She's takin' me back, ain't she?" he countered, looking Bonnie defiantly in the eye.

"She knows? Sherry knows that you…"

Preston shrugged again. "It's why she left me in Atlanta. Guess I got a little careless." He seemed boyishly amused by his own antics. "But hey, that's all over with. I really want to see if we can work this thing out this time. I'm through with all that cheatin' stuff. I called her last night, after seein' her at that Singles party. She just kinda broke down and said how much she missed me."

Remembering the way that Sherry had looked at Jeff Wells last night, Bonnie wondered how much of this part of the story was really true.

The waitress had returned and was placing their orders on the table. Bonnie looked at her salad, but felt no appetite for it. She felt a little nauseous, actually.

"Excuse me, miss," Bonnie spoke to the server. "I'm sorry to be such a pain, but would you mind wrapping this to go for me?"

"Aw, fer cryin' out loud," Preston said with disgust. He turned away from Bonnie and slung his arm insolently over the back of his side of the booth. The waitress glanced curiously at Preston, then back at Bonnie.

"Sure," she said. "No problem."

She picked up the salad again, turned to go, and nearly bumped right into Jeff Wells.

"Oh, excuse me, sir!" she said, trying to keep Bonnie's salad from spilling.

"Pardon me," said Jeff absentmindedly. He looked at Bonnie, then at Preston, then back at Bonnie again, coldness in his eyes. Ruth Newton stood behind him.

"Oh, hello, dear!" Ruth was the first to greet Bonnie. Preston looked up again and saw Jeff.

"Well, hey there, Dr. Wells!"

Preston thrust out his right hand to shake Jeff's. Hiding his reluctance, Jeff shook Preston's hand.

"Have we met?" Jeff looked a little confused that Preston knew his name.

"Well, it's been a while, but yeah, we met about five or six months ago, right before Christmas, when your church's bus broke down outside Duck Inn, up in Westdale. Guess I was dressed a little different that night, too."

Jeff rolled his eyes at the recollection. "Ah, yes," he said. "A night that will live in infamy."

"I couldn't make that trip," said Ruth, the sadness in her eyes momentarily erased, "but I heard the story. Oh, boy, did I hear the story!"

Jeff turned to her. "I don't think some of us will *ever* hear the end of it." Then, turning to Preston again, he said, "This is Ruth Newton. Forgive me, but I don't recall your name."

"Oh, that's all right," he drawled. "Ain't too many people as good with names as me! It's Preston Hardy. Pleased to meet you, there, Ruth."

"Preston," Jeff murmured, a note of recollection in his voice, as if something in the name jogged his memory. He looked at Bonnie again. Was that vindication she saw in his eyes?

"I s'pose you know my sweetie, here, Bonnie Martin. I mean Callaway. Man! Good as I am with names, I can't seem to make that Callaway stick!"

At the word "sweetie," Bonnie closed her eyes and shook her head slowly. So much for strictly business! One minute he's talking about reconciling with Sherry, and the next he's calling her his sweetie! This man was definitely trouble.

Ruth gave Bonnie a questioning look, but Jeff said, "Yes, Bonnie's a long-time member of my church. But it's just lately that I've really been getting to know her."

Jeff looked at her enigmatically, anger barely concealed in his eyes. Only Bonnie knew how much sarcasm was in his remark.

"Here you go, miss." The waitress had brought Bonnie's salad back to her, packed in a white paper bag. "Your check is on top, there."

Preston reached for the sales ticket on the bag. "Here, babe, let me get that."

"I've got it," Bonnie replied tersely, pulling the bag away from his reach while avoiding Jeff's eyes. Turning to Ruth, Bonnie squeezed her hand with her free one and said, "I'll call you soon."

"Thank you, dear," Ruth answered.

Without another word of farewell, Bonnie turned toward the cashier and got in line to pay her check.

CHAPTER 11

When Bonnie got home, she set the bag containing her chef's salad on the counter with disgust. Maybe she would nibble on it while she worked at her computer. At that moment, however, she couldn't decide who had made her angrier: Preston Hardy for being such an incredible jerk, or Jeff Wells for running Preston such a close second. All she wanted right now was to get out of her pantyhose and heels and into some shorts and a tee shirt and just try to *relax*.

Feeling much better after changing, Bonnie went to her office and pushed the button on her computer to begin booting it up. Then she looked over to her right and saw the red light blinking on her answering machine; there were two messages waiting for her. The first was from Betty and Claire confirming their order for the new menus and approving the mockup she had put together for them the previous Friday night after she had left Jeff's house. She had dropped it off at Grabbabite before going to Art's funeral service that morning.

The second message was most surprising. It was from Doctor Father from the Benevolent Council. To the best of her recollection, Father Blake had never called her at home. Indeed, their only contact had been at Council meetings and functions and the monthly after-meeting dinners. Father Blake's voice sounded grave, and the message urged her to call him as soon as she could. Jotting down the number, Bonnie picked up the phone at her desk and dialed St. Alban's. When his secretary put her through, Bonnie couldn't help but begin with, "Hi, Doctor Father. It was a surprise to hear from you! What's up?"

Bonnie heard Father Blake sigh deeply. "Something pretty terrible has happened, Bonnie, and I wondered if we could ask for your help."

"What is it? What's happened?"

"It's Loaves and Fishes. Someone broke in early this morning and vandalized it. The place is a real wreck."

Loaves and Fishes, housed in a building donated by a company owned by Art Newton, was the Benevolent Council's central location for distributing food, clothing, and, in some cases, money, to needy families in Chandler City and surrounding communities. It was also the site of an after-school program for latchkey kids in the immediate neighborhood.

"Oh, no," Bonnie moaned. "Who on earth would do such a thing?"

"Well, unfortunately, we know exactly who did it, and it's got Carolyn Perkins so upset, she's resigned her position on the Board."

Bonnie had to sit down. "Resigned? But why? I mean, I know this is a terrible thing, but—"

"It was JaMa'al Johnson," Father Blake told her gently. As if he were having trouble believing it himself, he repeated incredulously, "JaMa'al Johnson."

It was just too much to take in.

"Oh, Doctor Father, there's got to be some mistake! He's the sweetest—and Loaves and Fishes has done so much for his family! Are you sure it was him?"

Father Blake, normally so jocular, gave another weary sigh.

"Carolyn stopped by the place on her way to work this morning to drop off some canned goods donated by Franklin Unitarian. When she got there, she let herself in and was greeted by quite a sight. Food and clothes everywhere, all the after-school supplies scattered all around. Then she saw that the back door, you know, the service entrance, had been jimmied open. When she went into the office to call the police, there was JaMa'al, spray-painting—um, well, *words*, all over the walls. Naturally, when he saw her, JaMa'al took off like a shot. Practically knocked her over as he ran past her. I think she was in too much shock to try to stop him anyway."

Bonnie was speechless. What could have possessed twelve-year-old JaMa'al Johnson to do something like this? He had been one of the first to enroll in the after-school program when he was just eight. JaMa'al's mother had received any number of bags of groceries from the Loaves and Fishes food pantry, and JaMa'al and his younger brother and sister had received school shoes and clothes from its clothing ministry every year they had been in school. Carolyn Perkins herself had provided *pro bono* legal services to JaMa'al's mother on several occasions. No wonder she was devastated.

"Carolyn called the police and just left. Although I'm sure she probably felt like going home, she went on in to work. She called me from her office to give me the bad news, and then she said, 'You know, Doctor Father, if this is the thanks we get for everything we've done, for everything we've given, well, it's just not worth it. It's just not worth it. You'll be getting my written resignation in the next day or so."' Father Blake sighed again. "So...I was calling to see if you could spare any time to help clean the place up and get it back in order. I guess I'd also like to know if you'd be willing, at least temporarily, to hop back on board and fill in until we can find a replacement for Carolyn." Father Blake was slated to succeed Jeff Wells as Benevolent Council president.

"Oh, Doctor Father, you know I will," answered Bonnie. "But don't you think there's anything we can do to persuade Carolyn to stay on?"

"I'd certainly like to think so, but I can tell you, it won't be right away. After all she's done for JaMa'al and his family, to find him there, trashing the place like that, it was a real blow. Carolyn needs some time to recover."

"I guess you're right," Bonnie murmured, fighting tears herself. "Maybe I'll call her later tonight, when she's home from work."

Father Blake chuckled derisively. "I'd tell you to come by and pick up the keys to Loaves and Fishes, but there wasn't much point in locking the place up. From the way Carolyn described it, anybody else that wanted to break in wouldn't have much to steal. We'll have to have locksmiths change the locks, though, and I guess we'll have to have the back door replaced, too. Just let yourself in. Thanks for anything you can do to help."

"Since my name is still on the Council's checking account as an authorized agent, I'll take care of those arrangements and get the payments made."

"You're a gem."

Bonnie sat for a moment with her hand still resting on the receiver. She closed her eyes and began to pray: "Oh, dear Lord, be with Carolyn. I know that she isn't Your child, but just now she needs the comfort and healing that only You can give. Help me to reach out to her in Your name. Give me the right words to say." Then, knowing in her heart that something must be terribly, terribly wrong in JaMa'al's young life to bring him to do something so horrendous, she continued, "And Lord, I don't know why JaMa'al would do a thing like this, but forgive him. He's a young boy who needs guidance. Help us on the Council to reach out to him, too, to show him the love and forgiveness that You showed each of us."

Thinking quickly about what she would need to do in order to spend the afternoon working at Loaves and Fishes, Bonnie clicked her mouse through the shutdown procedure on her computer. She picked up the phone again to call Cheryl Summers to ask her to pick up Ben and Josh from school so they wouldn't come home to a locked house.

"Sure, I'll be glad to," said Cheryl, her voice full of concern for Bonnie. "Can you call the school secretary and let them know I've got your okay to pick them up?"

"Oh, yeah! Thanks for the reminder." Bonnie jotted a note to herself. "Okay if I pick them up around five? You won't be eating before then, right?"

"Bonnie, you aren't going to have time to cook today. Don't even worry about it. Just plan to have dinner with us, you and the boys."

"Oh, Cheryl, this is such short notice! Are you sure?" Bonnie breathed another prayer, one of thanks for the blessing of such a friendship.

"I won't even make you wash the dishes," she laughed.

"Thanks again for taking care of the boys. You're the best."

Bonnie hung up and dialed Ben and Josh's elementary school to make the arrangements for Cheryl.

Jeff loosened his tie roughly, slid the back tail out of the knot with a couple of quick jerks, and tossed it onto the bed. The sooner he got out of his suit, the better he'd like it. He was still agitated from having seen Bonnie Callaway at the Coffee Shoppe with that Preston Hardy character. All through lunch, he kept wondering what she *saw* in somebody like him. Having known Bill Callaway fairly well before he died, he couldn't help but marvel at what polar opposites Bill and Preston were. Even though he had taken himself out of the picture, Jeff still found himself more than a little angry at the way things had turned out. Why had Bonnie been so receptive to him last week? He was afraid that he hadn't been very good company for Ruth Newton.

Since Sundays were usually marathon days, with activities and meetings at church from eight-thirty in the morning until seven at night, three sermons to preach, and even after-church gatherings like the one at Jenny Pierce's house last night, Monday was Jeff's much-needed day off. Except when even that was superseded by obligations like the funeral he had conducted today or some other emergency affecting a member or family in his congregation. Today, he was looking forward to relaxing and finally sitting down to read the book a fellow pastor had lent him. When Jeff Junior got home from school, maybe the two of them could head over to the church gym and shoot some hoops together. Just as he'd finished tucking his t-shirt into his jeans, the phone rang.

Jeff closed his eyes and sighed. Now what? Maybe he wouldn't even answer it. It was his day off, for crying out loud! Didn't he *get* a day off?

"Jeff Wells," he said tersely into the phone.

"Hi, Dr. Wells, it's Sandra," said his secretary, apology in her voice. "So sorry to disturb you on your day off like this, but something's happened that I thought you'd want to know about."

Wanna bet? Jeff thought with a rueful smile. "What's up, San?"

"Father Blake from St. Alban's called while you were conducting the Newton funeral. There's been a bit of an incident over at Loaves and Fishes."

"Man, I can't believe it!" exclaimed Jeff when Sandra had told him of the morning's events. "Do they have any idea who did it?"

"Father Blake didn't say. He just asked that I pass the news on to you and ask that, if you could spare the time, you drop by the place and do what you can to start getting it cleaned up. I've already called Judy McKenzie, the director of the after-school program, to let her know not to show up today. I think it's going to have to be suspended indefinitely. Such a shame, so close to the end of the school year."

"Yeah, I guess some people just have no thought about the consequences of their actions," Jeff agreed. "Guess I'll head on over there. I've still got the keys to the place."

"One other thing, I just remembered," Sandra began again. "Jack Summers called to confirm your racquetball date for Wednesday morning. Guess he forgot that this is your day off."

"Not surprising, since he saw me at the funeral this morning. He probably thought I was working today. I'll give him a buzz at work before I head over to Loaves and Fishes."

"Yo, buddy!" was Jack's greeting when Jeff got through to him at his office. "What's shakin', dude?"

"Sandra said you called. Don't you know better than to bug me on my day off?" Jeff kidded his best friend.

"You're one of the few guys I know who has to work fairly regularly on his day off."

"Yeah, well, comes with the territory. Maybe I should've taken that window washing job Art Newton offered me years ago."

"Poor old Art," sighed Jack. "He was one of the good guys."

"That he was," Jeff agreed. "So, we're still on for wall ball on Wednesday morning?"

"Yeah, I was just calling to make sure. Bonnie won't be keeping you out late Tuesday night, will she?" Jack teased. "Seven o'clock comes awfully early."

Jeff sighed a small sigh and rubbed his eyes with frustration as he realized that he hadn't had the opportunity to tell Jack about breaking things off with her.

"Uh, no, I don't think so," he said, avoiding saying anything to Jack for now. Wednesday would be soon enough.

"So, what're you doing with what's left of your big day off?"

Jeff told Jack about Loaves and Fishes.

"Man, that's really tough. No rest for the wicked, eh?"

Jeff chuckled in response.

"So, you're probably gonna be pretty beat after all that manual labor…"

"Listen here, pal, I think I can hold my own in that department!" Jeff thought Jack was bantering with him again.

"No, seriously. I mean, it's not like you're going to want to come home and cook for yourself and Jeff Junior, right?"

"Oh, well, it won't kill us to eat burgers again. Maybe we'll order a pizza."

"Nothing doing, man," countered Jack. "You guys come over to our house this evening."

"Have you talked to Cheryl about this? I wouldn't want to spring any unpleasant surprises on her."

"Well, even if it's a surprise, it'll hardly be unpleasant. Especially for Amanda. She'll probably do back-flips when she finds out that Jeff Junior is coming over."

"Oh, yeah. Jeff Junior won't exactly be disappointed, either," Jeff said with a laugh. "Well, I really appreciate the offer. Cheryl's home cooking sounds great to me. What time do you want us there?"

"Five or five-thirty should do it. I'll give Cheryl a call right now. See you tonight!"

"Looking forward to it." Jeff smiled. What would he do without a friend like Jack? He headed downstairs, dashed off a brief note informing his son of his whereabouts and of their plans for dinner, and left for Loaves and Fishes.

CHAPTER 12

The sight that greeted Bonnie when she walked into Loaves and Fishes was enough to make anyone cry. JaMa'al Johnson had wreaked absolute havoc. Every shelf in the place had been overturned. Literally hundreds of dollars' worth of donated food lay mingled with perhaps thousands of dollars' worth of donated clothing. Broken glass from jars and bottles was everywhere. The soft drink that hadn't been shaken and sprayed onto the walls lay on the floor in puddles that harbored globs of ketchup and mustard. Flour and macaroni and rice carpeted the floor, creating a woefully inedible casserole.

Notebook and construction paper lay strewn and trampled throughout the after-school area. Crayons and chalk had been tossed over them and stomped into shards and powder. Long, thick rivulets of paint streamed down from their points of impact on the wall onto the floor. School glue had mingled with the papers and dripped from tables and chairs, hardening into a mess Bonnie wasn't sure how to clean. Precious little could be salvaged from the mess; most would have to be discarded.

"Where to start, where to start?" Bonnie asked herself aloud. Ironically, one of the few things that had escaped destruction was a large box of trash can liners. Bonnie stepped gingerly over and around the mess and took out two to start with: one receptacle for clothes that might be launderable, one for everything else. The first priority had to be getting the food mess cleaned up; if left out much longer, it would start to smell even worse than it already did. Looking at all the broken glass intermingled with everything, Bonnie found herself wishing she had thought to bring some type of work gloves. She really hadn't known exactly what to expect.

Item by item, Bonnie picked up clothes from the floor, inspecting them for stains that might come out with washing. She shook each salvageable piece gently but thoroughly to rid it of as much broken glass as possible, then stuffed it into one of the bags. She soon reached a point where there was little she could do until some of the overturned shelves could be moved out of the way. Eyeing them dubiously, Bonnie squatted down and grabbed the side of one set of very wide metal shelves. Had they not been quite so wide, she might have been able to lift them. As it was, when she lifted up on her side, the other end drooped down heavily so that she just couldn't manage to lift them on her own. Tears of frustration filled her eyes. Too bad this was a Monday. Who could she call for help that wouldn't be at work? Giving one more tug on the shelves, Bonnie was startled to hear a key turning in the front door. She turned to see Jeff Wells walk in.

A look of concerned reproach crossed his face. "Bonnie, don't try to lift those shelves! You could hurt yourself."

Bonnie said nothing, but wiped the tears away from her eyes with the backs of her wrists. Jeff walked over and around the mess.

"Here," he said gently, tactfully not remarking on her crying. "Let's see if we can do this together."

He squatted down on the other side of the shelves and grabbed the vertical bars. Bonnie followed suit and slowly, each looking blankly into the other's eyes, they lifted the shelf. She couldn't help noticing, to her own annoyance, that Jeff was quite a nice sight in his t-shirt and jeans. She rarely saw him when he wasn't wearing a suit and tie. She saw how the muscles in his arms flexed when he lifted up on the shelves and remembered that she had been held by those strong arms, however fleetingly, just the other night.

They went around the room, silently squatting and lifting until all of the shelves had been set to rights. The shelves themselves needed to be scrubbed down, but that would have to come later. At length, Jeff broke the silence that hung between them.

"How did you find out?"

"Doctor Father called."

Another long silence passed in which Bonnie resumed picking up and inspecting clothes. Jeff watched her a few moments, puzzled.

"What're you doing?"

"I think at least some of these things can be saved. I can take then to a commercial laundry and let them have a go at them."

"It'd nice to be able to salvage something from all of this."

Bonnie thought she detected a trace of irony in his remark, as if there were a double meaning in it. She fought the urge to shoot an angry look at him. He could be here, and he could help, she fumed to herself, but he *didn't* have to make small talk. Jeff stood watching Bonnie for a moment as she looked intently at her work. When he received no response from her, he frowned and turned away to find something else to do.

Bonnie tried to work without being so painfully aware of Jeff's presence, but the effort was futile. Only two weeks ago, before he had asked her to have dinner with him, before a strange twist of fate had provided an opportunity for Clara to fabricate an outrageous story about her, before Sherry Niles had walked smoothly into Jeff's life, they might have chatted pleasantly. Or, at least as pleasantly as circumstances like these would have allowed. The waste, the incredible waste all around them, was so disheartening. But now, Bonnie couldn't even be in the same room with Jeff and not want to vent feelings of tremendous anger. Yet she held back, both from the sense that, on some level, he was still the pastor of her church and some semblance of that relationship had to be maintained, if only for her children, but also from the persuasion that recriminations would be useless anyway.

Some time later, Jeff came back into the food storage room carrying the soggy remains of a collage of photographs of children and workers from the after-school program. Most of the pictures, happy faces of children in a safe place with workers who truly cared about them, had been splattered with glue and paint, rendering the figures in them virtually unrecognizable. He held the poster up, as if for Bonnie's inspection, and looked at it sadly.

"Who would do such a thing? Who could have such meanness in their heart?"

Bonnie's eyes flew to Jeff's in surprise.

"You mean, you don't know? Father Blake didn't tell you?"

"I didn't talk with him, Sandra did. She called me at home to tell me. Are you saying you *know* who did this?"

Bonnie nodded with a sigh.

"I'm not sure if you know him or not, but he's a boy from a family that has been helped quite a bit by Loaves and Fishes."

Bonnie then told him all that Father Blake had told her: how Carolyn Perkins had caught JaMa'al Johnson red-handed, spray-painting the walls in the office; how Carolyn had been so upset about it all that she had resigned her position on the Benevolent Council. Shock registered on Jeff's face.

"You can't be serious." The hand holding the poster dropped to his side. "JaMa'al Johnson did this?"

"So, you do know him."

"I've known him and his family a long time. He played on the children's basketball team at Foster Road for three years. It was only after he entered middle school and got too old for that team that he dropped out of the church's rec program altogether. I never could persuade him to come to church."

"It's hard for some black children to come to a mostly white church, especially if their parents don't attend either. You can't really blame him for that."

"I know," he said with a frown.

Squatting down near a hash of cans and bottles, Jeff grabbed a new trash bag and started to fill it with debris from the floor.

"But he's always been such a *good* kid—as nice and polite as they come. His mother always talked about how proud she was of his good grades in school, and gave plenty of credit to the help he got here in the after-school program. She always expressed gratitude that it helped to keep him from hanging out with the wrong kids. What could've made him do something like this?"

"I wish I knew." Bonnie sighed. "He did such a thorough job of destroying everything. It's almost hard to believe he did it all by himself."

"How do we know he did?" Jeff looked as if he were trying to piece something together in his mind.

"Well, Carolyn didn't *see* anybody else. Do you think he might have had help?"

"I can't say for sure, obviously, but you're right—this is an awful lot of work for one twelve-year-old boy."

Bonnie suddenly remembered how much trouble she, a grown woman, had had trying to lift the fallen, empty shelves. How could a slender young boy, not quite as tall as she was yet, have overturned those heavy metal shelves by himself when they had been laden with cans of food, sacks and sacks of rice and flour, and heavy bottles of juice and soft drink? He *must* have had help! His accomplices had simply managed to escape without Carolyn seeing them. Considering how shocked she must have been just walking in and finding the place as it was, that might not have been too difficult for them to do. But who would want to do something like this? And why? And why would JaMa'al want to help them? None of it made any sense.

Jeff's eyebrows knitted together as he continued throwing trash into the bag. Bonnie was just about to caution him about the broken glass when Jeff drew his hand back swiftly and hissed, "Oh, man!" A bright, red stream of blood was already dripping from his hand into the mess on the floor.

"Oh, Dr. Wells!" Bonnie picked her way back to the other side of the room and grabbed Jeff by the wrist. She could see the wedge of glass still sticking out of the wound. "Oh, dear!"

"It's nothing. I'll just put a bandage on it when I get home."

Bonnie gave him a look she might have given Joshua, her seven-year-old, for making such a remark.

"I don't think so." She turned and walked toward the office, pulling Jeff by the wrist as she went. "Come with me."

Jeff gave a little smile as he followed her dutifully to the back of the building.

There was a bathroom down the hall that, miraculously, hadn't been touched at all by the vandalism. Bonnie flipped on the light and held Jeff's hand under the faucet. With her slim, graceful fingers, she carefully dislodged the glass from his skin and glanced up at him ruefully as he winced a little. Rinsing the paint and glue and soda from his hand, she allowed the wound to bleed a little more into the sink. Still holding his hand with one of hers, she yanked three paper towels out of the dispenser on the wall. She patted his hand dry and then applied the towels to the wound and held them there.

Bonnie worked methodically, as if their closeness didn't really register with her at all. But Jeff watched her and was intensely aware of her nearness: the blue eyes intent on his hand, the soft hands that held his. Even though she wore shorts and a t-shirt, her hair and make-up were still nearly as perfect as they had been that morning at Art's funeral—she looked beautiful. And now that he stood next to her, that scent, that wonderful, enticing scent she wore, drifted up to him and he was taken back to last Friday night. Last Friday night when he had leaned over and kissed her for the first time.

For the last time, he reminded himself with a mental kick.

Leading him by the wrist again, Bonnie led him further down the hall towards the office.

"If JaMa'al didn't find it and trash it too," Bonnie informed him, but not turning to look back at him, "there's a first aid kit in here."

As they walked through the door, they both gasped at the obscenities JaMa'al had spray-painted on the walls.

"I…didn't know JaMa'al *knew* words like that," Jeff murmured. "But I guess most twelve-year-olds do, whether they say them or not."

Bonnie stared at the walls for another long moment and shook her head in disgust. Then she turned silently to the metal cabinet that housed the first aid supplies. As if his main intention had been to get the walls adequately spray-painted, JaMa'al had missed destroying its contents also. *Who knows* what *he might have done if Carolyn hadn't caught him when she had?* Bonnie thought. As it was, an expensive desktop computer, a printer, a telephone, and a fax machine sat unmolested on the desk. Bonnie opened the metal doors and pulled out a white box with a red cross on it. Not once did she release Jeff's hand or the pressure she held to his wound.

"I think I can take care of it from here," Jeff mumbled, beginning to feel a little embarrassed at the fuss Bonnie was making over him. Bonnie ignored his comment as she selected a bandage from the box.

Looking at him sternly, she said, "Hold this for a second," and she pressed the fingers from his other hand on top of the paper towels. She unwrapped the bandage and applied an anti-bacterial ointment to it, then nudged Jeff's other hand away. He pulled the paper towels aside, and Bonnie applied the bandage firmly, smoothing out the tapes on either side. All Jeff could think was, "Her hands are so soft. Her touch is so gentle."

"When was the last time you had a tetanus booster?" she asked, still not looking at him.

A sheepish look crossed his face. "That's a good question."

"Not funny," she said as sternly as she could, but Jeff could see a smile playing around the corners of her mouth.

"I know," he said more seriously. "I'll get it checked out."

Bonnie made no reply, but began disposing of the bandage wrappers and returning the contents of the first aid kit to the box. Jeff watched her again and hesitated. He wanted to take hold of her hands, to hold her in his arms, to kiss her again. He wanted her not to be involved with somebody else!

"Thanks," he told her.

"No problem."

She returned the box to the cabinet, closed the doors, and, without a parting glance or word to Jeff, walked down the hall to resume her work. Jeff watched her for a second, sighed, then flipped the light switch and followed her.

"She called the police. He ran out when he saw her."

"Do you suppose he's been arrested?"

"I…I don't know; Father Blake didn't say. I guess we could find out. Why do you ask?"

Jeff didn't answer her question, but turned back toward the office.

"I'll be back in a minute," he called over his shoulder.

Bonnie watched him go with a little frown, then turned with resignation back to the depressing task of reclaiming Loaves and Fishes. She was just about to begin looking for a broom and dustpan to sweep up some of the glass when Jeff came back, an eager look on his face.

"JaMa'al's been taken into custody. He's at juvenile detention."

Bonnie just looked at him, not knowing what to say. It was unthinkable that JaMa'al could do something like this with impunity, of course, but it still pained her somehow to think of the little boy she had once known, under arrest for vandalism. Breaking and entering, too, she imagined.

Jeff looked at her intently. "I want to go see him. I want to *talk* to him. I want to know why he *did* this!"

"Do you think they'd let you see him?"

"I don't know. I'd like to try, though. Will you come with me?"

Bonnie's eyes widened. "Come with you? Why do you want *me* along?"

Another remark, one about the propriety of their being seen together, was on the tip of her tongue, but she bit it back.

"He knows you. I'm sure he respects you. Maybe between the two of us, we can find out what in the world is going on with him."

Bonnie looked down, thinking hard. What could *she* possibly do or say that would help in this situation? After all, Jeff was the minister here. Frankly, the less time she had to spend in Jeff's company, the better off she knew she would be. Why couldn't he just go by himself?

Jeff saw her hesitate. "I'd really like you to come with me," he told her. "I could use the moral support."

Bonnie looked in his eyes and saw silent pleading there. Then she remembered the prayer she had prayed when she'd first found out about JaMa'al being involved in the break-in: a prayer about reaching out to him in love and forgiveness. She could feel God urging her to make good on that prayer.

"Okay," she sighed. "Let's go."

Jeff and Bonnie sat at a conference table that seated eight in a room with no windows and a door at either end. The only thing that broke the grayness of the room was matching rows of baseball-style caps mounted high on both of the long walls. Some of the caps bore the logos of popular sports teams from around the country, most the logos of local gangs.

Sergeant Ingram, the police officer who had shown them in, stood with his muscular arms folded across his massive chest and watched with a piercing glare for the door leading from the holding cell to open. The crisp midnight blue of his uniform accentuated his already imposing figure. Bonnie could well imagine young offenders thinking twice about crossing him. Jeff asked about the hats on the wall.

"It's a kind of intimidation factor," Sergeant Ingram replied, shifting his stance. "It's our way of showing the kids who come in here the victories we've had in combating gang activity here in town. They see one or two of their gang's hats and it gives them a little pause. We also try to put the hats of rival gangs next to each other when we can, just to tork 'em off."

"Gang activity? In Chandler City?" Bonnie was shocked.

Sergeant Ingram gave Bonnie an indulgent little smile.

"Gangs of one sort or another have made inroads into all but the most rural or remote areas. They're everywhere. We know they've been in Chandler City for at least seven years. That's how long ago we made the first arrest known to be gang-related."

Bonnie shook her head slowly in amazement; Jeff watched the police officer intently. Sergeant Ingram could tell that he was giving two people who ought to have known better a real education.

"It has to do with supply and demand in the drug trade," he explained. "Guys from L.A. and other places out west can fly here for a song and make a killing selling drugs here. What's plentiful out there is relatively rare here, so the asking price is much higher. Mostly crack cocaine, but we see a fair amount of marijuana, heroin, and speed, the whole gamut."

"Anyway, while those guys are here, they recruit for their gangs to help them peddle their dope. For most of the kids in the poorer neighborhoods, the money they get for dealing, or even just delivering for their bosses, is too good to pass up. It's certainly more than they could get flipping burgers anywhere.

"But when the bigger boys from around here start recruiting for members in their turf, it's the younger ones like your little friend JaMa'al who aren't really given much choice about whether they want to join. It's usually, 'Join, or pay the consequences.' The break-in at Loaves and Fishes was probably an initiation rite for JaMa'al's gang. The ones that get caught get an early start on their rap sheets."

He watched Bonnie and Jeff to see their reaction. They looked pretty blown away, all right.

"We got your guy on breaking and entering and destruction of property worth over a thousand dollars. Both are felony offenses."

Bonnie felt the bottom drop out of her stomach at the word "felony."

"I just can't *believe* it," she whispered. "I can't believe JaMa'al would join a gang. He *must* have been pressured into it!"

"And you're sure that JaMa'al acted alone?" asked Jeff.

Ingram looked at him with a raised eyebrow. "The person who reported the break-in only saw JaMa'al. Do you have reason to believe that others might've been involved?"

Just then, the door on the other side of the room opened and a uniformed police officer escorted young JaMa'al Johnson into the room. His head hung low, his chin nearly touching his chest, so they could see only the top of his head. They saw him peek up briefly to see who his visitors were and start with surprise; perhaps he had been expecting his mother. The police escort led JaMa'al to a chair and motioned for him to sit down. JaMa'al's lanky body, with its wiry, pre-adolescent limbs, slumped into the chair. He never looked up.

"Hello, JaMa'al," Jeff said, his voice almost a caress.

JaMa'al made no response.

Bonnie tried next: "Have you spoken with your mother yet?"

JaMa'al said nothing. He continued to stare bleakly at his sneakers, which seemed almost as if they had to be too big for a boy his age. His feet were growing faster than the rest of him.

Jeff turned to Sergeant Ingram. "Would it be possible for us to speak with JaMa'al alone?"

The sergeant seemed to mull it over a moment, then said to the escort: "Check him out again."

The officer tugged gently on JaMa'al's right arm and JaMa'al arose from his seat. The officer patted JaMa'al along the length of his body, then performed the same procedure on the inside of his legs. Bonnie closed her eyes in shame for JaMa'al.

"Checks out okay," said the escort.

"I'll give you fifteen minutes," Sergeant Ingram told them gruffly, throwing a stern glance at JaMa'al.

When the two officers had gone and the door closed behind them, Bonnie and Jeff stood together, as if on cue, and walked to the end of the table, sitting in chairs opposite each other, adjacent to JaMa'al. At first, neither spoke; it was difficult to know what to say. Jeff began first, trying to break the tension with a little bit of humor:

"You did quite a morning's work today."

JaMa'al's hands fidgeted in his lap and he bounced his legs nervously.

"Do you think you could give us some idea why? Did someone at Loaves and Fishes do or say something to make you angry?"

Still, JaMa'al made no response.

Then Bonnie saw a large tear roll a path down one of his cheeks. Putting a gentle hand on his shoulder, she said softly, "Oh, JaMa'al, please talk to us."

JaMa'al's head snapped up, his eyes flooded with tears, his young face a contorted mask of anger and pain.

"What did y'all come here for?" he cried. "Just go on home and leave me alone!"

CHAPTER 13

Bonnie and Jeff exchanged looks again.

"We came because we love you, JaMa'al," Jeff told him quietly. "We came because we know that you've always been a good boy, and that you wouldn't do something like you did today unless—Well, we just don't *know* why you'd do something like this. Can you help us understand?"

JaMa'al grimaced, tears flowing again, then hung his head. Bonnie looked at Jeff, once again grateful that making people feel comfortable in awkward situations always seemed to be his first aim. JaMa'al was obviously filled with remorse; it would do no good to make him feel any guiltier than he already felt. The anger she had been feeling toward Jeff was replaced for the moment with the warm admiration she was used to feeling for him.

"Did someone tell you to do this?" Bonnie's voice was soothing, as if she were speaking to one of her own sons. Jeff was so glad she had agreed to come with him. His heart warmed to her in spite of himself. *This* was the Bonnie he had asked to dinner last week, the Bonnie he had thought he knew. "Did someone *make* you do this?"

JaMa'al's head rose again slowly, and he looked incredulously through his tears at Bonnie, as if he were amazed that she knew he hadn't acted on his own.

"JaMa'al," she began again patiently, "I went to Loaves and Fishes today to help clean it up. But when I tried to put the shelves back upright again, I couldn't do it."

The hapless boy's tear-filled eyes were locked with Bonnie's; his lower lip trembled.

"Pastor Jeff had to *help* me lift them." She looked briefly at Jeff; there was silent encouragement in the look he gave back to her. "Are you telling me you were able to overturn those big, heavy shelves full of supplies all by yourself?"

JaMa'al looked almost relieved that Bonnie had revealed what he had wanted to tell them but couldn't bring himself to.

"My posse was with me," he managed to choke out. "I'm a member of the K.I.N.G.S. now."

"The Kings," Jeff repeated blankly, no comprehension in his voice.

Bonnie and Jeff exchanged looks of confusion as JaMa'al got up from his chair and walked to one of the groups of baseball caps that hung from the walls. He pointed up to a black cap with gold lettering.

"The K.I.N.G.S.," JaMa'al said again, as if repeating the name would make it more comprehensible. "'Killing Innocent Neighbors Gang-Style.' That's my posse now."

He said the name so matter-of-factly, as if he were completely unaware of its gruesome implications. Then he walked dejectedly back to his chair.

"So you *did* have help." Bonnie sounded almost vindicated.

"The other four broke the lock and busted in the back door. They were in charge of doin' stuff in the front rooms, but they got out before Miss Carolyn saw them. They told me to take care of things in the office."

It suddenly struck Bonnie that this was why things in the back of the building had escaped relatively unscathed, compared to the devastation that had been visited on the front area. She remembered the bathroom and the storage cabinet that were untouched, the expensive office equipment that had been left unharmed. When she thought of it, she realized that JaMa'al himself had done nothing to Loaves and Fishes that a couple of coats of paint on the office walls couldn't fix. It was obvious to Bonnie that his heart hadn't been in the project from the outset, and that he'd done as little damage as possible while still seeming to cooperate with his fellow gang members.

"What will your posse do for you now that you've been arrested?" Jeff asked, trying to keep anger out of his voice.

"Ain't nothin' nobody can do for me now," answered JaMa'al, resignation in his voice. "The boys in my posse'll take care of Mama for me, though, and Shaneetha, too." Shaneetha was JaMa'al's ten-year-old sister. "'Long as I'm in here, I'm a big man to the other guys in the gang. Daryl's only eight. He ain't got nothin' to worry about for a while yet." Daryl was the youngest Johnson sibling.

"Why would your mother and Shaneetha need to be taken care of?" asked Jeff, suspicion in his eyes.

JaMa'al looked at Jeff; his eyes seemed to plead with Jeff not to ask any more questions.

"Ain't got *nothin'* to worry about after you join the posse," he answered evasively.

Bonnie leaned forward. "And if you *don't* join the posse?"

JaMa'al looked down again in despair. After a long silence, he began again: "Shaneetha's only ten years old, but they don't care! Any girl counts for points. It'd kill my Mama if they got to her." He looked at Bonnie, pleading in his eyes. "It would kill Mama."

"'Counts for points'?" Jeff repeated incredulously. "Are you saying that they've threatened to—" He broke off when he saw Bonnie's cautioning look.

JaMa'al bowed his head again and his shoulders began to shake with sobs. Then he looked up, anguished remorse in his eyes, first at Bonnie, then at Jeff.

"I'm so sorry, Miss Bonnie, Pastor Jeff," he whispered. "I'm so sorry. I never knew they were gonna do what they did. They told me we were just gonna spray-paint the walls, to let everybody know Loaves and Fishes is on our turf. I never knew they were gonna do what they did."

"We believe you, JaMa'al," Jeff assured him, his hand on JaMa'al's shoulder, a kind of despair in his own voice. "We believe you, son."

He knew instinctively that JaMa'al would have been powerless to change anything had he known the gang's real plans.

"JaMa'al, you know Miss Carolyn Perkins, don't you?" Bonnie asked.

"Yeah," he answered eyeing Bonnie warily, suspicion in his voice.

"Well, she can help you, JaMa'al. She can help you, if you'll let her."

Even as Bonnie spoke the words, her heart pounded in her chest. She remembered quite well what Father Blake had told her earlier about Carolyn's feelings on this matter. She prayed silently that she wasn't making a promise she couldn't keep. Jeff looked at her as if she'd taken leave of her senses.

"*Help* me?" JaMa'al retorted in disbelief. "That lady called the police on me! She ain't gonna help me!"

"I know that she was the one who reported the break-in, but I think that if we explain things to her, she'll want to help you."

JaMa'al looked at her with doubt in his eyes and shrugged his shoulders in resignation. At that moment, the back door of the room opened and JaMa'al's escort leaned his head into the room.

"Time's up," he said, a kind of gentleness in his eyes as he looked first at Bonnie, then at Jeff.

JaMa'al arose and turned to go. Bonnie and Jeff stood also and stepped to his side.

"Could we have just one more minute?" Jeff asked.

The officer nodded once and closed the door softly.

"We have to go now," Jeff told JaMa'al. "But please know that we want to help you in any way we can."

The look of doubt and despair didn't leave JaMa'al's eyes.

"Could you do one thing for us?" JaMa'al turned questioning eyes on Jeff. "Would you pray with us?"

After a moment's hesitation, JaMa'al nodded curtly, his eyes downcast. Jeff reached for JaMa'al's right hand and held it in his. Bonnie saw Jeff's movement and looked at him, remembering the night at the Coffee Shoppe (had it only been a week ago?) when she had told him about the tradition of holding hands and praying at her house. She reached for JaMa'al's left hand and felt it grasp hers gratefully. She closed her eyes and waited for Jeff to begin his prayer. Then she felt Jeff's warm hand clasp hers in his. Tears filled her eyes. He would never hold her hand again, never have a reason to.

"Dear Lord," Jeff began, "We come to You for help today. Our friend, JaMa'al, needs our help, but most especially, Father, he needs Your help."

They heard the door opening again a few feet away. It was time for JaMa'al to go back to his detention cell.

"Lord, we know that You can forgive JaMa'al for what he did this morning. Help him to know that, too. We pray in Your name, dear Father, amen."

"Time to go back," said the escorting officer. JaMa'al slipped his hands out of Bonnie and Jeff's and turned to go, his shoulders slumped.

"We'll be in touch soon," Jeff told him. JaMa'al nodded his head, but looked at neither Bonnie nor Jeff as he walked out of the room.

Bonnie and Jeff stood motionless, watching JaMa'al as he left. It was only after a moment or two that Bonnie became aware that her hand was still in Jeff's. She glanced surreptitiously at their clasped hands, then pulled hers away.

"I…I really need to get going," she said, not meeting Jeff's eyes. "The boys are going to wonder where I am."

"Oh, yeah," said Jeff, looking at his watch. "I forgot to even ask where they were. School's been out a while."

"Cheryl Summers was kind enough to take care of them for me."

"Ah," was his answer. Jeff watched her as she looked intently through her purse for her keys. This was one of her little quirks, he began to realize: whenever Bonnie felt uncomfortable, she made a production of looking for her keys. He smiled sadly and reached into his pocket for his own car keys. He decided that, when he went home to pick up Jeff Junior, he wouldn't necessarily hurry over to Jack and Cheryl's. That way, with any luck, he wouldn't have to worry about seeing Bonnie a *third* time that day.

Ben and Josh ran to greet their mother as if it had been weeks since they'd seen her, instead of only since that morning.

"Hey, guys, what's the deal?" she laughed, hugging a boy to each side of her. "I thought you'd like a vacation from your ol' mom! 'Specially since you've been with your favorite baby sitter."

Bonnie looked over at Amanda and winked at her. Amanda smiled back shyly.

"My goodness, don't *you* look nice tonight!" Bonnie told her. It seemed that Amanda had taken a few more pains with her hair and make-up than she did when she came over to sit with Ben and Josh.

"Thanks," she murmured, blushing a little.

"So, have you guys done all your homework?" Bonnie asked, pretending to be stern. The boys basked in the attention.

"They have, indeed, and I was on hand to provide tutoring services," affirmed Jack as he entered the room. He went over to Bonnie and gave her a little squeeze around the shoulders and a peck on the cheek. "So how's the reclamation job going?"

"Oh, Jack, you've never seen such a mess in all your life. It was so depressing," she told him. "It's going to take a lot of work to get the place back in shape. Everything either needs cleaning or painting or both. And all the *food* that went to waste! Maybe we can have some kind of food drive at church or at some of the local supermarkets to replenish what was destroyed." Bonnie inhaled deeply, holding her stomach. "Speaking of food, though, something smells *fabulous*! I am starved. I wound up skipping lunch today, so you guys may not get much to eat unless you get to the food first!"

"Oh, yeah, we can look at you and tell you're a *really* big eater," kidded Cheryl as she came into the room wiping her hands on a towel. Then she announced, "Well, I decided that since we're having special guests for dinner tonight, I'd make my famous, super-deluxe seafood casserole: lump crab meat, shrimp, oysters, and eggplant."

"Oh, *boy*, does that sound good," sighed Bonnie. "Now, I know it's been a while since we were here for dinner, but I'd hardly call us special guests!"

"Well, not that you're *not* special," Jack grinned, giving her a gentle chuck on the shoulder, "but it's not every day that we have the pastor over to the house." He leaned back and peered out the living room window and said, "Speaking of the devil, the two Jeffs are pulling up right now."

Bonnie's heart began to pound and she felt her face flushing. Why hadn't Cheryl told her this morning that Jeff would be coming to dinner, too? She could have thought of an excuse to decline. Or maybe she could have just come clean with Cheryl, as she hadn't yet had a chance to do, and told her that Jeff had broken things off with her. Then it struck her that Jack and Cheryl probably thought they were doing her and Jeff a favor by having them over together! As if to confirm this idea, she saw Jack sneak a sly glance at his wife and smile conspiratorially at her. Cheryl winked back and wiggled her eyebrows playfully at him.

The doorbell rang and Amanda called out, "I'll get it!"

Bonnie couldn't help but smile at her eagerness. So, it was Jeff Junior that explained Amanda's good grooming. Well, at least one of the Jeffs would be a welcome sight to someone tonight. While the others all turned toward the door to welcome the Wellses, Bonnie walked over quietly and sat down on the edge of the sofa. She pretended to study the cover of one of Cheryl's home and gardening magazines and concentrated on looking as unflustered as possible for when she would finally have to face Jeff Senior.

Amanda and Jeff Junior greeted each other self-consciously, but clearly had eyes only for each other. It was really rather cute, Bonnie thought. Then Ben and Josh ran to the door calling, "Hey there, Pastor Jeff!"

"Well, hey there, boys!" he said, looking a little puzzled. "I'm surprised to see *you* two here. I'd have thought your mom would've been by to pick you up already."

Then he looked up at Jack and Cheryl, who turned as one to Bonnie. Bonnie arose, mustered a smile, and murmured, "Good evening, Dr. Wells."

"Why, Bonnie, what a treat! I'm getting to see you three times in one day." There wasn't a trace of sarcasm in his voice, and Bonnie could actually see sympathy in his eyes. He knew this was going to be an awkward evening, and it had only just begun.

"Well, Bonnie says she skipped lunch, and I know you guys've been working all afternoon, so let's not delay dinner any longer," said Jack broadly.

He put one arm around Jeff's shoulder and another around Bonnie's. Bonnie saw Jeff make a quizzical face at the words "skipped lunch," but made no comment on them.

They served themselves buffet-style in the kitchen; Jeff Junior, the Summers girls, and the Callaway boys sat together in the breakfast nook, while the four adults went into the quiet of the dining room.

And plenty of quiet there was—so much, that it drew more than one mildly questioning glance from Jack at Jeff and Cheryl at Bonnie. In fact, if they hadn't known better, Jack and Cheryl would have thought that Bonnie and Jeff were actually avoiding speaking to one another.

They tried, in turns, to draw Bonnie and Jeff into conversation by asking them about Loaves and Fishes. Jeff was more vocal than Bonnie, and he filled them in on their visit with JaMa'al Johnson at the detention center, as well.

"Goodness," said Cheryl. "How trapped he must feel! What a choice to have to make. He must've felt like he had no one to turn to, no one who could protect him."

"What was saddest to me," added Bonnie, "was that he seemed to feel that being in the detention center was actually a *good* thing. By being arrested for the gang initiation, he gets credit for being a member without having to actually participate in any more of their activities. He feels that he's protecting his mother and sister by being there."

After that, the conversation lagged again and uncomfortable silence hung heavy in the room. Feeling bad that Jack and Cheryl had unwittingly created an awkward situation, Bonnie felt compelled to help things along. She remarked on how good the casserole was, and Jeff agreed with her. Then Cheryl launched into a story about shopping for a prom dress with Amanda, doing so in rather hushed tones so that neither Amanda nor Jeff Junior, Amanda's intended date, would hear. Jeff and Bonnie listened politely. They looked at Cheryl, they looked at Jack, and they made concerted efforts not to look at each other.

"Hard to believe she's graduating already," sighed Bonnie. "When is the prom?"

"The seniors have two more weeks of school—they finish before all the other classes. The prom is on Saturday, the eighth of May, and graduation is on Sunday, the sixteenth," recited Cheryl. "But there'll be parties and rehearsals and receptions and goodness knows what-all between now and then. Are you ready for all this, Jeff?"

He smiled. "Guys have it lucky, I guess. They just have to rent tuxes, and those all look pretty much the same. But I remember what Terri went through with Becky when *she* was getting ready to graduate."

At the mention of Terri's name, Bonnie's eyes flew involuntarily to Jeff. It seemed he could talk about her calmly now, as though he had dealt with the pain and put it behind him. But the mention of Terri's name had also brought what little conversation there had been to an abrupt halt. There were several moments of awkward silence between the four of them, and they all concentrated on their plates.

"Speaking of Becky," Cheryl finally got inspired to say, "when will she be coming home for the summer?"

"Well, actually, she won't be coming home until the very end of the summer this year," Jeff told her. "She's lined up a summer internship with an architecture firm there in Chicago. She's really excited. Apparently, it's a pretty sought-after internship. They only pick two juniors, and she was one of them. And it's a *paid* internship," he added with a mischievous grin. "That's the best part of all!"

"Oh, Jeff," chided Cheryl. "Aren't you going to miss her?"

He sighed. "Oh, you know I will. It'll be the first time she's been away for the summer since she started college. But it's a great opportunity for her, and she tells me that one day it'll look great on her resume. I may try to surprise her with a visit to Chicago myself. Maybe when Jeff Junior is away on the Youth Mission Tour."

"Oh, that'll be great," agreed Cheryl. Then, with a mischievous look on her face, she said, "Anybody got room for dessert?"

Jeff leaned back and laid his hands on his stomach. "Oh, I think I could manage a bite or two, if you twist my arm. What've you got?"

"Only the best thing *you'll* ever eat," she said, her voice trailing away as she went into the kitchen.

"She's modest, too," Jeff kidded in an aside to Jack.

When Cheryl returned to the dining room, Bonnie's eyes opened wide. Cheryl was bringing in slices of the chocolate mousse pie she'd made on Saturday! Cheryl served generous wedges for everyone, then sat down to enjoy her own. Jeff took a bite, and a look of unvarnished pleasure washed over his face.

"Oh, Cheryl," he fairly groaned. "This *is* the best thing I've ever eaten! It's like eating chocolate air!"

Cheryl just smiled her mischievous little smile again and wiggled her eyebrows at Bonnie. Bonnie tried in vain to catch Cheryl's eye to signal to her not to go on so.

"You really like it?" Cheryl asked coyly.

"Listen, if you ever take a notion to leave this old dog here," he said, nodding his head toward Jack, "I'll marry you in a heartbeat if you promise to make me one of these at least once a week!"

Bonnie was mortified.

"Well," Cheryl drawled, "I have to be honest and tell you that I can't take any credit whatsoever for dessert. Bonnie, here, is the genius with chocolate. But I wouldn't go proposing to her too fast if I were you—she only treats us to these things once in a blue moon."

Bonnie wanted to crawl into a little hole in the wall and disappear.

"I was in the process of making it when you came by Saturday morning," Bonnie murmured, trying to get a word in edgewise so Cheryl couldn't say anything *else*.

Jeff looked like a rat caught in a trap, a flush of red creeping across his cheeks. He turned slowly to look at Bonnie and said in a much calmer voice, "This is really good, Bonnie."

"Glad you like it."

Bonnie rose with her plate and the casserole dish in her hands. She *had* to get away from that table.

"And just what do you think *you're* doing, young lady?" demanded Cheryl with a smile. "Didn't I tell you that you wouldn't have to wash the dishes?"

"Uh-uh," said Bonnie. "*You* picked up the boys for me, *you* shopped, and *you* cooked, but you're *not* going to do the dishes. I absolutely insist. Sit down and finish your dessert."

Bonnie was certain that Jack must have kicked Jeff under the table, because Jeff turned suddenly toward him with a questioning look. Jack made a funny face, jerking his head toward Bonnie.

"Let me help you," Jeff said without much conviction, and he rose with a dish in each hand himself.

"Oh! No," Bonnie stammered. "Really, Dr. Wells, you needn't feel obligated. I'm happy to do the dishes for Cheryl. She did such a big favor for me today."

"As did you for me," he answered as he walked behind her into the kitchen. "I didn't get a chance to thank you for coming with me to see JaMa'al."

"I was glad to do it," she murmured.

She set the dishes on the counter and went back to the dining room to retrieve another load and saw that Jack and Cheryl had already left the room. *Boy!* Bonnie thought. *What a couple of matchmakers. I need to talk to Cheryl, and soon.*

The silence in the kitchen was almost palpable as Bonnie washed and Jeff loaded the dishwasher. Bonnie felt her cheeks burning with embarrassment. She wished he didn't feel so obligated to be there with her; she was sure he must feel as uncomfortable as she did.

She remembered the look on Jeff's face earlier that day when he'd seen her with Preston at the Coffee Shoppe. When he had told her on Sunday that he was deferring to her previous relationship, as he had put it, his expression had been one of disappointment. Today, though, she had seen anger in his eyes. Yet, if one could tell by appearances, *he* seemed to be spending a good deal of time with Sherry Niles lately. Why should he care if she were seeing someone else?

At the thought of Sherry Niles, Bonnie debated about whether to ask Jeff the question that had been in the back of her mind ever since she had talked with Preston at lunch. What if he didn't know that Sherry was married to Preston? Wouldn't she be doing him a favor by telling him?

"Dr. Wells," she began slowly, not looking at him, "I *know* this isn't really any of my business…"

Jeff sighed. He didn't think that he would ever hear Bonnie call him by his first name. Especially not now.

"But?" he led her on.

"But," she hesitated, gathering her nerve, "I…I just thought I'd ask you if you knew that…" she looked up at Jeff involuntarily, "…that Sherry Niles is married." She looked quickly back into the sink full of sudsy water.

At first, Jeff started inwardly at the very idea that Bonnie thought he had any special relationship with Sherry Niles that would even make her being married an issue. Then he got mad. Of all the nerve! *Here she is, openly dating some other guy, and she has the temerity to intimate that I might be seeing a married woman!*

What was going on with her, that one minute she could seem to be every bit the strong Christian he had always thought her to be, the Bonnie he had seen today at Loaves and Fishes and with JaMa'al, and the next date someone who seemed not the least bit interested in Christian matters, who, indeed, had expressed disdain for them! The thought he'd had this afternoon as he was leaving the detention center came to him again: the less he saw of Bonnie, the better off he would be. For a long moment after Bonnie had asked her question, Jeff just glared down at Bonnie's blonde head.

"You're right," he answered finally, his voice tight with anger. "It *is* none of your business."

On top of the strained awkwardness that had hung between them all day, on top of the hurt that she still carried with her from his breaking off with her yesterday, Jeff's words stung Bonnie to the heart. *How could I have been so wrong about him?* Or was Jeff Wells simply that good at putting on a kind, understanding face when it suited him and being completely oblivious to people's feelings when it didn't? Struggling to contain the tears that threatened to spill from her eyes, Bonnie rinsed the last of the dishes, handed it to Jeff without meeting his eyes, and walked out of the kitchen without another word.

CHAPTER 14

Kneeling beside one of the children's worktables in the after-school area of Loaves and Fishes, Bonnie rubbed furiously at dried school glue with a wet washcloth and tried not to cry. A dull ache had settled into her heart, an ache closely akin to the one she had felt after the initial shock of Bill's death had subsided. That Jeff Wells could have spoken to her in such a way last night! After so many years of admiring him from a distance as her pastor, and then more closely as a fellow Benevolent Council member, and up until Sunday, as a man she'd looked forward to getting to know more personally, it had been almost like a physical blow to have him say to her, "It's none of your business."

Truly, she'd had his best interests at heart—after all, she didn't delude herself that there would ever be anything between the two of them *now*. She had been trying to look beyond her own feelings about him: if he were seeing a woman socially, wouldn't he want to know that that person was actually still married? That Jeff might even *contemplate* such a relationship was a staggering thought, but that he should be so angry with her that he could speak to her so coldly, was little short of devastating. Perhaps she had been right Sunday afternoon when she had thought she should find a way to leave Foster Road Baptist. Her heart ached and ached.

The locksmiths had promised to come to Loaves and Fishes between nine and noon, so Bonnie had decided to do what she could to continue with the cleanup process while she waited for them. Much as she would like to stay and help until the place was back in shape, though, she had work for her clients stacking up at home. And they couldn't eat at Jack and Cheryl's *every* night; she was going to have to do some grocery shopping and cooking of her own. Maybe she would even make a few casseroles to put in the freezer.

She heard the front door open and looked up, expecting to see the locksmith's crew. Instead, Cheryl Summers poked her head in.

"Oh, my goodness, what a mess," she said, trying to take it all in.

"According to JaMa'al, there were four older boys with him. They didn't fool around," Bonnie told her, rising to greet her friend. "What're *you* doing down here?"

"Well, I *did* think you could use some help," Cheryl said tentatively.

"I hear a 'but' in there," Bonnie replied with a smile.

Rolling her eyes in mock-defeat, Cheryl said, "Okay, I just *had* to find out what is going on with you and Jeff, and I knew you wouldn't want to be talking on the phone down here."

Bonnie sighed and looked at her friend with gratitude. It would be good to have someone to talk to about this, someone she could trust.

"Pick up a washcloth and I'll tell you a strange story."

Sparing no details (Cheryl's eyes had widened when Bonnie mentioned the kiss on Jeff's front porch), Bonnie helped her friend to understand why conversation had been so awkward over dinner the previous night.

"This is so amazing," Cheryl murmured, shaking her head. "It's true that Clara does have a lot of credibility with everybody at church. She actually grew up going to Foster Road, so nearly everybody knows her. I guess her word carries a lot of weight with Jeff, too. Do you suppose it would help if Jack said something to him?"

Bonnie stared hard at the floor and thought about Jeff seated across from Sherry Niles at the restaurant on Sunday, and then about his words to her as they had washed dishes together at Cheryl's the night before.

"No," she whispered, shaking her head. "Please tell Jack not to mention anything about this to Dr. Wells. The sooner this blows over, the better."

"And how long do you suppose *that* will take?" challenged Cheryl. "How long before you can look at him again and not feel angry and hurt?"

"I don't know," Bonnie answered, her eyes filling with tears again. "The whole thing just makes me so mad! I mean, just the whole idea that I didn't *ask* for any of this! I was doing just fine until he called."

Cheryl gave Bonnie a sympathetic look, then reached over and gave her a hug. She made no remark, however, about Bonnie's last statement.

"Well, it seems to me, things are going to be mighty awkward for you over the next few weeks, if not longer. Do you suppose he really doesn't know that Sherry Niles is still married to that Preston character? Maybe when he puts two and two together, he'll realize what a jerk he's been and make it up to you."

"I can't deny that I think he owes me an apology," said Bonnie, frowning as she scrubbed vigorously at the table. "But even if that happens, I think I've seen a side of him that tells me I'm better off the way things are. I've just got to get over my hurt feelings, and I'll be fine."

"Man, this is such a shame," said Cheryl as she worked at sorting salvage-able crayons from one of the smashed piles on the floor. "I mean, he's really such a great guy. Great sense of humor, lots of fun. He's Jack's best friend."

Bonnie looked with concern at Cheryl.

"I'm really sorry about last night. If I'd had *any* idea that Jeff would be there, I promise you I never would've—"

"Don't give it another thought," Cheryl told her. "There was no way you could've known. Jack called to tell me he'd invited Jeff to dinner about twenty minutes after I spoke with you yesterday. Considering what we thought were the circumstances, we *thought* it'd be a nice surprise for the two of you."

"Yeah, I kind of caught on to that." *And under other circumstances*, Bonnie told herself, *I would've been glad to have you play matchmaker.* "But Cheryl, I want you to know that I'll do my best to keep things from being awkward if the four of us are ever thrown together again. Mostly, I'll try to make sure that doesn't *happen*," she said with a wry smile, "but I don't want to make you and Jack uncomfortable."

When Cheryl left a while later, Bonnie looked impatiently at her watch and sighed. Eleven forty-five. Were those locksmith guys going to show up or not? Once again, she heard the front door open, and to her astonishment, Ruth Newton walked in, followed by three men in white work coveralls bearing the logo of Chandler City Lock and Key.

"Ruth! What brings you down here?"

Ruth smiled, weariness still in her eyes, and explained, "Well, dear, I don't know if you knew this, but this building is part of Art's—*was* part of Art's—real estate holdings. And since we own Chandler City Lock and Key, Ted, here, alerts us whenever they're called on to service one of our properties."

She gestured to the man immediately behind her, who tipped his work hat and smiled briefly through gritted teeth that held an unlit cigar. Looking up at Ted, who stood well over a foot taller than the tiny Ruth Newton, she said, "You boys go ahead and get started installing that new door."

Bonnie couldn't help but smile at the no-nonsense way Ruth dealt with these big, burly workmen, even calling them boys! Perhaps to a woman of Ruth's age, every man under the age of sixty was a "boy."

"So," Ruth began again, turning to Bonnie, "how about us having that lunch we talked about?"

"Well, but what about the workers? Doesn't someone need to be here with them?"

Ruth smiled again. "Ted's worked for us going on thirty years now. I think I can trust him to lock the place up when they're done. By the way, these are the keys to the new locks. Would it be too much trouble to ask you to a get a key to all the folks on the Benevolent Council who need one?"

"Oh, sure, I'd be glad to," said Bonnie, taking the ring of keys from Ruth. She made a mental list of those who would need them, secretly glad that Jeff Wells was no longer among them. "Um, where would you like to go for lunch?"

Bonnie asked the question, dreading that Ruth might want to go to the Coffee Shoppe. It seemed that every time she went there, she ran into Preston Hardy or Jeff Wells or both.

"Well, hmm," Ruth seemed to mull it over. "We both had lunch at the Coffee Shoppe yesterday, didn't we?" Bonnie made no reply; she didn't want to go into it with Ruth. "Do you know of anyplace close by?"

Trying to sound as casual as possible, she said, "Well, there's Grabbabite over on Troy Street."

"Oh, yes, that's right! That's only a couple of blocks away. We could just walk right over. It's been ages since I've been there."

Tremendously relieved, Bonnie went to the bathroom down the hall and washed her hands. Then she grabbed her purse and followed Ruth out the door.

When they arrived, Claire and Betty greeted them with pleased surprise.

"You know Ruth Newton, don't you?" Bonnie asked, by way of introduction.

"Actually," answered Claire with a conspiratorial smile at Ruth, "Ruth is our landlady. She owns this building. We couldn't have picked a more wonderful person to have rented from." Claire gave Ruth's hand an affectionate squeeze.

"Well, somebody had to help you ladies give Chandler City the best Quiche Lorraine in town." Ruth smiled fondly at the women.

"We'd be nowhere without you," added Betty.

"Ruth, let me say again how sorry I am for your loss," said Claire.

Ruth just pursed her lips and nodded, looking gratefully into Claire's eyes.

"Well," said Betty, "let me show you ladies to a table."

Bonnie was a little dismayed at how underdressed she was compared to nearly everyone else in the place. Workers from all over Chandler City's central business district had gathered there for lunch and were, of course, wearing their best suits and dresses.

"I wish I'd gone home to change first," Bonnie murmured, eyeing her own work-splattered jeans self-consciously.

"I think these folks've seen a pair of blue jeans before," pooh-poohed Ruth. "You've been working hard all morning, and you deserve a nice lunch."

Still, Bonnie couldn't help but notice that several men and women looked twice when she passed. Then she saw him. Was she going to run into Jeff Wells everywhere she went?

"Dr. Wells!" Ruth called, her face lighting up.

Jeff turned from the conversation he was having with Jack Summers and smiled when he saw Ruth. Then he noticed Bonnie next to her and the smile faded—perhaps only enough for Bonnie to notice, but faded nevertheless. Then Jack saw Bonnie.

"Hey, there, Bon!" he called. "Why don't you girls come join us for lunch?"

Bonnie saw the look on Jeff's face and hoped against hope that Ruth wouldn't want to accept. Ruth turned briefly to Bonnie, intending to ask her preference, but saw her looking down, obviously avoiding meeting *someone's* eye. Was it Jack Summers or Jeff Wells?

"Oh, you boys don't want to be bothered with all of our girl talk," Ruth said with a kind smile. "Besides," she added with a wink, "I'm treating Bonnie to lunch. I can't afford to buy for everybody!"

Jeff shook his head and smiled. "Yeah, right, Ruth. Well, enjoy! Good to see you both."

Bonnie turned to continue following Betty toward a booth, not looking at Jeff again. '*Good to see you both,*' Bonnie thought. *What a lie.*

When they had settled into their seats, ordered, and received their iced tea, Bonnie was surprised to see Jeff and Jack walking over to their table. Jeff stood next to Ruth and Jack next to Bonnie, a friendly hand on her shoulder. Bonnie looked up at him and smiled, but she saw the question in his eyes and looked away.

"So, I see you've been back to work at Loaves and Fishes," Jeff said.

But Bonnie didn't hear him. She had been so sure that he had come only to speak to Ruth that she was concentrating on the rivulets of condensation rolling down the side of her glass of tea, waiting for him to say whatever it was he had to say and leave. Ruth touched her hand softly.

"I think he was referring to you, dear," she said kindly.

Bonnie looked up with surprise, first at Ruth and then at Jeff.

"Oh, I'm sorry, I beg your pardon?" She could feel herself coloring at her blunder.

"I was just remarking that you must've just come from Loaves and Fishes," he said, giving her a look that seemed casual but behind which Bonnie could see almost a note of pleading, as if he wanted her to help him keep up an appearance of nonchalance. Unfortunately, this was just a bit beyond Bonnie at the moment.

"Oh, yes," she said, looking down again. "You'll have to excuse my appearance. I was just doing a little more work while I waited for the locksmiths to come. I'd forgotten that Art had donated the building to the Council. Ruth came in with the locksmiths."

With the possible exception of when Bonnie had greeted him at her door wearing green stuff on her face and a plastic bag on her head, Jeff thought that he had never seen Bonnie look bad.

"Well, don't expect to have to clean up the place single-handedly. I think a group from the Senior Adults is getting together a work party for Saturday."

Jeff smiled, but Bonnie wasn't looking at him. Ruth saw Bonnie looking down and looked quizzically at Jeff. He furrowed his eyebrows ever so slightly and shook his head briefly. Then he brightened again, an impish gleam in his eye. Turning to Ruth, he said, "Do you and Art own *everything* in Chandler City?"

Ruth looked surprised at first, then smiled as if each little joke Jeff made were making her feel better and better.

"Oh, I think there may be a couple of shops on Main Street that don't belong to us," she answered, the twinkle in her eye matching that in Jeff's, "but I'd have to check into it."

Jeff laughed and shook his head. "You're priceless, Ruth."

"Oh, I'll bet you say that to all the girls." Ruth was really enjoying the banter.

"Well, what I *did* come by to say, Ruth," Jeff continued, a little more seriously, "is that I hope you'll consider joining us this Friday night for the Seniors Banquet."

"Only if *you'll* consent to be my date," Ruth kidded him, a little mischief in her own eyes now.

Jeff looked momentarily uncomfortable and glanced at Bonnie. She was still not looking at him and, at that moment, he was glad.

"Oh, Ruth, you know I'd like nothing better, but I'm afraid I'm already spoken for."

So absorbed had she been with the idea of Jeff seeing the beautiful but married Sherry Niles, Bonnie completely forgot the conversation in which Anna Lee Adkinson had told her of the "date" Clara had arranged between herself and Jeff. Bonnie's face was aflame with embarrassment. Was Jeff *intentionally* trying to rub it in about Sherry Niles? And what must Jack be thinking? She felt his hand leave her shoulder and saw him cross his arms across his chest out of the corner of her eye.

"Isn't that always the way?" said Ruth airily. "The best fellas are always scooped up first."

"Well," Jeff said, obviously regretting his decision to come to the table to speak to Ruth, "I hope to see you there Friday. Enjoy your lunch, ladies."

"Catch you later, Bonnie," Jack murmured. "Good to see you, Ruth," he said, giving her hand a little squeeze.

Ruth waited a few moments after they left, turned to see that they were really gone, and then turned back to Bonnie.

"Want to tell me about it?" she asked, gently laying one of her cool, white hands atop one of Bonnie's.

"You're amazing," Bonnie told her, knowing what Ruth meant, but avoiding giving her a straight answer. "You just buried your husband yesterday, but today you're joking with Dr. Wells and taking care of business and having lunch with me. I don't know how you do it."

Ruth took a deep breath and sipped her tea.

"Honey, we'd been expecting Art to go any time over the last six weeks. His death was neither sudden nor a shock." Bonnie watched Ruth, still amazed at the strength in her face. "He'd been on a feeding tube for the last year and a half. But the day he looked me in the eye and called me 'Aunt Hattie,' an aunt of his who died forty years ago, *that* was when I knew I'd lost my Art. And that was over two years ago. Towards the end, that body in the bed at Rivendale Manor was just a shell waiting for the Lord to call Art home.

"As for the business, Randall and Roy gradually began taking over things when we started noticing the little lapses in memory and judgment Art was having, before we knew there was anything seriously wrong." Ruth's two grandsons, Randall and Roy, were just a little younger than Bonnie.

"When we finally put him into the nursing home, I was with him as much as I could be, but he was well cared for there. There was no point in my living there, especially toward the end. I tried to stay involved with my Sunday School class and the Seniors group, and, with the help of Doctor Father, I even kept up with Art's charity work. I think that's what's kept me going."

Then Ruth's expression changed and she looked sympathetically at Bonnie.

"So," she said, her voice gentle but imperious, "are you going to tell me about it or not? Did you and Cheryl Summers have some kind of falling out? I noticed you wouldn't even look at Jack."

Bonnie's eyes widened with surprise. Ruth didn't even *suspect* that it was Jeff whose eye she couldn't meet. But what could she say? How could Bonnie burden Ruth with what seemed so trivial compared to what Ruth had just been through with Art? But what kind of story could she make up that Ruth wouldn't see through immediately?

"Oh, no," murmured Bonnie. "Cheryl and I are still the best of friends. I don't know what I'd do without her."

"Well, don't *tell* me you've had words with the pastor! I've never *seen* anybody who was able to get along with so many different kinds of folks. He puts up with more than *I* ever could out of some people."

Bonnie wondered who she had in mind, but didn't voice her question.

"You're right, he's very good with people," Bonnie agreed, volunteering no more.

"But not with you," Ruth said, as if to finish the thought. She waited a moment, but still Bonnie said nothing. She just looked at her friend, almost as if willing Ruth to read the problem in her eyes.

"I'm a little surprised to hear him say that he's got a date for the banquet on Friday," she continued casually, watching Bonnie's face for a reaction. "I didn't know that he'd begun seeing anyone since Terri died."

At this, Bonnie looked down, and Ruth knew she had come close to the heart of the matter. "Truth to tell, I always thought maybe working on the Benevolent Council together would spark some interest between the two of *you*. But, as I said, I didn't know he was seeing anyone."

Bonnie was torn between telling Ruth what she believed to be true and still wondering if it could possibly *be* that Jeff Wells was seeing Sherry Niles, knowing her to be married. And what about Preston telling her that he and Sherry were discussing a reconciliation?

"Well," Bonnie began tentatively, "if it's who I think it is, she's an absolutely beautiful woman who just recently moved here from Atlanta. She works at Chandler City Bank."

Ruth's eyes flew open. "You couldn't possibly be talking about Jesse Niles's daughter, could you?"

"Do you know her?"

Bonnie's heart was pounding. What if she'd said something she shouldn't have? What if she was mistaken about Jeff and Sherry? Maybe their being together on Sunday hadn't meant what she thought it had!

"Yes, I know her, and I know her daddy, too," said Ruth. "Art and Henry Blankenship used to go hunting at Gus's place in Louisiana all the time. I know Henry just gave her a job as a favor to Gus when she left that…that *husband* of hers." Ruth had obviously bitten back the words describing her true feelings about Preston. "But to the best of my knowledge, they're still married. Jeff Wells would never go out with a married woman." She said it as if the whole idea were preposterous.

"I didn't know she was married when I saw them together," Bonnie admitted. "Maybe I was mistaken."

Ruth frowned. "Had to be. Because, you know, even if she were single, I just can't picture Jeff Wells with someone like Sherry. I've only spoken with her a couple of times on my trips into the bank. She's the sweetest thing you'd ever want to meet, but she's not exactly—well, you know what I mean, don't you? Terri was as sharp as they come. How could he go for somebody so different? That's why I always thought he'd be attracted to someone like *you*. Pretty, but with a brain, too."

Bonnie smiled and shook her head. She wanted to believe what Ruth was saying, that Jeff wasn't dating a married woman, but he had said himself that he had a date for the banquet Friday night. And to think that only last Friday, he was supposed to have had dinner with *her*!

"Well, if you go, maybe you can let me know who the mystery lady is." Bonnie gave Ruth a wry smile. "I'm sure that whoever Jeff arrives with will be the center of everyone's attention."

"True," Ruth agreed. "In that one respect, I don't envy *any* woman Jeff decides to court. Otherwise, he's one of the finest men I've ever met." Then, looking Bonnie directly and pointedly in the eye, she said, "A girl could do a lot worse than Jeff Wells."

If only, Bonnie thought wistfully, *I didn't think so myself.*

CHAPTER 15

When Bonnie woke up on Wednesday morning, it had been raining since the wee hours and showed no signs of stopping. Rather than forgo her daily run, she donned her running shorts and shoes and drove to the church's gym after dropping Ben and Josh off at school. The running track overlooked the basketball court from the second floor. Even at this early hour, there were walkers and joggers, mostly men and women from the Senior Adult group, making their circuits and counting laps. She had seen Clara Adkinson and Mertis Hargrove in the exercise equipment room pedaling side by side on stationary bicycles. Just as she rounded the curve in front of the plate glass windows fronting the racquetball courts, the lights went on and she saw Jack Summers and Jeff Wells entering, dressed for their racquetball match.

Jack saw her first and, though she couldn't hear him through the glass, she could see that he was yelling, "Hey, Bonnie!" and waving. She could see Jeff's unpleasantly surprised reaction to Jack's greeting and watched as he turned to see her pass. He waved at her somewhat automatically, as if his hand had gone up before he remembered that they weren't really speaking to each other, but there was no smile on his face. *Great*, thought Bonnie, *maybe I should have taken the day off after all.* She took a deep breath and forged ahead. Her ponytail bounced as she ran; her face glowed with exertion.

After Jeff's fourth straight miss resulting from Bonnie's passing by the window, Jack said, "Are you going to play, or are you going to watch her run?"

Jeff swiped at his forehead with his wristband and said, "Very funny." He walked over to his water bottle, laid his racquet down, and took a long drink.

"So who's your big date for the banquet Friday night?" Jack asked, accusation in his voice. "And when were you going to *tell* me that you've decided not to date Bonnie after all?" He took a noisy swig from his own bottle.

Jeff looked up at Jack with surprise, then smiled a wry smile. "No secrets in this town, are there?"

"She *is* Cheryl's best friend, remember?"

"No, I know. I was just kidding." Jeff appeared to be studying his shoe laces closely, avoiding meeting Jack's eyes. "Honestly, I was going to tell you this morning. I wish I'd known to tell you Monday, before we all had to endure that dinner together."

Jack was struck by the word *endure*.

"That bad, huh? What in the world happened?"

"Call me old fashioned, Jack, but my first time out, after not having had a date in over twenty years, I kind of wanted to be the only player on the field."

"Meaning?"

"*Meaning*," he began to explain, even as he wondered how much of this Jack already knew, "that when I found out Bonnie was already seeing someone, I just didn't feel like competing."

Cheryl had conveyed Bonnie's wishes to Jack about him not speaking to Jeff on her behalf, but Jack wasn't letting Jeff off the hook so easily.

"Well, I'm supposed to be sworn to secrecy on this, but I don't care. You really blew it this time, buddy."

"How do you figure?" Jeff asked, reaching down to retie his shoes and trying not to sound as annoyed as he was getting over the whole situation.

"Bonnie isn't seeing anybody else." He said it as if Jeff had taken leave of his senses for even thinking so. "She hasn't been out with anyone since Bill died. I think it was a miracle that she even said yes to *you*, but you would've been the first. Now, who knows how long it'll be before she even thinks about it again? You really kind of did a number on her."

"Look, I appreciate your concern, I really do, but I'm not going on second-hand information here. I saw her with the guy myself."

Bonnie passed by the window again and looked at Jack and Jeff in puzzlement when she saw them just standing there together talking. *Dear Lord,* thought Bonnie, *please don't let them be talking about what I think they're talking about!*

Waiting until she passed, as if she could actually hear them, Jack said, "Look, I know that what you saw may have looked funny coming on the heels of the misinformation you were given, but I'm *telling* you, Bonnie is *not* dating that guy. For whatever reason, Clara Adkinson gave you a bum steer. Although, I gotta tell you, I have no idea why she'd feed you such a pack of lies about Bonnie."

Jeff scowled but said nothing, remembering how Clara had not-so-subtly arranged for him to be her daughter's "date" at the upcoming Seniors Banquet. Then he felt that sinking feeling again that he'd had when, unable to conceal her tears, Bonnie had walked out of his office on Sunday. He should have trusted his gut instinct about Bonnie; how could he have doubted that Bonnie was everything he had always thought her to be? Now he'd fouled things up royally. What had he been thinking?

When Jeff made no reply, Jack continued, "And speaking of things looking funny, when I tell you who this guy is, you will know, *A*, that I'm giving you the straight scoop and, *B*, that you've got a little explaining to do yourself."

"What do you mean, 'who he is?' He's some guy that started coming to Singles functions after I gave him my business card. I met him in the bar we waited in when the church bus broke down in Westdale last December."

"Yeah, well you might want to talk to Tom Givens about that, because he's not exactly single."

Jeff eyed Jack suspiciously. "What do you mean, 'not exactly'? Either he's single or he's not."

"Well, I guess he *will* be single again if Sherry Niles goes through with their divorce."

Jack saw Jeff's shocked expression with some satisfaction. He figured there *had* to have been a breakdown in the information chain somewhere.

"That Preston guy is Sherry's husband?"

"So, you *did* know she was married, then?"

Jeff rolled his eyes and gave Jack a sardonic look.

"Of course I know she's married! That's how I met her. Norman Blake, the rector at St. Alban's, referred her to Foster Road Baptist for counseling. She's Catholic, but her husband was raised Baptist. Norman thought that if they were going to seek marriage counseling, the husband might respond more readily to someone from his own background. Judging from his general demeanor, though, I don't think any particular religious persuasion would mean much to him."

"So, you're providing marriage counseling to them?"

"No! Remember, I said I didn't even know who Sherry's husband was. She came to church last Sunday and introduced herself and told me the whole, long, sad story over lunch. She also told me that her husband wasn't interested in counseling, and especially not in pastoral counseling." At this, Jeff smiled and shook his head. "And I learned a long time ago, my friend, that pretty women and counseling with a male pastor are a dangerous combination. I wasn't about to get mixed up in that. I referred her to Susan Holland, one of the pastoral counselors at Southwest Methodist Hospital."

The longer they stood there, the more certain Bonnie was that they must be talking about her and Jeff. She was going to strangle that Jack Summers!

"So," Jack mused. "You're not counseling her."

"No."

"And nothing else is going on between you and her?"

Jeff rolled his eyes again and sighed. "Give me some credit here, Jack. I know it's been done, but it ain't been done by me!"

"You're aware that Bonnie thinks you're dating her?" Jeff made no answer, but Jack could see the truth in Jeff's guilty expression. "Yet you made no attempt to set her straight."

Jeff avoided looking at his friend, but didn't relent.

"Under the circumstances, I didn't see much point," he replied defensively.

"What about the *real* circumstances?" Jack persisted.

At that moment, Bonnie passed by again. Having caught Jack's eye, she made a face at him, as if to say, "You are in big trouble!"

Jeff didn't see her pass this time. He picked up his racquet and, without responding to Jack's question, said, "Let's get out of here. You've got to be at work soon."

Not having eaten breakfast, Bonnie decided to stop in at the Coffee Shoppe and grab a quick bite before heading over to the Warehouse Club. They were out of practically everything. What with the funeral and cleaning up at Loaves and Fishes, she felt like she'd hardly been home in the last few days.

Bonnie was pleased to find Della assigned to her table that morning.

"Della, what a nice surprise! I didn't think you worked mornings."

"No, I don't normally, but tonight's kinda special. John Reeves stopped in last night to tell me that Joanna finally had that baby! He was on his way home from the hospital, and he stopped in to tell me. Wasn't that sweet of him? I'm working a day shift so I can go visit her and the baby tonight. I figure that'll give 'em almost a day to do a little recoverin'."

"Oh, Della, that's great! I hadn't heard yet. What did Joanna have?"

Della couldn't have looked more proud if she'd had the baby herself. "I told everybody it was going to be a girl, and a girl it was!"

"How about that!" Bonnie laughed.

"But you ain't heard the best part yet, honey," Della said, leaning over conspiratorially.

"Oh? What's that?"

In uncontainable excitement, Della grabbed Bonnie's hands and told her, "John and Joanna said they wanted to name their baby girl after two of their favorite people. They named her Della Bonita. *Della Bonita Reeves!* Ain't that beautiful?" Della's eyes had welled with tears. "I never had no kids of my own," she continued, her voice still husky, "and I certainly never had nobody name a young'un after me! I liked to fainted when John told me last night."

Bonnie was momentarily overwhelmed by this piece of news herself. John and Joanna had named their daughter after her and Della? What an incredible honor! She made a mental note that, right after she finished at the Warehouse Club, she was going to have to run to the mall to get a gift for Della Bonita Reeves. And a very special gift it was going to have to be.

Browsing around the baby department in her favorite store at the mall brought back fond memories for Bonnie. The little blue outfits, the fuzzy little bears and bunnies that tinkled out lullabies when you wound them up, the downy-soft blankets: all reminded her of the shopping and dreaming she'd done when she was carrying Ben and Josh. But now she was looking for something pink!

"Have a good run this morning?"

Bonnie looked up to see Jeff Wells smiling down at her. She was so surprised to see him that, at first, she only stood and stared, her mouth slightly agape.

"Guess you must've heard about the Reeves baby, too, eh? I just got a call from John and figured I'd better go out and get a gift now, because tonight—"

The look on Bonnie's face stopped him mid-sentence.

Bonnie had collected herself. She looked around the baby department to see who else might be about. It was still relatively early, and the store was nearly deserted. The department clerk was standing far enough away that Bonnie ventured this reply in a stage whisper to Jeff:

"I don't know what kind of people you're used to dealing with, or if you think that just because you're the pastor, you can say or do anything you want." She saw Jeff's eyes widen with shock and surprise. "But it's just you and me standing here, and I want to tell you that you *cannot* just speak to me as coldly and callously as you did Monday night, and then turn around and greet me like nothing ever happened. Whatever you might think of me, whatever mistaken notions you might be laboring under, I *do* have feelings. I know it won't always be possible, but you and I both know it would be best if you just said nothing to me at all unless it's completely unavoidable!"

Bonnie could feel her cheeks burning, but she just couldn't go around pretending she hadn't been hurt. She could at least put him on notice not to pour any more salt into her wounds.

Nonplussed at first, Jeff looked at the floor for a moment. Then, with an incredibly abject look on his face, he said, "You're exactly right. What I said to you Monday night was totally uncalled for."

Bonnie didn't know what she had expected, but it wasn't this. She would never have thought he would acquiesce so easily.

"I know that I ask a lot in asking for your forgiveness, but I sincerely apologize for all of the hard feelings I've caused." The intensity in Jeff's eyes as he spoke nearly took Bonnie's breath away. "I only hope that, in time, you can forgive me, but for now, please accept my apology."

Bonnie stared at him wide-eyed, momentarily at a loss for words. Looking him in the eye only briefly, she cast her eyes downward and answered grudgingly, "Apology accepted."

The gift would have to wait. She strode out of the baby department and headed for home.

Joshua had never been to visit the maternity wing of a hospital, so he was thrilled to be going to see the Reeves baby. He lobbied for the privilege of carrying the gift that Bonnie had purchased after picking the boys up from school.

As they approached the front entrance of Southwest Methodist Hospital, Ben called out, "Hey! There's Pastor Jeff! And look! He's with that same lady he was with at the restaurant Sunday. Is that his girlfriend?"

He turned to look at his mother who, naturally, must know the answer to such a question.

"I...I really don't know, sweetie," she answered, wishing desperately that there were someplace she could hide before Jeff and Sherry saw her. "But let's not ask *him*, okay?"

She knew how bluntly direct children could be if you didn't head them off at the pass.

"Oh," said Josh, sounding a little mystified. "Okay."

Bonnie knew then that she had, indeed, at least partially circumvented an awkward moment.

As they neared Jeff and Sherry, who stood outside the hospital entrance in conversation with each other, Bonnie noticed that Jeff held a small white package bound with a pastel pink ribbon. A gift for the Reeves baby, no doubt. Ben ran ahead and called, "Hey, Pastor Jeff!" Bonnie steeled herself for nonchalance.

Jeff turned with surprise and smiled down on Ben and ruffled his hair.

"Benny Boy! Don't tell me you're coming to have your tonsils out tonight!"

Ben laughed, obviously reveling in the attention. Just then, Josh caught up with his big brother. Jeff bent over and swooped him up into his arms.

"Hey, there, tiger!"

Josh giggled with delight, smiling his partially toothless smile. Sherry looked on admiringly. As Bonnie walked up, it was Sherry who greeted her first.

"Hi! I met you last Sunday night, didn't I?"

Bonnie smiled as cordially as she could. "Yes, you did. Good to see you again, Sherry."

"Oh, I feel so bad. I never was any good at rememberin' names!"

Carefully avoiding Bonnie's eyes, Jeff took the initiative: "Sherry Niles, this is Bonnie Callaway."

"Bonnie! That's right! I remember now," said Sherry. "Are these your boys? They sure are beautiful!"

At the word "beautiful," Josh made a face.

"Boys can't be beautiful!" he said with great assurance. Then, he turned to his mother in doubt and asked, "Can they?"

The three adults got a laugh out of that, but Bonnie had no inclination to prolong this encounter.

"We really need to be going," she said. "I don't want to be late for Fellowship Supper."

Jeff looked at his watch.

"Oops! Neither do I! I'll talk with you soon, Sherry."

Sherry looked a little surprised, and then a little disappointed.

"Oh, okay. 'Bye, then. Good to see you again, Bonnie."

Bonnie smiled and held her arms out to Joshua. He allowed her to set him down on the ground again and they walked toward the door.

"Allow me," Jeff said, as he held the heavy glass door open for them. "Are you on your way to see the Reeves baby, too?" Jeff asked her.

Once again, Bonnie was struck by the incongruous timing that seemed constantly to bring her and Jeff to the same place at the same time.

"Yes, we are," she murmured.

They walked in silence to the bank of elevators, Bonnie torn between not wanting to have to make conversation with Jeff but conscious of the fact that her children were delighted to have run into the pastor.

"Guess what?" It was Josh who broke the ice.

"What?" answered Jeff with a smile.

"You know the baby we're goin' to see? They named it after Mom!"

Jeff's eyes widened and he looked up inquiringly at Bonnie. Her eyes neither denied nor confirmed what Josh had told him.

"Did they? They named their little girl Bonnie?"

"No, no, Josh has got it all backwards," corrected Ben importantly. "They named her after Della, at the Coffee Shoppe, *and* Mom."

"Della Bonita," Bonnie said matter-of-factly. "It's quite an honor."

Jeff held the elevator doors open as they stepped out. He wanted so much to say, "A well-deserved honor" or, "I hope that she grows up to be as wonderful as the ladies she was named after," but he knew that Bonnie was in no humor to accept a compliment from him, however sincere it might be. His fault. Entirely his own fault.

After visiting a pleasantly tired Joanna Reeves, Bonnie walked Ben and Josh down to the nursery area so they could see the new arrival. To her consternation, Jeff continued to walk with them.

"Whoa, look at all those little guys!" was Josh's awed exclamation when Jeff lifted him up to look through the window. There seemed to be quite a full house in the nursery just then.

"You were once a little peanut like that yourself, you know," Jeff reminded him. Bonnie wasn't entirely comfortable with how naturally Josh seemed to drape his arm around Jeff's neck.

"Really?" Josh looked again to his mother for confirmation.

With a wry little smile, Bonnie nodded in reply. Almost reflexively, she looked at Jeff to share the warmth and humor of the moment with him. When he looked back, she saw again the smile he had given her the night they had sat chatting so comfortably at the Coffee Shoppe, before Clara Adkinson had happened by. Then she remembered how angry she'd been with him this morning in the department store and looked away with a scowl.

When Bonnie and the boys got home from church later that evening, the light on her answering machine was blinking again. In a voice that sounded utterly weary, Carolyn Perkins had called to tell Bonnie that Joanna Reeves had given birth.

"And," Carolyn had added, "our good friend Della will be glad to know that the Reeveses are the proud parents of a healthy baby girl."

Bonnie felt a surge of guilt for not having called Carolyn before now. She had been so busy dealing with the aftermath of the Loaves and Fishes break-in (and wrapped up in her own inner turmoil about Jeff, if the truth be told) that she'd completely forgotten about her promise to Doctor Father to call Carolyn. After Ben and Josh were in bed, she dialed Carolyn's home number.

"Hi, Bonnie."

"Carolyn, thanks so much for calling to let me know about the Reeves baby." Bonnie tried to sound as upbeat as she could. "I hate to tell you, though, that I'd already heard about it from Della. Seems John made a special trip to the Coffee Shoppe just to fill her in."

"Ah, yes, I guess he would. Especially since it was a girl. Guess you know what they named her, then."

"Yes," Bonnie answered. "I was so flattered."

There was an awkward silence. Finally, Bonnie began again. "Carolyn, I've been meaning to call you ever since I heard about the Loaves and Fishes break-in. I'm sorry it took a call from you to remind me."

Carolyn sounded surprised. "Oh! I wasn't really expecting you to call."

"No, I didn't think you should be," Bonnie said. "But, well, I know what a shock it must have been for you."

"I can't remember being this disappointed in a long, long time," Carolyn said, the weariness back in her voice. "Do you know how many times—" She stopped mid-sentence.

"Yes, Carolyn. I know how much you've helped them. I know how much it had to hurt." Carolyn was silent. "Listen, Carolyn, I'd really like to talk to you about what happened."

"What's to talk about? I obviously misjudged the degree of gratitude I could expect from a family I tried to help. What else is there to say?"

"There really is more to this than meets the eye," Bonnie told her. "Would you be willing to have lunch with me to talk about it some more?"

"I'd like to have lunch with you, no matter what the excuse," Carolyn said. "I could use a friend right now."

"Why don't we meet at 11:30 tomorrow at the Coffee Shoppe?"

"I'll be there."

When Carolyn hung up, Bonnie prayed a silent prayer that the right words, the words that would lead Carolyn to forgive JaMa'al, would be hers tomorrow.

CHAPTER 16

As Bonnie got into her car the next morning, heading out to run errands and make deliveries before her lunch with Carolyn Perkins, she looked at the audiocassette sitting on the seat next to her and sighed. Jeff's secretary, Sandra, seemed to have made a point, as Bonnie had stood in the serving line at Fellowship Supper the night before, of making sure she got the tape of the previous Sunday morning's service she'd ordered. Despite her best intentions of becoming more attentive to what was being said in the services, though, she was reluctant to hear Jeff's voice at all, much less to listen to anything as lengthy as one of his sermons. Still, she remembered how much Cheryl had seemed to enjoy it and realized that, regardless of how unenthusiastic she was, she really *ought* to listen to it.

She glanced at the title typed onto the cassette label: *To Forgive, Divine*. It had been clear to Bonnie as she had left Jeff's office the previous Sunday afternoon that Sandra knew Jeff had broken things off with her. Was that why she'd seemed so anxious for Bonnie to have the tape? After the awkward and antagonistic encounters she'd had with Jeff Wells this week, Bonnie's feelings toward him were anything but divine. Grudgingly, she removed the tape from its case, pushed it into the tape drive with her forefinger, and backed out of her driveway.

She had a little time to prepare herself for hearing Jeff's voice: the first twenty minutes or so of the tape contained the opening hymns of the service, announcements, and an anthem sung by the choir. When she stopped in to see Claire and Betty at Grabbabite, the tape had advanced to an announcement Tom Givens had made about the after-church fellowship at Jenny Pierce's that night and a reminder for the Singles to register for the upcoming Memorial

Day Singles Conference. He had alluded to the mystery guest even then. What a fog she'd been in to have missed all this Sunday morning! She wondered again who the mystery guest was going to be. Well, she would find out: she had told Tom last night that she'd accepted his offer to lead a session at the conference.

By the time she stopped for gas, the Minister of Education had read the scripture passages on which the sermon was based that morning, and the choir was just about to sing its anthem. As she drove to the Coffee Shoppe to meet Carolyn, she listened as a father and son sang a kind of dialogue that told the story of the Prodigal Son, and the choir repeated a chorus of

> Rejoice! Rejoice! My son is coming home again!
> Rejoice! Rejoice! Go kill the fatted calf!

As she pulled into the restaurant parking lot, the last notes of the piece sounded, and the congregation had burst into applause. Bonnie remembered starting when she'd heard the people around her clapping and how her face had colored with the embarrassment of having attended so poorly that she didn't realize what a wonderful job the choir had done. *All because of one kiss from Jeff Wells,* she thought with self-disgust. She flipped off the cassette player just as Jeff was remarking on how moving the anthem had been. Then she turned off the motor and went in to meet Carolyn.

Carolyn had already been seated and waved Bonnie over with a smile. She took Bonnie's hand and gave it a squeeze; Bonnie could see pain in Carolyn's eyes.

"How are you?" Bonnie asked.

"I'm good," Carolyn answered.

Bonnie could tell it was an automatic reply, but she didn't press Carolyn for more candor. Just then, their waitress approached.

"So, what are you having today?" Bonnie asked, trying to help Carolyn relax a little.

"I've always loved the Reuben sandwiches here," Carolyn answered. "I'll guess I'll have that and a cup of coffee."

"And I'll have my usual chef's salad and a glass of iced tea."

"I suppose eating rabbit food is how you keep that gorgeous figure of yours," Carolyn teased her.

"I'd hardly categorize myself as gorgeous," Bonnie murmured, her face coloring. "And I think running three miles a day has something to do with keeping my figure."

"And I'm chained to my desk with law books and briefs all day." Carolyn shook her head with a rueful smile. "I know I should get more exercise."

The waitress came with their drinks, and there was an awkward pause in the conversation. Then Bonnie decided to stop beating around the bush and get to the real purpose of the lunch.

"Dr. Wells and I went to visit JaMa'al Johnson at Juvenile Detention Monday afternoon."

Carolyn concentrated on stirring her coffee, her eyes not meeting Bonnie's.

"So, they *were* able to arrest him. What's going to happen to him? It's probably his first offense. He'll probably get off relatively easy."

"That's why I wanted to talk to you, Carolyn. I don't know *what's* going to happen to him, but they're going to charge him with felony offenses."

"They should."

"Oh, but Carolyn! If he's found guilty, he could spend the rest of his youth in a juvenile correctional facility!"

Carolyn turned to Bonnie, her face a mask of cold anger.

"You don't think JaMa'al ought to be punished for what he did? He destroyed thousands of dollars worth of property. *Donated* property, things that were meant for needy people, for people like *him*!"

"But he *didn't*!" Bonnie's tone was urgent. "He didn't do it!"

Carolyn looked at Bonnie as if she'd lost her mind.

"Are you forgetting that *I* was the one who came in and caught him in the act?"

"I'm not saying he wasn't there," Bonnie answered. "I'm just saying that he didn't act alone. He was put up to it by the members of a gang he was pressured to join."

"Is that what he told you?" Carolyn scoffed. "Don't let him dupe you, Bonnie. There wasn't anybody there but JaMa'al."

Bonnie took a deep breath.

"I know you're angry, Carolyn. You have every right to be. Anyone who'd seen Loaves and Fishes Monday *would* be angry. But that's just the point. JaMa'al isn't *big* enough to do all the damage that was done. It took Dr. Wells and me together to lift the shelves that had been knocked over, and they were empty! There's no way JaMa'al could've turned them over by himself when they were all filled with supplies. JaMa'al says that there were four other boys with him, and that he didn't know they were going to trash the place the way they did. He feels terrible about what happened."

"Does he feel terrible about all the filth he spray-painted on the walls of the office?"

Bonnie's face heated up at the memory of the words and the knowledge that there was no denying that JaMa'al had done that.

"I'm not sure why you're telling me all of this anyway," Carolyn said dismissively. "What difference does it make whether JaMa'al had help or not? He and his family have been getting assistance from the Benevolent Council for as long as I've been involved with it, probably longer. Yet he still joined a gang and helped them to vandalize the place. He *deserves* to be punished."

"That's one way of looking at it, certainly, but Dr. Wells and I truly believe that he's sorry to have been involved in this incident. We believe that he was essentially given no choice about whether he wanted to join the gang or not."

Carolyn was unrelenting, but avoided meeting Bonnie's eye.

"You want ketchup for those fries, honey?" asked their waitress as she set their food before them.

"No, thanks, just more coffee," Carolyn answered. When the waitress had refilled her cup, Carolyn continued, "JaMa'al should've gone to somebody for help. He should've called the police."

"His mother isn't married. It's not like he could go to his father for help. Who could he have turned to? And it's not exactly like people in his neighborhood have a great relationship with the police, either." Bonnie paused. *Here goes nothing*, she thought. "Actually, I was hoping that *you* might be able to help him."

Carolyn stared at Bonnie incredulously.

"You have *got* to be kidding. Well, I can tell you right now, that is *not* going to happen. Besides, he'll have a public defender appointed to him."

It was Bonnie's turn to be angry.

"Oh, Carolyn, you and I both know that most lawyers who get assigned to those cases only take them because they have to. They won't care about helping him!"

"And you think that I *do*?" She made a derisive noise.

"Is there no way you can find it in your heart to forgive him?" Bonnie pleaded.

"Can *you*? Can you forgive him for being a part of destroying so much that was intended for good? For biting the hand that has fed him so many times?

After everything the Benevolent Council has done for him and his family, you can *forgive* him for that?"

Bonnie prayed a silent prayer for the right words and forged ahead.

"I don't want you to think I'm preaching at you, Carolyn, but, yes, as a Christian, that's exactly what I'm trying to do. Jesus asked us to forgive those who do wrong to *us* because God has forgiven us for the things we do to wrong *Him*."

"Yeah, well, I guess that's why I've never really seen much sense to Christianity." Carolyn's eyes met Bonnie's now; they flashed with defiance. "All this 'turn the other cheek' stuff! What kind of logic is that? And another thing: I've never done anything to God. I consider myself a good person. I don't see that I've ever done anything so terrible that I need His forgiveness. Not that there's probably any God out there to do any forgiving, anyway."

Bonnie's heart pounded with the shock of what Carolyn was saying. She realized that, because she spent nearly all of her time among people who believed as she did, hearing someone voice sentiments so opposed to her own would naturally be jarring, but still, it was unnerving. She took another deep breath before beginning again.

"In a very real way," she said in a small voice, "you've wronged God in the worst way possible."

It was Carolyn's turned to be shocked.

"And how do you figure *that*?" she demanded.

Their waitress came by again with the coffee pot. She glanced curiously at Carolyn when she heard the vehemence in Carolyn's voice, then moved quietly away. Carolyn took no notice of anything but the anger she was directing at Bonnie.

"Hang on a second," Bonnie spoke with a soothing voice. "Let me just ask you something, okay?"

Carolyn just stared at her plate, chewing her sandwich glumly.

"I know you don't have any children of your own, but I know you've heard stories of children who, for whatever reason, grow up only to reject everything good their parents have taught them. They lead lives of degradation and self-destruction, sometimes dragging their parents down with them. You've heard story upon story of drug-addicted children who steal from their parents to supply their drug habits, grown children who—"

Carolyn held up her hand. "You can stop right there," she snapped. "We've got one in our own family. I've got a brother in California who only contacts my parents when he needs money. They've tried and tried to get him into rehab. He actually did enter a clinic once, and my parents paid for it!" Carolyn's face was livid. "Three days after he got out, he was snorting coke with his friends again."

"How do your parents feel about him?" Bonnie asked softly.

Carolyn sat for a moment and fumed. "That's the most maddening thing about it! They *believe* him every time he says he's going to go straight! They'd forgive him in a heartbeat of everything he's ever done, every penny he's ever stolen from them!"

"Do you think they ought to disown him? Forget that he's their son?"

Carolyn gave Bonnie a derisive look.

"I know that parents can't *forget* their own child. I just can't believe they're not as fed up with him as I am! He's a blight on the family name! Heck, yeah, I think they ought to disown his sorry hide."

"But they love him," Bonnie reminded her quietly. "And they want the best for him, even if he doesn't want it for himself. That's exactly how God feels about us."

"What do you mean?" Carolyn asked, suspicion in her voice.

"God created us. He sees us as His children. He loves us and wants to have a father-child relationship with us. He wants to forgive us when we do wrong. But if you reject God completely, if you deny His very existence, you're treating Him in essentially the same way your brother treats your parents."

"How *dare* you compare me to my brother!"

Bonnie held up a hand and shook her head.

"No, Carolyn, I know you haven't been that kind of child to your parents. I'm only saying that, in God's eyes, *none* of us is any great shakes—we've all done things that go against God's way, and some of us, like you, have gone so far as to reject God Himself. Is God supposed to forgive you for rejecting Him? You judge your brother for rejecting your parents. Don't you think that God will judge you for rejecting Him?"

Carolyn took another bite of her sandwich and chewed in stony silence. Finally, she sighed and turned to Bonnie.

"Look, I understand what you're trying to do and, in a way, I can appreciate it. But you're not going to change my mind about JaMa'al. He can just take his chances with a public defender."

Bonnie tried not to cry. Poor JaMa'al! What would become of him? She picked at her salad, but it was like swallowing wood. At length, Carolyn made another stab at conversation.

"I suppose they're going to find a replacement for me on the Benevolent Council."

"Actually, I'm going to replace you until they can find someone else."

"Gee, I'm really sorry. I hope you don't mind too much. It was just something I felt I had to do."

"No, I don't mind."

Bonnie didn't know what else to say. After striking out with her pleas for JaMa'al, she certainly wasn't going to broach the subject of Carolyn reconsidering her resignation just now. Carolyn glanced at her watch and gave a little start.

"Oh, goodness, look at the time! Listen, I hate to eat and run, but I've got a one-thirty deposition to get to."

"Sure, I understand. I'll take care of the check."

"Oh, no, Bonnie! You don't need to do that!"

"It's okay, really. Go on to your meeting."

Carolyn hesitated. "Bonnie, I hope there won't be any hard feelings. I'd like to get together with you again sometime."

"I'd like that, too, Carolyn."

And with a wistful last look back at Bonnie, Carolyn left the restaurant. Bonnie flagged the waitress down and got their lunch check. She lingered over the candy at the checkout counter and picked out a couple of treats for the boys, then headed out the door to go home. It was time to catch up on some of the work she hadn't been able to get to lately.

As she passed by the row of cars parked nearest the building, Bonnie heard a couple of light beeps of a horn. She looked into the car on her right and saw Carolyn Perkins waving at her frantically. Climbing out of the driver's seat, Carolyn called, "Bonnie! Am I glad to see you!"

"What's the matter, Carolyn? I thought you had a meeting."

"Oh, this stupid car! It's got a loose thingamajiggy somewhere, and it won't start. This is the third time this week! The guys at the dealership *swore* they'd taken care of the problem."

"Can I give you a lift somewhere?"

"Well, you could, but I'm not sure how I'd get back." She looked at her watch again. "Oh, man, I am going to be so late! And old Judge Harkins doesn't take kindly to tardy attorneys."

"Listen, I have an idea. Why don't you just drop me off at home, and you can borrow my car to go to the deposition. Then, when you get back, we can call the guys at the dealership and have them come out here to bring your car in."

"Oh, Bonnie, are you sure that'd be okay? I can't tell you how grateful I'd be!"

"I'd be glad to."

Even as she said it, Bonnie was conscious of resenting that Carolyn hadn't been more receptive to the idea of helping JaMa'al.

Ben and Josh had been home from school a while. Their homework was done, Ben was practicing the piano, and Joshua and a neighborhood friend were playing Army when Bonnie heard a knock at the kitchen door. Giving her spaghetti sauce a quick stir, Bonnie wiped her hands on a towel; it was probably Carolyn, returning her car. She opened the door to see Carolyn standing there, her eyes swollen from crying. In her hand, she held an audiocassette.

Smiling through her tears and holding the cassette up for Bonnie to see, Carolyn said, "You did this on purpose, didn't you?"

Bonnie frowned and tried to make out the printing on the cassette's label. Then she recognized it: Carolyn had been listening to Jeff Wells's sermon on forgiveness!

"Carolyn, I—"

But Carolyn stepped into the kitchen and put her arms around Bonnie.

"Oh, Bonnie, I think I know what you were talking about now! I feel like I've been so blind!"

Joshua poked his little blonde head into the kitchen and looked at Carolyn curiously. Carolyn saw him and gave a little wave. Bonnie told him, "Joshie, this is Miss Carolyn Perkins. She's a friend of Mommy's."

His curiosity satisfied, he remembered his manners enough to say, "Hi, I'm Joshua Callaway. See ya!" and returned to his playmate.

Bonnie and Carolyn exchanged giggles, then Bonnie said, "Tell me what happened, Carolyn."

They walked to the round-topped table in the breakfast area and sat down. Carolyn occupied the same chair that Anna Lee Adkinson had sat in the other night.

"After I left the deposition meeting, I headed back here to bring your car back to you," Carolyn began. "After two hours of grilling deponents about family assets and trust agreements, I was ready to listen to a little music, so I turned on the radio. Or at least I thought I was turning on the radio. I didn't know you had a cassette in the player."

"Oh, yes," Bonnie confirmed. "I'd been listening to it this morning before our lunch. I didn't get through all of it, though."

"No," Carolyn acknowledged softly, "but you *do* seem to have stopped in a most strategic place. Dr. Wells was just about to begin a sermon on the topic of forgiveness, the very thing we'd been talking about over lunch."

"Carolyn, you know I had no idea you'd be driving my car today—"

"No, Bonnie! I'm not upset! Far from it! I feel like I've had my eyes opened." Carolyn played with Bonnie's car keys, which she still held in her hands. "I kept thinking about what you said during lunch, about my rejecting God. Even during the deposition, it was always in the back of my mind. And I was so angry, because I've always had everything all sorted out in my head. I didn't need God to *explain* anything."

"But?" Bonnie encouraged her.

"But I was wrong. I *didn't* have an explanation for everything. Like, why should my parents still love a child who has treated them so despicably? Like, why would anybody want to forgive such a capricious act of vandalism like JaMa'al's?" She sighed and smiled a wan little smile. "Then I turned your radio knob and heard Jeff Wells speaking. I recognized his voice, so I guess I was a little curious. Instead of ejecting the tape and finding a radio station, I kept on listening. And wouldn't you know it, he launches into a story that sounds just like it could be about my brother, Randy."

Bonnie smiled because she knew Carolyn must mean the parable of the Prodigal Son.

"Dr. Wells told story after story: a man has a hundred sheep and he leaves ninety-nine to find just one lost one; a woman loses one of her ten coins and turns her whole house upside down to find it. The father rejoices because the son he thought was lost to him forever turned from the error of his ways."

Carolyn looked sadly into Bonnie's eyes. "Then I realized that I was like the older brother in the story. I've resented my parents' repeated attempts to save Randy because I thought he should never have strayed in the *first* place! I'd hardened my heart against him for what he's done to my parents. But now I see that all my parents care about is getting their son back. Nothing he's ever done would matter, if they could only have their son back."

She paused, then began again. "Dr. Wells kept driving home the point that the whole thing is about reconciliation, about repairing relationships."

Tears of joy welled in Bonnie's eyes. "Yes," Bonnie whispered, "reconciliation." Suddenly, she couldn't help wondering if there would ever be reconciliation between herself and Jeff Wells. It seemed so hopeless.

"I mean, it's so clear to me now," Carolyn continued. "How it's so easy to condemn—to judge, to retaliate. It's natural and human to react that way, but it never brings anybody back together. It's so much harder to *forgive* a wrong, to resist the temptation to punish or strike back.

"But if you condemn those who wrong you, you can't be reconciled to them." Carolyn paused and took a deep breath. "And if we don't forgive JaMa'al, we'll miss any opportunity we might've had to bring him back from the ones who are trying to influence him for bad. If no one helps him, he'll just be another angry soul who feels outcast."

"Oh, Carolyn, I can't tell you how glad I am to hear you say that! Does this mean that you'll represent JaMa'al?"

"Yes," Carolyn whispered. "I'll help JaMa'al if I can."

"Oh, Carolyn, this is so wonderful! I know that Father Blake and JaMa'al's mother will feel so much better when they find out that you'll be helping him!"

Bonnie grasped Carolyn's hand; JaMa'al wasn't the only one that Bonnie was concerned about: "But Carolyn," she began again, looking earnestly into Carolyn's eyes, "what about you?"

"Me?"

"What does all of this mean for you? You've been talking about Jesus and forgiveness all this time, as if now they have meaning for you. Is that true?"

"Yes, I think it is," Carolyn answered with a little frown. "I can't really explain it very well, but can I ask you something?" Carolyn hesitated, and Bonnie watched her expectantly. "Have you ever felt like God was talking to you?"

Bonnie's eyes widened. "Yes, I have," she answered cautiously. "Many times."

"I mean, every time I've ever heard anybody say anything like that, I've thought they were either lying for effect, or that they were somehow delusional."

Bonnie smiled with understanding. She knew that if a person has never sought God or even acknowledged Him, the movement of the Holy Spirit is all but unrecognizable to him or her.

"But Bonnie," Carolyn began again in a hushed voice, "when I was listening to that tape, and Dr. Wells told the story of the shepherd leaving the ninety-nine to look for the one lost sheep, I could hear a voice inside me saying, 'I'm looking for you, Carolyn. I'm looking for *you*.' I actually had chills when I heard it!"

When Bonnie heard Carolyn speak the words she'd heard from the Spirit, she felt a chill and shivered herself.

"I never thought I'd hear myself say something like this, Bonnie, but I honestly believe that God had this *planned*, somehow—that I was *meant* to hear that tape today. I…I feel like God has sought me out! Is that crazy?"

"No, Carolyn, it's not crazy. Not at all." Bonnie reached out to hold Carolyn's hand again. "I think you're exactly right. The Bible tells us that God knocks on the door of everyone's heart. But we have to hear the knock. It's up to us to respond, to open the door. I can't tell you what joy it gives me that you've heard God's call to you."

Bonnie held Carolyn's hands tightly.

"I know I've already asked one major favor of you today," Carolyn began tentatively, "but I'm going to ask you for another now."

"Anything, Carolyn. What can I do for you?"

"I think it's time I *did* let God find me. But I need to know more. I want to know what I have to do. I want to talk to you and Dr. Wells about what it means to be a Christian. I'd like to get together with him—tonight, if he's available. Would you call Dr. Wells and see if we can set an appointment to talk with him?"

CHAPTER 17

The surprise in Sandra's voice when Bonnie told her she wanted to speak with Jeff Wells about setting up an appointment with him was unmistakable, but she put Bonnie right through.

"Bonnie, how are you?"

Nor was there any mistaking the incredulity in Jeff's voice. Hadn't she just told him that she didn't want him speaking to her? Why on earth, then, was she calling him?

Carolyn stood not more than a couple of feet away, eagerly watching Bonnie's side of the conversation. Looking at Carolyn with an affectionate smile, she told Jeff, "I have some good news, Dr. Wells."

Carolyn smiled back at Bonnie.

"I can't deny that I could stand to hear some good news right about now," Jeff answered, and Bonnie cringed a little inside.

"Do you remember I told you about how upset Carolyn Perkins was when she saw what JaMa'al and his friends did at Loaves and Fishes?"

"Of course."

"Well, a lot has happened since then, and, to make a long story short, Carolyn has had quite a change of heart. In fact, she wants to get together with you to talk about what it means to become a Christian."

"With you *and* Bonnie!" Carolyn called out into the phone.

"Wow," breathed Jeff. "This is really something. I can be over in ten minutes."

"Oh!" Jeff never ceased to surprise Bonnie with the way he responded to things. "Well, that's really good of you, Dr. Wells, but, uh, Carolyn's been having some car trouble and I need to help her get it to the dealership for repairs. Would it be possible for you to come over after dinner? Say around seven?"

"I'll be there at seven sharp. Thanks for calling."

Bonnie couldn't tell him, of course, that, if it had been up to *her*, Carolyn would have done her own calling and met with Jeff by herself, so she just thanked him and hung up the phone.

"All set?" Carolyn's eyes were filled with hope.

"All set," Bonnie answered. And to herself, she thought, *Here we go again.*

The folks at the dealership's service department had been most accommodating when Carolyn had brought her car back in, issuing her a loaner until the "loose thingamajiggy" could be found and finally eradicated. Perhaps their sudden burst of eagerness to please had something to do with her mentioning the fact that she was an attorney.

Carolyn, who rarely cooked for herself, subsisting on carryout or delivery at her desk at work and late-evening restaurant fare more often than not, had enjoyed a plate of homemade spaghetti and meatballs with Bonnie and her boys. Ben, fascinated with the idea of Carolyn's profession, plied her with question after question, usually beginning with, "What if…?"

Finally, Carolyn grinned and said, "This is some of the finest cross-examination I've ever heard! You've got a career as a lawyer ahead of you, young man."

Seeming sorry to contradict her, Ben answered, "Thank you, but I'm pretty sure I'm going to be a pastor when I grow up. One day, I want to be just like Dr. Wells, the pastor of our church. Do you know him?"

Bonnie smiled at Carolyn, then told Ben, "Miss Carolyn was on the Benevolent Council, so, yes, she know Dr. Wells. In fact, guys, Pastor Jeff is going to be over in just a little while to visit with Miss Carolyn and me."

Josh's eyes lit up.

"Pastor Jeff is coming over? Hot dog!"

After excusing himself from the table, he ran to his room to find his latest building block creation to show the pastor when he came. Bonnie sighed inwardly. Only a short couple of weeks ago, she had shared her boys' admiration for Jeff Wells and would also have been pleased, if not quite as excited as they, to be receiving a visit from the pastor. Now, it seemed that every encounter with him was an event to be endured, not enjoyed. The bell rang, signaling his arrival, and Ben and Josh raced each other to the front door.

Carolyn turned to Bonnie with a smile. "Looks like we've got some real Jeff Wells fans, eh?"

Bonnie could only manage a wan little smile.

After greeting Ben warmly and praising Josh's homemade starship, Jeff looked up and smiled at Bonnie and Carolyn.

"Good evening, ladies."

His eyes held Bonnie's for a moment, then he walked over to the kitchen.

"I've made some coffee, and I've got banana bread," Bonnie told him. "Would you care for some?"

For a split second, he thought about expressing disappointment at her not having another chocolate mousse pie to serve, but thought better of it. "That'd be great."

Jeff then turned to Carolyn as Bonnie went to the living room to set the boys up with one of their favorite videos and then to the kitchen to serve dessert. Carolyn told Jeff the story of her lunch with Bonnie and how she had later borrowed Bonnie's car and heard the sermon on forgiveness. Given Bonnie's terse speech to him the day before about not wanting him to speak to her, Jeff couldn't help but wonder at the idea of Bonnie actually listening to a tape recording of him, but he made no comment on it. Still, Bonnie hadn't missed his curious glance at her when Carolyn mentioned the tape.

"I guess you could say I listened in spite of myself," Carolyn said. "I'm sure you know that, up until now, I've been, if not exactly an atheist, then at least agnostic."

"Yes, I'd gathered as much," Jeff told her, kindness in his voice. "Do you feel that that's changing?"

Carolyn glanced over at Bonnie. There was encouragement in Bonnie's eyes.

"I…As I told Bonnie, I had the strangest experience when I was listening to the stories you were telling. And, believe me, I've *always* been skeptical when I've heard other people say this kind of thing. But it was like I could hear God *speaking* to me." She watched Jeff's face, as if she were afraid he'd scoff at her.

"Christians call that the movement of the Holy Spirit," Jeff assured her. "And different people experience it in different ways. When people say, 'I heard the voice of God,' or 'The Lord said to me,' it's so easy for those who've never experienced it to misunderstand. Rarely is anyone talking about an actual, audible voice."

Carolyn hung on his every word.

"It's more like an assurance inside, that either you're making the right decision about something, or that the Lord is leading you to do something. The more you hear it, and the more you attend to it, the more certain you become that what you're hearing really is the voice of God. In the case of new believers, it's the very presence of God, the sense of being persuaded that the words of the message of salvation are true, a sense that God is calling to them."

"Yes!" Carolyn almost shouted. "That's exactly what I said to Bonnie! I felt like someone was saying to me, 'I'm looking for *you*, Carolyn.' You know, when you were talking about the lost sheep that the shepherd goes off to find."

"The funny thing," Jeff told her with an understanding smile, "is that people hear the voice of God all the time, but they just don't know it, or they refuse to acknowledge it. Whenever a person's conscience pricks him at having committed a sin, I believe that's the voice of God. Whenever we experience the overwhelming grandeur of nature, that sense of smallness we feel as we contemplate the vastness of God's creation, that's the voice of God reminding us that He is the author of all things. It's just that most people become very adept at ignoring or denying what God has to say to them."

"I can certainly relate to that," Carolyn acknowledged ruefully, looking at her hands in her lap. "You want to think, 'Oh, well, God is okay for people who don't know any better, but if they knew as much as I did, if they were better educated or had experienced the same things I had, they'd know better.' Then that moment of clarity comes, when all the things you've heard about God suddenly ring true. Not only do they ring true, but you realize that they are all *meant* for you! I was thunderstruck."

"Jesus said that there is rejoicing in heaven when a lost soul finds the way back to God," Jeff told her, a warm smile in his eyes. "I know that there is rejoicing in heaven tonight."

He looked at Bonnie then, and she smiled back at him, in spite of herself, for sheer joy at what Carolyn was experiencing. Seeing Jeff's expression change at her smile, as if she were implying something more than happiness for Carolyn, she averted her eyes. With barely concealed disappointment, Jeff turned back to Carolyn.

"Would you like to pray with us here, tonight, to verbalize your decision to become a believer?"

"Is that all I have to do? Is there anything special I have to say?"

Jeff shook his head with a little smile. "Say what's on your heart, Carolyn. Tell the Lord that you want this to be just the first of a lifetime of prayers to Him, that you want to know what it means to be a Christian and that you want Him to teach you. Do you understand what it means to ask Jesus to be your Savior?"

Carolyn frowned a little. "I...I think so. I think it just means that now I know I *need* one, that I need to be forgiven of my sins just like everyone else, whereas, before, I really didn't believe that at all. Is it really that easy?"

Bonnie answered this time. "It's really that easy, Carolyn. God has promised us that any who seek Him will find Him, that those who turn to God for forgiveness will never be turned away."

Tears of joy and gratitude shone in Carolyn's eyes.

"Could one of you start for me?" Carolyn smiled sheepishly. "I'm kind of new at this."

"I'd be glad to," Jeff murmured. Then, without saying anything, he grasped Carolyn's hand and laid their joined hands atop the table. She looked a little surprised at first, then she saw him reach for Bonnie's hand to hold it, too. When she saw the look that Jeff and Bonnie exchanged as his fingers folded around hers, she wondered fleetingly if there were more to Bonnie and Jeff than Bonnie was letting on. Completing the circle, Carolyn moved to hold Bonnie's hand, too.

"Dear God," Jeff began, "we come to You tonight with grateful hearts because our friend Carolyn has come to know You. One of Your lost sheep is coming back into the fold. Be with her in the coming weeks and months, dear Lord, that she would come to know more and more fully with each passing day the joy of living with You in her heart, that she would know the joy of Your salvation."

There was a pause and Jeff and Bonnie could feel Carolyn taking a deep breath.

"God," she began in a whisper, "I feel as though I almost have no right to ask Your forgiveness after I've been so unforgiving with others." She sniffled a little, but went on. "I want to thank You, though, for being a God of forgiveness, for allowing me to hear the voice of Your Holy Spirit calling me to You.

"I *do* want to know You, dear God," she continued. "I do want to know what it really means to be a Christian. I want to know what You've said to us through the Bible; I want to learn how to pray. If Your promise is true, that You won't turn away those who sincerely seek You, then I know You'll help me, that You'll teach me. I thank You, dear God. I thank You."

There was another pause when Carolyn's prayer ended, and then the three of them opened their eyes. The presence of God there in Bonnie's kitchen was almost palpable.

"What you've done tonight is very important," Jeff told Carolyn softly.

He still held both their hands on top of the table. Bonnie wanted badly to pull hers away, but she wasn't sure how Carolyn would take it. This was Carolyn's moment; Bonnie didn't want to spoil any part of it for her.

"But it's just the beginning of what will be a lifelong process of developing a relationship with God. You'll want to spend time in God's word every day, spend time in prayer, form friendships with others who share your beliefs, and attend worship services."

"You're not trying to turn me into a Baptist already, are you?" Carolyn teased.

"I will be glad to see you attend any church you feel at home in, Carolyn. I mean that sincerely."

"I know you do," she assured him, "but actually, I think I would like to go to a church, at least at first, where I already know someone. Foster Road Baptist has classes for single adults, doesn't it?"

"Yes, it does," answered Bonnie. "I'd be happy to meet you there Sunday. We could get started there together."

Jeff looked at Bonnie with raised eyebrows at this remark, but said nothing.

"I think I'll take you up on that."

Carolyn smiled warmly. Squeezing Jeff's and Bonnie's hands and then glancing at her watch, she added, "Oh, wow, look at how late it's getting! It must be close to the boys' bed time, isn't it?"

Jeff didn't let go of Bonnie's hand when Carolyn unclasped her hand from his, so Bonnie slowly pulled her hand from Jeff's. He glanced briefly at their hands, then at Bonnie. Her eyes met his, but she was careful to keep expression out of them.

"Yes, I'll need to get them started on their nightly routine soon," Bonnie answered.

"Then I'll just let myself out."

The three of them stood. Carolyn grasped Jeff's right hand again shook it.

"Thank you so much for meeting with us on such short notice, Dr. Wells."

"Please, call me Jeff," he told her, glancing at Bonnie as if to remind her that he had made the same request of her not so long ago. "And, trust me, I'd *gladly* have meetings like this every night of the week."

Carolyn looked at Bonnie and could only smile with gratitude. "I'd thank you, Bonnie, but I have a feeling I owe you a debt I can never repay." She hugged Bonnie soundly.

"You don't owe me anything," Bonnie told her. "Your prayer tonight was all the thanks I'll ever need."

With a last smile and wave, Carolyn let herself out of the kitchen door.

There was a moment of awkward silence between Bonnie and Jeff in which they avoided meeting each other's eyes.

"I'd like to thank you for coming over tonight, too," Bonnie murmured. And for Carolyn's sake, she meant it.

"I was glad to do it."

Without looking at Jeff, Bonnie moved to the living room and called out, "Okay, guys, bedtime! Jammies on! Teeth brushed!"

Luckily, the credits of the video were rolling, so there were no protests to finish watching the end of the story. As if a sudden thought had struck him, Josh turned to Bonnie and asked, "Mom, would it be okay if Pastor Jeff tucked us in tonight?"

"Oh! Well, honey, I don't think—"

"I'd be glad to, if your mother doesn't mind," answered Jeff, now looking to Bonnie for her reaction.

Bonnie tried not to let her displeasure show. She felt she had no choice but to acquiesce, since he'd made the offer to the boys, but resented Jeff's not having consideration enough for her to refuse.

"Well, if he doesn't mind…"

"Get yourselves ready for bed, guys," Jeff said to the boys. "I'll be there in a minute."

And off they ran, as eager as Bonnie had ever seen them to be going to bed. She sighed deeply and turned back towards the kitchen to begin clearing their coffee cups and cake plates from the table. Jeff was behind her and picked up a cup and saucer himself. Bonnie looked up at him, finally allowing a little of her annoyance to show.

"You really needn't trouble yourself," she told him.

Seeing the look in her eyes, he silently put the dishes back on the table and headed to the boys' bedrooms.

Oh, dear Lord, Bonnie prayed, *how long will this hurt have to go on?*

When the dishes were loaded into the dishwasher, Bonnie headed back to see what progress was being made on bedtime. Arriving at Ben's doorway, she saw Jeff sitting on the bed, a boy on either side of him, reading a story out of one of Josh's Bible story books. Ben was sitting very close to Jeff, listening intently to the story, and Josh had leaned his head against Jeff's arm.

The scene immediately brought tears to Bonnie's eyes. Not only did it evoke memories of when Bill had been the man in between the boys, but, for a reason she couldn't explain even to herself, it brought back the feel of Jeff's arms around her last Friday night as he'd kissed her on his front porch. How could things have gone so far astray between them?

"Time for your prayers," Bonnie managed to say.

Ben got up and reached for Bonnie's hand and they walked over to the bed together. Jeff stood and held one of Josh's hands, while Josh reached out to hold his mother's other hand. Bonnie was at once relieved and disappointed that Jeff wasn't holding her hand again.

"Would you say a prayer for us tonight?" Josh asked Jeff.

"Sure," he said with a smile and a wink at the young boy. "Dear Father, thank You for loving us enough to be our savior. Help us to love each other as You loved us; help us to forgive each other as You forgave us. We pray in Your Name, amen."

Bonnie felt a flash of anger, as if that last part of Jeff's prayer had been directed at her. How dare he use a prayer to remind her that she hadn't really forgiven him? She felt her face burning with the shame of knowing that he was right, that she *should* be forgiving him, but she just couldn't let go of her hurt and resentment. Jeff pulled the covers up over Ben, then took Josh by the hand and led him to his bed.

"Goodnight, boys," he called to them when he had turned out Josh's light.

"'Night, Pastor Jeff. 'Night, Mom," they answered.

Bonnie and Jeff walked in silence into the living room. As they stood at the front door, he told her, "That was a real treat. It's been years since Jeff Junior's needed to be tucked in."

"I know it was a treat for them, too," she conceded, not meeting his eyes.

If she looked him in the eye, she was afraid she would—she was afraid she would *melt* and give up her anger and forgive him, as she knew deep in her heart she ought to do. She knew it was perverse logic, but how could she forgive him when he had just reminded her that she *hadn't*? Pride and resentment kept her arms folded and her eyes glued to the floor.

Jeff stood at the door a moment longer, hoping Bonnie would look up at him. If only she would meet his eyes, give him *some* indication that she was willing to forgive him for the stupid way he had acted.

But she didn't.

He had blown it, and he had blown it for good.

"Goodnight, Bonnie," was all he could manage to say.

When the door closed and the deadbolt was turned, the tears began to flow, and Bonnie wasn't sure then with whom she was angrier: Jeff or herself.

CHAPTER 18

Jeff looked in the mirror and adjusted his bow tie. When he was a seminary student, all those years ago, it would never have occurred to him that a pastor would need his own tuxedo. As one of Chandler City's most prominent and visible pastors, though, he was always being invited to charity and social events and banquets like the one being held by the Seniors tonight. And nearly all of them required formal attire. It had long ago ceased to be cost-effective to rent a tux for each event he attended.

As the pastor, he was more or less obligated to attend just about every function held at church, unless he was ill or had other, more pressing business. And he had been a pastor long enough to know, too, that if he *were* to have other business that kept him away too much, people would be offended. In the past, the Seniors Banquet had always been a fun, lighthearted affair that he and Terri had enjoyed going to. When he had attended his first one without her last year, it had been painful.

Missing Terri, however, wasn't the source of his lack of enthusiasm for the evening ahead: it just grated on him that Clara Adkinson was so obviously trying to play matchmaker between him and her daughter. He had hinted as broadly as he could that, while Anna Lee was certainly a nice enough young woman, he simply wasn't interested in dating her. And it was equally clear that Anna Lee wasn't interested in him. Why couldn't Clara see that?

The more he thought about it, though, the more he suspected that Clara had known Bonnie Callaway wasn't really going out with that Preston Hardy guy; she had only been trying to upset him enough to get him to stop seeing Bonnie. Maybe he was just mad at himself for having believed her so easily. He had never really known Clara to be a gossip, though, and he had been just nervous enough about beginning a new relationship with someone that he had swallowed everything Clara had told him without asking nearly enough questions. As naïve as it seemed to him now, it hadn't even occurred to him at the time that Clara would stoop so low in pursuing her daughter-marrying agenda.

So here he was, slated to spend an evening in which Clara smugly thought she had set up an actual date for him and Anna Lee. How he hoped that Clara didn't have the nerve to tell anyone that he and Anna Lee were "together." There was enough gossip flying as it was.

Before heading down to Fellowship Hall for the banquet, he stopped by his office to see if Sandra had finished typing up some of the correspondence he had dictated; if she had, he would take it home that evening and do some editing. As he sifted through the papers on his desk, he heard a soft knock at his door. He looked up to see a young woman dressed in an evening gown that would have been fashionable in about 1948. Nevertheless, she looked stunning—and vaguely familiar.

"Dr. Wells? I was wondering if I might have a word with you before we went in to the banquet."

He recognized the voice immediately.

"Anna Lee?" He couldn't hide his astonishment.

"I'm quite a sight, aren't I?" she said, looking embarrassed. "My mom really went all the way with this Rosemary Clooney thing. I don't have the blonde hair, though."

"Wow," Jeff finally managed to say. "I...I hardly recognized you. You look...you look great!"

And he meant it. Anna Lee usually took so few pains with her looks that when she did, the effect was almost startling. Then Jeff recovered himself.

"Please, come in and tell me what's on your mind."

Anna Lee sat down on the sofa at the front of his office and folded her white-gloved hands in her lap.

"This is pretty embarrassing," she began, "and way, way overdue, but I thought it was high time I got around to apologizing to you."

Jeff was at a loss. He had hardly ever had a conversation alone with Anna Lee (her mother was never far away), let alone had cross words with her.

"'Apologizing'?"

"Surely it's been as obvious to you as it has to me that my mother's been shamelessly trying to interest you in her daughter!" Anna Lee's smile was at once teasing yet sympathetic. Jeff looked down, embarrassed himself now.

"I…I don't know what to say."

"You don't have to say anything. I just wanted you to know that I haven't been a willing party to any of my mother's machinations. I've *never* had any designs on you." She said it with such emphasis that she immediately gasped and brought her hands to her mouth. "Oh! I didn't mean that the way it sounded! I…I mean, I think you're a wonderful person and one of the best pastors this church has ever had, but…"

Jeff raised his hands and laughed, his eyes bright with merriment.

"It's okay, I understand completely. No offense taken." He had come to sit in one of the wingback chairs across from the sofa. "Besides, didn't I understand Tom Givens to say that you and he attended Samford at the same time? That wouldn't make you more than about—"

"Twenty-seven," Anna Lee confirmed. "I won't be twenty-eight until next January."

"I'd be practically robbing the cradle," Jeff teased her mildly.

Anna Lee grinned. "That's just what I was telling Bonnie—" and again she gasped at her own careless words, covering her mouth again.

"Bonnie?" Jeff was all interest. "How did this topic come up in conversation with Bonnie Callaway?"

Anna Lee's face was aflame. "Let's just say…Boy, what an idiot I am!" Then she gave up trying to think of a little white lie to tell him. "I don't know how much of this you already know, but my mother hasn't exactly played fair in her little matchmaking campaign." Anna Lee's expression turned serious. "Her behavior toward Bonnie has been as embarrassing to me as her unabashed attempts to get you interested in me."

Jeff watched her intently.

"Somehow, my mother got the idea that you were interested in going out with Bonnie Callaway. Which, by the way, I don't happen to think is a bad idea, but nobody asked *me*."

She looked at Jeff, who said nothing, smiled at him, and took a deep breath.

"Anyway, I guess she saw the two of you together at the Coffee Shoppe after one of your Benevolent Council meetings or something, and it was all she could talk about for days!"

"She accused us of being 'out on the town' together," Jeff confided with a rueful smile. It had almost been comical at the time; it was anything but, now.

"Then, apparently she saw Bonnie standing with some guy the very next day at the Coffee Shoppe, and you could just see the wheels turning. Seems like by the end of the week, or maybe it was last Saturday, she had decided that you should know about this 'other man,' as she kept calling him."

"It was Saturday morning," Jeff informed her dryly.

Anna Lee looked at him for a moment, puzzled, then continued: "Well, when I found out that not only had she told you Bonnie was dating this guy, but that she had also hinted broadly that Bonnie had been more than a little intimate with him, I was just beside myself. She knew Bonnie wasn't dating that guy."

Jeff still made no answer, but she could see by his expression that he was thunderstruck.

"Finally, last Sunday night, I got up the nerve to go see Bonnie and apologize for my mother's behavior." She paused a moment, looking disgusted. "Seems that I'm doing a lot of that lately—apologizing for my mother's behavior."

"I'm sure you couldn't have stopped her if you'd tried," Jeff sympathized.

Anna Lee laughed derisively. "*That's* an understatement! But I wanted Bonnie to know how bad I felt about the whole thing, so I told her what my mother's real motivation was."

"And what did she say?"

Jeff hated gossip; he had been its victim often enough. But he knew, too, that, with Bonnie not speaking to him, any information he got about her would have to come from outside sources; he hung on Anna Lee's every word. Anna Lee looked momentarily uncomfortable as she remembered again how she had poured her heart out to Bonnie about her old college sweetheart; she wasn't about to tell Jeff Wells *that* part.

Choosing her words carefully this time, she said, "Bonnie understood that sixteen years is quite a difference in our ages."

Jeff smiled at Anna Lee's unwillingness to insult him, even inadvertently, a second time.

"So, I'm officially letting you off the hook of having a 'date' with me tonight, okay?"

"I don't know," he said, eyeing Anna Lee appreciatively, "I can think of worse things than spending an evening with you."

Anna Lee blushed and stood up quickly.

"See you in Fellowship Hall."

As Jeff walked down the corridor that approached Fellowship Hall, the rumble of voices and the tinkle of dinnerware grew louder. He rounded the corner and saw a knot of people, all dressed in their best finery, talking and laughing. From behind, he thought vaguely that he recognized the raven hair of Sherry Niles, but why would she be at a Seniors function?

"Oh, Dr. Wells! There you are!" Ruth Newton was the first to greet him.

The other people standing in the group turned to look at him, including Sherry Niles. Sherry was so beautiful; in the midst of ordinary-looking people, hers was a larger-than-life presence. She smiled radiantly at him—a little too radiantly for his comfort. With a pang of guilt, he remembered the words of admonition Jack had spoken to him the other morning: "You're aware that Bonnie thinks you're dating her, but you've made no attempt to set her straight." With an inward grimace, he forced himself back to the present.

"Evening, folks!" he called. "Ruth, I'm so glad you decided to come."

There was an unspoken message of empathy in his eyes, and she returned his look with gratitude in her own.

"Dr. Wells," Ruth began, turning to the distinguished older gentleman standing next to her, "I have someone I'd like you to meet. Dr. Jeffery Wells, this is my good friend, Henry Blankenship. Henry, this is our pastor, Dr. Jeff Wells."

Jeff held out his hand to shake Henry's. "Pleased to meet you, sir."

Just then, out of the corner of his eye, Jeff saw Clara Adkinson standing behind Ruth. He watched as Anna Lee leaned over, standing next to her mother, to whisper something in Clara's ear. Clara's face clouded with thinly disguised anger. What on earth had Anna Lee told her?

"Henry is the president of Chandler City Bank," Ruth told him. "He and Art were old hunting buddies. He's a longtime member of Covenant United Methodist."

Ah, Chandler City Bank! That must explain Sherry's presence.

As if to confirm his thoughts, Sherry herself spoke up: "Mr. Blankenship is my boss, Dr. Wells. He was kind enough to invite me tonight."

"Oh, so you two know each other, do you?" Ruth asked, interest written all over her face.

Sherry looked a little embarrassed at Ruth's question and glanced at Jeff as if for support. Tearing his eyes away from Clara and Anna Lee, Jeff explained, "Ms. Niles and I have a mutual friend who encouraged her to attend the Singles Sunday School class here and participate in the Singles' social activities. I met her after last Sunday's service."

"Oh, I see," said Ruth. "Well, when I told Henry about the banquet, he asked me if I thought it might be something she'd enjoy, too. I can't imagine why you young folks want to spend time with us old codgers, but we're glad to have you."

"Sherry's kind of new in town," added Henry, "and I thought it would be a shame if she sat at home by herself while there was good food and good fellowship to be had."

There was a mixture of affection and gratitude in the look that Sherry gave Mr. Blankenship.

"I couldn't agree more," said Jeff.

He put a light hand on the small of Sherry's back and led the group into the dining hall. Even as he did, he found himself wondering what Bonnie Callaway was doing on this Friday night.

Asking the blessing on the dinner was almost a ceremonial duty for Jeff at functions like this, but, having done it, he could more or less relax and enjoy the evening's festivities until it was time to dismiss everyone with a closing prayer. Or at least, that was the theory. But how could anyone enjoy himself with Clara Adkinson fairly scowling at him two seats away?

It was more or less natural, he thought defensively, for Sherry Niles to sit next to him; he had led her into the room. And Henry Blankenship had sat next to Sherry, and Ruth Newton next to Henry. Then, looking Jeff pointedly in the eyes, Anna Lee sat next to Ruth. That was when the scowling began. Not only was he sitting next to Sherry Niles (or Sherry was sitting next to *him*, depending on how you looked at it), but he was a country mile away from Anna Lee. Clara sat down primly next to her daughter, shooting Jeff a look that was honey on its surface but pure venom in her eyes. Jeff sighed inwardly and knew that it was going to be another long night.

To Clara's credit, she really *had* lined up quite an evening. The food, which had been catered by the ladies at Grabbabite and not provided by the more pedestrian talents of Foster Road's kitchen help, was elegant and delectable. And there was apparently no small measure of acting talent within this group, as an ensemble cast presented a delightful chapter of the old radio drama, *The Shadow*.

The true highlight of the evening, though, was Anna Lee. At some point, when the room had been darkened for the dramatic performance, she had slipped away from the table. When the lights went down again, a voice mimicking a radio announcer of old spoke in hushed tones:

"Ladies and gentlemen, I give you the vocal talents of the lovely Miss Rosemary Clooney."

A murmur went through the crowd as a spotlight went on above the make-shift stage erected for the event. There stood Anna Lee, looking as beautiful as anyone in the room had ever seen her look. A transformation seemed to come over her and, for a moment, Jeff believed, she *was* Rosemary Clooney. Or some famous, wildly popular singer who had captured the hearts of America. She opened her mouth to sing and Jeff could tell that nearly everyone in the room was transported back in time. Her voice floated over and around them like a rich, velvet cloud. When the last sultry note of "As Time Goes By" ended, there was a hushed pause before a thunderous burst of applause.

Anna Lee seemed taken aback by their response and smiled shyly as the adulation washed over her. Then the piano accompanying her began a lilting introduction to "Come On'A My House," and the crowd smiled up at her and tapped their feet. Jeff looked around the room: Clara seemed momentarily to have forgotten her pique with him and was basking in obvious pride for her daughter.

As his eyes scanned the dining hall, he saw something at the back of the room that made him start almost visibly: Bonnie Callaway, unnoticed by a crowd that only had eyes for Anna Lee, was leaning against the entryway watching Anna Lee herself! She wore blue jeans and a matching denim blouse, so she was obviously not there as an official banquet attendee. When the lights were lowered again for another slow song, Jeff leaned over to Sherry to excuse himself and slipped away from the table.

Making his way around the periphery of the room and walking as noise-lessly as he could, Jeff was by Bonnie's side before she even knew that he was approaching. He touched her elbow lightly and she jumped with a gasp. The people sitting at the table nearest them turned at the sound; they looked at Bonnie curiously when they saw how she was dressed.

"Sorry," Jeff whispered. "I didn't mean to startle you."

Bonnie just stared at him, her eyes wide. He searched her face earnestly for a moment, then turned to glance at Anna Lee.

"She's really fabulous, isn't she?"

"Oh, yes," Bonnie whispered back. "When she told me she'd be singing Rosemary Clooney songs tonight, I promised myself to try to break away from the boys' activity to look in on her. She's really outdone herself tonight."

In the back of his mind, Jeff vaguely recalled that the school-aged children were having their once-a-month video and popcorn night in another part of the building.

"I've always wondered why she never joined the choir."

"Good question," answered Jeff.

Bonnie was talking to him! For just this moment, she wasn't scowling at him or reminding him of what a jerk he'd been. He *had* to keep it going!

"Did you hear 'As Time Goes By?'"

A kind of dreamy look came over Bonnie's face and Jeff had an almost overwhelming urge to lean over, as he had last Friday evening, and plant a soft kiss on those lips that were suddenly so close to his again.

"Yes," she whispered.

Then there was applause and the lights began to come on.

"Oops! I've got to get out of here before everybody sees me in these blue jeans!"

Like Cinderella running from her prince at midnight, Bonnie slipped quickly away and was down the hall before Jeff could protest.

As he turned back to face the crowd in the dining hall again, he saw, much to his embarrassment, that almost every eye in the room was on him. Then he realized it was time for the closing prayer. For the sake of speed, he walked through the middle of the room this time, climbed the steps of the stage two at a time, and stood at the microphone.

"I don't remember when I've enjoyed an evening more. Anna Lee, you were sensational."

He held his hand out and Anna Lee joined him onstage, taking his hand shyly. The crowd burst into appreciative applause again. He glanced briefly at Clara; was the smug look on her face there because Anna Lee had performed so well, or because now he was holding her hand?

As Anna Lee slipped away, Jeff bowed his head and prayed the benediction. He said the briefest goodbyes at each table he thought he could get away with as he made his way back across the center of the room, then ran up to the second floor where the children's activity had been held. Jenny Pierce and a couple of other single parents who had stayed behind to clean up stray popcorn and rearrange tables and chairs looked up when he came to the door, but the activity itself was over. Knowing it was probably futile before he got started, he gave a quick smile and wave to Jenny and her companions, then ran back down the stairs. As he scanned the parking lot, he saw that he had arrived just in time to see the back of Bonnie's white minivan turning the corner as she headed for home.

With a frustrated sigh, Jeff returned to his office, picked up the papers Sandra had typed for him, and headed home to do some editing while he waited for Jeff Junior to return home from his date with Amanda Summers.

CHAPTER 19

It was Sunday again, and time to go to church. This week, though, Bonnie wasn't going, as she had last week, not knowing what would hit her during the course of the day. Although it was true, she wasn't *entirely* sure what to expect from her fellow church members, at least today she knew that there was something to wonder *about*. If people gave her inquiring glances or asked prying questions, she would be braced for it. And she did wonder: had word gotten around that she and Jeff weren't dating after all? If it had, surely people would be merciful enough not to ask her why. As she had done the whole previous week with each new awkward encounter with Jeff, she prayed for strength and grace.

And there *were* a couple of bright spots to look forward to on this otherwise beautiful spring Sunday morning: first, Carolyn Perkins had promised to meet her at the Singles Sunday School department. Carolyn had called Bonnie several times since their meeting with Jeff Thursday night, filled with questions: With so many different versions of the Bible, which one should she choose? Did it matter if she used "thee" and "thou" when she prayed? What could she expect at Sunday School?

Bonnie was unsure of the answer to that last question herself. She had called Nancy McLin, her Sunday School teacher from the ladies' class, to tell her that she'd decided to attend a Singles class for a while; she didn't want Nancy to find out from anyone else. The understanding with which Nancy received Bonnie's notice only added to the ambivalence she felt about making the change in the first place: Nancy had been a wonderful teacher; Bonnie would really miss her. The upside, though, was that the Singles met on the opposite side of the Education Building from where the married adult classes met. This would, she hoped, greatly reduce the chance that she would have to endure as many of the remarks and looks as she had the previous week.

The other thing she was looking forward to this morning was Ben's plan to make his profession of faith. She had thought about informing Jeff of Ben's intentions when he had been over to talk with Carolyn Thursday night, but she hadn't wanted to prolong his visit after he'd said goodnight to the boys. Bonnie knew, though, that this decision of Ben's would occasion another visit to Jeff's office, probably that very afternoon. Even as she prepared for Sunday School, she was psyching herself up for that encounter.

As she sat at her dressing table, she thought back on how Jeff had come to her at the Seniors Banquet, almost out of nowhere it had seemed at the time. She had seen him sitting with Sherry Niles. Why, then, had he made such a point of coming over to talk to her? Did her forgiveness mean that much to him? Bonnie doubted it.

How he could date Sherry so openly? Bonnie wondered. Ruth Newton knew that Sherry and Preston were still legally married; if Clara Adkinson didn't know, it was only a matter of time before she found out. Clara had tried to have Bonnie removed from her roles of leadership for the mistaken notion that she was dating two men at once, even though both of those men, as far as Clara knew, were single. What would Clara do if she found out that the pastor of their church was seeing someone who was married? There could be fireworks! What was Jeff thinking?

She *was* glad that it had been dark in the dining hall Friday night; Jeff couldn't see the red that had stained her cheeks as he had stood so near to whisper his conversation with her. Why did his nearness bother her so much? How could she be so angry with him and still feel so disappointed each time she parted from him without so much as having touched his hand? She fought back tears that came far too easily these days.

Maybe he was crazy, but Jeff actually took encouragement from his brief encounter with Bonnie Friday night. With no apparent acrimony or recriminations, she had spoken with him; however briefly, she had *spoken* with him! His only regret was that it couldn't have been for longer, that she had felt self-conscious enough about her dress to want to leave when the lights came on. She always looked beautiful to him. And whenever he stood close to her, as he had then, that scent she wore—musky and lemony at the same time…Oh, he smelled it in his dreams. He closed his eyes and sighed with a faint smile. *Enough daydreaming*, he thought. *Time to go to church.*

Opportunities to do the things *he* wanted to do at church were pretty limited on Sunday mornings. Like a bee buzzing from flower to flower, he tried to make at least an appearance in as many adult Sunday School classes as he could. Since it was a part of his duties anyway, he mused, he would just have to see that one of those appearances was in the Single Adult department, wouldn't he? After all, if Bonnie raised any objections about his presence (which he couldn't believe she would really do), he could always say that he wanted to check in on Carolyn Perkins and Sherry Niles (which wasn't entirely untrue, anyway). He just had to believe, though, that in time, Bonnie could forgive him. And if she could forgive him...

Carolyn Perkins was like a fish out of water on her first morning in the Singles Sunday School class. She was acutely aware that she was in a room full of people who, not so very long ago, would have been the object of her disdain. Neither of her parents had attended or brought her and her brother to church when they were children; she had virtually no background to help her through this experience.

What would these people say if they knew how she used to feel about Christians? She still knew so little about the matter; what if they asked her all kinds of questions she couldn't answer? What if, God forbid, they should ask her to pray aloud? What if they ridiculed her for being so ignorant of the Bible? Would she look like a complete idiot to them? But every person she met welcomed her and seemed glad to see her; she was heartened and gratified at how warmly she was received.

"Hi," Bonnie greeted her, an affectionate smile on her face. Carolyn was relieved to see her friend enter the room. "I see you got here a little early."

"Yes," Carolyn answered with a wry grin. "It's *amazing* how punctual you can be when you have a car that's working properly."

"What's the outlook on getting your own car back?"

"They're not *sure*," Carolyn answered, feigning surprise. "They think they may have *missed* something the first time they looked at it! Imagine that."

Bonnie could see nervousness in Carolyn's eyes even through her attempts to poke fun at the car dealership. Taking one of Carolyn's hands and giving it a squeeze, Bonnie told her, "I'm so glad you decided to come. I was afraid you might back out. You're going to do just fine."

"Don't think the thought didn't cross my mind! But this is something I really want to do. I'm glad you're here, though. I feel like I stick out like a sore thumb."

When Bonnie introduced Carolyn to Tom Givens, the Singles Minister, she mentioned that Carolyn was a new Christian. At first, he had stood still, his eyes wide. Then, he grasped Carolyn's hand and told her how wonderful he thought it was and that, if there was any way he could help her, to please let him know.

After he had left, Carolyn leaned over to Bonnie and asked, "Why is he making such a fuss over me?"

"Well, Carolyn, you might be surprised to know that it's actually pretty rare for people to become Christians as adults."

"Really? That *is* surprising. Judging by what you see on those religious stations on TV, I would've thought it was a fairly common occurrence."

"No, quite the opposite," Bonnie told her. "By and large, the adults who join our church are simply transferring their membership from one place to another. Most of the 'conversions' we see are children who have grown up in the church professing their faith before the congregation. So, you see, what happened to you is really pretty special."

This gave Carolyn pause. "I wonder why it's so hard for people to find God?"

Bonnie gave Carolyn a quizzical look. "Seems like you would know the answer to that better than anyone. Only a few short days ago, you weren't exactly open to God yourself."

Carolyn had to acknowledge that.

"In fact, one of the most difficult things you'll have to face in the coming weeks and months is the ridicule thinly disguised as kidding you'll get from people when they find out that you've become a Christian. Some may not even attempt to disguise it."

"Maybe that's why I haven't said anything to anyone at work yet," Carolyn conceded. "I guess I sort of intuitively know that very few of them will understand, so I pretty much kept it under my hat Friday. Even though there is one person I'd really like to have told."

"Oh?"

"Yes, we have a secretary who's a Christian. Her name is Jenny Pierce. I mean, she's pretty open about it. She's got all these placards and sayings about God and faith tacked up around her cubicle at work. At Christmas, she wears a little pin that says, 'Jesus is the reason for the Season.' I hate to admit it, but even though I never said anything to her, I always thought she was a little ridiculous, you know, kind of a religious fanatic. Some of the other lawyers in the office and I have made fun of her behind her back, calling her the 'Office Jesus

Freak.' I think she knows we talked about her, but she never said anything. Now, I guess *I'll* be on the receiving end of some of that."

Bonnie could hardly contain her smile. "I think you're in for a pleasant surprise. Don't turn around and look right now, but Jenny Pierce is standing on the other side of this room."

Carolyn's eyes flew open. "Are you kidding? Jenny Pierce comes to this church?"

"'Fraid so," Bonnie teased. "But you know what? I'm willing to bet that if you let Jenny know about your change of heart, you'll find that she could be a real ally at work."

Carolyn rolled her eyes. "Oh, yeah, if she can forgive me for being part of the crowd that made fun of her behind her back."

"Hmm, forgiveness." Bonnie gave Carolyn a knowing smile. "Isn't that how all this got started in the first place?"

Carolyn looked thoughtful at that and nodded. "That's what Dr. Wells kept emphasizing over and over in that tape I listened to: forgiveness and reconciliation."

As if on cue, Jeff Wells walked through the door to the Singles Department room and paused. Seeing Bonnie standing next to Carolyn, he put on his bravest smile and walked over to them.

"Good morning, ladies. So good to see you both."

Carolyn beamed. "Good morning, Dr. Wells. We were just talking about you."

"Oh?" he said, and cast a smiling glance at Bonnie. She felt herself coloring and looked down. "Nothing *too* bad, I hope."

"Oh, Dr. Wells, you know better," Carolyn chided him, chucking his arm gently.

"Speaking of knowing better," he said to Carolyn, "*you* should know that you don't have to call me 'Dr. Wells.' 'Jeff' is just fine with me."

He glanced again at Bonnie. Bonnie remembered the context in which he had first said those words to her, with his mouth so close to hers that warm Friday evening on his front porch. Even though she could feel flames of embarrassment licking her face, she returned Jeff's look with as much reproach as she could put in her eyes. There was no mistaking the meaning in Bonnie's glance, and Jeff looked away, glad that Carolyn didn't seem to have seen it.

"Thanks," Carolyn murmured. "Jeff."

"So!" boomed Tom Givens as he came up and slung an arm around Jeff's shoulder. "It takes two beautiful women to get you up to the Singles Department, does it?"

To Bonnie's surprise and amusement, she could see Jeff Wells actually blushing at Tom's remark. She had a feeling Tom would hear from Jeff later about *that*.

"Why, not at all," said Jeff, recovering himself. "I knew Carolyn was going to be visiting us this morning, and I wanted to make her feel welcome."

Not giving up his little dig, Tom winked at Bonnie and said, "A likely story."

At that moment, Sherry Niles entered the room. She saw Bonnie and Jeff and headed straight for them.

"Hey, everybody!" Then, turning to Bonnie, "It's Bonnie, right?" she drawled with a smile.

"Yes," laughed Bonnie. "Congratulations, you remembered!"

"I might be slow, but I catch on eventually." Sherry smiled self-deprecatingly.

Carolyn watched their exchange with interest.

"Carolyn, I'd like you to meet Sherry Niles," said Bonnie. "Sherry, Carolyn Perkins."

"Pleased to meet you," said Sherry. "Are you new here?"

"Yes," Carolyn murmured. "This is my first visit."

"Oh, well, you're gonna love it. Everybody is so *nice* here." Then, with a shy smile, she turned to Jeff Wells and said, "Good morning, Jeff. Wasn't that banquet just wonderful Friday night?"

Bonnie was not about to stand there and listen to them discuss their date in front of her.

"Excuse me a moment," she said, and headed for the door, nearly colliding with Anna Lee Adkinson as she turned the corner through the doorway.

"Hey, there, Bonnie," said Anna Lee, sounding a little surprised at Bonnie's haste. Bonnie called back a greeting, but didn't break stride.

Jeff watched as Bonnie hurried away. *Jack was right*, he thought with chagrin. *I should have set Bonnie straight about Sherry Niles a long time ago.*

There was a ladies' room just down the hall—the perfect hiding place. Fortunately, it was deserted, too, so she didn't have to make the pretense of really needing to be there. She opened her purse to look for her lipstick, just to have something to do, but she looked in the mirror and saw that it really didn't need touching up. Her heart had started to pound when she had heard Sherry mention Friday night, so she took a couple of deep breaths to calm herself. It looked like hiding out in the Singles Department to avoid contact with Jeff wasn't going to work, either.

Just then, the door opened and Cheryl Summers stepped in.

"Hey," she said, mild surprise in her voice. "Checking out the Singles class today, huh?"

"That's the plan," Bonnie answered, unable to hide her disappointment. "But it seems there's nowhere to run. Jeff just walked in, and Sherry Niles was right behind him. She seems pretty smitten. I think Preston was just blowing smoke when he told me they were talking about getting back together."

Cheryl hesitated. "Bonnie, there *must* be more to this than meets the eye. Maybe you're mistaken…"

"Maybe so," Bonnie answered softly, once again close to tears. "But it really doesn't matter now, does it?" She saw the sympathy in Cheryl's eyes.

"Listen," said Cheryl, glancing at her watch, "why don't we get together and talk about this over lunch? I really need to get back. I just left the kids working on the Bible puzzle activity, but they'll be finishing up soon."

"Oh, I didn't mean to keep you. I need to get back myself. Class will be starting any time now. Call me when you can get together."

Bracing herself, she walked back to the Single Adult classroom. To her relief, Jeff was already gone, and the opening assembly was in progress. She stood at the back of the room with a couple of others who had straggled in a little late and waited for class to begin. She would re-join Carolyn then.

Even though Tom Givens had invited him again, Jeff declined to go to lunch with the Singles after the morning service. He had gone last week because he thought it would be a good opportunity to introduce Sherry Niles to some of the other single adults, since it looked like that was the way she was headed. She had told him on Wednesday night when he'd run into her at the hospital that Preston had asked to move back in with her, but that he was still adamantly opposed to receiving any type of marriage counseling. Jeff had his suspicions that Preston's motives for wanting to "reconcile" with Sherry had as much to do with finances as any feelings he might have for her, but he didn't voice them to Sherry.

Last week's lunch had also been a good opportunity, or so he had thought it would be, to meet with Sherry to discuss her problems in an open-air setting. Whatever he did, he didn't want to meet alone with Sherry in his office or behind any other set of closed doors. It was the perfect way to get people talking. Unfortunately, his meeting with her at the restaurant, coupled with the several times Bonnie had seen them together since, had had just the opposite effect. Bonnie was coming to his office that afternoon with Ben to discuss the profession of faith he had made that morning; maybe he would try to talk to her about this business with Sherry when he had finished his discussion with Ben.

After grabbing a quick lunch with Jeff Junior at the fried chicken carryout (one of the few restaurants in town that didn't seem to be frequented by members of Foster Road), he headed back to his office at church to check his e-mail and straighten out a few other matters before Bonnie and Ben arrived; they had scheduled a meeting for three o'clock. Jeff Junior would spend some time practicing his free-throws in the church gym and then keep an eye on little Josh while he met with them.

Much to his surprise, the telephone rang in the outer office. Most people knew that, on Sunday afternoon, the church office was deserted and that no one was available to answer calls. He wondered if it might be Bonnie needing to postpone their meeting for some reason.

"Foster Road Baptist Church, Jeff Wells speaking," he answered after dialing in the code that allowed him to answer calls at his desk.

"Dr. Wells, this is Dean Hill." Dean, one of the oldest men in the congregation, was a deacon and one of the leaders in the Seniors Group. "I just want you to know that I'm behind you all the way. I think Clara Adkinson has bats in her belfry. I'll be at the meeting, don't you worry."

"Meeting?"

Hearing a noise, Jeff looked up to see Jack Summers standing with his arms folded, leaning against his doorway. Jack wasn't smiling.

"Listen, Dean, thanks for the call. I'll talk to you later."

And before Mr. Hill could explain any further, Jeff put the phone in its cradle, his eyes trained on Jack.

"That's me," Jack said grimly. "A day late and a dollar short. I was hoping to get to you before anyone else did. Gossip's already gotten back to you, eh?"

"That was no gossip, Jack! That was Dean Hill. He says he'll be there to support me at the *meeting*. What in the world is he talking about? What meeting?"

Jack covered his eyes with a hand and began to massage them with a thumb and forefinger. "What a nightmare," he muttered.

"Jack, what is going *on*?"

Jack walked into Jeff's office and slouched into a chair. He let out his breath with a noisy sigh.

"I think you picked the wrong woman to mess with."

"Are you talking about Clara?" He came from around his desk and sat in the chair next to his friend. Jack looked at Jeff with a cynical smile.

"Let's just say Clara doesn't approve of your *dating* Sherry Niles. And she's betting that everyone else will disapprove, too."

"Jack, you know perfectly well that I am not dating Sherry Niles! And everyone else *should* know better!"

"I don't guess Bonnie ever told you that Anna Lee Adkinson and she had a long talk about you?"

"Not Bonnie," Jeff answered. "But Anna Lee told me herself Friday night before the Seniors Banquet that she had spoken to Bonnie. She was apologizing for all the things Clara said about Bonnie last week. But she didn't say anything about their having discussed Sherry Niles."

"Just goes to show how quickly the conclusions people jump to can be converted to 'common knowledge.'"

"C'mon, Jack. Stop being so cryptic."

"Well, Clara called me this afternoon. The story she tells is that Anna Lee came home last Sunday night from some Singles party or something and told Clara that she'd been mistaken about you going out with Bonnie, that you were really seeing this woman Sherry Niles. And the relationship seemed to be moving pretty fast, since you were seen together at *two* Singles functions in the same day." He emphasized the word "two" with sarcasm.

"Oh, for crying out loud."

"No, wait, there's more. Clara tells me that, at first, she didn't believe Anna Lee, because she thought Anna Lee was just trying to protect Bonnie for some reason. She said that she didn't tell Anna Lee that she'd seen you and Bonnie 'smooching,' as she called it, on your front porch the Friday before. Which, by the way," Jack added with a pointed look at Jeff, "*you* didn't tell me, either!"

Jeff ignored Jack's last comment. "Well, if Clara didn't believe Anna Lee, why am I getting a call from Dean Hill about a meeting?"

"Ah! She said she didn't believe Anna Lee *at first*. But that was before your *date* with Sherry at the Senior's Banquet Friday night." Jack emphasized the word "date" with a twinkle in his eye. "Clara said that when she saw you two together, and Anna Lee pointed Sherry out as the one she'd said you were dating, well, Clara didn't need any more convincing. Especially, she said, since you were *supposed* to be with Anna Lee that night. You rogue, you."

The matter was really not funny, but Jack couldn't help but be amused at Jeff squirming in the corner he'd painted himself into.

"My *date* with Sherry?" Jeff spluttered. "I didn't even know she was going to be there! She came to the banquet with her boss, What's-His-Name Blankenship."

"Henry."

"Yes, Henry. She came with *him*. Sherry just happened to sit next to me."

"Oh, right," Jack said with a smirk. "I'm sure *that* was obvious to everyone. And what about Anna Lee? Where was she sitting?" Jack was playing his part of devil's advocate to the hilt.

"Well, that was actually the reason Anna Lee came to see me before the banquet: she said she wanted to 'let me off the hook,' as she put it, of being on the 'date' her mother had arranged for us that night. As I said, she's been pretty embarrassed by her mother's maneuvering. She sat across from me at our table."

"But you were sitting next to Sherry."

"Sherry was sitting next to me."

"Oh, give me a break, Jeff! A room full of people sees you, the widower pastor, sitting next to one of the most gorgeous women on the planet, and you don't think folks are going to want to know who she is and what your relationship is? Your ears should've been burning all day yesterday."

"So why was Clara calling *you*?"

"Guess she figured that the Chairman of the Deacons would be the one to approach about asking you to tender your resignation for unseemly behavior. So, you ready to resign, or what?"

"Jack, this isn't funny!"

"No, no, you're right," Jack answered more soberly. "It *isn't* funny, because Clara was perfectly serious about wanting me to ask you for your resignation."

It was Jeff's turn to rub his eyes. "What're you going to do?"

"The only thing I felt I could do under the circumstances—call a meeting so Clara can make her accusations publicly." At Jeff's open-mouthed, wide-eyed stare, Jack continued, "And then you can set her and everybody else, including Bonnie, I might add, *straight*. You've been playing this game *way* too close to the vest, my man."

"Good grief! This is humiliating! To have to justify these ludicrous accusations with a meeting!"

"It's not as ludicrous as you seem to think, Jeff. Need I remind you that any number of people saw you and Sherry together on several occasions? It looked like you were out together to *them*. What were they supposed to think?"

Jeff stared angrily at his feet.

"Yes, people should know better. But you and I both know that, when the gossip gets juicy, what's *really* true suddenly seems a lot less interesting. People believe whatever is most titillating to believe."

Jeff rubbed his face with his hands wearily.

"I love being a pastor, you know I do," he began. "But sometimes it all gets to be a little much."

Jack regarded his friend with sympathy now.

"Wouldn't trade places with you for all the tea in China."

CHAPTER 20

The phone rang just as Bonnie and her boys were getting ready to leave for Ben's meeting with Jeff Wells. She toyed with the impulse not to answer it, but they were running a little early. She picked up the receiver.

"Hello?"

"Hey, Bon."

It was Cheryl. Already, Bonnie didn't like the sound of Cheryl's voice.

"What's up, Cheryl? Sounds like something's wrong."

"Oh, yes," Cheryl confirmed. "Something is definitely wrong. You're going to be at church tonight, right?"

"Of course. Actually, we're on our way over there right now. Ben has a conference scheduled with Dr. Wells to discuss his baptism. What's the matter?"

"There's going to be a special called business meeting. They want everybody who's anybody to be there. Deacons, Women's Auxiliary, Brotherhood, Sunday School teachers, everybody. It's scheduled for during the Church Training hour."

"What's going on?"

Cheryl sighed heavily into the phone. "Clara Adkinson has really done it this time. She's calling for Jeff to resign—"

"What!" Bonnie broke in.

"You heard me right. She's calling for Jeff's resignation. She saw Jeff with Sherry Niles at the Seniors banquet the other night, and now she thinks he's having an affair with a married woman, of all things. The whole thing is just so absurd."

"Well, Cheryl, if Dr. Wells isn't exactly having an affair, he is certainly being very open about having a social relationship with her. She *is* still legally married to her husband."

Cheryl paused, as if unsure what to say. Finally, she broke the silence.

"Look, I haven't really talked to you about this because I know Jeff Wells has been a sore subject." She paused again. "And I *did* tell Jack not to say anything to Jeff about you and him, but…"

"Oh, yeah! I saw Jack talking to Jeff the other day when they were playing racquetball. I could've wrung his neck!"

"The point, though, is that Jeff is *not* dating Sherry Niles. Never has been."

"Oh, come on, Cheryl, I *saw* them together. Not just once, but several times."

"Just like Jeff and Clara saw you with Preston."

"That was different."

"No. That was the same—exactly the same. You jumped to a conclusion, and apparently, so did Clara."

With a start, Bonnie recalled her conversation with Anna Lee about Sherry Niles: "At least *you're* off the hook with my mom! Wait'll she hears about this!" Bonnie closed her eyes and shook her head slowly.

"Dear Lord, what has Anna Lee done?"

"I don't think Anna Lee has done anything wrong except have Clara Adkinson for a mother. Beyond that, Clara is turning into a really loose cannon."

"Guess I have to be there, huh?"

"Well, you *are* Chair of the Women's Auxiliary. But surely you don't want Clara to succeed? You couldn't harbor that much ill will for Jeff!"

"Well, no, it's not that I wish anything bad on Dr. Wells, because I don't. But now that I'm kind of out of the spotlight, it would sure be nice to *stay* out of the spotlight. I felt like everybody in Chandler City was talking about what a floozy I was or something."

"Yes, people were saying some pretty incredible things, but you're not going to just stand by and watch Clara try to ruin Jeff, just because you're mad at him, are you? Just to keep your own low profile?" Cheryl couldn't hide her incredulity.

A little warning bell went off in Bonnie's head. She seemed to be hearing her own voice as she had spoken to Carolyn Perkins this past week at the Coffee Shoppe when she'd tried to persuade Carolyn to forgive JaMa'al Johnson. But was this really the same thing? Hadn't Jeff stood by while Clara said all kinds of untrue things about *her*?

"I'll be there," Bonnie said, but Cheryl could hear grudging in her words.

"Not exactly the voice of righteous indignation," Cheryl remarked scornfully. "Bonnie, this doesn't seem like you. I...I always thought you liked Jeff Wells."

"I did. I do!" Bonnie was so flustered. "But—"

"But he hurt your feelings. He jumped to a conclusion about you and Sherry's husband, just like everyone jumped to a conclusion about him and Sherry. If you'd been in *his* shoes, how would *you* have felt if you'd thought there was another guy in the picture?"

But he should have known *better*, Bonnie thought. To Cheryl, she said, "I know, I know, you're right. I just can't get over this feeling that things won't ever be the same, that things have been tainted somehow by everything that's happened. I guess I feel like I can't trust him, and I'm pretty sure he doesn't trust me."

"Bonnie, as disappointed as I was that it didn't work out between you two, this isn't *about* you and Jeff right now. Why don't you cross that bridge if and when you come to it?

"Jeff's reputation, his *career*, is on the line here. The important thing tonight is that we stand behind Jeff Wells because he is our pastor, and because he's being accused of something that is patently false."

"Yes," said Bonnie softly. "You're right. You're absolutely right." She paused. "So, I guess I'll see you tonight. Can we sit together? Moral support and all that."

"Sure. Jack will be presiding over the meeting, so I'll need someone to sit with, too. I'll see you there."

"Cheryl?"

"Yeah?"

"Pray for me."

"I'm praying for both of you," Cheryl told her. "See you tonight."

Jeff was preoccupied with his impending confrontation with Clara, and Bonnie could see it as soon as she and Ben arrived for their meeting with him. When she knocked softly on his office door, he looked up at them, as if momentarily confused about why they were there. Then, recollecting himself, he said, "Oh, yes! Ben's meeting. Come on in."

Not wanting to involve Ben in an episode of church life she would just as soon he not know about, and still wanting him to have the best of the pastor's concentration for this important decision in his life, Bonnie looked Jeff pointedly in the eye and said in a quiet voice, "I understand that you have some pressing business this afternoon. If you'd like to reschedule our meeting, we will certainly understand."

He looked at her, surprised at first at the compassion inherent in such a gesture. Nearly overcome with gratitude and affection for her, he said, "Are you sure Ben won't mind?"

"Given the circumstances, I think he'd ultimately be more disappointed if we *kept* our meeting than if we postponed it."

"I…I really appreciate this, and I can't apologize enough that this had to happen today of all days."

He wanted so much to ask her if they could have dinner later. But Ben was standing there, and a room full of people was gathering for what felt like a public hanging. *His* hanging.

He smiled an ironic little smile as he watched Bonnie leave, her arm draped affectionately across Ben's shoulder. For some reason, the parable of the Good Samaritan came to his mind: Clara lived across the street from him, but who, indeed, was his neighbor?

Clara Adkinson sat primly on the front row of chairs that had been set up in the far section of the Fellowship Hall just for this impromptu meeting. Jeff Wells sat in a smaller row of chairs behind the podium and tried to catch her eye, but she studiously avoided meeting his glance. Mertis Hargrove sat next to her, having almost certainly been conscripted by Clara to be there. As many of the deacon officers as could be mustered on such short notice sat next to Jeff, all looking thoroughly disgusted. The folding chairs in front of the podium, much to Jeff's surprise, had filled up quickly, and people brought chairs in with them to add to the back of the rows as they came in. Word about this meeting must have spread like wildfire.

At a little after five o'clock, Jack Summers walked to the podium and opened the meeting.

"As most of you know," he began, "we're here today at the request of one of our longtime members, Mrs. Clara Adkinson."

Clara raised her chin slightly and looked down her nose proudly at Jack.

"Mrs. Adkinson has some rather grave charges to make against Dr. Wells, and she is calling for his resignation."

A murmur went through the crowd.

"In the interest of fair play, we will give Mrs. Adkinson the opportunity to explain her reasons for wanting the pastor's resignation, and we will give the pastor the opportunity to defend himself against her accusations. Mrs. Adkinson?"

Clara rose and, with one pointed look at Jeff Wells, went to stand behind the podium.

"Thank you, Jack. Thank you all for coming. I'm sure you all must know that it gives me no pleasure to be here for this purpose today."

Cheryl leaned over to Bonnie's ear and whispered, "Yeah, right."

"I've always been an admirer of Dr. Wells. That is, up until recently." She looked down at her hands, folded atop the podium. "It's always been my belief, however, that a man—a man *or* a woman," she continued, looking now at Bonnie, "who undertakes a position of leadership in the church should do everything in his or her power to demonstrate character as beyond reproach as possible."

"Oh, please," muttered Cheryl again. Bonnie could feel her cheeks burning at the insinuations in Clara's remark.

"But," Clara continued, "when a person is shown to be of questionable character, when a person's actions are in direct conflict with the teachings of the Bible, then it's the church's responsibility to confront that person and give him the opportunity to resign his position voluntarily because it is the right thing to do. The scriptures even speak to this issue."

At this she opened her Bible and read from I Corinthians 5: "'Shouldn't you put this man out of your fellowship?...are you not to judge those inside [the church]? Expel the wicked man from among you.'"

"Man!" Cheryl hissed. "She is really playing hardball!"

A couple of people sitting in the row in front of them looked back at Cheryl curiously. Bonnie elbowed Cheryl and gave her a stern look.

"Not long after the pastor's wife died," Clara began again after closing her Bible, "Dr. Wells, who is my across-the-street neighbor, began to see my daughter socially."

At this, Jeff Wells's eyes flew open and his jaw dropped slightly. He recalled vividly Clara Adkinson standing at his door with one of a seemingly never-ending supply of casseroles in hand.

"Naturally," she continued, not meeting the eyes of anyone in particular, "I wanted to do all I could to help the pastor at such a time of sadness in his life. Anna Lee and I both reached out in friendship to him."

At this remark, Bonnie glanced around surreptitiously. Interestingly, Anna Lee, who, it sometimes seemed, never left her mother's side, was nowhere around.

There were puzzled looks on some of the faces in the crowd; most had expected out-and-out accusations, delivered, perhaps, with some degree of hysteria on Clara's part. This measured, reasoned account of a heretofore unknown relationship between the Pastor and Anna Lee Adkinson came as a surprise; they followed Clara's every word.

"As time went on, I could see that Dr. Wells felt more than a passing interest in Anna Lee, but I'm afraid, as sometimes happens, the interest wasn't really returned on her part. I believe he *is* quite a few years her senior."

She smiled sweetly, sympathy in her eyes. Jeff just sat riveted to his chair, stupefied. Did she want people to think that he had been chasing after a woman who was much too young for him? And right after Terri died? She was attacking his character from every conceivable angle!

"And so, as I suppose it would be natural for any man to do, Dr. Wells turned his attentions elsewhere. At first, I thought that his affections lay with Mrs. Callaway."

Clara looked again at Bonnie, who could only stare back incredulously. Knowing what Anna Lee had told her, hearing Clara tell such barefaced lies was nothing short of astounding.

"I saw them out together on a couple of occasions. And, not wanting there to be any hard feelings between us about Anna Lee, I even mentioned to the pastor that I thought his seeing Bonnie was a fine idea, them both being widowed and all."

Leaving out a couple of details, aren't you, Clara? Bonnie fumed.

"Then I heard a report that alarmed me greatly. I heard that Dr. Wells was no longer involved with Bonnie Callaway, but that he was seeing someone relatively new to town. When I saw what a beautiful woman she is, I could understand how even someone as nice as Bonnie Callaway might not be able to compete."

"Sheesh! What a backhanded compliment," Cheryl groused to Bonnie.

Bonnie stole a glance at Jeff. He looked absolutely beside himself.

"But," Clara went on pointedly, "when I heard that this new woman was actually *married*, I thought that there must be some mistake. Surely, the Jeff Wells *I* knew was above *that* kind of thing. But, as many of you witnessed just this past Friday night, it is quite true: he *is* seeing this woman socially, and she is, indeed, married. The most surprising thing about it all, to me, is that he was so brazen as to think he could behave this way without anyone objecting to it." She paused, and then assumed a more defensive expression. "Now, those with a more liberal perspective on things might say that since Mrs. Hardy, Dr.

Wells's lady friend, is legally separated from her husband, that excuses his behavior, but I don't think most of you in this room put much stock in technicalities like that. And so if, like me, you feel that this kind of behavior is simply unacceptable in our pastor, I think you'll agree that we have no choice but to ask him to tender his resignation."

With pursed lips, she looked around the room once, then made a smugly dignified return to her seat. Jack seemed at a bit of a loss when he returned to the podium.

"Well. So. Now the matter is laid out before us. Does anyone have any questions for Mrs. Adkinson?"

There was a long, awkward silence before a reply came from the back of the room. All heads turned when Anna Lee Adkinson said in an ominous tone, "Yes, Mother, I have a question."

Bonnie's head snapped back to look at Anna Lee. Tom Givens and Sherry Niles were standing next to her; they must have come in together. Perhaps Tom had even called them to make sure they would be at this meeting.

"At what point did you *ever* think that Jeff Wells showed even the remotest interest in me?" Then, with a little smirk, she added, "And where was *I* when this was supposedly happening?"

Subdued chuckling went through the crowd, and all eyes turned expectantly back to Clara. Sherry Niles stood beside Anna Lee, wide-eyed with fright. Clara turned to look at her daughter, obviously shaken at Anna Lee's entrance.

"Anna Lee, how *dare* you speak to me that way?" Clara's face was a mask of anger and embarrassment. "Even if I *might* have been mistaken about Dr. Wells's intentions toward you, *you* were the one who first told me about his relationship with Mrs. Hardy."

It was Anna Lee's turn to look embarrassed. Bonnie noticed, too, that Sherry was now staring determinedly down at her shoes. Anna Lee closed her eyes and sighed. "Okay, fine. We were *both* mistaken, then, weren't we?"

"I'm not so sure we were," Clara argued, her chin tilted up defensively. "*You* told me you'd seen them at Singles functions together several times, and you saw them together at the banquet *yourself*."

At this, Anna Lee turned to Sherry, put a gentle hand on her shoulder, and gave her a meaningful look. Poor Sherry seemed terror-stricken. But seeing Anna Lee's smile of encouragement, she steeled her nerves and walked up to the podium. Jack stepped aside with a kind smile at Sherry.

"I...I'm sure most of y'all don't know who I am," she began softly. "My name is Sherry Niles. Um...Sherry Niles Hardy. I'm real new to Chandler City.

I'm originally from Louisiana, but I...I just moved here from Atlanta. A...A friend of my daddy's got me a job at Chandler City Bank."

She glanced nervously back at Jeff Wells, who returned her look with sympathy and concern. *To involve someone so new to the church like this is unconscionable*, he fumed inwardly.

"It's true, I am separated from my husband," Sherry continued, looking down now at her hands folded atop the podium. "That's why I left Atlanta, and it's how I met Dr. Wells in the first place. The priest of my new church thought that Dr. Wells could provide me and my husband with some marriage counseling."

She paused, struggling to continue. Then, in a voice choked with tears, she said, "But he ain't...he's not interested in goin' to a counselor. Says he doesn't want to tell all our troubles to some stranger."

She lifted her chin, trying to keep her composure. "Anyway, Dr. Wells referred me to a counselor over at the Methodist hospital. She's a real nice lady, but Preston won't go see her, neither."

"Did Dr. Wells ever ask you to date him?" prompted Anna Lee.

Sherry's eyes widened.

"No! No, indeed, not!" Sherry's look registered genuine shock. "He knew I was married! There was never any question—I mean, the idea never even came up!"

She checked the shrill tone of her voice and began again with a little more composure.

"Dr. Wells was very kind to me. He knows how hard it's been for me with my husband. He introduced me around to some folks in this church, and he told me about some of the Singles activities, but he never made out like he was doin' anything more for me than he would have for anybody else."

At this, Clara scoffed derisively. Sherry looked at Clara with a hurt expression.

"He was just doing what a good pastor *should* do, makin' me feel welcome and all. And I," Sherry said, looking Clara defiantly in the eye, "can't *believe* anybody would make up such a story about Friday night. I came to the Seniors Banquet with my boss—*he* invited me to be his guest. Him and Mrs. Newton. I was honored to be asked to sit at the same table as the pastor, but as far as I could tell, he was there by himself that night."

Jeff saw Clara shoot a meaningful glance at Anna Lee after Sherry's last remark. Sherry had said all she'd come to say. She then looked to Jack, as if unsure of what to do next. He stepped up next to her at the podium.

"Thank you for being concerned enough to come here today, Mrs. Hardy," Jack told her kindly. "Does anyone have any more questions, either for Clara, Mrs. Hardy, or the pastor?"

Silence reverberated in the room. Bonnie's pounding heart swelled with relief. She looked again at Jeff. He still looked angry, but there was obvious relief in his expression, too.

Bonnie knew that Anna Lee wasn't in the habit of talking back to her mother. Her standing up to Clara in an open meeting like that had obviously taken a good deal of courage.

"Dr. Wells, do you have anything to add?" Jack turned to face Jeff, a look of grim vindication on his face.

At first, Bonnie thought from the expression of disgust on his face that Jeff would say nothing, that he would be eager to have this whole farce of a meeting over with. But then, slowly, deliberately, he rose from his seat and walked to the podium. Jack moved aside as he approached.

Jeff looked at all of the faces in the crowd that had gathered, his own curiously devoid of expression. "I remember back when I was just getting ready to enter the seminary," he began slowly. "Seems almost like a lifetime ago, now. The night my home church in Bainbridge ordained me, they held a reception for me. And one of our dear old deacons, a man who'd been my Sunday School teacher when I was a boy, came up to me. I thought he was going to wish me luck, but do you know what he said to me?"

He paused, and the crowd before him leaned forward expectantly.

"He put his arm around my shoulder and he said, 'Son, you're gonna find out something about people when you enter the ministry. Folks can be mean and nasty anywhere you go, but when people get a bee in their bonnet and think God is on their side, you're gonna find out that there ain't no mean like Christian mean.'" He paused, shifted his stance, and folded his arms.

"I think what we've seen today is a woman who, in a very misguided way," and Bonnie marveled that he could be so magnanimous toward Clara, "was trying to right what she perceived to be a wrong. But what she wound up with was what my old friend would've called a good case of Christian mean.

"She's said some very embarrassing things about me and Mrs. Hardy and even her own daughter. And though they weren't mentioned today, she also said some things last week about Bonnie Callaway that were as unkind as they were untrue."

Jeff looked at Bonnie, apology in his eyes. Bonnie's heart skipped a beat when she saw his expression.

"And I am ashamed to say that, like many of you here today, I was willing to take whatever Clara said at face value, without questioning her motives or verifying the facts. Only *unlike* you, I didn't even give Mrs. Callaway a chance to tell her side of the story. And for that, I most humbly apologize. I can only hope at this point that Mrs. Callaway can find it in her heart one day to forgive me."

Finally, he tore his eyes from Bonnie's, and she looked down, near tears. Cheryl reached over, covered Bonnie's hand with one of hers, and gave it a squeeze.

"I'd like to be able to say that I'm sorry I didn't respond to Clara's attempts to bring me together with her daughter—"

At this, Clara opened her mouth in astonishment and two patchy red triangles of mortification appeared atop her cheeks.

"But, as Clara herself said, there just wasn't any interest there. On *either* of our parts."

Jeff looked back at Anna Lee, who smiled back encouragingly.

"I'm not sure why Clara would want her daughter to marry a poor preacher man, anyway." This got a chuckle from the crowd. "But I want to go on record that, except for a few brief moments when I *thought* I was going to have the pleasure of taking Mrs. Callaway to dinner, the only woman in my life since Terri died has been Becky Wells, my daughter."

At the mention of Terri's name, most people cast their eyes down guiltily. Jack walked to the podium again as Jeff returned to his seat.

"If there are no further questions, a motion has been made that we, as a church body, ask the pastor for his resignation. Does anyone care to second that motion?"

Silence resounded again.

"Our business here is concluded. See you all in church."

There was a loud rumble of conversation as people made their way up to Jeff Wells to shake his hand and to affirm to him that *they* had never believed Clara's accusations, anyway. Visibly rattled, Jeff shook hands a little absentmindedly, even as he scanned the crowd to see what Bonnie would do. He never did see her again, though, until he spotted her from the pulpit during the evening service.

Jeff returned to his office when church let out and slouched into his chair, emotionally spent. It had been all he could do to get himself through his survey of Ephesians.

Well, he thought, *if nothing else, Bonnie at least knows the truth now.* But had it made any difference in her opinion of him or how she felt about him? He didn't think so. He was grateful that she had come to the meeting at all, even though he wondered how much of that was attributable to mere obligation on her part. After all, she hadn't stayed after the meeting was over. The fact that he wasn't dating a married woman, he thought with a wry smile, didn't make him not a jerk.

He glanced to the side of his desk where he kept correspondence to which he needed to respond and picked up the letter he'd received on Friday from the seminary.

> Due to the retirement of three of its longtime faculty members, the Department of Theological Studies anticipates the need for professors of Hebrew, Greek, and Homiletics. Your contributions to the curricula in all of these areas during your doctoral studies is widely respected among your colleagues. If one of these positions interests you at all, we heartily encourage you to submit a letter of interest so that we may place you under consideration for the fall semester.

Maybe, he thought with resignation, *I just ought to send them that letter of interest.*

CHAPTER 21

May went by in a flurry of activity: Jack and Cheryl were busy with Amanda's Senior Prom and graduation and preparations for the annual Youth mission tour. This year, a group of over fifty young people ranging in age from thirteen to seventeen, along with their adult chaperones, were headed to a mission church in the mountains of Oregon. There, they would conduct a Vacation Bible School for a church that was struggling to establish itself within a population that had little religious affiliation of any kind. They would leave the Tuesday after Memorial Day and be back in time to assist with Foster Road's own Vacation Bible School in mid-June.

Carolyn Perkins had enlisted the help of John Reeves to have JaMa'al Johnson released from Juvenile Detention on probation. John led his church in sponsoring the relocation of JaMa'al and his family to Greenville, South Carolina, where JaMa'al's mother had family. Unknown to all but Carolyn and John, much of the funding for this relocation was provided by Ruth Newton. The firm for which Carolyn worked was handling Art's succession; when Ruth heard about JaMa'al and the threats his gang had made against his mother and sister, she had become a "silent partner" in helping JaMa'al and his family find a safe place to begin a new life. Carolyn heard through John that JaMa'al and his brother and sister were doing well in their new town and were looking forward to going to new schools in the fall.

The Chandler City police had kept JaMa'al's release a closely guarded secret until he and his family were safely out of town. The police had also put the Johnson house and Loaves and Fishes under plain-clothes surveillance. No one could say for sure whether the members of the K.I.N.G.S. who were arrested for trying to break into the Johnson's old house had been involved in the break-in at Loaves and Fishes, but JaMa'al and his family felt safe again, and Loaves and Fishes again went unmolested.

Carolyn was making new friends in Foster Road Baptist's Singles Department and had also joined a Friday night Bible study for singles.

"I can't believe I used to think that Christians were just a bunch of nerds," she admitted with chagrin to Bonnie. "This group really knows how to have a good time. And they're so willing to share…I've learned so much already."

As Bonnie had anticipated, Jenny Pierce, after she had overcome her initial shock at seeing Carolyn in church in the first place, became something of a mentor to Carolyn. It was actually a two-way relationship: Jenny was studying to be a paralegal, and Carolyn assisted her freely with her homework; Carolyn was a new Christian with everything to learn, and Jenny shared books and devotional guides with Carolyn and became her prayer partner.

Bonnie and Anna Lee Adkinson, someone with whom Bonnie would never have thought herself as having anything in common, were becoming fast friends. Her mother, Anna Lee had told Bonnie, was visiting other churches in the area sporadically, but staying home from church more often than not. After her humiliating failed attempt to have Jeff Wells ousted from his pastorate, she had no plans to return to Foster Road Baptist. Bonnie was not surprised, of course, but could take no real pleasure in this knowledge.

After having felt for so long that Clara was watching his every move, Jeff was acutely aware now that suddenly, he never saw her anymore. Not only was she not sitting on the first row of pews behind the deacons every Sunday these days, but he no longer saw her peering through her curtains when he drove into or out of his driveway. And, of course, the homemade casseroles, pies, and cookies were things of the past.

Much to the disappointment of many, though, Sherry Niles had also stopped coming to Foster Road. She hadn't attended the service after the showdown with Clara Adkinson, and she wasn't in Sunday School the next week. Bonnie had even tried calling her.

"I don't belong there," Sherry told Bonnie tearfully. "I ain't married and I ain't single. I feel like I don't belong anywhere. And if people think I'm trying to chase after your preacher, well, I just *can't* go back."

Jeff had made a discreet call to Norman Blake, who confirmed that Sherry had attended mass at St. Alban's a couple of Sundays running. Bonnie, of course, had no way of knowing that. Nor could she ever confirm or deny whether Sherry and Preston had reconciled, as Preston had said they would. Now that his true marital status was known at Foster Road, he no longer showed up at Singles-sponsored activities. Bonnie couldn't be sure of this either, but she thought that he must be spending less time in Chandler City than he had been; she never saw him anymore, either at the Coffee Shoppe or at Grabbabite.

Bonnie, who had her own hands full with preparing to direct the fifth- and sixth-grade Vacation Bible School class and conducting the seminar on single parenting at the upcoming Singles Conference, was secretly glad that Jeff Wells planned to accompany the Youth on their mission trip. She had no doubt, just because it was the way her luck was running these days, that he would attend the Singles Conference, and that she wouldn't be able to avoid seeing him there. They had rescheduled Ben's conference for the week after the showdown with Clara, and Bonnie had to admit that it was a little less tense than it might have been before he had apologized to her in front of everyone. But his going on the Youth trip meant that there would be almost three weeks (including two Sundays) when she wouldn't have to worry about seeing him at all or running into him if she went to the Coffee Shoppe or Grabbabite or anywhere else!

And yet, she felt as guilty about being relieved as she felt relief at his going. She shouldn't *have* to feel this way about her pastor! Of course, Jeff had long since ceased to be merely her pastor. The old argument she had played in her head a thousand times since that Sunday afternoon in Jeff's office—she wanted to change churches, she couldn't bear to change churches—repeated itself with every pang of guilt.

On the Thursday evening before the Singles Conference was to take place, Cheryl called Bonnie.

"Hey, there!" said Bonnie. "So, you've come up for air long enough to call me, huh?"

"Listen, I am so sorry it's been so busy. I've really missed getting to talk to you. What are you doing for lunch tomorrow?"

"Having lunch with you, I hope! Where would you like to go?" They agreed to meet at the Golden China House at noon the next day.

Bonnie could see that there was something on Cheryl's mind as soon as she saw her. The smile on Cheryl's face didn't quite reach her eyes.

"So," Cheryl said, obviously trying to sound cheery, "are we going to be good girls or bad girls today? I'm craving a big plate of sweet and sour pork and almond cookies for dessert!"

Bonnie arched an eyebrow at her friend.

"In that case, I'd say you're definitely going to be a *bad* girl. I'm having lunch at the Singles Conference tomorrow, and a group of us may go out to dinner afterwards, so I'd better put myself into a fat gram deficit for now."

"Oh, that's right! The conference is tomorrow. Are they expecting a big turnout? Got your seminar all ready?"

"Tom Givens says that over three hundred and fifty have registered from around the tri-state area. I thought that was pretty good. And that's not counting Foster Road's own singles. As for my *seminar*, as you call it, well, I prefer to think of myself at this point as a facilitator, not a teacher. I mean, I really don't see myself as having any great wisdom to impart. I think people will get a lot more out of it if they can just share their experiences with each other."

Cheryl looked as if she were only half-attending to what Bonnie said.

"Hmm, probably right," Cheryl murmured.

Well known for her candor, Cheryl was no shrinking violet about saying what was on her mind. Her pensiveness had Bonnie watching and waiting for what Cheryl would say.

When they had finished their lunch, Cheryl nibbled at one of her almond cookies.

"I've missed you," she finally began. "It's just been so incredibly busy lately. But there was a special reason I wanted us to have lunch today."

I could see that, Bonnie thought with an inward smile, but she waited for Cheryl to go on. Bonnie looked into her friend's eyes and saw pain there.

"I've got some good news and some bad news," Cheryl said, trying to smile.

"What's the good news?" Bonnie asked warily.

"The good news is," Cheryl began, her voice suddenly catching, "you won't have to put up with me and my pushy ways for much longer."

Bonnie looked at her, puzzled.

"The bad news is, Jack's being transferred by his company. We're going to be moving."

Nothing could have prepared Bonnie for this. She felt the bottom drop out of her stomach and, for a moment, she could only stare at Cheryl in disbelief. Cheryl's eyes had filled with tears, and Bonnie looked down to hide her own.

"When?" was all Bonnie could manage to whisper.

Cheryl dabbed at her eyes with her napkin and cleared her throat.

"We've got an appointment with a real estate agent on Saturday to discuss putting our house up for sale. We're going to New Orleans to look for a house while Amanda's on the Mission trip. We need to be settled in time for Carrie to start school in August. Seems like the school year starts early there."

Bonnie's head snapped up.

"New Orleans! Are you kidding? That's where I'm from! My sister and my parents still live there!"

"Yeah, I know." Cheryl smiled weakly. "So maybe we'll still get to see each other sometimes."

"Oh, yes, absolutely! Thanksgiving and Christmas and during the summers! It won't be like having you in the same town, but at least you won't be in Timbuktu!"

"No." Cheryl grinned. "I don't think Southeastern Distributors has any offices in Timbuktu yet."

"Oh, dear, Cheryl," sighed Bonnie. "This is terrible. How can I be losing you? What am I going to do without you?"

"The same thing I'm going to do without you: miss you a lot."

A thought occurred to Bonnie. "Has Jack told Jeff Wells yet?"

"Jack just found out that the position and transfer were approved yesterday. I called you last night after dinner, as soon as Jack told me. We didn't say anything about it before, in case the deal fell through. Anyway, Jack was supposed to tell Jeff over lunch today, too." She glanced at her watch. "They're probably together, even as we speak."

Jeff stared at Jack, wide-eyed.

"You can't do this to me! Who am I going to beat at racquetball now?"

Jack pursed his lips and shook his head. "One of life's little trials, my boy."

"It's for sure?"

"Got the word from Corporate yesterday," Jack confirmed.

"Major bummer," Jeff murmured. "What am I going to do without you?"

"You've got an e-mail account. You can tell me your troubles over the Internet."

"Won't be the same." Then he paused. "Well, at least Amanda and Jeff Junior had the prescience to enroll in the same college. *They'll* still see each other."

"Maybe we'll see each other at the wedding," Jack joked.

Jeff shook his head with a smile, as if he hadn't thought about *that* before.

"You may be right. Let's just hope you're not right for at least another four years!"

Fellowship Hall positively swam with people, and the roar of conversation was nearly deafening. Tom Givens was just about beside himself with pride.

"What a turnout!" he yelled to Bonnie over the din. "This will be our best Singles Conference ever!"

"I'm glad I decided to come," Bonnie answered.

But she was just being polite. She was actually close to panicking. What *had* she been thinking? Until fairly recently, she hadn't even thought of herself as *single*, and now here she was jumping right into the middle of things by attending a Singles conference—and leading a session in it, no less! Would everyone think her horribly presumptuous? She tried not to think about it and found herself wishing it were just over with.

"Look, there's Carolyn Perkins. Excuse me, would you?"

Carolyn met her friend with a smile.

"Man, what a crowd! I never expected this!"

"Yeah, Tom Givens is just about to bust his buttons. I guess you heard about the Mystery Guest, huh?"

"Uh-huh. Wonder who it could be?"

"I don't know," Bonnie answered, "but it had better be somebody good, or Tom may have a stampede on his hands."

"Nonsense," said Carolyn. "I hear this conference has some *excellent* session leaders!" She chucked Bonnie playfully on the shoulder.

"Yes, and I hope I get to *hear* one of them!" Bonnie countered. Then Bonnie saw Anna Lee. "Anna Lee! Over here!"

Bonnie was pleased to see that, while Anna Lee had worn blue jeans like most everyone else, she had also worn a mauve silk blouse and suede loafers in a matching shade. There were tasteful gold earrings at her lobes and her hair was caught back in a French braid that cascaded gracefully down her back. A transformation of sorts had come over Anna Lee after her night of glory at the Seniors Banquet. Or perhaps it had been after she had stood up to her mother the day Clara tried to have Jeff Wells ousted. Whatever had effected the change, Bonnie had never seen Anna Lee look more attractive. The defeated air she used to wear all the time seemed to be gone now, too.

"Hi, guys," said Anna Lee shyly. "Great crowd, huh?"

"Yeah," answered Carolyn. "Better grab a doughnut and some coffee before they're all gone."

She peered around the room. Then, in a dreamy voice, she asked, "Are either of you the type to go to functions like this and wonder if the man of your dreams is in the crowd somewhere?"

Bonnie's eyes widened, but she said nothing, even as she felt herself blushing at the sudden thought that Jeff Wells would almost certainly make an appearance today.

Anna Lee gave Carolyn a sidelong glance that said, "Get real!" Then she responded quietly, but emphatically, "I don't think so."

Carolyn shot Anna Lee an amused look. "Hey, I can dream, can't I?"

"Dream about what?" asked Jeff Wells as he approached the three of them.

"Ah!" said Anna Lee, linking her arm playfully in Jeff's. "Speaking of the man of my dreams!"

Jeff smiled sardonically and shook his head.

"Anna Lee, you are bad to the bone."

With a mock-innocent grin, she replied, "I try, Dr. Wells, I try."

Bonnie couldn't tell if it was just Jeff's standing next to her, or Anna Lee's linking her arm in Jeff's that made her face burn with embarrassment, but she knew she couldn't just stand there and watch.

"I just thought of something I need to tell Tom Givens," she lied. "Excuse me."

She felt bad about just leaving Anna Lee and Carolyn like that, but they had made plans to sit together at the brunch. She would see them again then.

Jeff wondered with despair, as he watched Bonnie walk away, if she was going to find excuses to leave the room every time he ever came around.

The first session, during which she would hold her discussion of Single Parenting issues, was set to begin in just under ten minutes. Bonnie thought she probably ought to head on down to the room. She read the signs with the titles of each session as she went down the hall: "Managing Your Money: Stewardship and Security," "Daily Devotions: A Journey and a Journal." Anna Lee Adkinson was leading that one.

The next title she read really caught her eye: "Bringing Jesus on Your Date." *What a name*, Bonnie thought with a grin. She was still shaking her head and smiling as she passed the open door.

"It's rather a catchy title, isn't it?" said a masculine voice.

Bonnie started and looked up into one of the most devastatingly handsome faces she had ever seen. The man who had spoken to her stood and towered over her as he walked toward her.

"Sam Washington," he said, extending his right hand to her. His voice was deep and velvety.

"Oh!" said Bonnie, recollecting herself and shaking his hand. "Um, Bonnie Callaway. How do you do?" Then she recognized the name. "Sam Washington? The author?"

Sam Washington was a bestselling author of several books on Christianity and singleness. Was *he* the special guest Tom had been so mysterious about? If so, it was, indeed, quite a coup on his part.

Washington didn't even try to appear modest. "The very same," he said with an indulgent smile. "Are you familiar with my work?"

Nothing wrong with this man's ego, Bonnie thought a little derisively. *But goodness, he's good looking!*

"Um, no, I, uh, haven't been single that long."

Good grief, she thought. *What an idiotic thing to say.*

"Ah, divorced?"

Bonnie didn't exactly care for the condescending way he said this, or the way she saw the interest in his eyes slightly diminish.

"Uh, no. I'm a widow."

"Ah," he said again. To her amazement, Bonnie saw the interest in his eyes rekindle. "I'm sorry."

But she could tell that it was a perfunctory thing for him to say. Just then, the hall began to fill with people looking for the sessions for which they had registered.

"Guess I'd better get to my classroom," Bonnie told him. "I'm leading the session on Single Parenting."

"Oh!" he said in a mockingly grave voice. "*Definitely* not my area of expertise."

"No children?" Bonnie asked.

With a meaningful look, he informed her, "Never been married."

Bonnie ignored the look, trying not to think about what he was implying.

"It was nice to meet you, Mr. Washington."

"Please," he said smoothly. "Call me Sam. Maybe I'll see you again at the break."

Smiling a deliberately weak smile, Bonnie said, "Yes, perhaps so."

Great, she thought. *Now I have somebody else to avoid.*

She found her room and began to put on each chair a handout she'd made up on various resources available to single parents. People began to file in: mostly women, as Bonnie had suspected might be the case. The only one she recognized was Jenny Pierce. Then she reminded herself that there were a lot of people here from out of town; she couldn't expect to know *them*.

To her astonishment, the room filled up and several of the men in atten-dance began to bring in more folding chairs from the dining hall. She soon ran out of handouts. Ducking her head out of the door, she saw Tom Givens talk-ing to Jeff Wells at the end of the hall. Taking a deep breath, she walked up to the two men, who broke off their conversation when they saw her.

"Sorry to interrupt," she said, avoiding looking at Jeff. "But could you do me a favor? I've run out of handouts for my session. Do you think you could make me about ten more copies?"

Before Tom could answer, Jeff took the original from her fingers and said, "Here, let me take care of that. I was going to attend your session anyway." When he saw the surprised look on Bonnie's face, he pretended to be defensive and said, "Hey, I'm a single parent, too, you know!"

Bonnie turned to walk back to her classroom and thought, *Yes, and your youngest* child *is getting ready to go to college in the fall.*

Knowing that there would almost certainly be enough problems to discuss, Bonnie decided to begin her session on a light note. She went around the room, asking each attendee to give his or her name and then tell either their fondest or their funniest memory of being a parent. By the time they had got-ten back to Bonnie, the atmosphere in the room was relaxed, and laughter rang down the hall.

Just then, Jeff peered into the room, a sheaf of Bonnie's photocopied hand-outs in his hand.

"Looks like I've come to the fun session," he grinned. He handed fliers out to those who didn't already have them, then seated himself.

Why me? Bonnie groaned inwardly. *Of all the sessions they're holding today, why does he want to come to* mine? She took a deep breath and began fielding responses to the questions she had prepared to get discussion going. She soon found herself mostly listening; these single parents had plenty to say and seemed grateful for a forum in which to air their feelings with others who shared the same trials. As she looked around the room, she stole a glance at Jeff. He didn't have much to contribute, of course; his own children were mostly grown. But he seemed avidly interested in what the group was sharing.

As if he could sense her looking at him, he turned briefly to Bonnie and returned her gaze. She couldn't exactly read his expression, but there seemed to be kindness in his eyes. She thought once again about the night they had found themselves alone in the booth at the Coffee Shoppe, how the kindness in his eyes had made her feel better after she had brought up Bill's name. How she wished, at times, she could turn back the clock to that time! Everything had been so innocent then; now, every meeting with him was awkward and uncomfortable.

The man publicly apologized to you, for crying out loud! she chided herself. *Are you going to carry a grudge forever?* Reluctantly, she returned his smile with a diffident one of her own.

Carolyn had attended Anna Lee's session on devotionals just down the hall from where her own session had been held, so Bonnie walked to the convocation with them. Jenny Pierce joined them and walked beside Carolyn. As they passed Tom Givens, Bonnie stopped for a moment.

"I want to thank you," she said.

"Thank me? What did I do?"

"For asking me to do this session. I have to be honest and tell you, I had a lot of doubts and second thoughts. But this has been a real blessing for me. I'm sure I got as much out of it as anyone in the room."

"I'm glad you feel that way," he said, "but really, we owe you a thank-you. I saw your handout. You did some really great research."

"So," Bonnie said with a knowing smile. "Sam Washington, eh? Was *he* the special mystery guest you advertised?"

"Who, Sam?" Tom seemed genuinely surprised at the idea. "Oh, no! Sam's publishing company called to ask if he could lead a session. Good PR for his books, I guess.

"No, the mystery guest is about to make his appearance." Then, with a decidedly smug gleam in his eye, he put an arm around Bonnie's shoulder, began leading her down the hall, and added, "Honey, you ain't seen nothin' yet!"

CHAPTER 22

Perhaps it was anticipation and curiosity about the identity of the much-talked-about mystery guest; perhaps it was that over four hundred people had gathered under one roof to celebrate their Christianity and their singleness: the atmosphere in the sanctuary was positively electric. Tom Givens had called on everyone to stand and sing a rousing rendition of "How Great Thou Art." Bonnie listened to Anna Lee as they sang; she marveled once again at how beautiful her voice was.

When the crowd sat down again, Tom smiled and looked around the sanctuary.

"What a fabulous gathering!"

There was a spontaneous burst of cheering and applause.

"And it's fitting that so many should have come today," he continued, "because we really do have a very special musical guest."

He paused again, hardly able to contain his excitement.

Anna Lee leaned over and whispered to Bonnie: "Boy, he's really milking this one!"

Bonnie laughed. Tom did seem pretty proud of himself, whoever it was he had gotten.

"A lot of you may not know this, but I had quite a special roommate in college."

At these words, the crowd started to chuckle, as if Tom were trying to pull some kind of joke, but Anna Lee's hands went to her mouth and she drew in her breath sharply.

"No way," she whispered.

Bonnie looked at Anna Lee quizzically.

"He's really a man who needs no introduction nowadays," Tom continued, smiling broadly. Then, his voice dropping dramatically, Tom leaned into the microphone and said, "Ladies and gentlemen, I give you...*Mr. Mark Miller.*"

There was stunned silence at first, then gasps of surprise from all over the sanctuary. The first few chords of "Spirit in the Sky," the song that had been playing on everyone's radio since early that year, came rumbling over the sound system. No one appeared on the stage at first, and people began looking around, almost frantically, to see if Tom Givens had, indeed, been playing a trick on them. Finally, one of the doors leading onto the dais opened, and the man himself, dressed all in black right down to his boots and playing a black lacquered electric guitar, strolled onto the stage. People all over the sanctuary stood spontaneously and began to cheer and applaud.

"Oh, Lord, I don't *believe* it," Anna Lee mumbled under her hands. Her head dropped into a deep bow.

Bonnie started inwardly as she suddenly remembered what Anna Lee had told her about having fallen in love with the singer when they were both in college.

"Oh, my goodness, it's Mark Miller," she whispered.

She looked again at Anna Lee, who was absolutely dumbstruck. Her hands still covered her mouth. Gently, Bonnie pulled one of Anna Lee's trembling hands away from her face and held it in one of her own. *What must Anna Lee be going through right now?*

"Oh, Bonnie, I've got to get out of here!"

This would be much easier said than done, since they had made a point of getting good seats fairly close to the front of the sanctuary. If Anna Lee got up and left, it *wouldn't* be inconspicuous.

Carolyn leaned over and looked inquiringly, first at Anna Lee, then at Bonnie. Bonnie gave Carolyn a cautioning look.

"Anna Lee, please don't go," Bonnie whispered back. "Isn't it good to see him again at all?"

The look Anna Lee gave her was a mixture of pain and panic. Then, with resignation, she sighed deeply and slumped back against the pew.

"Not if he sees *me*," she moaned.

Nearly the entire audience was on its feet now, save Bonnie and Anna Lee, swaying and clapping along with the music. Faces fairly shone with the excitement of having such a famous and celebrated performer in their midst. When the last chords of the song faded away, the audience cheered with unrestrained fervor. Mark Miller smiled a self-deprecating, somewhat lopsided smile and bowed slightly.

"Great to see everybody!" he shouted over the roar.

The roar just got louder. Miller grinned and looked over to his friend, Tom Givens, who was seated on the front row of pews. Tom looked back and gave Mark the "thumbs up" sign. Jeff Wells, seated next to Tom, seemed pleased with such an enthusiastic response, too. He turned around in his seat to scan the crowd. Then he saw Bonnie and his gaze rested on her face. As if she could sense that he was looking at her, she turned and her eyes met his. Each was looking for some kind of sign in the other's eyes, some silent message of forgiveness and reconciliation. But the searching was all they saw in each other.

Effecting a mock-country accent, Mark Miller addressed his audience: "Hoo-whee! Calm down, now! Ain't y'all never heard nobody *sang* before?"

It wasn't until he began playing the notes to the next song, slow, meditative notes, that the crowd began to seat itself again and grow quiet. He played the introduction a couple of times through until everyone was seated. When all of the notes could finally be heard, Anna Lee groaned again.

"I don't believe it!"

"What's the matter now?" asked Bonnie.

"We used to sing this song together all the time at the BSU at school. I can't *believe* he's going to do this song!" She just sat back and closed her eyes.

As he continued to run through the introduction to the song, Mark spoke soothingly into his microphone.

"Now, I know a lot of you guys were plannin' to duck outta this conference after lunch and get a head start on goin' home, so don't try to tell me you weren't."

Self-conscious laughter rippled through the audience.

"Well, nothin' doin', y'all. I want everybody right back here after this afternoon's session. We'll have a little concert and sing-along. How's that sound?"

There was subdued, but nearly universal, applause. He grinned that slow, lopsided grin of his again, and Bonnie could definitely see how Anna Lee could have fallen for him.

"Alright, then, no sneakin' out."

He continued strumming the chords of the song he was about to sing.

"Now, don't get mad, y'all, but this next song I want to sing ain't for you guys. You can listen if you want to," he joked, and the audience laughed again, "but I want it to be a little stroll down memory lane for an old friend of mine that I'm told is here today. I hope she remembers it as fondly as I do."

"Oh, dear Lord," Anna Lee groaned, covering her eyes this time.

Mark then launched into the first verse of "Sing Allelujah to the Lord." The words and the melody were haunting, almost mesmerizing. Bonnie saw people all around her listening with their eyes closed. All except for Anna Lee. Carolyn was still sneaking curious looks at Anna Lee periodically; Bonnie would have to fill her in later.

After the words of the first verse trailed smoothly up and away, Mark spoke softly again. "This is one of my favorite songs of praise, but you know, it just doesn't sound the same unless you have someone with you to sing the descant." He continued to strum the chords of the song on his guitar.

"No," whispered an agonized Anna Lee.

"I don't know where she's sittin', but I surely would be honored if my old singing partner would come up and help me with the second part of this song."

"*No*," she whispered again, almost in tears.

Then, before she knew he had even gotten up from his seat, Tom Givens was by her side, extending his left hand to her. Bonnie nudged Anna Lee gently and pointed to Tom. Anna Lee just looked at him, wide-eyed.

"There she is," Mark said gently. "My old buddy Tom has found her. Would you come up and sing with me, Anna Lee, for old times' sake?"

Instantly, every eye in the place was on Anna Lee Adkinson. There was a smattering of applause, encouraging her to acquiesce. How could she say no in front of all these people? Slowly, reluctantly, she took Tom's hand and allowed him to lead her to the stage. She walked up the steps, and the audience applauded again softly.

For the first time in over six years, Anna Lee stood next to the man whose heart she had broken because she'd been too timid to stand up to her mother. He smiled that crooked smile again, and this time, it was just for her.

Then, he launched into the words of the second verse. When it was time for Anna Lee to sing her part, he looked down at her expectantly. There was uncertainty in her eyes as she met his gaze, and she had to lean very close to his face to share the microphone with him, but her voice rang out as clearly and sweetly as it had when she had sung at the banquet the week before. It was an electrifying moment, and a chill went down Bonnie's back.

After Mark and Anna Lee had sung several rounds of the song, Mark invited the audience to stand and sing along with them. Spontaneously, people began to join hands as they sang. People standing at the ends of their pews walked out into the aisles to join hands with those across from them. Bonnie looked to her left at the two women she now counted as friends: Jenny Pierce, whom she was just getting to know, and Carolyn Perkins, whom she considered her miracle friend. God had drawn them together just as surely as he had spoken to Carolyn through Jeff's sermon all those weeks ago. She and Carolyn and Jenny often had lunch together now; their lunches were as much prayer sessions as they were social outings. Cheryl was leaving Chandler City, and no one could replace her, but it seemed that the Lord was giving her ample compensation in the three women she was sitting with today.

Since Anna Lee was up on the dais, Bonnie walked into the aisle to join hands with the person across from her. She looked up to see that it was Sam Washington, the man she had met earlier as she was going to her classroom. She started a little when she recognized him, then smiled to cover her surprise. Perhaps she had smiled too broadly, she thought, because she felt herself coloring at the warmth in the smile he gave to her in return. For the first time since the afternoon she had left Jeff's office in tears, she found herself actually wishing that it was *his* hand she was holding.

When the last words of the chorus had been sung, Bonnie saw Anna Lee looking up at Mark, and she seemed to search his face. He looked down at her, a gentle kindness in his eyes, and he leaned over and kissed her cheek. Without looking at him again, she walked back into the audience and sat down next to Bonnie. Bonnie watched Jeff Wells as he walked to the podium and then glanced at Anna Lee. Her head was bowed and tears rolled silently down her cheeks.

As people entered the dining hall for lunch, they looked around to see if Mark Miller were there yet. Gradually, they gave up looking for him and settled down to eat their meals. But it was Tom Givens that Anna Lee Adkinson was looking for. She found him in the kitchen, and anger sparked from her eyes.

"How could you do that to me?" she demanded without preamble.

Tom looked a little confused at the vehemence with which she spoke, but said, "Oh, Anna Lee, you sounded fine! You may not be a star like Mark, but you have a beautiful voice. It was great to hear you guys sing together again."

Anna Lee stopped and stared at Tom. She could see it in his face: he didn't know! How was it possible that he had roomed with Mark and not known of their ill-fated relationship? She closed her eyes and took a deep breath.

"Let's start at the beginning," she said. "Tell me exactly how it was that Mark came to be here today."

"Well, I know you guys kind of lost touch with each other after we all graduated, but Mark and I have kept in pretty close contact over the years. He was best man at my wedding."

He paused, as if that were somehow explanation enough. Anna Lee was trying to be patient.

"Yes? And?" She urged him on.

Looking at her in puzzlement, Tom continued, "Well, and so when Lisa and I saw him at Christmas, he told me that he was planning to take a little R&R after his concert tour ended this month. Said he thought he would head down to Panama City Beach, or maybe Mexico Beach where it's a little quieter. He said he'd be going down there over Memorial Day weekend, so *I* got the brilliant idea of asking him if he'd condescend to grace our little gathering with his presence. He agreed to do it, but only on the condition that we not use his name in any of the promotional materials we sent out. Probably a wise decision. We would've been mobbed, otherwise. Not to mention the press, which he's trying to get away from for awhile."

Tom watched Anna Lee's face, still wondering why she was so intent on knowing how this had come about. He had rather thought that she might get a kick out of seeing her old singing partner again, especially since he had become so famous.

"Any other questions?"

Anna Lee sighed, the wind having been taken from her sails.

"Just one. Did Mark know that—"

Before she could finish her question, though, Mark Miller himself walked up behind Anna Lee and finished it for her: "Did I know that you were going to be here? Let's just say I took out a little insurance policy. I just reminded Tom about how well you used to do leading our Bible studies at the BSU, so it wasn't exactly his own idea to ask you to lead a session today."

His eyes gleamed with mirth. Tom just stood by, incredulously, and watched Mark and Anna Lee, an unbelievable thought forming in his head. Was there something he had missed between these two all those years ago? Something that Mark hadn't told even his best buddy? Could it be that Big Man on Campus Mark Miller and dowdy little Anna Lee Adkinson had once been an item? Judging by the looks that Mark and Anna Lee were giving each other right now, it certainly appeared so.

Anna Lee was momentarily speechless. Finally, she managed, "Wh...why would you do that?"

"Why don't we grab a couple of plates and chat about it over lunch?" Mark answered. "Your pastor was kind enough to lend me his office to have my lunch in. We all felt my presence might be a little disruptive."

Anna Lee smiled and rolled her eyes. "That's an understatement if I ever heard one."

"Let's get out of here," he told her, leading her by the hand.

Tom just looked on, shaking his head in wonderment that he had never seen it before.

Carolyn had gotten beeped by her office and had to dash over just as lunch was beginning.

"On a holiday weekend?" Bonnie complained.

"I'll be back in time for the afternoon session, I promise."

So Bonnie and Jenny Pierce sat next to one another at a table that was still nearly empty. Jenny had just asked Bonnie what she knew about the relationship between Anna Lee and Mark Miller when a deep voice inquired, "Mind if I join you ladies?"

They looked up to see Sam Washington smiling down at them, plate in hand. Jenny took one look at him and her mouth fell open slightly.

Bonnie could see that Jenny was incapable of replying coherently, so she said, "Sure, have a seat."

"Well, that was quite a treat, wasn't it? Did you have any idea that *Mark Miller* would be here today?" Sam asked, looking at Bonnie.

Jenny continued to stare at him.

"Um, no," Bonnie answered, trying to suppress a smile at the star-struck look in Jenny's eyes. "That was Tom Givens's closely guarded secret. I don't know how he managed to keep it under wraps so well. He must've been the only one who knew Mark was coming." She turned to Jenny then and said, "Jenny, I'd like to introduce you to Mr. Sam Washington. Mr. Washington, Jenny Pierce."

"Oh, please," he said, reaching his hand out to Jenny, but looking at Bonnie. "Please call me Sam." Jenny said not a word.

Bonnie found herself wishing intensely that Carolyn and Anna Lee hadn't had other places to be for lunch; at least Sam Washington wouldn't have been able to sit directly across from her. Then, as if she weren't uncomfortable enough already, Jeff Wells came and sat next to Sam, across from Jenny.

"Mr. Washington, I can't tell you how excited I was when Tom told me you were going to be speaking at the conference this weekend," he told Sam. "I just finished your book on Christianity in the workplace and enjoyed it immensely."

Once again, Bonnie was amused to see how quickly Sam's attention was diverted at the mention of his own work. She also noted with an inward smile that Mr. Washington didn't suggest that Jeff call him Sam. To her great relief, though, Jeff actually said very little to her and Jenny; he was mostly occupied with discussing Sam's book with him. *Not a bad development after all,* Bonnie thought with an inward smile.

"If you'll excuse me," Bonnie said when she had finished her dessert and there was a pause in the conversation between Jeff and Sam, "I'd like to freshen up before the next session begins," and she rose from her chair.

"Oh!" said Sam, as if taken off guard. "Is it that time already? I'm sorry we hardly had time to chat at all. Do you think you might like to join me for dinner?"

Bonnie was shocked that he would ask her to dinner on so short an acquaintance, but tried not to show it. Did the man think he was that irresistible?

"Oh, well, thank you for the invitation, but I really don't think I could get a sitter on such short notice. But it was very kind of you to have asked. Excuse me."

Without giving Sam or anyone else the chance to say anything more to her, she hurried away to the ladies' room. If she played her cards right, she would miss seeing Sam Washington again until after the conference and the concert were over and escape with her boys back to the house for dinner.

Mark Miller brought the house down a second time with his concert that afternoon. He didn't ask Anna Lee to sing with him again, though, leaving Bonnie to wonder if that were a good sign or a bad one with regard to their lunchtime reunion. The older youth had been in charge of childcare for the children of conference attendees, and they had stayed in the church gym during lunch and the morning and after-lunch seminars. But word had gotten out that *the* Mark Miller was giving a concert in the sanctuary that afternoon, so the youth workers led their charges up to the balcony so that they could enjoy it, too.

When the Single Adult Conference was over for another year and everyone who wanted one had gotten Mark Miller's autograph, attendees from neighboring cities began their journeys home. Carolyn and Anna Lee stood chatting a moment, and Bonnie wondered whether Anna Lee was filling Carolyn in on her reunion with Mark Miller. She'd like to know how their lunch had gone herself.

Jenny went to pick Jason up from his father's house. Bonnie started out for the gym to look for her boys, but they found her first. Jeff Wells, Jr., was right behind them.

"Wow, Mom, that was awesome!" Ben greeted her, his eyes shining.

"Mr. Jeff and Miss Amanda let us all come in to hear the music, too!" said Josh proudly. "We need to buy some of his CDs."

Bonnie laughed. "Well, you've got a birthday coming up in July," she told him. "Maybe we'll get you some Mark Miller music for your birthday present."

"Alright!"

"Thanks for watching the kids today, guys," Bonnie told Jeff Junior and Amanda.

"Oh, these guys are fun to have around," said Jeff Junior, ruffling the top of Josh's hair.

At that moment, Tom Givens came up to Carolyn and told her he had someone he wanted her to meet. Looking back, she waved goodbye to Bonnie and Anna Lee. Bonnie watched with no little surprise as Tom led Carolyn to the front of the sanctuary where Sam Washington was standing. They stood there in conversation for several minutes and then, after Bonnie saw Carolyn nodding her head, Sam led Carolyn out of the sanctuary.

Hmm, thought Bonnie with an amused smile. *Carolyn should be able to hold her own with him.* Then Tom was back. Jeff Wells was with him this time.

"So, what've you guys got planned for the evening?" Tom asked, looking alternately at Bonnie and Anna Lee.

"Well…" Anna Lee started, but hesitated.

"Ben and Josh and I are going to go home, have some dinner, and rest up for church tomorrow," Bonnie told him.

Ben and Josh just looked up at the adults and watched the conversation.

"Well, Lisa, Jeff, and I wanted to take Mark out for a thank-you dinner, and we were hoping you might want to come along," Tom said to Anna Lee.

"Oh! Well, I…I mean, did you ask Mark? I mean, does *he* know you're asking me?"

"Any reason why he'd object to having his old singing partner along for the ride? It'll be like a class reunion!"

"I…" Anna Lee looked a little panic-stricken, as if she didn't know how to respond. On impulse, she turned to Bonnie. "Bonnie, would you like to go with us?" There was pleading in her eyes. What must have gone on between the two of them that afternoon that had Anna Lee so panicky about the idea of seeing Mark again? Much as she would like to help Anna Lee out, she, herself, didn't relish the idea of spending the evening with Jeff Wells, even if there would be four other people along. Besides, she couldn't exactly bring Ben and Josh with her.

"Oh, I'd really love to go, but I've got the boys—"

"Hey, Jeff," Jeff Senior piped up, "how'd you like to earn a few extra bucks?"

"What'd you have in mind, Pop?"

"I know you and Amanda had a date planned for tonight, but if you'll take the guys back to Mrs. Callaway's house, I'll spring for pizza."

"Oh, no," said Bonnie, looking at the young lovers. "I wouldn't want to spoil your plans to go out."

What was Jeff doing, for goodness' sake? But Jeff Junior and Amanda were exchanging looks that indicated they definitely didn't mind spending time with her boys if it meant that the two of them would have time alone together after the boys were in bed.

"No," said Amanda, and Bonnie had to admire the innocent look of which she was capable, "we really don't mind at all. Free pizza sounds great." Then, turning to Ben and Josh, Amanda asked them, "How does that sound to you guys?"

"Pizza! Alright!" they chorused.

Bonnie looked at Jeff, her eyes full of questioning. There was the faintest hint of a smile in his eyes, and he gave her just the briefest of winks. Bonnie remembered suddenly that Jeff hadn't volunteered his son's babysitting services when Sam Washington had asked her to dinner. *Clever, Dr. Wells*, she thought. *Very clever.*

"Well, it's all settled, then," said Tom, smiling broadly. "Let me go round up Mark and Lisa, and we'll all go together in our van. How does *Chez Andre* sound?"

"Expensive," said Bonnie.

"I think the honorarium fund for the Conference will handle it," Tom answered smugly. "After all, Bonnie, Anna Lee, and Mark all provided their talents today."

"Hey, don't forget, I made copies!" Jeff joked.

"Fine, we'll buy you a glass of water and a toothpick. Let's get going."

As they walked out of the church to the parking lot, couples formed: Lisa and Tom led the way, Anna Lee walked next to Mark, and Bonnie had little choice but to walk with Jeff.

Feeling as if she ought to say something to break the silence between them, Bonnie remarked, "It was really nice of Jeff and Amanda to agree to stay with the boys, especially since they've been with them most of the day already. Guess it's hard for teenagers to turn down free pizza."

She was trying to be nonchalant, but she knew her words sounded trite and contrived. When Jeff made no reply, she turned to look at him. He was smiling a very knowing smile that made her face begin to flush.

With one arched eyebrow, he leaned over and whispered in her ear, "Free pizza, indeed."

CHAPTER 23

As apprehensive as she had been about spending an evening in which Jeff Wells was part of the company, Bonnie found herself having a really good time. For one thing, it was a treat just to see how Anna Lee glowed in Mark Miller's presence. And it seemed pretty clear that whatever ill will he had felt resulting from their long-ago breakup, he was rapidly getting over it. Tom Givens, whether he had known he was going to or not, had done quite a day's work.

Tom had been right about one thing, though: the reunion of the four college mates (Tom and his wife, Lisa, had met at Samford, also) had Bonnie and Jeff listening eagerly, but required little contribution from them toward the conversation. This was just fine with Bonnie. The day on the whole had been quite taxing; she was glad not to feel obligated to make conversation with Jeff. As the four chattered away about what they had all been doing since they had left their *alma mater*, Jeff sneaked sideways looks at Bonnie, and Bonnie glanced at Jeff now and then when she thought *he* wasn't looking. Once, their eyes did meet, and for a long moment they looked at one another. Again, as they had earlier that afternoon when they had seen each other in the sanctuary, each searched the other's face for some sign that reconciliation was possible.

Perhaps Bonnie thought he should know that her very presence with them at this dinner was an indication that she had forgiven him; perhaps Jeff thought he would see something in her eyes that would tell him they could go forward from their false start. A smile from either of them might have done it, but each was so worried about the other's reaction that the moment passed, and they both looked away uncomfortably.

As the party of six headed back to Chandler City, Tom decided he would take Bonnie, Jeff, and Anna Lee back to the church parking lot before bringing

Mark to his motel room. Mark alighted first and held his hand out to Anna Lee to help her descend from Tom's minivan.

"I'll walk you to your car," he murmured. Anna Lee made no protest.

Jeff was sitting nearest the door, blocking Bonnie's exit, and he made no move to get out as Mark and Anna Lee walked across the parking lot. Bonnie looked at Jeff to see why he was delaying getting out of the van.

"So," Jeff began, with a knowing smile at Tom, "you think he'll try to kiss her goodnight?"

Bonnie's eyes widened and she stared at Jeff.

"Oh, I think he's going to go for the gold," grinned Tom.

"Tom Givens!" Lisa chided, but there was an uncontrollable smile on her face. "You two are acting like a couple of high school kids!"

"Hey, we call 'em as we see 'em," Tom told her.

"They haven't seen each other in six years," Lisa reminded them. "I don't think they're going to—"

"Okay, they're at the car," Tom broke in. "He's telling her he had a good time."

"A hush falls over the crowd as Miller lines up his next shot," Jeff said in whispered imitation of a golf tournament announcer's play-by-play.

"You guys!" Lisa giggled.

Bonnie just stared at Jeff in fascination. This was the playful side of him she had often seen at their dinners after Benevolent Council meetings. It was good to see it again after what now seemed like a very long time.

There was a moment of silence, and the four of them watched as Mark Miller leaned over and gently placed a kiss on Anna Lee's lips.

"He shoots! He scores!" shouted Tom.

"Touchdown!" Jeff called out. Tom and Jeff gave each other the high five.

"Are you believing these guys?" Lisa asked. "Who needs to have children when you've got Tom around?"

Bonnie just shook her head and smiled.

"On that note," Jeff said as he climbed out of the van, "I believe it's time to call it a day. Sunday morning comes early."

He extended his hand to Bonnie and helped her out of the van.

"Thank you," she murmured, only briefly meeting Jeff's eyes. "Thanks again for dinner," Bonnie called back into the van.

"Thanks for coming," returned Tom.

"Goodnight, everybody," Bonnie said, so she wouldn't have to say goodnight specifically to Jeff. But Jeff said his "goodnight" directly to her. She looked at him again and gave an awkward little wave. She drove from the parking lot, watching as Anna Lee and Mark began to make up for six years of separation. She thought back to her one, brief kiss with Jeff Wells and sighed a very lonely sigh.

All Anna Lee had to do was meet Bonnie's eyes the next morning in Sunday School and she began to blush.

"Quite a day, yesterday, eh?" Bonnie asked her, trying hard not to sound like she was teasing her. Anna Lee just smiled shyly, her cheeks glowing. "Did you tell your mother that you saw Mark?"

Anna Lee looked shocked.

"Are you kidding? She despises the very mention of his name! Ever since she found out that he's become a famous recording star, I know she's been kicking herself that she talked me out of marrying him. Although she'd never admit that to *me*."

"Do you have plans to see him again?"

Anna Lee cast her eyes down. "I…I don't know." She shook her head. "I don't think so. At least, not anytime soon. He's going to sing at the eleven o'clock service, but then he's got plans to take a little vacation time in Panama City."

"Ah," said Bonnie. "Well, now that you've seen each other again, maybe he'll get over his hard feelings about the way you broke up, and you'll get to see each other now and then."

Anna Lee shrugged. "I kind of doubt it. I mean, he lives in Nashville. I doubt that he'd be interested in a long-distance relationship. And I don't know for sure that he's not already seeing someone. The subject didn't really come up yesterday. It *is* good to know that at least he doesn't hate me anymore."

Bonnie could hear the tentative note in Anna Lee's voice, as if she were willing herself not to get her hopes up about anything developing between her and Mark again. Soon, Carolyn Perkins came into the room. She didn't look exactly angry, but she had a rather sardonic smile on her face.

"Hi, guys," she said in a deadpan voice.

"Hello, yourself," Bonnie answered with a quirk of her head. "How are you this morning?"

Jenny Pierce joined them, catching the tail end of the conversation.

"Remember how I asked you guys yesterday morning about meeting the man of your dreams at the Singles Conference?"

Anna Lee and Bonnie stared at her.

"Yes," answered Bonnie cautiously.

"Well, that did *not* happen."

Bonnie and Anna Lee exchanged looks.

"Are you talking about Sam Washington?" Bonnie asked, trying hard to hide her amusement.

Carolyn nodded with an ironic smile. "Don't get me wrong, we had a great dinner last night, the three of us."

"'The three of you'?" Bonnie echoed.

"Me, Sam, and his ego."

At this, Bonnie couldn't restrain her laughter. Anna Lee just looked on; she hadn't met Sam yesterday. Finally, Carolyn grinned in spite of herself and shook her head.

"I think my self-esteem is pretty well intact, but I have to admit I was rather flattered when he asked me out to dinner, especially having just met me."

"Hate to burst your bubble," Jenny broke in, a mischievous smile on her face, "but Bonnie got to him first."

"Jenny!" Bonnie chided.

"Oh, that's just great!" Carolyn kidded. "Now I'm second choice, too! Well, it became painfully clear, as the evening went on, that his chief interest in me was that I just happen to be an attorney specializing in corporate law and intellectual property matters. It seems Mr. Washington wants to expand his niche in the publishing world and, silly girl that I am, I was a treasure trove of free legal information."

"Poor Carolyn," said Jenny. "Well, at least you had nice scenery to look at."

Carolyn arched an eyebrow at her and grinned.

"Can't deny that. He *is* easy on the eyes."

There were a few older members of the congregation who had not heard of Mark Miller, but his presence in the eleven o'clock service that morning caused nearly as much stir as it had at the Singles Conference the previous day. He sang a song from one of his earliest albums, and it struck a familiar chord with nearly everyone there, since many soloists had sung it in church over the years. Bonnie noticed that Anna Lee Adkinson was in the spot that she used to occupy with her mother each Sunday, and no one was more surprised than Anna Lee herself when Mark left the dais and went down to sit next to her. Once again, Bonnie could see Anna Lee's face redden, but she obviously basked in Mark's nearness. Bonnie just knew that Anna Lee wouldn't have seen the last of Mark after today. She just knew it.

To round out his weekend with the Singles Conference, Sam Washington gave a brief account of the previous day's events, along with an overview of some of the important issues facing single adults today which, coincidentally, he just happened to have discussed in one of his recently published books. Bonnie tried to hide her smile at Washington's self-promotion for Carolyn's sake; Carolyn herself, however, didn't seem to be trying hard to hide her own disdain. Still, she smiled blandly enough when Sam came and sat next to her. Carolyn wouldn't be regretting Sam Washington's departure for Atlanta as Anna Lee would be Mark Miller's for Nashville.

Bonnie and the boys joined the Singles at the Chinese buffet again, something they did on a fairly regular basis now. After that first Sunday, when Jeff had spent all of his time in conversation with Sherry Niles, Bonnie never saw him there again. Today was no exception. Carolyn was there, Sam Washington in tow, surprisingly enough, but Anna Lee didn't show up. Bonnie wondered if she were having a farewell lunch with Mark Miller.

She didn't have to wonder long.

At about three o'clock that afternoon, Bonnie was putting some last minute touches on the layout for Grabbabite's new menu when the phone rang.

"Bonnie, this is Jeff Wells."

At the sound of his voice, her heart began to pound. Just the sound of his voice on the phone, and she fell apart a little inside.

"I know this is short notice, but Anna Lee Adkinson asked me to call you."

Bonnie gasped. "Is something wrong?"

"No," Jeff laughed softly. "Everything is just great, actually. There's going to be a wedding."

Bonnie felt her knees go weak. "A wedding?" she whispered.

"Anna Lee would like for you to stand up with her as her matron of honor. What are you doing after church tonight?"

Bonnie laughed at the offhand way he said it, as if they planned for weddings with five hours' notice every day.

"I'd be honored! Oh, my goodness! They're really doing it? They're really getting *married*?"

"Seems like they've both been waiting six years for this," he said. "That sounds like a long enough engagement to me, doesn't it to you?"

"Oh, yes," she laughed. "I just can't believe it! When I talked to Anna Lee this morning in Sunday School, she sounded as if she didn't know if she'd ever see him again after today."

"That sounds like Anna Lee, always so unsure of herself. But I've never seen a guy so happy to be reunited with anyone." There was an awkward pause after that remark. "I guess you realize, too, that this is top secret business."

"Oh, sure, I guess it would have to be, wouldn't it?"

Bonnie thought of Clara and wondered just how she would react when she found out. Would she be angry that Anna Lee had married the man Clara had rejected all those years ago, or would she be glad that Anna Lee was finally marrying into money? It was a strange relationship Anna Lee had with her mother; anyone would have thought that a mother would be happy for her daughter at a time like this. But Bonnie could see why Anna Lee wouldn't want to take chances on her mother trying to talk her out of anything again. She'd been paying for *that* mistake for six years.

"Would it be okay if I told Cheryl? I was going to ask her if she could watch the boys for me, maybe feed them some dinner after the service."

"Actually," Jeff said, "I was going to offer to let Jeff Junior stay with the boys again, if you thought that would be okay."

"Well, no, I don't mind, and the boys certainly wouldn't mind. They're crazy about him," Bonnie told him. "But do you think Jeff Junior will want to? How much babysitting can he take?"

"Oh, he's just as nuts about them as they are about him. He revels in all that hero worship they heap on him. They're like the little brothers he never had."

Bonnie drew a deep breath at that comment.

"Well, sure, then, that'd be great. So what's the plan?"

Jeff filled her in on the logistics of how the ceremony would take place when everyone had cleared out of the sanctuary after the evening service. Her heart nearly bursting with excitement, Bonnie went to pick out a dress that would suit an impromptu matron of honor.

"Are you nervous?" Bonnie asked Anna Lee as she helped her to zip up the tea-length white dress she had hurriedly purchased at the mall that afternoon.

"I guess I should be," said Anna Lee, catching Bonnie's eye in the mirror, "but I've waited so *long* for this. It just feels so right. When Mark and I are together, it's as though we were never apart. He told me that he kept up with me through Tom Givens all these years." Her eyes brimmed with tears. "He never forgot about me, Bonnie. He says he never stopped loving me, even though it took him a while to get over his anger with me."

"Don't you dare cry, young lady," Bonnie teased her. "We want your make-up to be perfect when Mark sees you."

Anna Lee's eyes glowed with excitement, then she whirled around and hugged Bonnie.

"Oh, Bonnie, I'm going to miss you! We haven't been friends that long, I know, but what a friend you've been to me!"

Bonnie thought back on the twists and turns that had brought them together and marveled at how funny things could turn out at times.

"I'll miss you, too, Anna Lee." Then, holding her at arm's length, she said, "Have a wonderful life with Mark."

"I think I will," Anna Lee whispered.

"Come on, lady. Let's go get you married!"

Lisa Givens had been busy that afternoon, too. She had practically stood over the florist who put together the bouquets that Anna Lee and Bonnie carried, but they were resplendent. Mark had told Lisa to spare no expense. Lisa had also contacted Betty and Claire of Grabbabite. By the time the wedding party arrived at Bonnie's that evening after the ceremony, the two restaurateurs, who were only too happy to be involved in the conspiracy, would have a small but delectable array of finger foods, a bowl of punch, and a miniature wedding cake spread out for the last-minute reception.

Everything went by so quickly: Carolyn had looked at Bonnie quizzically when Bonnie told her she wouldn't be going to the after-church Singles fellowship, but gave no reason why.

"I'll fill you in tomorrow, I promise," Bonnie told her; she had invited Carolyn to spend Memorial Day with her and the boys. The sanctuary seemed to clear out in record time; Ben and Josh, thrilled to be taken out to the Coffee Shoppe for dinner with Jeff Wells, Jr., waved gleeful goodbyes to their mother.

Not wanting to attract attention from anyone who might still be in the building, Anna Lee walked down the aisle accompanied by no music, even though Lisa had offered to play the "Wedding March" on the piano.

"We have a lifetime of music ahead of us," Mark had told her.

Lisa had never seen her husband's friend look so happy. She realized now that, all those years she and Tom had known him since college, there had been a trace of sadness in him that now seemed miraculously to have disappeared. Instead of playing music, then, Lisa provided her services as wedding photographer.

When Anna Lee had become Mrs. Mark Miller, there were hugs all around. Only Jeff and Bonnie, unnoticed in the excitement of the moment, failed to embrace each other. As she hugged Anna Lee again, Bonnie started as her eyes strayed to the back of the sanctuary. On the very last row of pews sat Mertis Hargrove! When she saw that Bonnie had seen her, Mertis rose and exited through the back doors. With widened eyes, Bonnie looked at Jeff, who, having performed the ceremony, had to have known she was there. He lifted his eyebrows as if to confirm that he had, but said nothing.

Bonnie could tell that Mark and Anna Lee were anxious to leave; it was almost a two-hour drive down to Panama City. But Tom and Lisa were able to convince them that they couldn't get married without at least some semblance of a reception. Besides, Lisa had argued, there were still a few shots left on the disposable camera she had bought on which to capture the wedding.

The small but excited wedding party headed over to Bonnie's house; Jeff Junior had already let himself and Bonnie's boys in, and the children were dressed for bed.

"Say congratulations to Miss Anna Lee, guys!" Bonnie told them. "She just got married to Mark Miller."

"Whoa!" said Ben, as if he truly grasped the gravity of the event.

"Can I have some wedding cake?" asked Josh, and everyone laughed at the significance the occasion had for him.

"I promise to save you a big piece," Bonnie told him, and Jeff Junior led them off to their bedrooms. When he was certain that the boys were safely asleep, he let himself out and headed home to make a belated call to Amanda Summers.

Anna Lee couldn't believe what Bonnie and Lisa had been able to put together on such short notice.

"Oh, look at everything!" she sighed.

Lisa took pictures of the cake and the food before the hungry crew demolished them. As Bonnie had expected, though, Anna Lee and Mark didn't linger. Not wanting to attract her mother's attention, Anna Lee hadn't packed any of her own things before leaving for church that afternoon. Instead, she had gone on a miniature shopping spree earlier that day when she went to buy her wedding dress. What few things she was bringing with her were already in her car; they would drive it to the Gulf Coast for their honeymoon. Bonnie anxiously wondered why Clara wasn't calling to chew them all out for holding the wedding behind her back. Surely, Mertis had filled her in by now. Bonnie was secretly grateful for the silent telephone.

"We can't thank you all enough," Anna Lee said as they stood at Bonnie's front door, ready to leave. "We'll be back next week to pick up my stuff at my mother's."

Then she gasped.

"My mother! How am I going to let her know not to worry about me when I don't come home tonight?"

Everyone looked sheepishly at one another. No one relished the idea of bearing this particular piece of news to Clara Adkinson.

Finally, Jeff raised his hand.

"Don't worry, Anna Lee. I'll talk to your mother." He didn't sound thrilled at the prospect.

"Thanks, Jeff," said Mark. "I owe you one."

"Yes," Jeff said with an arched eyebrow and a smile, "you *do*."

Everyone had to laugh. Then, as if suddenly remembering something, Anna Lee turned to Mark.

"Hang on a second, I nearly forgot one of the most important things!"

She ran over to the kitchen table where she and Bonnie had lain their flowers and picked up her own.

"I've got to throw out my bouquet!"

Lisa chuckled. "Well, Anna Lee, since there's only one single woman in this crowd, the destination of *that* bouquet is a no-brainer."

Realizing who she meant, Bonnie felt her face begin to color.

"Oh, Anna Lee," she began, "that's not really nece—"

But before she could finish, Anna Lee had lightly tossed the ribbons and flowers in Bonnie's direction. Bonnie plucked them out of the air, in spite of herself.

"Well," remarked Lisa with a wide grin, "looks like you're next!"

Bonnie smiled weakly and thought, "*Yeah, right.*"

After Mark and Anna Lee had gone, Tom stuffed a few more of Betty and Claire's canapés into his mouth.

"Boy," he remarked. "Am I glad tomorrow's a holiday! This has been some kind of weekend!"

"I'd like to get the holiday started right now, if you don't mind," said Lisa. "Let's help Bonnie get this place cleaned up and clear out of here."

Before Bonnie could respond, Jeff said, "Oh, no, you guys don't need to worry about that! I'll stay and help Bonnie clean up. You two go on home."

Tom looked at Bonnie, and she knew exactly what the question in his eyes was, but she said nothing.

"Alright," he said with mock resignation. "I had counted on doing some more work tonight, but if you insist."

And then, he and Lisa were gone. All that was left were plates full of crumbs, a half-eaten wedding cake, and two uncomfortably silent people.

"You really don't have to stay," Bonnie told him without meeting his eye. She picked up a couple of plates and brought them to the kitchen. "There's not that much to do, and I'm sure you've had a long day."

Jeff's only response was to begin bringing plates and punch cups into the kitchen so that Bonnie could prepare them for the dishwasher. Bonnie sighed. Why did he feel it necessary to do this? Didn't he feel as awkward as she did?

When the last of the plates and cups had been arranged in the dishwasher, Bonnie stood at the sink wiping her hands on a towel, desperately trying to think of something casual to say. All she could think of was whether Jeff would ever try to kiss her again. Might *this* be the night that they brought this whole awful business with Clara and Sherry and Preston to a close? On such a happy occasion as Anna Lee's wedding, it seemed somehow fitting that it would. She glanced over at Jeff, who stood at the kitchen table absentmindedly fingering the flowers and ribbons on Anna Lee's wedding bouquet.

Without any other introduction, and without looking at her, Jeff began, "I wanted you to be the first to know."

Bonnie just looked at him and her heart began to pound. She didn't like the gravity of his tone.

"Yes?"

"When we get back from the Youth Mission Tour, well, actually, the Sunday after Foster Road's Vacation Bible school…" He looked as if he were still trying to figure it out himself. "I guess there's no best time to do this, but I *do* want at least to wait until VBS is through…"

"What is it, Dr. Wells?"

Man! he thought. *Not even now can she bring herself to call me Jeff!* Well, it didn't matter anymore now, anyway, did it?

"After the service that Sunday morning, I'll be reading my resignation to the congregation." He hesitated. Bonnie felt her knees go weak.

Trying desperately not to cry, Bonnie murmured, "That'll come as quite a shock to everyone."

"Yes, I suppose it will to some." Then he looked at her. "Perhaps not to others."

Bonnie looked away. She wanted to ask him where he was going, what he would be doing, but she knew that if she tried to speak, she would break down and cry.

"Well," she finally managed, "I wish you well wherever you go."

"Thanks," he said tersely. "But, um, listen. I haven't told anyone about this yet except for Jack—and now you. I'd appreciate it if you could keep this under your hat until I actually announce."

She looked at him, wondering if this was his only concern about what she would do about this news. "Oh! No, I won't say a word."

"Thanks. As I said, I…I wanted you to be the first to know."

She wasn't looking at him now. She could make no further reply.

She didn't even ask me where I'm going!

What did you expect? He chided himself. *She's never going to forgive you for all that business with Clara. Well, at least you know now you've made the right decision.* He reached into his pocket and pulled out his car keys.

He was going to leave, and Bonnie didn't know what to say to him. Just before he opened the front door, Bonnie blurted, "Have a great trip with the youth!"

He smiled a weak smile, and Bonnie could see pain in his eyes.

"I know I will," he said, and he closed the door behind him.

CHAPTER 24

Bonnie's mother heard the sadness in her daughter's voice when they spoke on Memorial Day.

"What's the matter, honey? You don't sound well."

"Oh, I'm alright," she fibbed. "I just had a really busy weekend."

"Excuse me," her mother replied briskly, "but I think I know my own daughter a little better than that! What's going on with you?"

"Oh, Mom, I wish we could have lunch so I could tell you all about it."

"Well, why don't we, then? Pack those boys in the car and come on over!"

Bonnie thought about it. Vacation Bible School wasn't for another three weeks yet. Cheryl and Jack would be in New Orleans on a house-hunting trip—maybe they could go to dinner together while she was there! She was mostly caught up on work for her clients, and she usually took the boys to see their grandparents over the summer anyway. Why not?

"Are you sure you and Dad won't mind company on such short notice?"

Mrs. Martin scoffed. "Get yourself in that car and I'll have dinner waiting for you tomorrow evening. How does crawfish bisque sound?"

"We'll be there!" Bonnie laughed.

After hanging up with her mother, she picked up the phone and called Bill's parents to let them know that she would be returning to Georgia by way of Jackson so that the boys could get in a visit with them, too.

Somewhere between Arkansas and Oklahoma, the bus full of youth and chaperones heading for Oregon got very quiet. Heads began to nod as the early hour at which the bus had departed from the church parking lot began to take its toll. Jeff looked up from the book he was reading and watched Interstate and billboards flash past; somehow, Sam Washington's work held a little less interest for him since he had heard Washington ask Bonnie out to dinner right in front of him.

Of course, that wasn't all that distracted him from his book. Outside of the huge success of the Singles Conference, which *he* certainly couldn't take any credit for, and Anna Lee and Mark Miller's wedding, which he was also not responsible for bringing about, he could think of very few things that had gone right in the past couple of months.

His across-the-street neighbor was no longer speaking to him. To make matters worse, she blamed him, somehow, for Anna Lee and Mark's elopement, as if they wouldn't have gotten Tom Givens to marry them if he hadn't been willing to. When he had arrived home from Bonnie's Sunday night, Jeff Junior had reluctantly given him a message that Clara had called.

"She sounds pretty torked, Dad," his son had warned him.

He wasn't surprised, of course, that Mertis had told Clara about the wedding she had inadvertently witnessed. Truth be told, Mertis had done him a favor; he only had to listen to Clara heap abuse on him after the fact. The task of actually breaking the news to her had at least been spared him.

What he really couldn't get off his mind, though, was Bonnie and the way they had parted Sunday night. He'd had such high hopes for a reconciliation with her after he had publicly apologized to her at that ridiculous church business meeting. But Bonnie had let him leave the other night without so much as asking him where he would be going when he left Foster Road Baptist. He sighed deeply.

He was doing the right thing, he was sure. With Jeff Junior going off to college in September and his best buddy moving away sooner than that, there was really nothing to keep him in Chandler City. He needed a new start. So why did he feel so lousy about it?

Ben and Josh had begun the trip with noisy anticipation. They had packed books and travel games to keep themselves occupied in the back seat, and fought a little bit over who would play with which thing first. Eventually, though, they settled down, and each selected a book to read. Bonnie glanced into the back seat periodically. About the fourth time she looked, the excitement and the early hour at which they had risen had gotten the better of them; each boy was fast asleep, their heads tilted back and their mouths slightly agape.

Alone with her thoughts, about the same time that Jeff Wells was scanning the landscape outside of his bus window, Bonnie thought back again to Sunday night. *You should have said something,* she berated herself.

For what? another part of her argued. He was leaving. What could she possibly say to change that? *Fat lot of good it had done to forgive him,* she thought bitterly. She found herself not just a little angry with God at that particular moment. She had prayed about this long and hard, hadn't she? She had tried to do the right thing, forgiving him when she felt like *she* had been the wronged party. What good had it done her? She took a deep breath and tried to think of something else. She needed to listen to some music or something.

She lifted the lid to the storage compartment between the two front seats and flipped through the audiocassettes stored there as she held the steering wheel with her left hand. In her disgruntled mood, nothing she saw really interested her. The car in front of her was slowing down, and Bonnie felt like passing it. She grabbed a tape without looking at it and popped it into the tape player, then accelerated to get ahead. As soon as she had settled back down to cruising speed, she reached over absentmindedly and twisted the "on" knob.

"...the choir for such a fine job this morning."

Oh, great. It was the voice of Jeff Wells, and it sounded like he was just getting ready to begin one of his sermons. Annoyed that this was what the luck of the draw had produced for her, she let the tape continue to play while she began shuffling through the tapes in the compartment again.

"I want to read to you from the fifteenth chapter of Luke: 'There was a man who had two sons. The younger one said to his father, "Give me my share of the estate."'"

Bonnie's hand went still. This was the tape Carolyn Perkins had listened to, the sermon Cheryl had found so moving the day it was preached. Something inside her, a small voice she hadn't attended to in far too long, reminded her that *she* had intended to listen to this tape herself, that she had ordered it from Jeff's secretary expressly so that she *could* listen to it. Wasn't it about time that she did?

The tape continued to roll, and Jeff's voice came out to her, as if he were speaking just to her. She realized, with a pain that tore at her heart, that it was the voice of the man she loved, of the man who was leaving her life for good. She listened to him, cherishing every word he said, knowing that every word he said was true: God meant for us to be reconciled to Him, and He meant for us to be reconciled to each other.

But that was never going to happen—not with her and Jeff—because she had been too proud to let him know she had forgiven him. She had no one to blame for her sorrows but herself. For the first time in a long time, without the boys or anyone else to see her, she allowed the tears to flow.

It was so good to be back in the house she had grown up in, sleeping in the room that had been hers when she was a little girl. She could almost forget about the pain gnawing away at her, forget about the hopelessness of things between her and Jeff Wells. Knowing that Jeff planned to leave Chandler City, even Bonnie's mother could see no way that Bonnie and Jeff could get back together. All she could do was offer the comfort of a mother's love.

Bonnie went to dinner with Jack and Cheryl once when they were in town; it looked liked they'd found a house they liked out in Kenner, a suburb to the north and west of New Orleans. While Bonnie's father took Ben and Josh fishing in his little boat out on Lake Maurepas, Bonnie had lunch and café au lait and beignets with her mother. She even took her morning runs on the playground of her old elementary school. It seemed almost like old times. The only thing missing was Sally, Bonnie's big sister, who was away on business in Chicago. Bonnie had decided to come to New Orleans so suddenly that Sally hadn't had a chance to change her plans. She would be back at the beginning of next week.

On the day Sally was to arrive, Bonnie and her mother drove out to the airport while Bonnie's father stayed home with the boys. They stood at the entrance to the concourse and waited as streams of travelers passed from the emptying planes. Bonnie dawdled at one of the airport's many gift shops and toyed with the idea of buying t-shirts for Carolyn and Jenny. They would get a kick out of wearing shirts with dancing crawfish on them, she was sure.

"Bonnie," called her mother, "here comes Sally."

Bonnie looked up to scan the onslaught of people striding down the concourse, and her breath caught in her throat. She squinted, because she was sure she must be seeing things. But the closer Sally got, the more certain Bonnie was that Sally was walking side-by-side with none other than Jeff Wells! How could this possibly be? Bonnie's mouth went dry.

"Hey, guys!" Sally called, giving her little sister a bear hug. "Look who I found on the plane from Chicago! The pastor of Bonnie's church!"

Jeff looked at Bonnie as her sister hugged her; the look in his eyes was almost guilty. All Bonnie could do was stare back at him, utterly dumbstruck. What on earth was Jeff Wells doing in New Orleans?

"Mrs. Martin," Jeff greeted Bonnie's mother. "So good to see you again."

"Dr. Wells! What a surprise to see you!" Bonnie's mother plastered a smile on her face, sneaking glances at Bonnie for her reaction. "What brings you to New Orleans?"

"Well, as Bonnie knows, I left Chandler City the day after Memorial Day to go on the mission tour with our youth. After Vacation Bible School was over there, I flew out of Portland to Chicago to visit my daughter. She's working an internship there this summer."

Bonnie suddenly remembered their conversation the night they'd had dinner with Jack and Cheryl. Jeff had told them then that Becky would be in Chicago for the summer.

"Since our own VBS won't be starting until next Monday, I thought I'd sneak down here to visit some of my old seminary buddies."

"Oh, that's right," said Mrs. Martin. "You got your doctorate here, didn't you?"

"Yes, ma'am, I did," he answered on a deep breath.

Bonnie could tell he was anxious not to prolong this encounter, and she felt the same way.

"Well, hey," piped up Sally before Bonnie could find a polite way of bidding him goodbye, "while you're in town, why don't you come to the Martin house for dinner? Nobody makes better gumbo than my Mom!"

"That's very kind of you," he murmured, glancing briefly at Bonnie, "but I'm sure Mrs. Martin has her hands full with Bonnie and her boys."

"Oh, nonsense!" answered Sally, "There's always room for one more!"

She looked to Mrs. Martin for confirmation. Instead, she saw her mother making the strangest face at her.

"I'm sure Dr. Wells would like to spend his short stay in New Orleans with the people he really came to see, Sally." There was just the slightest emphatic edge to her voice.

Sally suspected something was amiss when her mother hadn't seconded the invitation, but when her mother made *that* statement, she knew something was up! It was going to be an interesting ride home.

"Thank you for understanding, Mrs. Martin. Perhaps I'll be able to accept your hospitality some other time. It was very good to see you again."

With a nod to Bonnie and Sally, Jeff Wells continued down the corridor toward the rental car kiosks. For what felt like the first time since she'd seen him walking off the plane with Sally, Bonnie exhaled.

"Thanks, Mom," said Bonnie.

"You *are* going to tell me what's going on, right?" Sally said as they made their way to the luggage retrieval area.

"Film at eleven," Bonnie told her.

Bonnie could only hope that when she got to be her friend's age, which she reckoned to be at least eighty, she would have as much energy and resilience as Ruth Newton. Ruth was one of the "cookie ladies" in Vacation Bible School—instead of teaching a class, she worked with several other women from the Senior Adult group serving refreshments to the children coming in from their recreation breaks. How they stood the noise and clamor in the dining hall was beyond Bonnie, but Bonnie was glad for the chance to see Ruth each day.

"So, how are you surviving fifth- and sixth-graders?" Ruth said with a wink. "I don't envy *you* a jot."

"Oh, it's not so bad," Bonnie said with a smile. "They just get a little hyper when they start running around on their break."

"What do you hear from the newlyweds?"

"I think Anna Lee is having the time of her life," Bonnie answered. "Apparently, Mark is getting ready to record a new album, and she's going to sing backup for him. She's thrilled to pieces!"

"What a fairy tale romance," Ruth said.

There was a look in Ruth's eyes that Bonnie couldn't quite read.

"I sat with Dr. Wells at fellowship supper last night," Ruth continued.

Bonnie could tell now that Ruth was trying to get some kind of reaction out of her. What had Jeff told her?

"Did you?" was all Bonnie replied, her face carefully nonchalant.

"Yes. He mentioned that he ran into *you* in New Orleans, of all places."

Ruth was getting at something, Bonnie just knew it. But what a poker face!

"You could've knocked me over with a feather when I saw Jeff walking off of that plane talking to my sister," Bonnie laughed.

"Wonder what he was doing there?" Ruth baited her again.

"He said he was visiting some of his old friends from the seminary."

"Ah, yes, he mentioned that to me, too. Did the two of you get together at all while you were both there?"

Bonnie felt herself blushing in spite of herself. That innocent look in Ruth's eyes wasn't fooling Bonnie one bit. Ruth was up to something.

"Get together with him?"

"Well, you two *are* good friends, aren't you? I mean, after serving together so long on the Benevolent Council."

"Well, yes," Bonnie fibbed, "but…"

"I just thought you might've had him over for dinner, or that maybe you two might have shared dinner at one of those fabulous places in New Orleans. After all," she continued, a more pointed tone in her voice, "the Coffee Shoppe and Grabbabite aren't the only two restaurants in the world. In fact, I've heard that there are a couple of really *great* seafood places down at Mexico Beach."

Now Bonnie knew exactly what Ruth was getting at. Jeff must have told Ruth about their date that was cancelled the day that Art died. Had he told her about all the rest, as well? Bonnie was grateful that it was time for her class to get back upstairs.

"I've gotta get going," she mumbled, trying hard not to give Ruth the reaction she was trying to elicit. "Talk to you later."

That Sunday morning, when Jeff Wells read his letter of resignation to the congregation, there was stunned silence. Even Tom Givens, to whom Jeff had said nothing save asking him to postpone the closing prayer until he made a final announcement, sat and stared, wide-eyed, when Jeff left the dais through one of the choir entrances. Finally, Tom rose from his seat and said the briefest prayer he could manage. The choir sang its benediction, and Tom was after Jeff like a shot. There were tears in his eyes as he closed the door to Jeff's office. Jeff looked up, dreading the confrontation he knew was coming.

"You never said a word to me," Tom said, accusation in his voice.

"I'm sorry. It was tough decision. I only told a couple of people before-hand."

"But not me."

"I'm sorry, Tom. What do you want me to say?"

Tom chewed at his upper lip. "Is this about Bonnie?"

Jeff started. How did Tom know? He'd never said the first thing—Then he remembered that there were probably very few people in church who didn't know that, at least at one brief point, there had been something going on between him and Bonnie. Tom had simply never said anything to him about it.

"I guess you could say that Bonnie factored into the decision."

"'Factored into.' Oh, that's just great. Great way of putting it," Tom scoffed. "Why didn't you ever get together again after you'd found out what a pack of lies Clara had told about her?"

"What makes you think that Bonnie wanted to?"

"She told you she didn't want to see you anymore?"

"She didn't have to."

Tom hesitated, as if unsure of whether he should say what was on his mind. At length, he folded his arms and began again: "Well, you won't be my boss for much longer, so I can say this to you now."

Jeff raised his eyebrows curiously.

"I think you're wrong, and I think you've made a big mistake." He got up to leave Jeff's office. Taking a deep breath, he said, "But I wish you luck wherever you're going."

Moving day came and went for the Summers family. Bonnie and her boys were on hand to help with the packing, and they made another trip to New Orleans to help with the moving in. Moving into a house in late August in New Orleans was like taking a job in a giant sauna: the heat and humidity were oppressive. One evening, when Cheryl had gone to the store to pick up cold drinks and ice for everyone, Bonnie sat with Jack on the front steps of their new house and felt the perspiration trickle down her back. *Only for a best friend*, she thought wryly.

"So how are you doing?" Jack asked her.

It had been months, probably not since the day they had talked on the phone after her aborted date with Jeff, since Bonnie had spoken with Jack alone, but she knew exactly what he was referring to. She chose to ignore it.

"I'm good," she told him, not meeting his eye.

"Wish I could say the same for Jeff," Jack said. He swiped his sleeve across his forehead.

"What's wrong with him?"

"Nothing that a little romance wouldn't have cured."

Bonnie couldn't hide her annoyance as she gave him a sidelong look. "And you're telling me this because...?"

"Bonnie, Jeff hasn't been himself ever since you guys broke off with each other last April."

"'Broke off with each other?' I think you're forgetting a couple of details there." Bonnie was losing patience. "And I still don't see your point. What could I have done differently? What could I have done, period, that would've made any difference?"

"Okay, fine. Maybe things were bound to happen the way they did. Just tell me one thing: did you care for him?"

"Jack, do you really think it matters any more?"

"Just answer the question, Bonnie. Did you care for him?"

Bonnie folded her arms and rested them on her knees, then rested her forehead on her arms. She sighed deeply, trying hard not to cry in front of Jack. She lifted her head and shook it slowly, her eyes still closed.

"For what it's worth, Jack, yes. I did care for him. I've often asked myself, I've often asked *God*, why Jeff was allowed to enter my life so briefly and make me care for him the way I did. Why did God think I needed that?"

Jack put a sympathetic arm across her back and rubbed her shoulder. "No way you could swallow your pride and let Jeff know that?"

Bonnie looked at Jack as if he'd taken leave of his senses. "For what, Jack? To make him feel better when he leaves Chandler City?"

As the date of Jeff's last Sunday at Foster Road Baptist Church approached, Bonnie found herself growing more depressed. It didn't help that she felt so alone: the boys were spending two weeks at their Callaway grandparents' house; Cheryl and Jack and Anna Lee were gone; Carolyn was vacationing in Europe for three weeks. For the second Sunday in a row, she just couldn't roll out of bed and bring herself to go to church, to ride there without the boys, to sit in Sunday School without Carolyn. Jenny was there, it was true, but truth be told, she just couldn't go and listen to Jeff anymore. She couldn't sit and look at him for an hour, even from a distance. Maybe when he had gone to wherever it was he was going, which wouldn't be long now, she could go back.

At just about twelve-twenty, the doorbell rang. Bonnie was still in her bathrobe, not having even felt motivated enough to get dressed yet. Who in the world was calling at this hour? Anybody she knew was still in church, or just getting out, at best. She thought back to that Saturday morning when she had been wearing the plastic bag on her head and Jeff had come calling in his Sunday best. At least she didn't have to worry about him seeing her *that* way again, she thought with an inward chuckle.

She opened the door and peered around its edge. There stood Ruth Newton, looking trim and stylish in a light blue seersucker suit.

"Ruth!" Bonnie couldn't hide her surprise. "What brings you here?"

"More to the point," said Ruth, walking through the front door without waiting to be asked in, "What keeps you *here*? Were you planning to come back to church any time soon?"

Bonnie felt herself flushing with embarrassment. Lost in her own self-pity, she hadn't thought that anyone would even notice her absence.

"I…" She really didn't know what to say to Ruth.

Ruth took her by the hand and led her to the sofa. "Bonnie, dear, you know how special you are to me." Bonnie just looked down. "Won't you tell me what's bothering you?"

Did she dare? Ruth had had her hands full with Art for so long that Bonnie had never wanted to burden her with her own troubles. But it would be so nice to have her to confide in. Ruth was like having a Mom away from home. Before Bonnie could say anything, though, Ruth asked her, "Is it Jeff?"

Bonnie stared at her, dumbfounded. "How did you know?" she whispered.

Ruth gave Bonnie a look that said, "You ought to know better than that," but she patted Bonnie's hand. "Oh, I keep my ear to the ground," she told Bonnie, not revealing any more.

"You are one fascinating woman," Bonnie told her, admiration in her eyes.

"And you are one stressed out woman," Ruth said, never one for sentimentality. "And Dr. Newton has just the cure."

Bonnie grinned in spite of herself. "Tell me, please!"

"What do you say to a little time on the beach? The summer's almost gone, and the boys will be back in school soon. Why don't you take them down to Panama City for Labor Day weekend?"

Bonnie smiled and rolled her eyes. "Yeah, like I could get reservations for Labor Day now! Like I could afford them if I could get them!"

Ruth picked up Bonnie's hand again and gave it a little shake. "How many times do I have to tell you that I have a condo down there that is yours to use anytime you want it?"

"Do you mean it's not rented out for next weekend?" Bonnie's heart beat faster now.

"That's *exactly* what I mean!" Ruth reached into her purse and pulled out a key ring. With a twinkle in her eye, she told Bonnie, "If you and those boys aren't down there next weekend filling my living room with sand, I'll come over here and drag you down there myself!"

Bonnie reached down and hugged the petite little dynamo. "Oh, Ruth, thank you so much!"

"Helps to have friends in high places, doesn't it?"

CHAPTER 25

Bonnie slid Ruth's key into the lock and let herself and the boys in. The property managers had been by to prepare for their arrival; the air conditioner was blowing blessedly cool air. The dusky quiet inside the condo was a welcome contrast to the blaring heat of the Florida summer sun. She would have liked nothing better than to slide into one of Ruth's big, overstuffed chairs with a glass of iced tea and just enjoy the cool and quiet for a half hour or so. But she knew that Ben and Josh were impatient to be in their swimsuits and out in the water.

"Okay, guys," she told them. "Help me bring the stuff in from the car, and we can hit the beach."

"Alright!" they chorused.

Making quick work of carrying in the suitcases and the bags of books, games, and videos they had brought to occupy themselves in the car and when they couldn't be on the beach, Ben and Josh presented themselves to Bonnie, swimsuits on and sand castle paraphernalia in hand.

Bonnie looked at their eager young faces and smiled. "Here we go, guys!"

Armed with a hat, sunglasses, and a novel she'd been waiting for time to read, Bonnie set up their beach chairs under a large, striped umbrella, stacked their towels onto one of the chairs, and sat down to watch the boys play. They splashed with each other in the beautiful aquamarine water, allowing the waves to knock them over and the sinking sand to trip their attempts to run at the water's edge. Then they grabbed their buckets and sand shovels and began work on sculpting the pristine white sand into castles and moats and bridges. Bonnie smiled at their antics and thought, once again, how wonderful it was to have a friend like Ruth Newton—a friend who could sense her troubles and wanted to help.

Shaking off the sadness that threatened to engulf her, she opened up her book. Ruth had been right: she needed to get away from everything that had been dragging her down emotionally and spiritually all summer. Bonnie, herself, knew what she really needed: to pray.

Setting the novel aside for the moment, Bonnie bowed her head. As the roaring waves pounded rhythmically onto the shore, she prayed: "Oh, dear Lord, I've always felt closest to You near the sea. I see what You've made, and I realize that the vastness of the water stretching before me pales in comparison to the whole universe that You created. Yet, in all Your vastness, in all Your power and glory, You still love men. You still want us to know You, to love You, to walk with You beside us in our lives.

"I'm afraid I haven't stayed very close to Your side these past few months, dear Lord. I've been caught up in feelings of anger and sadness. I've struggled with forgiving Jeff. I think that I *have* forgiven him, but I can't seem to forget how I once felt about him. And how I *thought* he felt about me. Continue to be with me, Lord. Help me to overcome my feelings for him so that I can get on with what should be the main focus of my life: living for You and serving You."

Bonnie lifted her head and felt her heart lighten a little. This pain in her heart would pass; with God's grace, she knew it would. She glanced at her watch. It was getting close to twelve-thirty already, the hottest part of the day. She had probably better get the boys out of the sun; she didn't want them exposed too much on their first day out.

"Hey guys!" she called to them, "How do burgers, fries, and shakes sound to you? Anybody hungry?"

"Oh, yeah!" They came running.

"Can we go to a restaurant with a playland?" asked Josh.

"Only if it's indoors," she answered. "Slides and crawling tubes sitting out in this sun would be no fun to play on."

Hauling in all of their beach gear, they went back to the condo, washed up, and headed out for lunch. On the drive down Highway 90, the boys scoped out miniature golf courses and go-cart tracks they wanted to visit later. They also noted local theaters showing the latest children's movies.

"You guys are planning to keep me busy, aren't you?" Bonnie laughed.

After wolfing down their burgers and fries, Ben and Josh spent over an hour clambering about in the indoor play area of the fast food restaurant they had gone to. They crawled through clear plastic tubes, slid down the slide and the fireman's poles, and threw colorful plastic balls at each other in the ball pit. Bonnie was able to persuade them, however, to wait until early evening to play miniature golf. The afternoon heat was nearly unbearable after the air conditioning of the restaurant.

Back at the condo, Bonnie played Monopoly with the boys; Ben, who was getting pretty good at that sort of thing already, swallowed up everyone's money and property with relish.

"Bet I can beat you at Trouble!" challenged Josh.

Bonnie picked up her book again while they played a noisy game of sending each other, in turn, back to their home bases. As luck would have it, Josh did win that game and crowed loudly over his big brother.

"Okay, you wheeler-dealers," Bonnie said when the game was over, "I think it's time for a little shuteye."

"Aw, Mom," Ben protested. "We're on vacation. Why do we have to take naps on vacation?"

"For just that very reason," she explained. "You can't enjoy your vacation if you're all tuckered out, can you?"

Grudgingly, they went to the room Ruth had furnished with twin beds for her own two grandsons for their visits to the beach. One of those grandsons was already grown and a father himself now.

"Can we at least read until we fall asleep?" Ben cajoled.

Bonnie sighed. "I guess so, but I don't want to hear any noise in here, alright?"

"Okay, Mom," Ben agreed with the straightest face he could muster.

Bonnie saw Josh bring his hands up to his mouth to cover his wide grin; his eyes danced with mischief. Bonnie looked from one boy to the other lying innocently on their beds, books in hand.

"I mean it!" she warned, then walked to her own room.

Boyish giggles followed her down the hall, but she heard Ben warn his younger brother not to get them into trouble. She smiled and stretched out onto the satin bedspread. Its cool surface actually sent a chill through her.

Picking up her book, she dived back into the story: a romance with a plot that was already getting juicy. The heroine meets her love interest, a dark, shadowy character with something mysterious lurking in his past. Despite her initial instinctive resistance, she is drawn irresistibly to him and finds herself wrapped in his arms, savoring his forbidden kiss. Her eyes suddenly weighty with the heat and the long drive and the early hour at which she had risen that morning, Bonnie's hand went limp and the book folded closed over her thumb. And she suddenly found herself in the arms of the man she had been resisting for so long.

She and Jeff were back in the office at Loaves and Fishes; she was putting a bandage on the cut on his hand. She looked up from his hand and Jeff gazed searchingly into her eyes. Then he leaned over and kissed her, gently, tenderly, but endlessly, endlessly. She wrapped her arms around Jeff's neck, holding him close to her. Then she felt a strange tapping on her shoulder.

"Mom," she heard Ben whispering. "Mom!"

Unwrapping her arms from around the pillow she was hugging, Bonnie looked up at Ben in puzzlement.

"Mom, it's almost five o'clock. Can we get up now?"

Glancing at the digital clock on the night stand to confirm Ben's information, she pulled herself up a little groggily and said, "Oh, yes, sweetie. I didn't mean to sleep so long. Did you guys have a good nap?"

She heard Josh giggling behind Ben.

"You guys didn't sleep at all, did you?" Bonnie asked them, trying to sound stern.

"Big mouth," Ben muttered to his little brother.

Bonnie smiled. She knew two boys who would have no trouble falling asleep later that night.

"Well, I tell you what, guys," she said, seating a boy on either side of her on the bed. "I've been looking forward to going out to a seafood restaurant ever since we started planning this trip to the beach."

"Do they have hamburgers there, too, Mom?" Josh asked. The Callaway boys hadn't yet acquired a taste for seafood.

"Well, they do," she said, "but you guys had hamburgers for lunch! I'll order you some shrimp. I'm sure you'll like that. Oh, and we're going someplace special tonight, so I want you to go put on the outfits I brought for you to eat out in."

Josh wrinkled his nose, as if not convinced that he could really make a meal of shrimp, but went off with his brother to dress. While Ben and Josh readied themselves for dinner, Bonnie took out the sundress she'd brought to wear. It had hung in the closet long enough, she'd thought as she had packed it for the trip. Just because she had bought it for her dinner with Jeff didn't mean she couldn't wear it again, she'd told herself sternly.

She reached into her make-up case and pulled out a small atomizer of her perfume. Grudgingly, she had admitted to herself some time ago that part of the reason she wore it so often now was because Jeff Wells had told her how good she smelled with it on. Well, so what if it had been Jeff? If it smelled good, then she would wear it!

She twisted her hair up and pinned it in place, then slid into her high-heeled sandals. Looking in the mirror, she was pleased with what she saw. She wondered fleetingly if Bill would have liked her dress; she knew that Jeff had. Well, tonight, she'd have *two* dates, she told herself. Ben and Josh would be her escorts for the evening.

Ben and Josh sat on the sofa waiting for her.

"Wow, Mom, you look nice!" Ben told her.

"Thank you, sweetie." Looking in her purse for her keys, she murmured to Ben, "Could you go and make sure the back door is locked?"

"Sure," he said, and went through the kitchen to the back door. Just as he was leaving, Bonnie and Josh heard a key turning in the lock of the front door. Her heart pounding, Bonnie pulled Josh to her side and watched in horror as the door opened.

To Bonnie's utter astonishment, *Jeff Wells* poked his head around the door, and he looked around the room. His eyes flew open wide when he saw Bonnie, mouth agape, frozen to the spot where she stood.

"Pastor Jeff!" Josh squealed, and ran to greet him.

Still looking warily at Bonnie, Jeff walked through the door and swung Josh into the air, then held him in his arms.

"Hey, there, Partner!"

Equally surprised at seeing them there, Jeff Junior tousled Josh's hair and said, "Hey there, Pipsqueak, what're *you* doing here?"

As if to echo his son's question, Jeff turned to Bonnie and looked at her inquiringly, but she was still too shocked to speak. Jeff let Josh slide back down to stand on his own feet again, then held a set of keys aloft.

"Ruth Newton offered to let us use her condo this weekend," he explained quietly. "It would appear that she made a similar offer to you."

"Y…yes, she did," Bonnie stammered. "We got in about nine-thirty this morning."

"Ah," he said with a disappointed look. "Well, possession is nine-tenths of the law, so I guess we need find a place to spend the night," Jeff said to his son. "After all, I did promise you a weekend at the beach."

Bonnie was just beside herself. Could Ruth have really engineered this?

"I…I can't imagine how Ruth could have forgotten and lent the condo to two different people for the same weekend!"

"Well," Jeff said, a knowing smile on his face, "she's had a lot on her mind lately."

Bonnie could tell by the look on his face that he didn't believe this any more than she did.

"We were just going out to eat," Bonnie said tentatively, hoping Jeff would catch the hint and leave.

He gave them an assessing look, as if just noticing their dinner clothes.

"Yes, I guess you were," said Jeff, but he didn't move. Then, a thought seemed to strike him. "You know," he began slowly, "I, um, I never did get a chance to take you to Cap'n John's, did I?"

Bonnie said nothing, but felt herself coloring. Jeff Junior, however, caught the drift of his father's words right away.

"Hey, guys," he said to Ben and Josh, low excitement in his voice, "did you know that the world's best pizza is made right *here* in Panama City, Florida?"

"Yeah?" Josh took the bait.

"Absolutely," he confirmed. "I was gonna take my dad there, but if *they'd* rather get seafood," he said this with some disdain, "I'd be glad to take you guys with me. And it's right next door to one of the best go-cart tracks in town!"

The look on Josh's face was unmistakable: he might just escape those shrimp after all! Both boys turned eagerly to Bonnie.

"Can we go, Mom? Can we?"

Bonnie looked first at Jeff Junior, who was wearing a completely innocent smile, then at Jeff, whose smile was much more knowing. Jeff, however, didn't look at her.

"I...Well, I don't think it's right to interrupt Pastor Jeff's plans," she stammered.

"Pastor Jeff won't mind just this once. Will you, Pastor Jeff?" Ben asked, his voice not too far from pleading.

"Not at all," he confirmed quietly.

"Alright!" they shouted in unison, as if Jeff's acquiescence was sufficient permission. "Let's go!"

"Here, let me give you some money for the boys," Bonnie said, reaching into her purse.

"You can pay me later." Jeff Junior flashed them a smile as he corralled the boys out the door. "Have a good time, you guys!"

When the door had closed behind them, Bonnie and Jeff turned slowly to look at each other.

"Ready to go get some seafood?" he asked, his face devoid of any expression that Bonnie could read. From his look, Bonnie thought, he could just as well be asking Ruth Newton to join him for dinner. Bonnie smiled back weakly and nodded. She thought back to the evenings when she and Jeff had both been invited to Jack and Cheryl's for dinner and when they had joined the Givenses, Anna Lee, and Mark Miller after the Singles Conference—how awkward the conversation had been, how long the silences. Tonight, there wouldn't even be Jack and Cheryl to help. What on earth would they talk about?

As it turned out, very little. It seemed to Bonnie that while they filled their conversation with banal topics like the weather (hot, of course) and what was on the menu (seafood, of course), the air between them hung heavy with unanswered questions: Where was Jeff going now that he was leaving Foster Road Baptist Church? Had Bonnie forgiven him? Did Jeff still care for her at all? Had the events of last spring really been too much to overcome? Bonnie couldn't say how Jeff felt, but for her, the tension was almost unbearable.

When Jeff and Bonnie got back to Ruth's beach house, all was dark and quiet. Jeff used his key and carefully pushed the door open. On the sofa, bathed in the flickering blue glow of the television screen, sat Jeff Junior, a sleeping Callaway boy under each arm. Jeff Junior raised an arm from behind Josh and laid his index finger over his lips with a smile.

"Let's not go in just yet," Jeff whispered. "Jeff Junior looks like he's got things well under control. Let's take a walk on the beach."

Bonnie looked at her feet and tried to hide a sigh of frustration. Why was he doing this? Hadn't dinner been as tortuous for him as it had for her? Why did he want to prolong their time together when they clearly had nothing to say to each other? It just didn't make sense. Nearly all summer, they had been thrown together constantly: everywhere she went, Jeff seemed to turn up. But not once had he ever mentioned a desire to go out with her again. Maybe it was different for him, but that night when he had held her hands, when he had kissed her ever so softly, a threshold had been crossed, and she couldn't pretend that it hadn't. She couldn't be around him without wanting to hold him, and she hated that he seemed to be suffering no such inner turmoil.

Jeff closed the door quietly and put his hand gently on Bonnie's back to guide her back down the steps. They turned right at the driveway and were soon picking their way past the sea oats and into soft, white sand. Bonnie's sandals, with their two-inch heels, were sinking deep with every step.

"Hang on a second. These shoes have got to go."

She lifted one foot and teetered a little as she reached down to slide a sandal off. Jeff caught her other hand to steady her. He held it until she had the straps of both sandals hooked over her forefinger. When she righted herself, she pulled away the hand that Jeff was holding, and he resisted letting go ever so slightly. Bonnie looked into his eyes briefly, a look of confusion in hers. Jeff thought he saw accusation, stifled a sigh of resignation, and let her fingers slip from his.

They walked along in silence, kicking up sand with every step as waves lapped the beach inches below where their feet fell. A melancholy manila moon lit up the gently rolling Gulf of Mexico and then vanished behind a column of cloud that was threatening to rain. Bonnie stole occasional glances at Jeff, but she couldn't read his expression. He looked straight ahead or to his right at the condos, hotels, restaurants, and bars lining the beachfront. Music and laughter wafted over to them intermittently, but only those sounds broke the silence between them.

What on earth is he doing, Bonnie wondered for the millionth time. *Why are we here, if he can't even talk to me?* As they walked on, the strains of amplified guitar music and adolescent male voices grew gradually louder. A look of recognition came across Jeff's face and his head snapped to the right to look at the young men singing.

With a pleased smile, he turned to Bonnie and said, "That's Gerald Markham's boys, Nathan and Jim!"

He pointed at the group. Bonnie looked and saw four boys, two of whom she recognized from church and two she didn't.

"It sure is," Bonnie confirmed. "Nathan and Jim have sung duets at church lots of times, but I didn't know they'd gotten a little band together. They must be pretty good if they were able to get a paid singing engagement here at the beach."

"I wouldn't be too sure," said Jeff with a conspiratorial smile. "Sometimes the Christian coffee houses will take anybody who'll play for free, but the groups are usually glad to do it for the practice and the exposure. Want to stop and listen a bit?"

"Sure," Bonnie said.

It was time she said to Jeff some of the things she had been holding in for far too long.

CHAPTER 26

They walked over to the fence that separated the coffee house from the beach. Jeff leaned against the fence, his chin resting on his crossed arms. Bonnie stood to the side a bit, her hands clasped lightly behind her back. In their best Country and Western twang, the boys were playing and singing a haunting old Hank Williams gospel tune, "Can't You Hear the Blessed Savior Calling You?"

Bonnie stole a glance at Jeff. There was a strange expression on his face, as if he *could* hear God calling to him. The last chord was strummed on the guitars and a long moment of silence held until it was broken by polite, scattered applause. The next song the boys played was something of a spoof and had the audience laughing intermittently at its satirical lines. Without turning his head, Jeff began to speak, almost as if to the air, as if there were no music playing.

"Funny thing about when the Savior calls you," he mused. "No matter how plain it is, sometimes you still ignore it, or deny that you hear it, because you think that what God is saying couldn't possibly be directed at you."

Bonnie looked at him in surprise. To hear a minister make such an admission was startling. Jeff turned to Bonnie now, his arms folded and his shoulder leaning against the fence.

"About a year after Terri died, I began having thoughts that I should start looking for another place to serve, that my time was just about up in Chandler City."

Bonnie looked down. He was leaving, and she knew it, but she hated the thought that soon they would be separated forever. It was probably better that way, considering the state of their relationship, but it still hurt to think about it. She wished he hadn't brought it up, but the fact that he was leaving was even *more* reason for her to say the things that were on her mind. She waited for Jeff to finish.

"And I thought, 'This can't be right!'" he continued. "'I *love* it here. And people like *me* here. Things are going great at this church, Jeff Junior is happy in school. Why would I want to think about leaving?'"

"Because maybe God thought it was time?"

Bonnie looked up at him with a smile tinged with sadness she couldn't hide. Jeff wondered how many other women would have known a thing like that. He looked down at her, admiration in his eyes.

"Sounds like you're a little quicker on the uptake than I am," he grinned.

"Oh, I don't know about that." She folded her arms in front of her, shoes dangling from one hand, and kicked the sand with her big toe. "I've done my share of asking God, 'Who, me?'"

"But then the signs get more and more unmistakable, and you realize that, yes, God *is* talking to you. Then you know you're doing the right thing, even if it isn't what you would've planned for yourself or even if it scares you to death. Guess that's what happened with me." He paused awkwardly, glancing at Bonnie. "The signs telling me it was time to leave just got to be unmistakable."

Bonnie wondered with a pang of guilt whether her failure to forgive him had been one of those signs. Had she helped to drive him away?

He had never talked with Bonnie about the specifics of his leaving, and he didn't know what he expected her to say now. He couldn't exactly expect her to say, "We'll miss you" or even a more impersonal, "Everyone will miss you." He didn't know why he had even brought it up.

The last notes of the silly song sounded and Nathan Markham, the elder Markham brother and lead singer, addressed their tiny audience.

"Thanks, ladies and gentlemen. You're a great group. We're going to take a little break now, but we'll be back in just a few. In the meantime, we'll pipe in some tunes for you and you can get up and dance if you feel like it."

"I don't think Mark Miller has anything to worry about for a while," Jeff said with a smile, "but they're not bad for a bunch of local guys."

In the silence that followed the group's exit from the stage, Bonnie gathered her courage, said a silent prayer, and looked up at Jeff.

"Dr. Wells," she began.

With a look of chagrin that she *still* had never called him Jeff, he turned again to face her.

"I know this is long overdue, but I hope it's not so late to say this that we can't somehow bury the past."

Jeff's eyes widened, but he said nothing.

"I...I know I should've said something to you that day of the meeting—Clara's meeting, when you apologized to me in front of that whole group. In fact, I've had several chances to tell you that..." What was it that she really wanted to say, now that he was leaving, now that he would be out of her life for good? "To tell you that I hated the way everything happened. I guess it's my turn to ask for forgiveness, for holding on to my anger and pride for so long."

"And here I was thinking that you'd never forgiven *me*," he said, a gentle smile on his face.

"Oh, Jeff, I forgave you long ago! And yet, somehow, I was too stubborn and proud to actually let you know!" She hung her head and shook it sadly. "What a hash I've made of things. I...I just couldn't bear the thought any longer of you leaving and still feeling—still angry with me."

Jeff hesitated for the briefest moment when it registered with him that Bonnie had just called him "Jeff," the first time he could *ever* recall her doing so. Then, as the Markham boy had promised, the sound system began to play again and the haunting words and music of "Unchained Melody" wafted out over the warm summer evening.

Jeff reached for Bonnie's hands. Bonnie tossed the shoes she was holding aside and let her hands slide into his. When the words "Oh, my love, my darling" rang out, their eyes met and held for a long moment. Bonnie caught her breath at the look on Jeff's face; there was unmasked longing in his eyes. She looked down, tears threatening to flow, and began to pull her hands back. Jeff said nothing, but held tightly onto her hands. Bonnie looked first at his hands holding hers, and then up at him. Wordlessly, he beckoned her with eyes that pleaded with her not to say no. Almost as if in a dream, Bonnie walked toward him, her eyes locked with his. He put one arm around her waist, his hand touching the skin on her back.

Bonnie closed her eyes and breathed deeply when she felt Jeff's touch. She felt him pull her a little closer and found her arms reaching around his neck. Why was she allowing herself to do this? Why was she holding him this way, when he was leaving? Did she want to add the feel of his arms around her to the memories that would torture her when he was gone?

The words of the song swirled around them and pierced them with the immediacy of the truth they held. Afraid to meet Jeff's eyes now, she felt his forehead come down to rest lightly on hers.

"We both really made a mess of things, didn't we?" His voice held no recrimination.

Bonnie shrugged. "What's done is done," she whispered, her voice catching on a sob.

His other arm still around her waist, Jeff lifted Bonnie's chin with his finger. The longing in his eyes was still there, more intense than ever.

"But we've forgiven each other, haven't we?" she whispered. His mouth was so close to hers. "Isn't that what's important?"

Jeff closed his eyes and shook his head slowly. "So much wasted time."

Seeing the anguish on his face, Bonnie laid a hand gently on his cheek. Jeff cupped his larger hand over hers, turned his face into her palm, and kissed it. Bonnie slid her hand further back, behind his head, and gently pulled it down, bringing his lips to hers.

"Oh, Bonnie," he breathed, just before their lips met.

The kiss was tentative at first, as if Jeff couldn't quite allow himself to do it. Suddenly, Jeff's hands held Bonnie's face, and he began to kiss her with the pent-up urgency of three, almost four, months' longing. Bonnie responded in kind, relishing the feel of finally holding Jeff close to her.

Their kiss lasted a long, wonderful time. When their lips finally parted, Jeff pulled Bonnie close into an embrace, as if, now that he finally held her in his arms, he wasn't going to release her again so soon. Each could feel the other's heart pounding. Jeff breathed in her heady, intoxicating scent. He reached his fingers tentatively into the hair at the nape of her neck and thrilled to its cool, silky touch.

"So beautiful," he whispered.

A voice in Bonnie's head chastised her for allowing Jeff to hold her, to kiss her again, for *making* it happen herself! In her heart, she knew that it would only hurt more now when he left. But right now, for this moment, she didn't care, *couldn't* care. Not when she was wrapped in the arms she knew now she had wanted all along.

After a long moment of holding Jeff, her heart still pounding, Bonnie heard the rumble of thunder in the distance. How fitting that it should rain, she thought ruefully. She remembered how it had stormed that long-ago night when she had dashed away from him at the Coffee Shoppe. It was time they parted again.

Her head bent, Bonnie whispered, "I've got my keys with me. Why don't you go on back and room with Jeff Junior for the night. It's too late to find a motel now, even if you could on a holiday weekend. I'll be in in a little while."

Jeff tilted her head up again with his finger under her chin.

"I don't want to leave you now!" His voice was urgent. "Not when I finally have you in my arms. I can't tell you how long I've wanted this."

Probably as long as I've wanted it, Bonnie thought bitterly. But now it was too late. Bonnie turned her head to the side so Jeff wouldn't see her tears.

"Oh, Bonnie, love, what's wrong?"

"You're leaving Chandler City at the end of next week, and you have to ask me what's wrong?"

He pulled her close and held her tightly.

"I'm sorry, I don't mean to lash out at you," she said through her tears. With a heavy sigh, she told him, "Timing has never been on our side, has it?"

Jeff knew it was selfish of him to continue to hold Bonnie this way. She was absolutely right. He was leaving, and this simply should not have happened. Yet he held her still. She allowed herself to be held.

"But, you know, I think that God has been speaking to me, too," she told him. "I think it's time I cleared out of Chandler City, myself."

"Oh, Bonnie, you don't have to say that just for me. Where would you go?" He knew that, as a self-employed person, she had to be where her clients were. Anywhere she moved, she would have to start all over again.

"Well, my parents have been after me for a long time to move back to New Orleans to be close to them. And I have a standing offer from the company I used to work for there to come back to work for them."

Jeff leaned back and held Bonnie at arm's length.

"Did you say New Orleans?"

Bonnie looked at him quizzically.

"Well, yes, I thought you knew that that's where I grew up."

"I did, but I never really thought you'd move back there! This is fantastic!"

"It is?"

"Do you remember when we ran into each other at the airport back in June?"

"Sure."

"Well, I wasn't completely honest about why I was there."

"You weren't there to visit your old Seminary friends?"

"I was there to *interview* with my old Seminary friends. That's where I'm going—to teach at the Seminary in New Orleans."

Bonnie just stared at him. "Are you serious?"

"Cross my heart," he told her. Then, looking at her with a gleam in his eye that made her want to giggle nervously, he said, "You know, I've heard Tom Givens performs a mean wedding ceremony when he has the chance."

"And so you think you might be able to throw a little work his way, do you?"

"I'm certainly hoping so."

"Maybe we can get the Markham boys to sing for us," Bonnie teased.

"Anybody you want, my love, anybody you want!"

Bonnie wrapped her arms around Jeff's neck again. Now it was she who couldn't get enough. They held each other for a long, long time. Bonnie had begun to relax, and now she felt like being playful.

"Clara Adkinson sure is going to be mad when she finds out what a wicked woman you've decided to marry."

"You must think I'm the biggest jerk on the planet."

His expression told her that he was only half-joking. Bonnie smiled a mischievous smile.

"Well, maybe not the planet," she teased. "Maybe just this hemisphere."

"Clara!" Jeff scoffed, shaking his head ruefully. "That woman could make the Pope look like a bad guy!"

"Tsk!" Bonnie chided him playfully. "To say a thing like that about her after all those goodies she brought you!"

"Oh, man!" He shook his head again. "I gotta tell you, I hope Anna Lee can afford a maid now that she's married to Mark Miller. That girl can't cook for beans!"

At this, Bonnie looked at him, mouth slightly agape, and burst out laughing. She laughed until tears came to her eyes.

"What?" Jeff asked. "What did I say?"

"Oh, never mind," Bonnie shook her head. "Clara's *really* gonna be ticked when she finds out that *I* will have access to all of your millions. I really think she believes that you rich guys should keep it all to yourselves."

Bonnie linked her arm in Jeff's and rested her cheek on the warmth of his arm as they began strolling back toward Ruth's condo.

"My millions?" Jeff looked at her skeptically.

"I hate to break it to you, Dr. Wells, but, according to Anna Lee, the money you inherited from Terri was a large part of your appeal to Clara."

Jeff walked in silence for a moment.

"Hmph," he said. "And here I thought it was my devastating good looks."

Bonnie looked up at him and made a face.

"Well, *I* hate to break it to Clara, but she'd have been in for a severe disappointment if I had wanted to marry her daughter."

"Oh?"

"You betcha. Except for some money that was put in trust for the kids' education and the money I used to pay off the mortgage, I didn't keep any of Terri's millions. What do I need with that kind of money? I'm a minister, not a mogul!"

"Well, what did you do with it?"

"Part of it went to oncology research to fight the kind of cancer that took Terri," he told her soberly. "The rest went to a scholarship fund in Terri's name at Mercer University, her *alma mater.*"

"Wow," said Bonnie. "So, you're not a millionaire after all?"

"Disappointed?" Jeff asked her with a mischievous smile.

Bonnie didn't bother to answer his silly question. Instead, she asked him one: "Who should we break the good news to first, Jack and Cheryl or Ruth Newton?"

"Considering that it was her little scheme that brought us together tonight, I'd say Ruth ought to get a call first thing in the morning."

As they walked back toward the condo in no particular hurry, Bonnie opened her eyes and looked heavenward. The moon, now a dazzling white, presided triumphantly over a clear midnight sky. The cloud that had threatened rain was nowhere in sight.

About the Author

Melissa Lea Leedom is a native of New Orleans, and has also lived in Florida, Virginia, Alabama, and Maryland. She holds degrees in English and Professional Writing from Troy State University at Dothan, Alabama, and Towson University in Maryland.

Ms. Leedom was single-again for over five years and was a member of Single Adult Sunday School classes in New Orleans and the Metro-D.C. area. A part-time developmental math instructor at Central Texas College in Killeen, Ms. Leedom lives in a suburb of Austin with her husband, two sons, and two noisy parrots. Please write to her at forgive490@yahoo.com.

0-595-29495-2

CPSIA information can be obtained
at www.ICGtesting.com
Printed in the USA
LVHW091744040921
696729LV00005B/1